For the Cause of
Freedom

MY BROTHER'S FLAG
BOOK 2

For the Cause of
Freedom

BY REBEKAH COLBURN

Other Books

by Rebekah Colburn

OF WIND AND SKY SERIES
Through Every Valley
The Whisper of Dawn
As Eagles Soar

MY BROTHER'S FLAG
On Grounds of Honor
For the Casue of Freedom

For the Cause of Freedom
Copyright © 2016
Rebekah Colburn

Cover Design by Jody Christian, Christian Graphic Solutions
Back Cover Union Soldier, Courtesy of Library of Congress ID# 31085

Back Cover photo of woman, courtesy of Bill & Ann Turpin. Cover photo of Bloomingdale, courtesy of Ward and Betty Lee Taylor.

Scripture quotations are taken from the NKJV, New King James Version of the Bible. Copyright © 1982 by Thomas Nelson.

This is a work of historical fiction; the appearances of certain historical figures are therefore inevitable. All other characters, however, are products of the author's imagination, and any resemblance to actual persons, living or dead, is coincidental.

Dedicated to

Juanita Deskins & Emma Edwards:

Two women who played the role

Of grandmother in my life

And to whom I am very grateful.

Acknowledgements

I would like to extend special thanks to the following:

Ward and Betty Lee Taylor for generously allowing me to use their home, Bloomingdale, as the setting for the story as well as in the cover art.

Becky Marquardt of the Queen Anne's County Historical Society for invaluable help with researching the Civil War in Centreville, and for pointing me to Emory's *Queen Anne's County Maryland*, a historical account.

My parents, Leroy and Mary, for their enthusiasm and support in this endeavor, and for always believing in me.

My husband, Ben, and daughter, Grace, for tolerating my constant preoccupation with research and writing, and allowing me to hide away in my office at all hours of the day and night.

I would also like to thank the following for their feedback, creative suggestions and editing assistance: Sarah Smedley, Nikki Link, Teresa Martinoli, and Ann Turpin. I couldn't do it without you!

And my gratitude to Jody Christian for another beautiful cover!

Finally, to all my readers who've sent notes of encouragement and appreciation, you will never know how much it has meant to me.

All My Best,

Rebekah   *Colburn*

*"Is not life more than food,
and the body more than clothing?"*

Matthew 6:25

Prologue

December, 1863
Point Lookout Confederate Prison Camp
Scotland, Maryland

A damp, biting wind blew in from the Chesapeake Bay and seeped its way under the thin woolen blanket Charlie shared with another prisoner. Pressing closer against Wilson's back for warmth, he closed his eyes and tried to block out the sounds of merriment coming from the garrison where the guards welcomed the newly arrived colored troops. Beneath him, the ground was as hard and cold as a block of ice. A shiver rattled his teeth, and Charlie curled his knees into his chest.

Many Rebels had died in this camp since they were taken prisoner last summer at Gettysburg. Some were shot in cold blood, while others suffered a slow and degrading death brought on by dysentery and dehydration. Starvation took some, while others froze to death from exposure to the elements.

I must survive, Charlie Turner reminded himself as another violent shiver overtook his thin frame. *I will survive*, he vowed, grinding his teeth together to cease their chattering. If for no other reason than to return home and see his father and Jeremiah again, he must endure this frozen hell.

In a gray haze of semi-consciousness, a memory drifted into his thoughts like fog rolling in from the bay. It had been a beautiful spring day, and Charlie had clutched the newspaper tightly in his hand as he urged the mount under him into a full gallop, racing up Turners Lane between the corn fields toward Laurel Hill.

He'd been so eager to share the fateful news with his brother that Fort Sumter had fallen into Confederate hands and President Lincoln was calling for volunteers to suppress the rebellion. Charlie had felt a twinge of guilt at the excitement pulsing in his veins at the prospect of war. Perhaps within every man there was a warrior crouching in repose, waiting until the moment when he should be called upon to fight.

Against his father's wishes and his brother's counsel, Charlie had been with the first wave of men to enlist with the Rebels. He'd taken the buckskin gelding, Archie, under cover of darkness and rode through the night to catch a ferry across the Chesapeake Bay and enlist with the First Maryland Infantry of the Confederate States in Richmond, Virginia.

He'd been so sure it was the right course to follow in the footsteps of his grandfather, who'd fought in the war of 1812 to suppress tyranny and defend freedom. But nothing seemed clear anymore.

"I'm sorry, Jeremiah," Charlie moaned as he drifted into tortured sleep.

He awoke with a start as the bugle sounded the morning Reveille and demanded the prisoners assemble for roll call. The sky was still dark as he forced himself upright, running a dirty hand over his tired face. Beside him, Wilson groaned in greeting to another day. The circular Sibley tent quickly converted into a cramped mass of elbows and knees as the men rose from the ground where they huddled against one another for warmth and stumbled toward the flap.

The air outside the tent was even colder than within, where at least there was a barrier against the wind, and the body heat they generated had filled the small space. Charlie shivered as the air struck his face, and he folded his arms across his chest in a reflexive posture against the assault, although his thin arms inside the tattered uniform provided no protection against the bitter cold.

On the eastern horizon, the sun pushed back the darkness and a pale rim of orange light glowed as the fiery orb climbed into the sky. But the weak rays it produced were useless at dispelling the chill that gnawed deep into the prisoners' bones. The long months of summer when they had sweltered in the burning sand like bacon on a griddle seemed no more than mere hallucination.

Their sunburned skin had faded to pale white, tinged with blue from cold or the gray pall of approaching death. Scurvy and malnutrition had weakened them all until there was no fight left in them. They ate whatever they could find, as the rations served were barely enough to keep them alive. Before the bay's waves were capped with ice, they had been permitted to search for clams, lobster, or fish in the enclosed area behind the stockade where they bathed and washed their clothing. Now, the only protein to be added to their paltry diet was rats, hunted out of sheer desperation. As firewood was scarce, it was reserved for roasting the filthy rodents.

As the Confederate prisoners fell into line for the roll call, it was to the jibes and jeers of the black troops sent to guard them. They inspected the emaciated forms of the men in their torn and faded garments, laughing at just how low the mighty had fallen. Many of these Negroes had once been enslaved to the white men of the South. This was indeed an unexpected twist of fate, to be both celebrated and exploited.

"Looks like the bottom rung's on top now!" Charlie heard one of the darkies taunt his former master, the barrel of his rifle jabbing the prisoner in the ribs.

If the guards of their own skin color had treated their execution as a sport, how much worse would it be now that the colored troops had arrived? Numb with cold and his awareness that the specter of Death followed in every shadowed footstep he took, Charlie acknowledged this new threat calmly. Every Confederate soldier present had survived the bloody battle of Gettysburg, and many battles before it, only to fight hunger and inclement weather here at Point Lookout. There were a thousand ways that death could claim a man: gunfire, grenade, smallpox, dysentery, blazing heat or freezing cold... Each of the prisoners was, at any given moment, only a breath away from passing into the next life.

Sometimes it was difficult to remember why he must keep his spirit firmly rooted in this wretched mortal body. It would be easier to goad the guards into shooting him and ending this perpetual misery.

But Charlie was determined to survive, if his determination alone were enough to ensure it. He kept his eyes lowered and his mouth shut. He did what he was ordered, and did nothing to bring attention to himself. He was simply another gaunt face, another name on the long list of prisoners held in the "bull pen." And that was the way Charlie wanted it to remain. He combated the hunger and the cold with the same unwavering resolve. He *would* survive.

Standing at attention, eyes straight ahead, though unfocused on anything in particular, Charlie listened for his name as the register was shouted out into the frosty morning air. He was aware of the colored guards slowly circling the prisoners, gloating over their elevated status, but he paid them no heed until one of them jerked his head at the call for "Private Charles Turner."

The dark-skinned soldier's eyes narrowed on Charlie as he

barked out his response. In the gray light of dawn, Charlie scrutinized the black face staring back at him. There was something familiar about it... Then recognition suddenly slammed into place. *Henry?*

The Federal blue uniform and erect posture had tricked Charlie's eyes for a moment, but he was certain that it was the slave, Henry, from Laurel Hill. At the precise moment that acknowledgement registered on his face, Henry shook his head ever so slightly, his hand lifting for a brief second to cover his lips with his forefinger. It was a subtle message to keep their association silent.

And for the first time in months, Charlie felt a small spark of hope fan to life within his chest.

Chapter One

December, 1863
Bloomingdale
Queenstown, Maryland

Beyond the glass window panes, snowflakes drifted slowly from the gray clouds above and disappeared into a landscape obscured by a thick veil of white. It was Christmas Eve, and company would be arriving shortly. At any moment Abigail Sterret would be called upon to descend the stairs and greet the guests as they entered the main hall of Bloomingdale and exclaimed over the splendor of the eight foot spruce tree decorated with crimson ribbons and white candles to be lit at midnight.

Peering in the mirror, Abigail studied her reflection. Her dark hair had been curled and carefully pinned into a waterfall style, with one spiral curl artfully draped over her shoulder, and she wore a garnet necklace around her slender neck. She looked lovely in a fitted burgundy gown with black lace trim at the neckline and rosettes at the shoulders. The wide skirt flared out like a bell, the hoop and layers of petticoats beneath swishing with every move she made.

But the festive dress she wore had lost its sheen and the hem had been mended more than once. Perhaps she could have pressed her mother for a new gown, but it hardly mattered when this year there would be no young men to dance with.

In one way or another, the war had claimed them all. Those who hadn't enlisted—either with the Federals or the Rebels—had been drafted into the Union Army once Maryland's fate was secured. A few had lived to return home, but these wounded veterans were quickly seized by eligible women who knew their pickings were scarce. The future would hold many spinsters as the number of eligible men steadily dwindled.

Abigail ran a hand over the smooth fabric of her burgundy taffeta skirt with a sigh. She had no right to wish for a new frock or a handsome dancing partner when so many of the women who would grace Bloomingdale's hall that evening would arrive in the somber hues of mourning. It was as if a cloud of doom was fixed on the horizon, unmoving, and it cast a gloomy shadow even on what should have been a cheerful occasion.

Shaking off such somber thoughts, Abigail tugged her black lace shawl more tightly around her shoulders. Stepping away from the mirror, she moved as close as she dared to the flames crackling in the fireplace. The warmth seeped into her, yet there was a chill she could not chase away.

For two and a half years this war had dragged on, and still there was no end in sight. The conclusion had been predicted many times over, and yet still there was no finality. Battles were won and lives were lost. But neither side would relent. Instead, they dug their heels in deeper and fought all the more fiercely.

There would be no talk of politics tonight, Abigail was certain. Her mother would see to that. Not only did tempers flare and passionate arguments ensue whenever the topic was raised, but there were too many divided families with sons who had come to opposing conclusions on the war. Positioned between the North and the South, Maryland did not truly belong to either.

A brisk knock at the door startled Abigail, and Esther

bustled in. Her young face, dark as ebony, was excited as she announced, "Miss Abigail, ma'am, Mrs. Sterret say she need you come right down! The guests is here!"

"Tell her I'm on my way," Abigail nodded, pausing to glance in the mirror one last time. Then, gathering her full skirts in one hand, she descended the staircase to the great hall below. Her other hand trailed the mahogany railing as she navigated the steps in her black leather boots.

On either side of the white double doors, narrow glass windows allowed Abigail to observe as her guests stepped from the carriage. Above the doors, an arched window shaped like a sunburst allowed light from within to spill out into the snowy night. She smiled as she recognized her friends, Jeremiah and Clara Turner, along with Clara's sister, Jane Collins, and her escort, Judson Shephard.

The young slave girl, Esther, stepped to the side as the guests were ushered in, the ladies' hoop skirts swaying as they stepped into the brick Colonial manor house. Persian rugs muffled the sounds of their heels as they entered the great hall.

"I'm so pleased to see you!" she said to the four of them, sincerely. "I was afraid no one would dare brave the snow!"

Her father, Irving Sterret, interjected, "I suspect my peers will decline in favor of their parlors tonight, but at least you'll have some company."

Gratefully, her father had neither enlisted in the Rebel Army or been drafted into the Union Army, either of which had at one point seemed a possibility. Mother had made it very clear that he would be an ungrateful soul if he left the Aunts to fend for themselves when they had so graciously taken the family in and given him such a generous position. Margaret had also stated that if he left, he could plan on not returning.

There was little need for such threats however, as Irving was as gentle as the terrier Sam, lacking the killer instincts necessary in a soldier. When the mandatory conscription began, Margaret was in a flurry of anxiety, determined that they would pay commutation fees or send a substitute in his place if Irving was given orders. The maximum age, however, was forty-five, and as Irving was two years above it, he was exempted from the draft.

Abigail patted her father's arm in consolation. "I'd be happy to share with you," she grinned. Her father's forehead wrinkled as he laughed in reply. Her mother, Margaret, beautiful in an emerald green ball gown, appeared less amused.

"Please make yourselves at home," Irving instructed his guests. "There's drinks in the library for the men, and punch and hors d'oeuvres for the women in the drawing room."

As more guests began to arrive, Abigail retreated with the women into the drawing room.

"I always forget how grand this place is," Jane commented, lowering herself onto a damask settee the burgundy hue of rich claret.

The focal point of the room was a fireplace, with an elaborately carved mantle standing five feet high, and arched recesses built into the walls on either side of it. The thirteen foot ceilings, white crown molding, and silk wallpaper the shade of summer roses, contributed to the stately atmosphere.

Abigail paused to appreciate her surroundings, remembering how she had felt when her family first came to live with the Aunts. Before their installation at Bloomingdale, the Sterrets had lived in a townhouse in Baltimore where her father held a law practice. They had been doing quite well, but Sallie and Mary Harris were getting advanced in years and wished to employ a family member who could be trusted to look after their interests rather than an opportunist who would profit from their father's work.

Bloomingdale was a plantation of over two thousand acres. In addition to growing corn and wheat as staple crops, the plantation also boasted beef and dairy cows, hogs, and Merino sheep. Of Spanish origin, this particular breed was reputed to have the finest and softest wool of any sheep, lightweight yet warm, and with a unique property which wicked moisture away from the skin so that the wearer remained dry.

Abigail's younger brother, ten year old Harris, named after Sallie and Mary Harris, certainly had flourished in the fresh country air on the Eastern Shore, becoming an eager student of all their father taught him. Like a faithful puppy, he followed Irving around the plantation whenever he was allowed, eager for the day when he would step into his father's role.

Jeanine, Abigail's sister, would have surely loved Bloomingdale too, but she had passed into the next life when she was only twelve years old. Influenza had swept through the family, and all had recovered except her. Abigail had been fifteen at the time, and the girls had been very close. She had never known loneliness until her friend and confidante fell asleep for the last time.

Leaving Baltimore, where Jeanine had died, had been difficult for the family. But the new surroundings and the serenity and beauty of the plantation had the effect of a balm on their grieving hearts. Now, Bloomingdale was home, and Abigail couldn't imagine ever living anywhere else.

The awe and wonder had long since been replaced with grateful acceptance. Sometimes it was easy to forget that she had not always been so fortunate.

Clara, resting in an ornately carved chair with plush velvet cushions, smiled at her sister. "I must agree. Bloomingdale is one of the few places it's easy to forget that there's a war. It seems so untouched."

For these two sisters, the War Between the States had irrevocably altered their lives. Not only had their younger brother, Edward, been drafted into the conflict only to be killed, Jane's fiancé had died in the battle of Antietam, and Clara's husband had been wounded at Gettysburg.

Abigail had first met Clara when Jeremiah was honorably discharged from the Union Army for his injuries. His hand had been amputated above the wrist, and Abigail had been instrumental in introducing him to Judson, who had suffered a similar injury, and could point him to a doctor who could fit him with a useful prosthesis.

"I was pleased to see Jeremiah here tonight," she told Clara. "I wasn't sure if he would come."

The smile that touched Clara's face as she replied said everything. Adoration was evident in her eyes as she said, "I just can't tell you how thankful I am that you were able to introduce him to Judson. Having a friend with the same malady makes him feel less like uncomfortable with it. And Dr. Greene's device has been a godsend!"

The most modern design, the prosthesis was made of leather which strapped to the forearm and could be used in a variety of ways with interchangeable tools, as well as a rubber hand for formal occasions. Abigail's friend, Judson Shepherd, had been the first man in Queen Anne's County to obtain one, and he had been more than happy to persuade Jeremiah of its usefulness. When Jeremiah had first returned home as an amputee, he had been bitterly discouraged by his disability.

Jane nodded. "If you didn't know it, you wouldn't realize that either of them men are missing a hand."

Abigail didn't want to embarrass Jane, but she was pleased that she had arrived on Judson's elbow. It was wonderful to see her coming to life again since her fiancé's death.

"I believe that's one of the reasons Jeremiah came tonight," Clara admitted. "At home, however, he enjoys being able to transform his arm into different tools. Men! I declare, I don't know if the hook or the fork gets more use."

"But isn't it his left hand?" Abigail raised a brow in confusion.

"It is. Now he wants to have a fork in each hand," Clara giggled.

Abigail laughed. "You shouldn't tease me at your husband's expense!" she admonished.

Clara only grinned, wholly unrepentant, and Abigail could only smile in return. She was pleased to see Clara so happy after all she had been through.

Growing serious, Clara said, "I am thankful he's here. He seems to be adapting to his amputation and the tools have made his work much easier."

"And has he had any reply to his letters?" Jane wondered.

At Abigail's questioning look, Clara explained, "He's been trying to get a letter through to his brother, who's being held at the Confederate prison in Southern Maryland. But there's no way to be sure that his letters have been delivered. There's been no response."

Abigail had forgotten that Clara's brother-in-law had joined the Rebels. There had been many families on the Eastern Shore, and throughout the state of Maryland, who had been torn apart by the war. It was an impossible mess which her father predicted would forever scar the nation.

President Lincoln may have ensured that Maryland did not secede, but he couldn't outlaw the strong Southern sympathy which still flourished among many of its citizens. Some subscribed to the president's view that secession was a form of rebellion and must be suppressed, but her father was not one of them. Irving Sterret and his cohorts referred to the conflict as "The War Against Northern Aggression" among themselves. In public, they had enough good sense to keep their views quiet— and Margaret Sterret would have boxed her husband's ears if he had brought any trouble with the Provost Marshall or the Home Guard to their door.

To the Far North and in the Deep South, there was outspoken resentment for the opposing party. But in Maryland, a border state seized by the Federal Government, it was far more complicated and convoluted. Families and friendships were redefined, and trust was a precious commodity. Only the closest of friends knew where any man or woman truly stood on the subject.

Although the sweep of arrests which upset the state at the outbreak of the war had ceased, they had left a lasting impression. Anyone implicated as a Confederate supporter had fallen under scrutiny, and many had been imprisoned without charges.

Now, those who harbored strong anti-Union sentiments had either gone south or learned to keep their mouths shut and salute the Stars and Stripes when it was required. Ironically, Abigail had heard that down in Dixie the song "Maryland, My Maryland," was still a celebrated anthem, even though the state was not included in the Confederacy. Its passionate expression of distaste for the "Northern Scum" had made it a Rebel favorite.

Clara's forehead creased as she continued, "Jeremiah's very worried. They say the conditions at Point Lookout are far from pleasant."

Abigail reached for her friend's hand, giving it a reassuring squeeze. "Then we shall keep him in our prayers."

Chapter Two

Crouching low to the ground, Charlie moved stealthily along the perimeter of the stockade, Wilson at his heels. The lapping of the waves on the beach beyond the wooden wall muffled the sound of their footsteps in the sand. Alert to every movement and noise around him, Charlie's eyes searched the darkness as his hands felt for a breach in the wall which signaled an opening.

There was a deadline within ten feet of the wall, and any prisoner who crossed the line could expect a bullet in his back. As the guards didn't need a reason to shoot, it was foolish to provide them with justification. The only reason they dared to slink in the shadows, cautiously making their way to the rear gate, was confidence in the two former slaves of Laurel Hill, Henry and Eli, who had been stationed as guards at Point Lookout with the Third Maryland Colored Regiment. Meeting secretly with Charlie in the dead of night, they had devised a plan of escape, risking their own lives to set him free.

Never in his years growing up on the farm had Charlie imagined a day when his fate would rest in their black hands. The Turners had always had an amiable relationship with their slaves, but they were nonetheless subordinates. Life had certainly taken many unexpected turns.

Despite their lack of education, Charlie learned that these Negro men were both intelligent and wise. For months, Henry and Eli planned and prepared for the perfect opportunity. As they waited for the weather to warm into spring, they made careful observations of every detail at Camp Hoffman, as the prison camp was officially named. They noted the patterns and behaviors of both guards and prisoners, and learned the connections between the cycle of the moon and the tides.

Tonight, by random coincidence, the two Negro men were both assigned to the second night shift, while everyone else on the Point lay sleeping. When utter silence reigned over the stockade and the darkness was so deep that Charlie could barely see his hand in front of his face, they would execute their plan. While Eli stood guard, ready to interfere if anything went awry, Henry crept around the exterior of the stockade to permit their exit through the rear gate.

A canoe, stocked with a few days' worth of hard tack and salted pork, was beached behind the "bull pen." Fresh water was scarce on the Point, and Henry could only provide one small canteen. Wilson, Charlie's comrade since the beginning of the war, had been invited to join in the escape both for the sake of friendship and necessity. Charlie wouldn't be capable of rowing across the bay alone. Although Eli and Henry had smuggled extra rations to him when they could in hopes of building his strength, Charlie remained anemic and thin as a rail.

Clouds, like tufts of gray wool, drifted across the sky and obliterated the moon's pale radiance. Fleeting slivers of light slipped through, cutting a path across the undulating inky surface of the bay as the three men crept quietly toward the beach.

In a low whisper, Henry ordered, "Head due east," as he placed a map and a compass in Charlie's palm. "You's gots to row all night, Mister Charlie, hard as you can. Take turns, but don't stop. It gonna take you all night and then some to get 'cross that bay, then head north and hug the shore. They's lots a islands and rivers out there, they say, and can be confusing. Be real careful. The Home Guard's keeping a watch out for Rebels."

Charlie tucked the items into his pocket. He extended his hand and gripped Henry's firmly as he replied gruffly, "Thank you..." He wanted to say more, but was at a loss for words. How could he ever thank this man for the risk he was taking? Especially when Charlie didn't deserve such compassion or kindness.

Wilson also shook the black man's hand. "I'm indebted," he said, sincere gratitude layering his voice.

Henry nodded in acknowledgement. "Get going, now," he eased the canoe into the water and held it steady as Charlie and Wilson climbed into the shallow craft and took up the oars. "Be safe, and Godspeed," the Negro guard encouraged, giving the canoe a hefty shove that sent it gliding out into the rising tide. Then turning on his heel, he quickly disappeared into the shadows.

Together, the prisoners silently rowed out into the open water. The lapping of the waves against the side of the canoe was the only sound other than the splash of the oars as they broke the surface. Charlie and Wilson bent into their work, eager to put distance between the Point and themselves.

It didn't take long for a burn to grow in Charlie's shoulders, which spread down into his back and biceps. Perspiration beaded his brow and dampened his clothing, and his breath came heavily. Wilson too strained against the oars.

When the beacon of the lighthouse had diminished into a mere pinprick in the distance, Charlie whispered, "Let's rest for a minute, then I'll take the first shift."

Wilson groaned as he eased the oars down into the canoe and flexed his sore shoulders. "Just for a minute," he agreed. "I feel weak as a kitten, and hungry as a tiger."

Charlie concurred with the sentiment. It was only the lure of freedom that gave him the strength to press on.

Through the long hours of the night they alternated rowing the canoe across the Chesapeake Bay, the one at rest lying down in a ball on the floor of the canoe to catch a few quick minutes of sleep to gather his strength for the next shift. The current tugged at the canoe and tried to pull them off course, but at the end of each shift, they checked the compass to be sure they were staying due east.

As the horizon glowed with the promise of dawn, Charlie had a fleeting thought for the safety of the guards who had freed him, hoping they would not be held accountable for the escape. But his tired mind was unable to stay fixed for long on anything beyond the present moment, the rhythm of his oars, and the threat of capture.

The sun made its slow progression into the sky, and Charlie sighed with relief as a row of islands appeared before them. Steering toward the one closest, they pushed the canoe up the bank into the reeds and sank down on the ground in exhaustion.

"Stay here with the canoe," Charlie managed to rasp out, his eyelids tugged by lead weights. "I'll go in search of fresh water." Their meager resource was already depleted.

Wilson barely nodded, his head sinking down onto his arm as he drifted into sleep. Charlie surveyed his gaunt friend, knowing he looked just as wretched. Cheekbones protruding, color sallow, and clothing worn, they were a pathetic pair. If he ran into anyone on the island, he would likely frighten them with his appearance.

Slipping carefully through the tall grasses, Charlie spied a farmhouse further inland. Although he didn't see anyone about, he skulked along the fence line and in the shadows of the barn in search of a spigot.

"Hi there," a boy's voice nearly made him jump out of his skin as it sounded behind him. Spinning around, Charlie looked down into the upturned, freckled face of the little urchin.

"Hello," he replied, in what he hoped was a friendly manner.

"You lookin' for my daddy?" the boy wondered.

"No," Charlie hastened to assure him, holding up the empty canteen. "I was out fishing on the bay and ran out of drinking water. Would you mind showing me where I can fill this?"

The boy studied him cautiously, taking in Charlie's attire. His uniform was so faded that it hardly appeared gray, and only the yellow stripe on his arms and the buttons gave it away. He nodded slowly. "It's this way."

"Which island is this?" Charlie wondered, trying to get his bearings and determine how far north they would need to travel.

"Holland Island," the child answered. "That's Smith Island that way," he pointed south, "and Bloodsworth Island over there," he indicated the opposite direction.

"Thank you, son," Charlie replied as he quickly moved to the well to fill his canteen before the boy's father appeared. "Appreciate your kindness," he added, taking a draught of the cold water. Then with a wave, he set off in the direction he had come, hoping the boy would forget to mention the stranger's visit to his father.

Returning to the beach, Charlie was relieved to discover that

Wilson had upturned the canoe and supported it with driftwood to create a makeshift shelter, covering it over with reeds and grasses to camouflage it. Offering his friend the canteen, Charlie slid underneath and within seconds was fast asleep.

They did not awaken until dusk. If anyone had tried to apprehend the fugitives, they would have faced little resistance. The boy had either kept Charlie's appearance secret, or his parents supported the Southern cause. On this side of the bay, the Confederacy had many spies and allies.

Quickly consuming a small portion of their hardtack and pork, followed by a measured drink from the canteen, they retrieved the map and tried to ascertain the most effective route in the fading pink light. The goal was Centreville, in Queen Anne's County. It could take them as long as a week to get home, assuming they weren't intercepted.

Uncovering the canoe, the Confederate prisoners carried it down the sandy beach to the bay. They pushed off from Holland Island and headed back out into the channel, bypassing Bloodsworth Island as well as a string of other islands, invisible in the darkness. Their eyes scanned the water around them cautiously. The Union, having taken control of Maryland, had also seized possession of the Chesapeake Bay. Charlie and Wilson were lucky not to have encountered a Navy ship in route to Annapolis or Baltimore thus far, and they prayed their luck would hold out. Their hope was to make it as far as Tilghman Island by morning, just past the mouth of the Choptank River.

Charlie leaned forward then pulled back on the oars, struggling to cut a clean path through the water as the canoe dipped and lurched in the waves. Despite the hours of rest they'd grabbed during the daylight hours, Wilson lay huddled in the floor of the canoe. Although Charlie could not see him there, enveloped in thick shadows, he knew Wilson was lost in the oblivion of sleep brought on by malnutrition and overexertion. Although he fought the exhaustion that claimed to overtake him as well, Charlie resolved to let Wilson sleep for as long as his strength held out.

They both resembled scarecrows with their clothes hanging limply from their gaunt frames, but there was an increasing absence growing in Wilson's glassy eyes. It was as if his spirit was tethered to his body only by one thin tie, and if it were to break, Wilson would drift away like an air balloon floating into the sky.

Wilson had been with Charlie from the beginning. They had both been in attendance at the secret meetings held in support of the new nation, the Confederate States of America. They had somehow believed that if they held their ground, the United States would grant them sovereignty: America would be comprised of two nations, both born from the pursuit of freedom.

With a band of like-minded men, they had headed south to Richmond and enlisted in the army of the Confederacy, under President Jefferson Davis. The First Maryland Infantry, CSA was without weapons and ammunition until Captain Bradley Johnson's wife, from North Carolina, was able to obtain such for them.

They were taught the Manual of Arms and drilled side by side until the orders were instinctive, requiring no forethought. It was as if it was the musket in their hands obeying the commands, transitioning quickly from shoulder to chest, to resting position. The days of training had been charged with excitement that quickly yielded to fear as they were sent into the fray in Manassas, Virginia—the first large scale battle of the war. Charlie and Wilson had faced the fear and the horror of battle together, earning the title of soldier as they fought with valor and courage.

In Front Royal, Winchester, and Bolivar Heights, they had fought under General "Stonewall" Jackson. They had stood shoulder to shoulder at Harrisonburg, the Battle of Cross Keys, and at Gaines' Mill, frequently referred to as Cold Harbor. All this they had survived, only to be taken prisoner at Gettysburg and sent home to Maryland as prisoners of war.

Wilson stirred, pushing himself up groggily into a sitting position. He twisted his head to spot the white crescent of the moon in the sky overhead, and realizing that Charlie had neglected to wake him, climbed onto the bench and took up his oars. "I'll row," he insisted, though the weakness in his voice was far from reassuring.

Charlie pulled his oars into the canoe and stretched his neck and shoulders. If he didn't ache from the long hours pulling the small craft through the rocking waves, he would have insisted that Wilson rest. But the truth was he needed the break.

He sighed as he ran his fingers through his hair. They had to survive.

Charlie relieved Wilson one more time before morning broke. They successfully reached Tilghman Island and pulled the canoe into a marsh thick with cattails and tall grasses. Thus hidden, they both lay upon the floor and slept through the day.

"You think we're going to make it?" Wilson asked as they prepared for another long night. The shadows beneath his eyes had deepened, and his cheekbones were sharp enough to pierce his skin.

"We'll make it," Charlie answered, his voice firm with conviction, wishing his resolve could somehow strengthen Wilson and keep him going. If the smoke wouldn't have signaled their location, Charlie would have made an effort to trap a muskrat or catch a fish to roast for their dinner. As it was, they were surviving on next to nothing.

But they were getting close, and that knowledge spurred them on. If they could just hang on for another day or two, they'd be home.

They rowed the canoe northward, around Tilghman Island into the Eastern Bay, and from there made their way to the Wye River, following it until it narrowed into a creek that wound its way through forests and fields. When this stream mustered out, they pushed the canoe onto the bank and continued their journey on foot.

Traveling northeast toward Centreville, they made slow progress through the undergrowth and bramble. Cursing the difficulty of negotiating the untamed terrain of the woodlands, they were thankful nonetheless for its protection. Hidden deep in its shadows, they were concealed from prying eyes.

After some time, they stumbled out of the forest onto a dirt road. With a glance in either direction, they crossed over it in the pale moonlight. Suddenly, what had appeared to be no more than a shadow lunged forward, yelling, "Halt! Stop right there and report—"

Charlie and Wilson sprinted into the tree line opposite them, the thud of hooves behind them echoing in their ears. Adrenaline surged through their weakened frames and propelled them forward until, in the darkness and underbrush, the mounted pursuer was forced to abandon the chase.

Through the stillness of the night, a voice shouted, *"You aren't getting away! I'll find you. I know where you're headed!"*

Once confident that they were no longer at risk, the men sank to the ground, heaving. Leaning against the trunk of a tree, Charlie gulped air into his burning lungs. Beside him, Wilson panted as he gripped his side.

"Know that stitch you get when you run too much?" he wheezed. "I hate that."

"That was close," Charlie gasped out.

"Home Guard?"

"Yeah. And I'm guessing they know it's us. Must have got word from the prison to keep an eye out for us. Probably figured we'd head for home." Charlie closed his eyes. What had ever made him think this scheme would succeed?

He took a few more deep breaths, then decided, "All right, let's head south for a bit, just to throw them off. We'll spend the night out here, then tomorrow, we'll make our way back toward Centreville."

Wilson nodded, a slight movement that seemed to require all his strength and willpower.

"You all right to keep going?"

Wilson nodded again. "Can't wait here like sitting ducks."

They set off a pace that was far too slow for Charlie's liking, but was all they could manage in their impaired state. The escaped prisoners kept clear of every lane or street they encountered, staying within the safety of the shadows. As the sun pushed back the darkness, and dawn spread like wildfire across the eastern horizon, they took refuge in a shallow depression hidden by a grove of ancient oaks. Burrowing into the leaves like squirrels, they quickly fell into dreamless sleep.

"Hey, I think we found 'em!" the cry alerted Charlie to their discovery.

He sprang to his feet, but swayed dizzily, trying to ascertain the direction of the voice. Wilson's expression was calm as he stared up at Charlie, resigned to his fate. He was in no condition to outrun the patrols again.

Charlie spun in a circle, crouched like a caged tiger, ready to fight with whatever strength remained in him. A voice replied to the first man, softer than his counterpart's, and Charlie squinted through the foliage to spy five blue bellies on horseback. Without hesitating, he grabbed Wilson by the elbow and yanked him to his feet.

"Run!" he ordered, dragging Wilson with him as they stumbled through the leaves and thistles.

A shot cut through the stillness and Wilson's body jerked before crumpling to the ground. Charlie paused only long enough to see the emptiness in his friend's eyes before he set off in a zig-zag motion, darting between the thick tree trunks. Another shot rang out, and the bullet imbedded harmlessly in the bark. Heart thundering in his ears, Charlie dodged to the left, only to hear the whine of another bullet as it sped through the air over his head. Ducking now to the right, he feared he was fleeing the inevitable.

No sooner had he prepared for the end, than Charlie saw his opportunity and hurled himself at it without regard to the risks involved. A ravine opened up just ahead, enclosed by thick snarls of ivy and thistles. He launched himself over it, heedless of the consequences. The thorns snagged his clothing and ripped his skin as he somersaulted head over heels down the slope, slamming hard into a tree. Stunned, Charlie shook his head and tried to regain his bearings.

Above, the vehement cursing of the Home Guard affirmed that the blue bellies had no intention of leading their mounts into such dangerous terrain. Instead, they aimed the barrels of their guns into the morass of greenery and fired. Shots echoed around Charlie, and he darted behind the tree which had stopped his fall. But not before a bullet had found its way into his right side.

As soon as the barrage had ceased, left hand clutching his wound, Charlie staggered to his feet and clambered from the ravine.

Chapter Three

Bloomingdale Plantation
Queenstown, Maryland

Beneath a wide oak with towering limbs, Abigail rested on a bench, her pink-checked skirts spread out around her with a calico cat purring in her lap. Stroking the silky fur absently, Abigail watched the men in the fields as they ploughed through the hard earth which had lain dormant since fall.

Nearby, her black Staffordshire terrier sniffed the ground, excited by the smells of fresh growth and budding flowers. Sam periodically left his task to return to Abigail, shoving his wet nose into her lap and giving the cat, Sprightly, an affectionate lick. When he eventually wandered off, following a particularly interesting scent, Abigail barely noticed, confident that he wouldn't stray very far.

Spring always brought with it a renewal of hope, a promise that all which dies will one day live again. Abigail basked in the warmth of the golden sunshine, soaking it in with gratitude after the long winter months. The yellow daffodils and the purple crocus, the rich green of the lawn, and the powder blue of the sky above, were such a welcome sight after the gray emptiness of the preceding season.

The sound of Sam's barking brought Abigail sharply from her reverie. The black dog bounded toward her from a nearby copse of trees, stopping a few feet away from her and raising a noisy racket. The intensity of his barking was unusual, and Abigail narrowed her brows in concern.

"What is it, boy?" she wondered.

Coming to her feet, Abigail gently placed Sprightly on the bench with the command, "Stay here," as if the cat could do otherwise.

The calico had been just a kitten when her hind legs had been severely broken by a misplaced hoof in a horse stall. It was a miracle she had survived, and without Abigail, she wouldn't have lived another hour. The stable master, the slave called Washington, had intended to end the animal's misery. But Abigail had heard the commotion and run into the barn to investigate. Seeing the wounded creature, she had begged him to let her save it. Reluctantly, Washington had yielded the mangled kitten to the master's daughter.

Abigail had arrived at the kitchen, the bodice of her gown soaked with blood, and begged Lizzie the cook to help her save the calico kitten's life. Lizzie had complied, applying herbs to the site of the injury and binding the tiny legs with linen bandages. Abigail had committed herself to its recovery, and had defied her mother by keeping the animal in her bedroom. The kitten had pulled through, but was rendered lame.

Sprightly meowed in protest as Abigail left her to follow the dog, who was running in frenzied circles around her, barking wildly.

"What is it?" Abigail demanded again, and Sam took off in the direction of the woods. As they approached the thicket, Sam lunged ahead, forcing Abigail to lift her skirts and break into an unladylike run. Still, Sam reached the site of his concern before her.

Abigail arrived panting, her chest heaving as she stepped around a dense shrub to see the source of the dog's distress. Her hand flew to her mouth as a gasp escaped her lips. A man lay face-forward in the leaves, his head resting on his forearm. A stain of crimson colored the right side of his gray uniform.

Staring at the wounded man, a million thoughts raced through Abigail's mind. Why was he here? How had he been shot? And who was he? But all these were quickly erased by one more pressing question.

"Is he still alive?" she wondered, taking a tentative step toward him.

Leaning cautiously over him, she noted the shallow rise and fall of his chest. Peering over his shoulder, she could see the contours of his left cheek. "Barely," she whispered, horrified. Gaunt, his skin as gray as his uniform, he appeared to be clinging to life by only a fragile thread.

"Oh dear God," Abigail whispered. "Sam, you stay with him," she ordered the dog, who seemed to understand as he lay down next to the injured soldier and licked his hand.

Turning on her heel, Abigail hurried back to the house, rushing into the kitchen in a hurricane of whirling skirts and rushing words.

Lizzie huffed, wiping her dark hands on her apron as she stepped away from the stove to command, "Calm down, child!" Taking in Abigail's wide eyes, she queried, "What on earth's the matter?"

"A man!" Abigail tried to explain, "in the woods—" she pointed in the general direction where he had been found. "He's been shot, and he's barely breathing!"

"Lawd have mercy!" Lizzie exclaimed. Turning to the

young black girl sweeping the kitchen floor, she snapped, "Ruthie, you take those biscuits out when they gets gold brown on top and stir that pot, you hear?"

Ruthie nodded obediently, the broom held immobile in her hands.

"We gonna need some help bringin' him in," Lizzie thought out loud. "Better see who's in the stable."

Abigail followed Lizzie breathlessly to the barn, standing back as the cook explained to the stable master and groom, "We gots a 'mergency what needs your help. Follow me!"

Washington and Abel immediately dropped their tasks and made to follow her. Lizzie turned to Abigail, who quickly led them to where Sam waited with the invalid. They found him exactly as Abigail had left him, head resting on his arm, unconscious.

"Good boy, Sam," Abigail patted the dog's head as he left his vigil to stand beside her.

Washington lowered his bulk to the ground beside the young man, shaking his head. "He ain't too good off, Missy. I think he half-dead already."

Lizzie knelt down beside Washington, her nimble fingers pulling back the layers of clothes which covered the wound to examine the bullet's point of entry. "I bets I could get that shot out," she mused. "Ain't infected yet... I's thinkin' he just plumb worn out from runnin' and never havin' no good food."

The stable master stared at the cook incredulously, his dark eyes round and his second chin wobbling beneath his first. "This here ain't no kitten, Lizzie. That's a Rebel soldier!"

"You think I don't know that?" the little woman retorted,

unperturbed by the large frame towering over her. "Bring him to the house. I hide him in the cellar."

Abigail released the breath she didn't realize she'd been holding.

"You can't hide no Rebel at Bloomin'dale!" Washington sputtered. "You out of your ever-lovin' mind!"

"What you gonna do?" Lizzie came to her feet, just barely taller than the big man when he was kneeling. Hands on her narrow hips, she lifted her black eyebrows in challenge. "Shoot 'im? He ain't one of your horses."

The stable master's black skin flushed red as he growled in reply. "You gots to promise to tell Mastah Sterret. I ain't risking my hide for no damn Johnny Reb."

Abigail stepped forward. "I'll tell Papa. I know he'd want us to help." Her mother, on the other hand, was an entirely different story.

Shaking his head and grumbling, Washington heaved himself onto his feet. "Let's get 'im on his back," he instructed Abel. Carefully flipping the limp body onto his back, Washington slid his hands under the armpits while Abel hefted the unconscious man by the ankles.

"Good thing he don't weigh much," Washington muttered as they slowly made their way back toward the house.

Reaching the edge of the trees, Lizzie commanded them to wait while she searched the area for anyone who might observe their strange cargo. With a wave of her hand, she directed them into the open and across the lawn to the kitchen. Once inside, she pointed a finger at Ruth and said, "You don't see nothin'!" as she lit a candle and preceded the men down into the cellar.

The musty smell of dampness and potatoes assaulted Abigail's nostrils as she followed them into the earthen cave beneath the kitchen. The flickering light of the flame danced in the closed space, the shadows it cast eerie as they moved across the uneven surface of the walls. A shiver skittered down Abigail's spine.

"Just lay 'im here," Lizzie pointed to an open space on the floor between crates of potatoes and leather-britches-beans. To Abigail, she said, "Tell Ruthie find some blankets for the poor soul. This floor ain't nothing for him to lay on."

Abigail was happy to comply, breathing the fresh air greedily into her lungs as she emerged from the black cellar and into the light. Once delivering Lizzie's orders, she hesitated, reluctant to return to the cramped space below. Deciding to wait for Ruthie and carry the blankets down herself, Abigail suddenly remembered that Sprightly still waited for her on the bench.

Once having retrieved the cat, who was peeved at having been thus abandoned, she situated the calico on a chair in the kitchen just as Ruthie came through the door with a stack of blankets on her arms. Accepting them from the slave girl, Abigail took a deep breath before she climbed back down into the hiding place.

"Slide this one under him," Lizzie directed the men, who obeyed with more gruffness than was good for the patient. "Now get on out of here," she waved them toward the door. Without a word, they readily complied.

"I gonna need someone to hold the candle steady," Lizzie's face, even blacker in the shadows, was stern. "If you can't stomach watchin', then you either need to look away or gets Ruthie to hold it from the start."

Unused to being spoken to by slaves in this manner, Abigail

merely nodded. She understood the gravity of the situation. "I'll do it," she promised.

Lizzie nodded in approval. "I get my things and be right back," she said, bustling up the steps and leaving Abigail alone in the shadows with the wounded soldier.

Holding the candle high in the air, Abigail approached the resting figure slowly. He sported a short, but unkempt beard, the same brown as his hair. She guessed he couldn't be much older than she was, and from the looks of him, he'd had a rough time of it before he ever met the wrong end of the firearm.

Lizzie soon returned with a basket swinging from the crook of one elbow and a bowl of water in her hand. Wordlessly, she knelt down beside the young man and uncovered the wound. Curious, Abigail wanted to watch the procedure, but the sight of fresh blood and the gaping hole in his flesh brought a wave of nausea which compelled her to look away.

Fastening her eyes on the dirt floor, she listened to the sound of Lizzie's confident ministrations. The soldier groaned and flinched, but never awakened.

"All right, then," Lizzie announced, "I'm going to need your help dressing the wound."

Slowly lifting her eyes, Abigail saw that Lizzie had covered the bullet wound with a bandage held firmly in place with her left hand, while her right hand held a roll which they would need to wrap around his waist.

"Oh…" Abigail said as she realized what she needed to do and came to join her. Together, they rocked his slight frame to one side and then the other, until the bandage was secured around him.

"Do you think he will make it?" Abigail studied his wan

face in the wavering candlelight.

"If God wills," Lizzie replied, coming to her feet.

.

Chapter Four

When Charlie opened his eyes, he was surrounded by darkness so thick it was as if he were blind. His heart thumped against his ribcage as he gasped for breath, lifting his hands above his head in wild panic, expecting to feel the wooden encasement of a coffin.

He had heard that soldiers were sometimes buried with a string tied to their finger, attached to a bell above the ground to alert someone if a man presumed dead should awaken in his grave. The administration of chloroform, which slowed the heart rate, and the chaotic conditions of the field hospital, had combined to lead to more than one false proclamation of death.

But instead of meeting the ceiling of a coffin, Charlie's hand stretched upward unhindered in the blackness. Reaching to the side, his hand was met with the damp surface of the earth. Had he been buried without a coffin, thrown into an open hole in the ground?

Fear propelled him into a sitting position, and it combined with the pain which seared his side to create a guttural cry which ripped involuntarily from his lips.

Suddenly the sound of a door scraping open filled the silence around him, and a yellow circle of welcome light flooded the dark space. The sound of footsteps descending wooden stairs was accompanied by a voice saying, "Hush now. You all right. You just fine. You in my cellar. I brought you some water."

The candlelight revealed a black woman's face, thin and angled, with her head bound by a white cloth. He hesitated as she pressed the cup into his hand.

"I's a friend," she assured him, sensing his distrust.

Thirst cried out to be slaked, and Charlie accepted the water and greedily pressed it to his lips.

"Slow sips," the mysterious woman cautioned.

Charlie obeyed, grateful for the fresh liquid as it eased down his parched throat. Next she pressed a cracker into his hand. He ate it slowly as well, surprised by how quickly the small portion filled him.

When she took the cup of water from his hand, she replaced it with another. Charlie sniffed it carefully. Laudanum. "It help you rest," she explained. "You gots to rest if you gonna get better."

Leaning heavily against the moist wall of the cellar, Charlie welcomed the oblivion which the opiate would bring. His side throbbed and burned, and his entire body ached with weariness.

"Now, you gots to be quiet," his black angel of mercy admonished gently. "No one can know you here."

Nodding imperceptibly, Charlie winced as he leaned back to lay upon the blanket which covered the hard ground. He wanted to ask her name, but the laudanum had already taken effect.

When he awakened again, it was with the same terrifying fear that he had been buried alive. But as memory returned of the Negro woman and the care she had given him, Charlie's heart slowly calmed to a steady rhythm. He was safe, at least for the moment.

But where exactly was he?

For what seemed like hours, Charlie lay silently in the dank cellar, listening to the sounds of scraping chairs and busy feet above him. He slept intermittently, startled awake by the pain that jabbed through his right side with even the slightest movement. Sliding a hand down the protruding bones of his ribs, he gingerly felt the bandage and rubbed his fingers together. It was wet. He must have reopened the wound somehow. It would need fresh dressing, and he longed for another drink of water and a handful of crackers. But he dared not call out for fear of jeopardizing his own safety, as well as those who harbored him.

He had no concept of night or day, no way to mark the time in this never-ending darkness. Left alone, with no one but himself for company, there was nothing to do but stare into the black space above his head and think. In the quiet loneliness his life flashed before his eyes in a series of memories, like a parade of ghosts taunting him as they went past, reminding him of choices which would haunt him forever.

Regret, self-loathing, and bitterness marched in circles around his head, crowding out every other thought and feeling until the blackness within him was as dark as the blackness around him. Charlie no longer cared if the Negro woman reappeared with provisions for him. Death would be a welcome solace.

And yet... There was so much left unfinished.

The scraping of the door signaled that he was no longer alone. Charlie closed his eyes in despair, feeling a unity with the darkness. But something was different about the fluid grace of the approaching footsteps, and curiosity turned his head for him. The small flame illuminated another face this time, one far more youthful, pale, and beautiful.

His heart caught in his throat. He hadn't seen a woman, not

a woman like this, in longer than he cared to remember.

"I've brought you some bread and soup," she said softly, lowering the tray which held the items and the candleholder to a small table which Charlie was certain had not been there before. A chair also seemed to have materialized, and Charlie wondered if someone—if she—had sat with him, watching over him while he slept.

"Do you think you can sit up... or do you need my help?" she asked innocently, her wide almond eyes studying him with concern.

Wincing, Charlie managed to bring himself upright, using the wall for support. He feared he may not be steady enough to hold the bowl with one hand while he spooned the broth into his mouth with the other, but he didn't dare express this concern aloud. He watched as the young woman removed the candle from the tray and placed it on the table, then carefully situated the tray in his lap.

With hands trembling from hunger and pain, or so he told himself, Charlie slowly lifted a spoonful to his mouth. It was only soup, but it was real soup, made with chicken stock, meat, carrots and peas. He savored every bite, then reached for the bread. Fresh and warm, it was thick and hearty, and he relished every crumb.

"There," she said maternally, "that feels better, doesn't it?" She bestowed a smile upon him that nearly took his breath away as she leaned down to retrieve the tray.

Charlie waited, but she showed no sign of leaving, studying him quietly as if she was rolling a question around in her mind before she asked it. Having no desire to answer questions of any kind, and feeling uncomfortable with himself in this condition in her presence, Charlie eased back down to the ground and supported his head with his arm. He closed his eyes, intending to shut her out.

But her voice, sultry and sweet, floated in the space above him. "Are they looking for you?"

He nodded, ever so slightly. "As soon as I'm able, I'll be on my way," he promised.

"No hurry," she answered calmly. "I just wanted to be sure."

"You're in danger harboring me," he warned, just to be certain she understood the risk she was taking.

"We know," she replied, sounding wholly unconcerned.

"We?" Charlie asked, hoping she did not refer to her husband.

"My father knows you're here. He tried to visit with you yesterday, but you were sleeping." Charlie felt odd knowing a stranger had watched him sleep. "My mother doesn't know, and must not find out," the young woman added. "Only four of the slaves know you're here. They've been given strict orders to keep your presence a secret."

Charlie wondered who it was who had found him, and who had carried him down into the cellar. But he didn't ask. It didn't really matter.

"Are you a fugitive or a deserter?" she finally voiced the question which he suspected was the one she had been contemplating all along.

Considering his answer truthfully, Charlie replied, "Both."

"Ah," she replied noncommittally.

The silence lengthened, and once again Charlie hoped she would consider the conversation closed. He preferred to be left alone with his misery.

"What's your name?" she asked softly.

"Where am I?" Charlie evaded the question.

"Bloomingdale," she told him without hesitation. "My father is Irving Sterret, and I'm Abigail."

In the long pause that followed, he knew she was waiting for his answer.

"You can call me Johnny," he finally offered.

~

"Harris Sterret, I declare! You are not a common farmer's son." Margaret Sterret scolded the ten year old boy as he proudly produced a fat green frog from his pocket. "*Please*, would you behave like a gentleman?"

Having received the reaction he hoped for, Harris flashed his older sister a smile marked by two missing front teeth as he released the amphibian onto the porch floor. It hopped across the white painted boards with Harris bounding behind it, while on Abigail's lap, Sprightly expressed her regret at being unable to chase it.

"And *you*, Miss Abigail," Margaret turned to her daughter, "with that animal on your lap! I declare, my children have no appreciation for their social distinction." She huffed irritably, her narrow foot rocking the white wicker chair back and forth in agitation.

Abigail, seated on the wicker divan across from her mother on the hexagonally shaped porch, held her tongue as she had been taught. It was rare that anyone performed to Margaret's expectations in any capacity. They had all grown accustomed to the incessant nagging which characterized her presence.

Stroking the cat's soft fur, Abigail let her thoughts wander to the root cellar, where the wounded soldier lay resting. She had yet to visit him today and she hoped he showed some improvement. Lizzie had commissioned Ruthie to help her with Johnny's bandages, insisting it was not appropriate for the young miss. Lizzie said that the wound was healing up nicely, but the greater problem was the young man's malnourishment. His bones and muscles had been weakened from what she suspected was years without a proper diet.

"Nothing but skin over bones!" Lizzie had fussed. "I ain't never seen nothing' so skinny in my life," the Negro cook had shaken her head sadly.

Johnny's tattered rags had been infested with vermin, and Irving had insisted that the soldier change into fresh clothing, and his uniform be burned. Too weak and in too much pain to manage himself, Irving and Abel had assisted in seeing Johnny dressed.

Lizzie had taken a basin of hot water and lye soap to the cellar and washed his hair, as well. "Yo' head ain't no place for bugs," she'd insisted.

Johnny had endured their attention with sullen gratitude. When Abigail mentioned his demeanor to her father, Irving had simply replied, "The boy's been through a hell of a lot, Abby. It's going to take time for him to mend from the inside out."

Although Abigail looked more like her mother, she had inherited her father's personality, a fact which she considered a gracious act of God. Irving was a plain looking man, of average height and with a balding head. There was little in his person to distinguish him. But he had a quick mind and a kind heart, and he was loved and respected by his children.

Margaret Sterret was still an attractive woman despite her advancing years, and while she did possess a loving heart, it was overshadowed by the sharpness of her tongue. Like the children, Irving had learned to turn a deaf ear to her when possible, and to placate her when necessary.

Irving often quoted the Proverb: *"Better is a dry crust with peace and quiet than a house full of feasting, with strife."*

Abigail loved her mother, she simply loved her more in her absence than in her presence.

If Irving hadn't been a compassionate man, Abigail doubted she would have been able to persuade the slaves to hide Johnny. He would have been turned over to the authorities, where she doubted he would have lived for very long. And if Sam hadn't found him, Abigail was certain he would have died right there, within yards of the house.

The dog had sniffed out that the young man was down in the cellar, and had taken up residence in front of the door. When given opportunity, he ran down the stairs to greet the wounded soldier with affectionate and slobbery kisses.

Lizzie said she thought it did Johnny good to have the company. They just hoped the terrier didn't give the fugitive's presence away.

With a sly wink directed at his sister, Harris approached their mother nonchalantly, releasing a beetle from between his cupped hands when she glanced up at him. Squealing in surprise and alarm, Margaret waved her hands frantically at the winged creature as it buzzed away to safety.

Harris clutched his belly and laughed, "It was just a beetle,

Mama! It can't hurt you!"

Margaret sprang to her feet, taking the boy by the ear as she screeched, "What you need, young man, is a good spanking. And I shall be sure your father delivers one to you this evening!" With an injured huff, she swept into the house with her skirts rustling behind her.

Unperturbed, Harris grinned at how easily he had disposed of their mother and scampered off to find Lizzie's son, Billy, who enjoyed frogs and beetles as much he did. Abigail shook her head in amusement. They both knew that Irving wasn't going to whip the boy for such an innocent prank.

Carrying Sprightly in her arms, Abigail made her way to the kitchen. Lizzie stood at the table kneading dough for biscuits, an apron tied around her thin waist. She looked up from her work as Abigail entered, relaxed upon seeing it was only her, and returned to the task at hand.

"'Afternoon, Miss Ab'gail," Lizzie greeted her with a distracted smile. At the sound of her voice, Sprightly meowed.

Lizzie grinned as she answered, "'Afternoon to you too, Kitty." The cook referred to every feline on the plantation as "Kitty," and there were many of them. Their job was to manage the rodent population in the barn and corn cribs, and under normal circumstances they were barred from the house. Sprightly was the one exception.

"You can go on down," Lizzie said, knowing why Abigail had come. "He just as pleasant as always."

"Delightful," Abigail muttered as she lit a candle and descended into the dank coolness below.

Johnny blinked against the brightness of the flickering light, obviously disturbed from his sleep. "I'm sorry to wake you,"

Abigail apologized, "but I thought you might like a bit of company." A blank stare was his only reply.

"Lizzie said that you enjoyed my dog Sam's visits, so I brought you another pet of mine. I had a female dog, Sophie, but she became aggressive toward Sam and I sent her to live with the miller's family."

"Aggression is nature's way of weeding out the weaklings," he grumbled.

"This is Sprightly," Abigail ignored his comment as she placed the calico cat on his lap.

"You have a sick sense of humor," Johnny observed as he took in the animal's bent, withered legs. "What happened to it?"

"She wandered into a stall where she didn't belong and met with a misplaced hoof," Abigail replied, pausing for a brief second before explaining, "She has a sprightly spirit, even if not a sprightly gait."

Johnny raised his eyebrows in mockery. "Sprightly spirit, eh? Whatever that means. So, how does it hunt its food now?"

"She can't, she's completely lame. I feed her scraps from the kitchen, and she stays in my bedroom for her safety," Abigail answered.

The invalid snorted. "I don't know which of the two of you is more spoiled."

Abigail bit her tongue, reminding herself that he had endured many hardships she couldn't even imagine. With a forced smile, Abigail ignored the jab and asked instead, "Do you like cats?"

"No," he replied flatly, although Sprightly purred contentedly on his lap as Johnny scratched her behind the ears.

"I find her company peaceful," Abigail replied, hoping the cat would have the same effect on this young man. He resembled a human scarecrow, with his baggy clothing hanging from his gaunt limbs and his freshly washed hair tumbling onto his forehead above a thin face, hidden behind a layer of thick stubble.

Folding her hands in her lap, Abigail made no further attempt at conversation. She wished she knew what to say to him.

"Any chance I could see a newspaper? I'd love to know what's happening," he finally broke the silence. His eyebrows drew together in curiosity as he asked, "You know who's winning the war?"

"Who can say?" Abigail shrugged. "The Rebels won a battle in September, in Tennessee, at Chickamauga. But they paid for it with a defeat in November, at Chattanooga. The end has been predicted a thousand times over, so who knows when or how it will end?"

Rubbing a skeletal hand over his scruffy face, Johnny sighed heavily. "If there are any newspapers from the last few months lying around, I'd like to read them," he repeated.

"I'll talk to my father," Abigail promised.

"He's a brave man, and kind, to hide me here," Johnny offered, his eyes softening for the first time.

"Thank you," she replied, pleased to hear him express gratitude. "When I found you, I knew he would never turn you away."

A dark look returned to his eyes, and Abigail wondered what she had said to revive it.

"You seem to be in the habit of saving pathetic souls— trampled kittens and wounded soldiers." It sounded like an accusation.

"If I can save a life, why shouldn't I?" she challenged.

Johnny scowled. "Maybe some lives aren't worth saving."

Chapter Five

By the light of an oil lamp Mr. Sterret had provided when he delivered the last few weeks' worth of newspapers, Charlie's eyes scanned over the small block print. As the flame within the glass chimney flickered, the shadows danced eerily along the earthen walls.

Raking his hand through his hair, Charlie read that the War Department had reduced the rations for Confederate prisoners in retaliation for reports of mistreatment to Union prisoners of war. It seemed hardly possible that the prisoners at Point Lookout could subsist on less than they already received. And the cruelty inherent in such an order made him cringe. There was no shame or regret, certainly no mercy, in such a statement. You starve our boys—we'll starve yours.

Charlie had heard rumors about Andersonville, down in Georgia where Union prisoners of war were kept. What the Federals didn't understand was that the Rebels didn't have enough resources to feed both themselves *and* their enemies.

The resentment which had spawned the war had multiplied with each bloody defeat into seething hatred, on both sides of the Mason-Dixon Line. It was rare to find kindness and compassion in this world. Charlie had seen so little of it in the last three years that he hardly knew what to think of it, and certainly was uncomfortable receiving it.

Abigail Sterret must have learned these traits from her father, who had treated Charlie as his equal from the first introduction, despite that he knew nothing about Charlie, other than that he was filthy, starving, and wounded. He admired the Sterrets' determination to care for him without regard for the cost, and yet it made Charlie feel something he didn't like: indebtedness. And perhaps a bit of guilt, knowing how undeserving he was.

Refocusing his thoughts on the newspapers, Charlie read an account of a Confederate ironclad ship, the *Albemarle*, which was able to defeat the Federal Navy on the Roanoke River and take the garrison at Plymouth, North Carolina. Although he was a deserter for all intents and purposes, as he had no intention of reporting to the Confederate Army and returning to active duty, Charlie still felt a thrill of victory as he read the report.

The feature article in the next newspaper was about a new phrase which had been approved to be printed on coinage. The words, *"In God We Trust"* would begin to appear on all of the Union's coins. It was interesting timing. Lincoln found it expedient to quote scripture and to present himself as a spiritual man fighting for a moral cause, when as far as Charlie could tell, the President was no more than a tyrant determined to hold on to his empire.

If there were any saints in the world, they weren't to be found in the government or the military, whether Federal or Confederate. Whatever ideals had existed at the onset of the war, freedom of the states to govern themselves or a belief that the Union must be preserved, they had been polluted over time with bloodshed and political rhetoric.

The phrase, "In God We Trust," originated with the *"Star Spangled Banner"* in the fight against the British in 1812, and was used as a battle cry by the 125th Pennsylvania Infantry at the Battle of Antietam. Lincoln's statement was clear: God was on the side of the Union and whatever they did to achieve victory was sanctioned by Providence.

In Charlie's opinion, this war was the result of man's hubris and the only spiritual force he could see at work in it was the Devil.

A sound at the door to the cellar jerked Charlie's attention from the paper. Sam, the black dog, came bounding down the stairs and planted his paws squarely on Charlie's shoulders, pushing him against the wall as he covered his face in exuberant kisses.

Pushing the dog away with a wince of pain, Charlie looked up to find a young boy standing in the circle of lamplight, mouth open as he gaped at the stranger. His gaze shifted to Sam, observing the familiarity the dog demonstrated, even as he continued to regard Charlie with mingled curiosity and distrust.

"Who are you?" the child demanded.

Holding up a hand in caution, Charlie whispered, "I'm here with your father's permission. Please close the door!"

Backing away slowly, eyes still riveted on the unexpected interloper, the boy did as he was told. He returned immediately to the very spot he had vacated and repeated his question. "Who are you?"

"I'm Johnny. I'm just staying here for a bit until I'm strong enough to move on," Charlie explained.

The child's eyes narrowed suspiciously. "Why are you hiding?"

"Because I don't want to be found," Charlie retorted, stating the obvious.

The little boy's eyes widened in awe. "You're a real Rebel, aren't you?" he exclaimed enthusiastically.

"I promise it isn't as exciting as it sounds," Charlie replied drily.

"I'm Harris," the boy announced, stepping forward and offering his hand. Charlie accepted it, amused by both the serious expression and the firm handshake which accompanied the introduction. "I'm a Rebel too. Only my mother would kill me, so I can't tell anyone either."

In battle, Charlie had seen lads as young as this toothless fellow shot down as they beat their drums for the soldiers to march in rhythm. Many of them had run away to join the fighting, doing what they could for the cause they believed in.

"Well, we'd best keep it a secret then," Charlie agreed. "How did you find me?"

"Sam was scratching at the door, whining. I thought maybe there was a snake down here. Turned out it was only you," Harris said as he pulled up the chair and settled into it, as if anticipating a lengthy visit. "Who brought you here?" he inquired.

"A young woman, whom I'm guessing is your sister."

"Abby? Yes, she's my sister. And that doesn't surprise me a bit." He grinned, the space where his front teeth were missing showing pink gums. "We love to do things that aggravate Mama."

Feeling compelled to defend Abigail's motives, Charlie stated, "I don't think that's why she hid me, son."

"No," Harris agreed. "It was just a bonus."

Sam flopped to the ground and rested his head in Charlie's lap. He rubbed the dog's head absently as he considered the boy in front of him. Dressed in a brown linen suit sporting fresh dirt stains on the knees, his brown hair neatly combed down the middle, and a spattering of golden freckles across his pert nose, Harris was the definition of precocious. Charlie couldn't help but like him.

"Harris... Isn't Bloomingdale owned by the Harris sisters?" he struggled to remember. The life he had known before the war almost seemed to belong to someone else.

"Yes, they're my great aunts. I'm named after the Harris family," the child explained. "My papa manages the estate for them. I like it here. There's much more trouble to get into than when we lived in Baltimore."

Charlie felt a smile shaping his lips, the first he had worn in longer than he could remember. "I'm sure you could find trouble wherever you went," he responded positively.

Harris grinned, feeling no need to dispute the statement.

"How long have you been here, Johnny? I wish I'd known you were here sooner," the boy confessed.

"Only a few days," Charlie reassured him. "But your cook has taken good care of me, and I'm getting stronger every day."

"What happened to you?" Harris wondered. "You don't look too healthy."

Charlie hesitated. He hadn't confided in Mr. Sterret, Abigail, or the slaves. But somehow his newfound friend was different. "I was taken prisoner at the Battle of Gettysburg," he admitted. "I escaped, but was shot by the Home Guard's night patrol."

The admiration in Harris' eyes deepened. "Where?" he asked, leaning forward eagerly. "Can I see it?"

Again, Charlie felt the unfamiliar pull of a smile at the

corner of his lips. "In the side," he answered, lifting his shirt to reveal his bandages.

"You're awfully skinny!" Harris observed. "I like to sneak cookies and cakes from the pantry. That's where I was going when I saw Sam whining at the door. You want some?"

"Sure," the renegade replied, his mouth salivating at the mention of such delicacies.

Harris beamed. "Don't tell nobody," he admonished. "And I won't tell nobody I know you're here," he added, conspiratorially.

~

A fine mist fell from the sky, the morning light filtering through a gray layer of clouds. From the second story portico, Abigail gazed out at the lush grass dampened with rain. From this vantage point, she could see for miles around: the sprawling green lawn and the winding drive lined with poplars; the fields tilled for planting and the fields where new sprouts were just beginning to push through the earth; the barns, stable, and slave quarters; and the birds nesting in the trees opposite where she stood.

"Do you think I could climb up there?" Harris wondered aloud, studying the tall maple curiously. Leaning forward, shoulders just forward of the railing, the boy's eyes searched for foot and hand holds on the thick trunk.

"Harris! Get back from there!" their papa barked, stepping out onto the porch.

Startled, and unaccustomed to Mr. Sterret raising his voice, Harris spun around and stepped away from the railing.

"Papa?" Abigail raised her delicate brows in question. "What's wrong?"

Irving came to rest a hand gently on Harris' shoulder. "I didn't mean to startle you, son. I just didn't want you to fall."

"Papa, I lean over the railing all the time and I ain't never fallen."

"You haven't fallen," Irving corrected patiently. "And I don't want you to lean over the railing again. I suppose it's one of those things we just don't think about until something tragic happens. I was just reading in the paper this morning that President Jefferson Davis' son died from such a fall. He was on the porch of the family's home and fell to his death."

"I wasn't going to fall," Harris insisted.

"That's awful, Papa!" Abigail exclaimed. "And Harris Sterret, you don't ever lean over that railing again! I don't want to have to worry for even a second." To her father, Abigail reminded him, "If Mama heard you call Jeff Davis 'President,' she'd have a conniption."

Irving's lined face creased into a smile. "Then it's a good thing she wasn't here." Taking his son by both shoulders, he added, "Don't harass your mother with insects."

"Yes sir," Harris answered, but almost immediately an impish twinkle danced in his eyes as he broke into a toothless grin. "Reptiles would be better!"

Irving chuckled. "Let me rephrase that: Don't harass your mother. Now, isn't Mr. Reynolds waiting for you to begin your day?" he cocked an eyebrow, emphasizing the wrinkles which creased his forehead.

"Yes sir," Harris groaned, the toes of his black leather boots scuffing the floor as he dragged his feet to demonstrate his reluctance to report to the tutor's room for his lessons.

As soon as the boy was out of earshot, Irving whispered to his daughter, "Keep an eye out for visitors. Yesterday, in Centreville, I heard that the Home Guard is searching for two escaped prisoners of war believed to be in the area. If the Provost Marshall or any officers arrive and demand to search the premises, I'll have to comply to avoid suspicion. I'll distract them while you get word to the kitchen.

"For now, warn Lizzie, and tell her to take the lantern and newspapers up right away, and to get Abel to help her set up a false floor in the bin where the beets and turnips are stored. I know our guest is in no condition to be moving about, so have Ruth stay close to assist him into it, if necessary. Hopefully, we won't be bothered."

Abigail nodded, swallowing down the fear that rose like a knot in her throat. "What happens if...?"

Irving shook his head, brushing the question aside. "Avoid the kitchen other than to deliver the message to Lizzie. We don't want to draw attention."

"Yes sir," Abigail felt the pulse in her throat accelerate. Could her father be imprisoned in Fort McHenry as Cousin Severn Teackle Wallis had been when he was a member of the General Assembly, for failure to take a Union Oath? As the property was legally owned by the Aunts, and they knew nothing about Johnny, Bloomingdale should not be in danger of confiscation.

After delivering the message of warning to Lizzie, Abigail set up an easel on the second level porch and began sketching with colored pencils. She was far from gifted as an artist, but it was one of the subjects she had been encouraged to pursue as a lady of refinement. Under the guise of inspiration, she could keep watch on the driveway for approaching visitors.

Even if she had possessed a talent for drawing, her mind was so distracted that she could hardly concentrate on the details of the landscape she was attempting to duplicate. Using shading to create depth and dimension had always been her greatest challenge, and she cringed to think what Mr. Reynolds would say if he were to see her pathetic rendition of nature's beauty.

She was examining her pencils for a darker shade of green when something from the corner of Abigail's eye caught her attention. Her dark hair hung loosely over her shoulder, and she brushed it aside as she studied the carriage rolling down the lane. Her eyes narrowed, mind racing.

If it were the Provost Marshall or a member of the Home Guard, they would most likely have arrived on horseback. Still, her heartbeat did not steady until she recognized the conveyance as belonging to the Turners.

Abandoning the attempted artwork, Abigail descended the stairs to welcome Clara to Bloomingdale. She tried not to stare at her friend's rotund shape as she struggled down from the carriage. Abigail knew that Clara was expecting, but hadn't seen her since she had begun to show. Her swollen belly looked both uncomfortable and unnatural beneath the navy blue dress which had been sewn especially to accommodate her girth.

"You shouldn't be travelling in your condition!" Abigail worried. "I'm surprised Jeremiah would let you leave the house."

"He's rather distracted today," Clara admitted, her own brows knit together with worry. Even her face was fuller than Abigail remembered.

"What is it?" Abigail detected that this was more than a

mere social call, and whatever troubled her friend was the primary reason for her visit.

"Can I please sit down?" Clara sounded short of breath, and Abigail hurried her inside.

Retreating to the drawing room, Abigail seated herself strategically in a position which afforded her a view of the yard. It took Clara longer to lower herself into the plush velvet chair she preferred.

"Now, what's wrong?" Abigail demanded.

Glancing nervously over her shoulder, her auburn hair tucked up in a snood, Clara leaned forward to whisper, "Marshal Goldsborough came to Laurel Hill yesterday and scoured the entire property. He said they received word from Point Lookout that Charlie had escaped with another prisoner, and they suspected he was trying to return home. There was a report that two men had been spotted near here, and one or both of them may have been shot, but only one body has been located. Charlie is still missing. If you hear anything, please let me know."

Abigail schooled her face to hide her inward reaction as Clara continued.

"Jeremiah is worried sick. He wanted to send men to search the area, but feared he was under surveillance. I'm sure they know I'm here, but after all, I'm only a woman," Clara added, as if that placed her above suspicion.

Abigail carefully guarded her response to this announcement, although her mind was reeling. "Johnny" was actually Charlie Turner, Jeremiah's brother!

She desperately wanted to assure Clara that her brother-in-law was safe, but feared bringing her into the secret might increase the danger for all of them. Abigail hoped her encouragement sounded more like reason than knowledge as she leaned forward to rest a hand on her friend's arm.

"If they haven't found him yet, he must still be alive, hiding somewhere. I'm sure he's safe, and he'll get word to Jeremiah when he can."

"I hope you're right," Clara fretted. "Jeremiah is desperate to see him again."

Chapter Six

Charlie's heart pounded wildly against his ribcage as he was awakened by the scrape of the cellar door against the kitchen floorboards. The sounds above had long since quieted, and he suspected it was the dead of night. A visitor at this hour did not bode well.

Rolling onto his left side, he carefully eased himself onto his knees, wincing at the pain which throbbed below his right ribcage. In the blackness, he couldn't make out the turnip bin where his hiding place was concealed, and he had no time to reach it before the light of the intruder's lamp would give him away.

Having no other alternative, Charlie raised his hands in the air, prepared to surrender.

"It's only me," a female voice whispered as the pale light spilled down the steps into the earthen cave.

Charlie sank to the ground, relief coursing through him.

"I'm sorry I frightened you," Abigail whispered as she closed the door behind her and descended the crude steps, walking around the bins and baskets which filled the space to where Charlie huddled in the far corner.

"What time is it?" he wondered.

"I wanted to wait until everyone was sleeping," she explained. Her chestnut hair was plaited into a thick braid which fell over her shoulder, ending in a mass of loose curls. She hugged a knit shawl about her tightly as she lowered herself onto the floor beside him, despite the abundance of petticoats which layered her calico dress and made the effort appear awkward.

"What's happening?" Charlie feared that their secret was out and he would need to move quickly to another location, though he was hardly in any condition to do so.

The young woman sighed, folding her hands in her lap as she leaned back against the wooden bin behind her. Beautiful and elegant, Abigail was decidedly out of place on the dirt floor with a crate of leather-britches-beans as her backrest.

"I needed to talk to you, Charlie," Abigail said softly. "I couldn't sleep until I did."

"What's wrong?" he leaned forward, fresh fear surging through his veins.

She stared at him wordlessly, her eyes boring into his as if he should somehow know the answer. It took a moment for it to sink in.

She had called him Charlie.

"How did you find out?" he ran a hand through his hair. There was no point in denying it.

"You are an escaped prisoner of war?" she asked, her eyes soft with fresh compassion. Charlie had to look away, touched by the kindness and concern in their depths.

"I am," he admitted.

"You said you were a fugitive *and* a deserter," she reminded him. "You don't wish to report back to your superiors?"

"No. I'm done with the war." Slouching wearily, Charlie let his hands fall limply to his lap. "They're just two sides of the same coin. Neither is right; both are wrong."

"But you joined the Rebels... why?" she cocked her head to the left side, her expression sincere and questioning. The candlelight played across her delicate features, and Charlie was reminded how young and naïve she was.

His voice was hardened with bitterness as he replied, "I believed in the cause of freedom; in maintaining the rights of the states to govern themselves; in preventing the Federal Government from growing larger than it was ever intended to be and diminishing the liberty of the people within this nation who fought with such dedication to preserve it.

"All of those *ideals* were what inspired me to enlist. But the truth is what has led me to desert. Whatever led to the outbreak of war is not what propels its continuance. Now it's just a matter of stubborn pride and raging evil. I don't want anything to do with it."

"But... don't you believe in freedom anymore?" Abigail persisted, her brows creasing in concern.

Charlie sagged against the dirt wall behind him. "I do, more than ever. I believe in my own freedom."

"The Federal Government has taken over Maryland," Abigail stated. "My Aunts have a cousin, Mr. Wallis, who was imprisoned for months because he refused to take an oath of loyalty to the Union. He was one of twenty-seven members of the General Assembly arrested and held without ever having committed a crime. If the due process of law hadn't been interrupted, Maryland would have voted for secession and become a part of the Confederate States.

"We are being held by force, prevented from leaving the Union, under the thumb of General Butler. Twice the United

States had to fight Britain for her independence, to stand alone as a Republic—a form of government which fostered the freedom of her citizens. If the South gives up, what will that mean for America?" she finished, her voice impassioned and sincere.

Charlie chuckled derisively. "You would make a lovely spokeswoman for the Southern Cause."

"You mock me," Abigail's eyes flashed angrily.

"You misunderstand me," he sighed. "You voice the position well. And you are lovely." If he wasn't an invalid, her father might have thought twice about leaving her alone with him. "The problem is this: the soul of mankind is corrupt. Wholly and thoroughly. And every government which springs to life will inevitably become corrupt, no matter how well meaning it begins. Because power feeds corruption."

"You have a very jaded perspective," she accused softly.

"And you, ma'am, have a very sheltered perspective," he countered.

"Enlighten me," Abigail challenged, her dark brows arching defiantly.

"Both the Federal Government and the Confederacy have been forced to rely upon Mandatory Conscription, bounties, and threats of jail time to maintain their armies. Both sides are taking from their citizens, against their consent, to feed their armies and fuel the war. It's a rich man's battle, but a poor man's fight. While they—the presidents and generals—sit in their offices and sign orders, we are the ones sent out to die. Do you know how many soldiers have been sent into battle, forced to march into the muzzles of their enemies' weapons, knowing they advanced into a slaughter? I've seen enough ruthless killing and brutal mistreatment to last a lifetime. I'm done with all of them!"

he hissed in the effort to keep his voice down.

Sitting across from him in the dim light, the young woman looked as if she had been slapped. Shame crept into Abigail's cheeks as she admitted, "You're right, Charlie. I haven't seen the things you have. I'm sorry you had to endure that."

Remorse for speaking to her so harshly immediately flooded Charlie, and he sighed as he confessed, "I'm glad to know that there is still kindness and goodness to be found in the human heart. I've been the recipient of its generosity more than once, and I'm grateful."

"Is that how you escaped?" she perceived.

Charlie nodded, but offered nothing more.

"How long were you there?" Abigail wondered.

Narrowing his brows, Charlie remembered that she had yet to answer his question. "How did you find out who I am?"

"The Home Guard is looking for a man named Charlie Turner. I assumed it must be you," she replied matter-of-factly, but Charlie noted that her eyes shifted as she spoke, as if she was withholding something. He found the honesty inherent in such a reaction charming, and decided to pretend it had gone unnoticed.

"Bloomingdale," he said thoughtfully, as if trying to place his location. "Isn't it owned by two elderly women?"

"Yes, my father's aunts, Sallie and Mary Harris," Abigail replied with apparent relief that he hadn't pressed for the source of her knowledge. "My father manages the estate for them."

"It's quite an estate, isn't it?" Charlie recalled.

"Yes, it is," she admitted. "They named it 'Bloomingdale' when they inherited it. It was previously called 'Mount Mill.'

Now only the gristmill is referred to by that name."

"I've heard stories about your great-aunts," Charlie reflected. "Especially Sallie Harris... Do they know I'm here?"

"No. Only my father and I, and the four slaves," she assured him.

Charlie resisted a smile. Harris had kept his secret from his sister, too. "Well, as soon as I'm able, I'll be on my way. I don't want to bring trouble to the old ladies," he assured her.

"There isn't anywhere for you to go," she countered. "You'll need to stay here."

"I'm a grown man, miss, and I can make that decision for myself," Charlie snapped before he had time to catch himself.

Carefully maneuvering herself to her feet, Abigail stood, staring down at him with an injured expression. "Of course," she said quietly. "Good night." The pale circle of candlelight followed her from the cellar.

In the wake of her departure, the darkness seemed blacker than ever before.

Chapter Seven

Irving lowered his black felt bowler over his eyes, clutching a briarwood pipe between his lips. As he spoke, his gaze scanned the area around them for eavesdroppers.

"Isn't that an interesting coincidence," he mused. "Charlie Turner of Laurel Hill."

Sitting on the bench, Abigail huffed, "I know he's been through an awful lot, Papa, but I still don't understand why he's so rude. He has every reason in the world to be kind to me, and yet he isn't."

"Never judge a man unless you've walked in his shoes, Abby. Pain shapes each of us differently," he admonished gently.

Abigail looked down at the cat napping in her lap. Since her accident, Sprightly was terrified of horses. And Sam, since Sophie had attacked him, approached other dogs in cautious submission. Even Abigail, since Jeanine's death, grew anxious every time Harris contracted the sniffles, remembering how her sister had languished in bed with the influenza before her death.

"You're right, Papa," Abigail admitted. "I really know nothing of his story."

Releasing a cloud of smoke, Irving adjusted the lapel of his coat as he glanced up at the brilliant blue sky overhead. "I can't imagine being locked in a dungeon does much for a man's spirits. His health is improving, and I think he could be moved soon. But where?" he finished thoughtfully.

"He could hide in the hayloft of the barn," Abigail suggested.

Irving considered this for a moment before shaking his head. "The risk of exposure is too great. There are any number of slaves who might discover him, and it would be an obvious place for the patrols to search."

"Then where? We need to be able to smuggle food to him," Abigail considered.

Mr. Sterret puffed quietly on his pipe for a moment as he considered the alternatives. His thick brows, once dark as Abigail's but now speckled with gray, drew together as he searched his mind for another idea. Finally, he sighed as he said, "Well, at least he can stay in the cellar until we think of someplace else."

"I know!" a voice startled them as it came from the limbs of the oak tree overhead. Looking up, Irving and Abigail peered into the thick camouflage of green leaves above them. A pair of black boots, badly scuffed, and a pair of brown linen trousers slowly came into view as Harris shimmied down the tree.

"I have an idea!" he exclaimed, willing to risk punishment in exchange for sharing it. "The attic!" he cried.

"Harris Sterret!" Irving scolded. "What were you doing up in that tree, and why didn't you make us aware of your presence sooner?"

Sincere but mild contrition colored Harris' expression as he lowered himself like a monkey onto the bench beside Abigail. "I just wanted to hear what you were saying," he asserted. "I already knew he was there. And I haven't told nobody, not even Billy. Why do you think he said his name was Johnny?"

"How long have you known?" Abigail demanded. "And how did you find out?"

"Not long," Harris assured her. "I followed Sam down there. I thought maybe there was a snake."

Abigail and Irving glanced at one another nervously.

"He'll need to be moved without the dog knowing," Irving advised, glancing over at the animal where he napped in the sunshine near Abigail's feet.

"But why did he lie?" Harris persisted.

"I'm sure he has his reasons," Abigail answered, although she wondered the very same thing.

"The attic?" Irving considered. "I'd be afraid someone would hear him walking up there and investigate."

A wide smile, devoid of two front teeth, split Harris' freckled face. "Didn't Aunt Sallie say she saw Grandpa's ghost once? We could just say it came back!"

There was a widely spread account of a knock upon the door of Bloomingdale, late at night after the slaves were in the quarter sleeping. Aunt Sallie had answered the door in her nightcap to find her nephew, William Sterret, standing on the doorstep. The pale figure had entered the house, despite the horrified response of Sallie and her friend, Mrs. De Courcy, who was staying over that night.

William had drowned in a race by the old mill, yet they said he walked up the stairs to his old room, and right through the locked door. By the time Aunt Sallie was able to retrieve the key and enter the room, it was empty. The quilt upon the bed, however, bore the impression of a body in its center.

Irving shook his head. "It's nothing but absolute nonsense. I don't know what those two ladies were drinking that night—or how much—but I don't believe it for a second."

"No, Papa, he's right!" Abigail exclaimed, noting the crestfallen expression on her younger brother's face evaporate as she added, "The only ones to go up to the attic are Esther and Ruthie, to clean. You know how superstitious the slaves are. If Ruthie says she saw a ghost, no one else will go near it!"

Tapping the bowl of his pipe thoughtfully against his chin, Irving considered the idea. "But if the house is searched, where can he hide?"

"Oh, that's easy!" Harris' face lit up. "There's a loose panel at the top of the stairway. All he has to do is pry it open and step inside. He's just got to be real still and quiet, and sometimes it gets awfully stuffy, but no one would ever think to look there!"

Cocking one eyebrow quizzically at his son, Irving asked, "And how do you happen to know about this?"

With a sheepish expression, Harris confessed, "Sometimes I hide there, from Mr. Reynolds."

Shaking his head in exasperation, Mr. Sterret promised, "I will be speaking to your tutor about this."

"Yes sir," the boy acknowledged, hanging his head.

"But," Irving continued, "I think you might be on to something." Harris lifted his face, beaming.

"We'll have to move him at night," Abigail cautioned, having failed to mention to her father that she had been to visit their secret guest under cover of darkness more than once.

"I'll speak to Washington and Lizzie," Irving replied. "I'm sure the poor boy would love to see daylight again. But he'll need a bath first."

Abigail had to agree. Anyone who approached the attic would smell him long before they saw him. She suspected he hadn't washed in months.

Having worked out the details of their plans, Irving and his children returned to the house, then parted their separate ways. Abigail hoped Harris was able to keep their secret, although it seemed he had more than a few secrets of his own.

"Ma'am," Esther appeared in the main hallway as Abigail let herself in. "I gots a letter for you," the dark-skinned girl pointed to the envelope leaning against the porcelain vase on a marble-topped mahogany table, carved with roses and scrolls.

Nodding her thanks, Abigail retrieved the letter and stepped into the drawing room to read it. It was from Jane. Opening the folded page within, Abigail smiled as she read: *Clara has delivered the baby. Mother and child are well. She has a daughter, and they have named her Henrietta after Jeremiah's mother.*

Deciding it best to give the Turners time alone to adjust before stopping by to meet the sweet little one, Abigail sent a quick prayer of gratitude to heaven for keeping Clara and her daughter in good health.

As she came to her feet, a somber thought disrupted her sense of celebration. Charlie was this baby's uncle, but Jeremiah had no way to inform him of Henrietta's birth. It didn't seem right to withhold something so joyous.

Abigail resolved to tell Charlie that she had overheard the announcement in town. She was sure he would be delighted to know.

~

By the light of a single candle, with the curtains drawn and Lizzie and Washington posted as guards at both entrances to the kitchen, Charlie sank down into a tub of hot water for the first time in longer than he could remember. A sigh escaped his lips as the warmth relaxed his muscles.

Working the soap into a lather, he marveled at the comforts he had once taken for granted, but which he now appreciated as luxuries. Privacy, a warm bath, and soap—with clean clothes to put on when he had dried himself using a fresh towel. He had forgotten how wonderful such basic pleasures could be.

The simple act of breathing air that didn't smell of dampness, potatoes, and turnips felt like a gift. After weeks in the underground root cellar, Charlie had begun to feel like a mole, losing both his eyesight and his sense of humanity. He eagerly awaited the morning's sunrise, longing to see the brilliant colors of the sky as the sun painted the earth with light.

Once he had scrubbed himself clean and donned the clothes set out for him, he felt like a new man. Washington had set out a mirror, razor, and shaving cream, and when he was finished taking care of himself, Lizzie had promised him a haircut.

He felt more like an honored guest than a man on the run. How could Charlie ever repay their kindness?

He opened the interior door quietly, finding Lizzie waiting as she had promised.

"Hope I don't take off your ear without no light in here," she grinned as she took up scissors. Charlie remained as still as possible, hoping she could see well enough to watch his ears even if not to give him a decent haircut.

"You all done," she announced moments later. "Now let's get you up them stairs without no one knowing."

She left the candle in the kitchen, commenting, "I know you can see like a cat after being down in that cellar so long," as she led him through the dining room to the main hall, and up the stairs. She didn't explain how she could see in the dark.

Trailing behind her in his bare feet, Charlie held his breath as they reached the second level where the family was sleeping. Even in the darkness, Charlie could feel the extravagance of the mansion in its spaciousness, with hulking shadows of furniture along the walls.

An open staircase led to a third floor loft, with bedrooms opening off on either side of it, used only on rare occasions to house family members for holiday parties or weddings. Lizzie guided him to the room on the right, the farthest from the stairwell. Ruthie had set out extra blankets for him and he was instructed to sleep on the floor behind the bed, to provide an additional boundary should anyone happen to look in. During the day, he would store these blankets under the bed, and remain alert for anyone who might be searching for him.

By now word had certainly reached Laurel Hill that he was suspected to be in the area. Feeling much like the prodigal son, Charlie wondered how he would be welcomed by his father and his elder brother should he ever make his way back home.

For now, he was grateful to have a place of refuge.

"Thank you, Lizzie," he whispered quietly, "for everything."

She nodded, reaching out to pat his shoulder before disappearing into the shadows.

Alone again, Charlie lay down upon the wood floor and gazed out the window at the faint glimmer of moonlight visible in the sky above. Stars twinkled in the distance, pinpricks of light in a sky like gray velvet. He had made it this far. He only wished Wilson had too.

He awoke with the very first rays of dawn, his eyes struggling to adjust to the presence of light. As the sky glowed with hues of ochre and rose, Charlie watched the sunrise in rapt fascination. Slowly, by degrees, the sun edged higher in the sky and the darkness faded into light. It was like witnessing a miracle.

When the colors of sunrise had faded into powder blue, he began to look around the room he now inhabited. Careful to move quietly, he searched for the hiding place Harris had generously shared with him. After several minutes, he found the lose panel and eased it open, revealing a space between the walls which was barely large enough for him to fit between. In an emergency, it would suffice, but it would not be comfortable.

By measuring the position of the sun and the angle of its light, Charlie was able to track the passage of time. He spent the quiet, lonely hours watching the breeze rustle the leaves outside his window, and the birds as they soared in the sky or perched in the tree limbs. He was captivated by the world beyond the window, unlike anything he had been privileged to see in months.

Ruthie made a very brief appearance in the late morning with a platter of eggs and sausage. In the evening, while the family gathered in the dining room, a plate was delivered with ham, peas, and biscuits. Both times, a container of water was delivered as well.

As his strength slowly returned and the gunshot wound healed, he felt restless. It was far better to be concealed in the attic than in the root cellar, but Charlie still felt trapped, a feeling he despised after his time spent in the prison camp.

Freedom had proven to be an elusive objective many times over.

His own words came back to haunt him, spoken in naïve passion. *"I'd rather be killed as a rebel than live as a prisoner,"* he'd declared to his father and brother in defense of his decision to drill with the Scott Rifles. He'd used the term "prisoner" symbolically then, to illustrate the tyranny of the Federal Government over its citizens. Little could he have imagined in the spring of 1861 just how literal the word would become to him.

Now, he was willing to suffer prison as a means of survival. When all the pretentions and ideals were stripped away, the human spirit clung to life above all else, even above freedom.

When evening fell and the sun sank back below the horizon, the darkness returned and Charlie lay down upon the floor to rest. He closed his eyes, but his mind raced with questions. How long would he be forced to live this way? How soon could he return to Laurel Hill? And how would he be greeted when he arrived?

As there were no answers to be found to any of these questions, his mind eventually quieted and he drifted into troubled sleep.

During the night, he was awakened by a rustling sound. Charlie lay rock still and waited, heart thumping, afraid to move. Silvery moonlight spilled across the floor, causing the room to glow with an eerie light. As a figure appeared at the end of the bed, he realized it was Abigail.

She wore a pink silk kimono robe over her white nightgown, her dark hair draped over her shoulder in a long braid. Kneeling down on the floor, she presented him with a stack of newspapers and books.

"I thought you might want these," she whispered, "since you have light now to read all day."

"Thank you," he replied softly, forcing himself to look away from her round eyes, framed in dark lashes, and to focus on the reading materials she had delivered instead.

"They're old newspapers," she stated the obvious, staring down at her hands, clasped in her lap. "So you can read about events you missed while you were in prison."

Was it his imagination, or was there a nervous, breathy quality to her voice? He noticed the shyness which had suddenly appeared in her expression. Remembering that he had received a haircut and shave since she last saw him, Charlie was tempted to smile. But any mutual attraction they might feel only made his situation more torturous.

"I should go," she said as she began to rise. She hesitated, lowering herself back into a kneeling position on the floor. "But I did want to tell you something that I thought you might like to know. I heard in town that your brother and his wife just had their first child. A daughter. They named her Henrietta."

Charlie was surprised by the knife that sank into his chest, the sharp edge of pain which pierced his heart. Relief that

Jeremiah was safely home mingled with regret and self-loathing. He was overjoyed for his brother's happiness, thrilled to know that a new Turner had entered the world. Yet he felt so distant from his family, estranged and exiled.

Attempting to hide the strong emotions which swept over him, Charlie stammered, "Do you—do you know how he is? Jeremiah?"

Abigail tilted her head slightly as she answered, the moonlight playing along the curve of her cheekbone and the line of her delicate jaw.

"He's well," she answered. "He was wounded at Gettysburg and his arm was amputated below the elbow, but he wears a prosthetic hand now and functions quite normally. I think he and his wife are very happy, especially now that they have their daughter."

"I—I've been away a long time," he said, observing the way she studied him in the pale light.

"Yes, of course," she assured him quickly. "I should go," Abigail repeated, this time rising to her feet and offering a brief nod before she made her exit.

Charlie stared at the emptiness where she had been.

Henrietta. Jeremiah had named his daughter after their mother. Homesickness for a time, distant and gone, nearly choked Charlie as he rolled onto his side and closed his eyes.

Chapter Eight

A s Abigail slid under the woven wool coverlet in her bedroom, Sprightly meowed either to welcome her back or to protest that she had left in the first place. Snuggled against the cat, which slept on her own pillow in the bed, Abigail pressed her face against the soft fur.

Tonight, something had changed. For a brief moment, Charlie had given her an unwitting glimpse into the suffering within his soul. In his eyes, she had seen that he was tortured by things Abigail could only guess at, things she may never be able to understand.

She had to admit, although reluctantly, that he was no longer simply a scruffy fugitive in her eyes. Not only had she seen the vulnerability Charlie hid behind his gruff exterior, she had also realized that he was far younger and more attractive than she had first presumed.

It shouldn't matter, but it did. When she first looked up and saw the transformation, she'd felt her heart do a peculiar flip-flop in her chest, something it had never done before. Beneath that ragged beard and unkempt hair was a very handsome man, the contours of his features revealed in the soft moonlight. Even unhealthily lean and pale, he was still one of the most appealing men she had ever seen.

Sprightly's rough tongue licked Abigail's cheek, as if the cat sensed her inner turmoil. She wished she could talk to someone about these new feelings, but that was impossible. The only ones to know of his presence at Bloomingdale were her father, Harris, and the slaves. None of whom Abigail was comfortable taking into her confidence in matters of romance.

For the next three days, Abigail made it a point not to visit Charlie. Not only would it be better for her to keep a distance from him, but she didn't want to endanger him by drawing attention to his hiding place. She had hoped that by avoiding him, she could avoid the confusing feelings he had evoked. Unfortunately, the handsome young man with haunted eyes could not be chased from her thoughts.

Finally, she decided to pay a visit to Clara and meet her newborn daughter. Although she feared that Charlie might not receive adequate warning if the Provost Marshal arrived to search the place, she reminded herself that Lizzie and her father would do all they could to protect him.

Abel drove Abigail into Centreville. The carriage rolled over dirt roads between fields and pastures until reaching town, where the streets were paved with crushed oyster shells. Passing homes and stores on Commerce Street, Abel turned onto Turners Lane and directed the horse toward Laurel Hill.

The driveway wound up a slope between the fields of new green corn, no more than a foot tall. The white house was perched atop the hill, stately and elegant in a less ostentatious manner than Bloomingdale. Flanked on either side by immense locust trees, and surrounded by colorful azalea bushes and blooming flower gardens, Laurel Hill was a beautiful spot.

Upon entering the house, Abigail could hear the sound of female laughter upstairs. "Missus Clara invite you upstairs," the slender black woman gestured to the staircase. "Miss Jane here already."

At that precise moment, Jane appeared at the top of the stairs. "Abigail! Come up and meet sweet Henrietta! She's the most adorable thing you've ever seen!"

Abigail chuckled. "I'm sure she is, although you might be a bit partial, Auntie Jane."

Jane laughed in acknowledgement. "Perhaps a bit," she admitted as she led Abigail to Clara's bedroom.

Clara wore a pale blue dressing gown over her white nightgown, and she sat in bed, propped up by thick, feather pillows. Abigail had never seen a woman so soon after delivering a child, but after several days of recovery, she had expected Clara to look more robust. Her face was still pale, and the fact that she still was abed meant she had not recovered her strength.

Pushing her concern aside for the moment, Abigail turned her attention to the bassinet next to the bed, over which Auntie Jane was perched like a mother bird over her nest. Inside the oval basket draped with lace was a diminutive bundle swaddled in a white knit blanket. The face which appeared above the fuzzy wool was pink and round, with a pert little nose and bow shaped lips. Her dark eyelashes fanned out against her smooth skin as she slept, her tiny hands balled into fists. A lacy cap of matching white was tied under Henrietta's chin.

"Oh..." Abigail leaned forward, completely captivated. "She's beautiful!"

Clara's smile was pleased and proud as the two women peered into the bassinet, exclaiming over how adorable and precious the infant was. After a moment, Abigail pulled a chair up to the edge of the bed and left Auntie Jane to watch her niece as she slept.

"How are you feeling?" she asked the new mother.

"I'm just tired," Clara replied. "She needs to nurse every two hours, day and night, and it's difficult for me to sleep."

"Are you sure that's all?" Abigail pressed, worried by the lack of color in her friend's cheeks. Against her auburn hair, her skin was as white as a marble tombstone.

"Well," Clara admitted reluctantly, "I had a few complications during delivery, but nothing to worry about now. Henrietta and I are both doing well, and I'll be back on my feet very soon."

Abigail wanted to press for more information, but knew it was improper for a married woman to speak of such things with a single woman. And after all, it was probably better for young women not to know the details of all that childbirth involved.

"Is Jeremiah pleased?" Abigail asked, watching the grin that spread across Clara's face in response.

"He is completely enamored!" she laughed. "I thought he might be disappointed that I didn't have a son, but he doesn't seem to be in the slightest."

"How could he be?" Jane retorted. "She's perfect!"

"I do hope Auntie Jane doesn't spoil her," Clara commented indulgently. "Although I imagine I'll be tempted to do the same when I become an aunt."

Abigail turned curious eyes on Jane.

"No! No, she's speaking very optimistically and theoretically," Jane clarified. "I do not have a beau in my life."

"Although she has a friend who would like to be," Clara informed Abigail with a knowing smile, "if Jane would only give him the nod."

"I thought so," Abigail replied. "It didn't look to me like Judson Shephard escorted you on Christmas Eve as a mere favor."

The blush that crept into Jane's cheeks was answer enough.

"He's a good friend," Jane protested, "and I do enjoy his company, but… I'm just not sure that I feel that way for him."

Clara and Abigail exchanged glances, then burst into laughter. "Why is her face so flushed?" her sister teased.

"He is very handsome," Abigail added, gauging Jane's response. Her blush deepened and she resembled a child caught with her hand in the cookie jar.

"He is… Very handsome," Jane finally admitted. Her hands twisted in her lap as she sorted through her thoughts, her expression growing somber. "I was a different person when I fell in love with Louis," she said of her fiancé, who had died in battle. "It's easy to celebrate romance and dream of the future in a time of peace. Now romance seems superfluous and foolish. The excitement and the thrill are overshadowed by fear and the dark reality of war. I still believe in love, it's just a far more serious prospect now that I know how painfully it can end."

Jane sighed, running a hand over her face as if wishing she could wipe the thoughts and feelings away. "I count down the days and the hours until I can see Judson again. I think about him in the morning when I wake up and when I fall asleep at night. I feel my heart come alive when I'm with him… But I'm so afraid to love in the world we live in now. Love isn't a prize to chase after anymore, but a risk to enter into cautiously."

Clara wiped a tear from her eye, pressing her lips together. Abigail suspected memories of the challenges she and her husband had faced in Gettysburg had drifted to the surface.

Clara reached for her sister's hand as she whispered, "I understand, Jane. I do."

Abigail took Jane's other hand, squeezing it gently in sympathy. Though she didn't say it aloud, she too understood.

~

The floor boards beneath Charlie's feet creaked as he shifted positions to follow the movement of the sun through the window, basking like a cat in the warm shaft of light. His hands, holding the newspaper in his lap, were the shade of fresh milk, as fair as any lady's skin. He longed to be outside, to turn his face up to the sky and feel the warmth upon his cheeks.

He tried to remain as still as possible throughout the day, reading newspapers or novels, so as not to draw attention to his presence in the attic. At night, when he hoped everyone lay sleeping, Charlie allowed himself to get up and move about. His muscles ached from disuse, and as his body healed from the gunshot and malnutrition, he longed to be active again.

The honest hard work of farm life held an allure he never imagined possible. His family's farm was nothing compared to this plantation. The Turners worked in the fields alongside just a handful of slaves, cultivating the soil, planting the seeds, and harvesting the crops. There was always work to be done, if not in the fields or orchard, then in the care of the hogs, chickens and turkeys they kept.

Laurel Hill was just a faraway dream, a distant memory of when life was simple and peaceful. Remembering it the way it was before the war was painful for Charlie, because that life was gone forever.

Closing his eyes, Charlie leaned back against the bedframe. He wanted to know what had transpired during the months he had been imprisoned, but there were some things he found torturous to read about. Mr. Sterret had two different newspapers, each with opposing points of view. One was in support of the Union; the other in support of States Rights. It was only a matter of time until only one voice was allowed.

In Baltimore the previous fall, three newspapers sympathetic to the Southern Cause had been shut down by military officials. Churches and public buildings had been ordered to display American flags to demonstrate their loyalty to the Union, and pictures or music of a Rebel nature were forbidden.

The hostile nature in Baltimore had further been demonstrated by the arrests of those participating in the funeral of Captain William D. Brown, CSA at Green Mount Cemetery. When the service concluded, all but the ministers were taken into custody.

Both of the Centreville papers had reported on the address President Lincoln delivered at the dedication of the Gettysburg National Cemetery, with very different conclusions. The States Rights paper declared the two minute address to be nothing but ludicrous and flat utterances; the other quoted the brief oration word-for-word and praised it as eloquent and steeped in meaning.

The National Cemetery was to commemorate the service of the Union soldiers who died there. Buried in shallow graves at the battlefield to prevent the spread of disease as the corpses rotted in the sun, their remains were disinterred and relocated to a more dignified resting place.

The deceased Confederate soldiers were not given such an honor.

Gettysburg... The name itself had become like a curse to Charlie. Not only had he been taken captive at the Pennsylvania town, he had made a decision in the heat of the moment which haunted his every waking moment. He tried to push down the memories, keeping them at a distance where they could not rise up to strangle him.

He exhaled slowly, the gun smoke and the cries of the battle receding as the present reasserted itself. The words on the newspaper in his lap shifted back into focus, and he forced himself to concentrate fully on its content.

Curious how Lincoln could justify the atrocity of Gettysburg, where over ten thousand United States citizens had been killed, Charlie read the words the President had spoken at the cemetery in November of 1863.

"Four score and seven years ago our fathers brought forth on this continent a new nation, conceived in liberty, and dedicated to the proposition that all men are created equal.

"Now we are engaged in a great civil war, testing whether that nation, or any nation so conceived and so dedicated, can long endure. We are met on a great battlefield of that war. We have come to dedicate a portion of that field, as a final resting place for those who here gave their lives that that nation might live. It is altogether fitting and proper that we should do this."

Grinding his teeth together, Charlie resisted the urge to verbalize his response to this manipulative rhetoric. The superiority of the Northern scum were what had precipitated the war. If they hadn't looked down their noses at the South because they were agricultural and not industrial, and if they had been willing to allow equal representation within the government, all the lives lost in this war could have been spared. Even so, if Lincoln had simply allowed the States of the Confederacy to peacefully secede from the Union, reverting back to their former independence, all of this bloodshed could have been averted.

"But, in a larger sense, we can not dedicate, we can not consecrate, we can not hallow this ground. The brave men, living and dead, who struggled here, have consecrated it, far above our poor power to add or detract. The world will little note, nor long remember what we say here, but it can never forget what they did here. It is for us the living, rather, to be dedicated here to the unfinished work which they who fought here have thus far so nobly advanced. It is rather for us to be here dedicated to the great task remaining before us—that from these honored dead we take increased devotion to that cause for which they gave the last full measure of devotion—that we here highly resolve that these dead shall not have died in vain—that this nation, under God, shall have a new birth of freedom—and that government of the people, by the people, for the people, shall not perish from the earth."

Political drivel! Unfinished work... so nobly advanced... for us to be here dedicated to the great task remaining before us... these dead shall not have died in vain... this nation, under God, shall have a new birth of freedom... shall not perish from the earth.

How could any intelligent human being not recognize the calculating choice of words Lincoln had constructed? He was elevating the preservation of the Union to a higher cause, speaking as if the North were a conglomeration of saints and philanthropists, while the South was comprised of villains and scoundrels.

Every general who served for the Confederate States Army had once served for the United States. Did it not beg the question: why were such a large number of patriots and citizens willing to defect from the Union to band together in the creation of a new nation?

Lincoln wanted to convince the country that both he and the Union were *"dedicated to the proposition that all men are created equal."* Anyone willing to search for the truth could quickly find contrary evidence. In 1858, in a debate against Stephen Douglas, Abraham Lincoln had made his personal position and purpose clear.

"I will say, then, that I am not, nor ever have been, in favor of bringing about in any way the social and political equality of the white and black races—that I am not, nor ever have been, in favor of making voters or jurors of Negroes, nor of qualifying them to hold office, nor to intermarry with white people; and I will say in addition to this, that there is a physical difference between the white and black races which I believe will forever forbid the two races living together on terms of social and political equality. And inasmuch as they cannot so live, while they do remain together there must be the position of superior and inferior, and I, as much as any other man, am in favor of having the superior position assigned to the white race."

Politicians would say anything to motivate those people who were not independently minded to think as they wished them to, and therefore to do as the politician wished them to. Lincoln was no exception.

As for the Union, the Constitution drafted in 1787 permitted and regulated the holding of slaves. It was all very inspiring and compelling language, and Charlie could see how many were persuaded under Lincoln's peculiar charm. However, the irony in the matter was that Lincoln would condemn the slave master as a tyrant, while he had suspended the writ of habeas corpus in order to arrest anyone who stood opposed to him, and had issued the Emancipation Proclamation as an executive order so as not to be thwarted by a government *of the people, by the people, for the people.*"

Charlie did not deny that slavery was a questionable institution. But his choice to enlist in the Confederate Army had not been hinged upon the subject. He had enlisted to defend the nation against a tyrant who would strip the states of their sovereignty by imposing laws upon them, and denied their right to secede from a compact they had entered into by choice.

Lincoln's argument was that perpetuity was implied in the Constitution, that when the states joined the Union they once and for all surrendered their sovereignty. Unfortunately, the individual states were not aware that they had forfeited their freedom when they joined the Union.

To not only allow, but to continue a war which would take the lives of thousands of American citizens over the use of "implied" language was not the action of a protector, but of a tyrant determined he would not relinquish even a smidgeon of his power.

Of course, Charlie had to admit that the Confederacy had been corrupted by its power just as easily.

He tossed the newspaper aside. No one was guiltless.

Chapter Nine

Moonlight filtered through the lace curtains at the window. Lying in the four poster bed, the coverlet over her woven from merino wool sheared from Bloomingdale's sheep, Abigail studied the pattern of silvery light cast upon the wood floor.

Her mind could not rest. Jane's troubled expression as she admitted the feelings she had for Judson Shephard replayed in her thoughts. Love was no longer a prize, Jane had said, but a risk. Truer words had never been spoken.

At twenty-three years old, Abigail was uncertain if she would ever marry. Before the war broke out, there had been plenty of eligible young men to choose from. Now so many were away in the war, and the number of those who lived to return did not equal the number of young ladies in need of a husband.

Although she reaped the benefits of living at Bloomingdale, the fact of the matter was that she was a lawyer's daughter, with nothing but her family connections to the Harris sisters to recommend her. She was attractive enough and pleasant enough that a man might take an interest in her, but life held no guarantees.

She had found certain men to be handsome in the past, but without feeling particularly drawn to them. Abigail had always been content to be alone, finding satisfaction in life on the plantation with her pets for companions.

Perhaps Charlie had invaded her thoughts simply because of his dramatic entrance into her life, and because there was an element of excitement which accompanied the danger of hiding him at Bloomingdale. She did have a penchant for saving pathetic souls, as Charlie had pointed out. Maybe her interest in him was as simple as sympathy mingled with common curiosity.

Abigail also hadn't anticipated his transformation from an unkempt fugitive to an attractive young man. Perhaps it was the unexpected surprise which had so affected her.

Deciding it was foolish to entertain any thoughts or feelings outside of concern for his wellbeing, Abigail threw off the coverlet and reached for her kimono. She imagined the poor man was lonely, locked away in the attic, and would benefit from some companionship.

Giving her cat a gentle pat on the head, Abigail padded quietly from the bedroom, peering into the darkened hallway cautiously before making her way up the stairs to the third floor loft. Not wanting to startle Charlie, but afraid of being overheard below, Abigail tip-toed into the room where he resided.

In the pale light, she could make out his form on the floor behind the bed, but could not ascertain if he was awake or asleep.

"Charlie?" she whispered.

"I'm still here," he replied softly in the darkness.

Kneeling down upon the floor, Abigail tucked her nightgown around her ankles. "Did I wake you?"

"No," he answered, pushing himself into a sitting position. "I couldn't sleep."

"How are you feeling?" she asked, thinking it was discomfort which kept him awake.

"Fine," he replied. "Just thinking."

She sensed his desire for conversation, and was glad she had put her foolishness aside to pay him a visit. Abigail couldn't imagine living as secluded as he had been forced to in the last few weeks.

"About anything in particular?" she encouraged, careful not to pry if her curiosity was unwelcome.

Silence lengthened before he finally answered, his voice thick with emotion: "Gettysburg." There was more contained in the one word than Abigail could comprehend. Perhaps talking about what troubled him would help him to heal.

"You fought there?" she prompted.

"That's where I was taken captive," he replied. "I didn't think anything could be worse than the life of a soldier. But I was wrong."

"How long were you a prisoner?"

"Nine months," he sighed. "Although I feel like I traded one prison for another." Quickly he added, "I don't mean to sound ungrateful. I'm deeply grateful... I'm just tired of being confined."

"Understandably so," Abigail sympathized. When he did not make an immediate reply, she made no effort to force further conversation. When he was ready, she suspected he would talk.

For a moment, it seemed Charlie had forgotten she was there. His eyes were fixed on the silver moonlight, gazing out past the window into the sky. She sensed he was far away, returning to a time and place imbedded deep in his memory.

When he spoke, his voice was distant. "It's funny the things you remember. As we were marching toward Gettysburg, we met a stray dog. She was friendly, and one of the men fed her. I guess she lifted our spirits with her wagging tail and wet tongue. We adopted her, and she marched the rest of the way to the battlefield with us. We named her Grace.

"We had become her family, and when the fighting began, she led the charge up hill. Grace was barking at the Yankees, excited by the noise of the gunfire and cannons, and the air quickly grew thick with smoke. When she ran back to us, she saw that some of her boys had fallen. Grace whined and licked them, nudging at the dead bodies with her nose. Then she ran back into enemy lines, as if to avenge their deaths. I heard that when she was shot, the Yankees tried to save her. When Grace died, they saw fit to give her a proper burial."

Abigail had to strain to hear his hushed whisper, her mind struggling to create the scene which his words described. But there was nothing in her experience to aid her imagination in conjuring such images. In this one short reminiscence she glimpsed the full horror of war, its evil and destruction.

"The poor dog," she said, though Abigail also was moved with pity for the soldiers, blue and gray, who had lost their lives in such a violent and senseless manner. And for the men who survived, like Charlie, who would never be the same again.

Charlie bent his knees and leaned forward to rest his elbows atop them, his chin perched on his forearm. "I guess the Yankees figured she couldn't be held accountable for getting in on the wrong side of the war."

The moonlight on his handsome face carved deep shadows into the hollows of his cheeks and eye sockets. He sighed, the sound so burdened and weary that Abigail's heart ached for him.

"How many battles have you fought in?" Abigail asked, wondering how many similar experiences he had endured.

Charlie quietly counted them out in his head before answering, "Eight or nine. Some worse than others."

"I just can't imagine…" Abigail confessed, her voice raspy with emotion.

When he cleared his throat, she realized he had been moved by her compassion for him. "You do what you have to," he explained. "In times like that, you find out what you're made of. All of the pretenses and the polish are stripped away, leaving the soul exposed. I don't see how anyone who's ever been to war could say that humanity is essentially good. I can tell you it isn't. The essence of the human being is wicked. There are a few men who aren't fundamentally selfish and cruel, but they're rare."

Abigail bit her lip thoughtfully. She wanted to ask Charlie why he had been angry upon learning she was responsible for bringing him to the safety of Bloomingdale. He has said that some lives weren't worth saving. Was he speaking of himself, and if so, what had led him to that conclusion?

She phrased the question carefully. "What did you learn about yourself in battle?"

"I guess I'm still trying to figure that out," he answered darkly.

"It isn't the same," Abigail was sure to preface her statement, "but when my sister Jeanine died, I saw how it affected each member of my family differently. We all grieved, but some of us were made more compassionate for it, while others seemed to grow harder."

"Your mother?" he guessed.

Nodding, Abigail hastened to clarify, "She's not a bad person. She just doesn't always know how to let her words reflect her heart."

Charlie offered a nod in response, and she sensed that he was withholding a different opinion. But she could hardly blame him for having a jaded perspective. He had witnessed the very worst in humanity.

"If more people were like you," he said instead of whatever negative response had come to mind, "the world would be a better place."

Grateful he could not see the blush which crept into her cheeks for the shadows which encompassed them, Abigail ducked her head in embarrassment. She was sure the compliment was not meant to be of a personal nature, but she still felt warmed by the praise.

Trying to steer the attention away from herself, she replied, "The Bible tells us, *'Bear one another's burdens, and so fulfill the law of Christ.'*"

"I'm surprised you didn't go to the battlefield as a nurse," Charlie commented.

"I would have," Abigail admitted. "But I knew after Jeanine's death that my family couldn't risk losing me. They needed me here, and my first obligation is to them."

"It would have crushed you," Charlie replied thoughtfully, "to see all of the suffering. And a woman as young and pretty as you are would have received more attention than you could manage. It was better that you didn't go," he assured her.

Heat spread down her face into her neck as Abigail searched for some response. She told herself that he was merely making an impartial observation. Why was she so easily flustered by this man?

"At least I was able to help you," she whispered, uncertain how to respond.

"Yes," he said, his eyes studying her intently in the pale light. "You did save me."

~

Long after she had left, Charlie could see Abigail in his mind's eye, her dark hair tousled from lying abed before her visit. In her nightclothes, with her braid dangling over her left shoulder, she was even more beautiful than he remembered.

He'd been painfully aware of her absence in the last week, and had been far more pleased by her unexpected appearance than he should have been. But then, he asked himself, what red-blooded man would not enjoy having his isolation disrupted by a beautiful young woman? Especially one so easy to be with.

His only other visitors had been Mr. Sterret, who had made a brief appearance to deliver more newspapers and to inquire after his health, and Ruthie, who continued to make routine deliveries with breakfast and dinner.

Sometimes Charlie feared he would lose his sanity, left alone so much to himself. He feared that the years spent in military service, prison camp, and now in hiding, had ruined any manners or social graces he'd once possessed. Never before had he considered how essential it was to remain in continuous contact with his fellow human beings.

Even at Point Lookout, he'd had the other prisoners to commiserate with. He never would have been able to successfully execute the escape plan without Wilson to share the work of rowing. Charlie grieved that they had come so close to freedom, only for Wilson to meet his end with a Yankee bullet.

Now, the only variation to the monotony of Charlie's existence was the unannounced arrival of the Harris sisters' niece, who cared for him the way she would a wounded puppy. Still, he was indebted to Abigail for both her kindness in saving his life, and for the companionship she had offered since. She was the one ray of light in what was otherwise a dark and empty life.

Reading the newspaper did little to lift his spirits or to distract Charlie from his preoccupation with the war. He wished there was more to fill the pages than reports of battles, the corresponding lists of casualties, and political predictions and analysis.

Unable to fall back to sleep, Charlie waited for the sun to brighten the room enough to read, hoping to divert his thoughts. But today's report was of a battle in Spotsylvania and Orange Counties, Virginia. It had been fought in a heavily wooded area, referred to as "The Wilderness." The Federals had suffered heavy fatalities, but the Rebels had a smaller army to begin with, and therefore were more impaired by their losses. It was also reported that although Grant's Army of the Potomac had withdrawn during the night, they had continued to advance southward instead of retreating north toward Washington.

In addition to this disparaging news for the Rebels, Lee's "Old Warhorse," Lieutenant General Longstreet, was inadvertently shot through the shoulder by his own men. Although he survived, he was badly wounded.

Charlie scrubbed a hand over his face. He had deserted from the war, but still he found that his heart was with the South. Only last summer, General "Stonewall" Jackson, that great man who had led the First Maryland Infantry on the Valley Campaign, had died due to complications from an accidental gunshot by Confederate pickets. The general's arm had been amputated with the hopes of preserving his life, but eight days later pneumonia had claimed him. His death had been a devastating blow for the Confederacy, both militarily and in terms of morale.

How much longer would—

Charlie's thoughts were interrupted by the pattering of feet rushing up the stairwell. He recognized the light step as belonging to Ruthie, and knew immediately that she had come with a message of warning.

"Hide!" she whispered in panic. Quickly they opened the panel for him to slip into the narrow gap between the walls. Ruthie secured it behind him, then rushed back down to the kitchen.

It was a confining space, and it didn't take long for Charlie to feel cramped and short of breath. A sweat broke out on his skin, soaking his clothes. There was no movement of air within the passage, and the combination of May heat and fear of capture combined to stifle him.

He could hear the deep rumble of voices and the heavy fall of masculine steps as the house was searched. Mr. Sterret's tone was casual and accommodating as he led the Provost Marshal on a tour of Bloomingdale, as if it were a social call and not a question of his loyalty or a threat to his safety. As the voices grew louder, Charlie's heart began to thump within his chest.

A salty rivulet of sweat dripped into his eye, and he blinked it away, resisting the urge to lift his hand to wipe it. His lungs felt short of oxygen, and he was sure the walls were closing in on him. Charlie squeezed his eyes tightly shut, all of his focus channeled on keeping his breathing quiet and even.

Even after the silence had reigned for what seemed like hours, Charlie was afraid to move. He resolved to stay utterly still until he was assured the threat was gone.

After what seemed an interminable amount of the time, he heard a feminine voice on the other side of the wall. "It's me," Lizzie assured him as she loosened the panel for him to slip through. "They gone."

Stepping out into the open air, Charlie gulped it greedily into his lungs. He thumbed the sweat from his eyes, then wiped his forehead with the back of his sleeve.

"We gots to move you," the slave woman informed him anxiously. "Mr. Sterret out in the carriage, waiting for you." Genuine concern was evident in her dark eyes as she added, "But you gots to wear this." She held up a dress and a woman's straw hat with a blue ribbon tied around it.

Charlie lifted an eyebrow, "You can't be serious."

"They's probab'ly got someone watchin' the house, Mr. Sterret say," Lizzie explained. "You put them clothes over yours, and you be Mrs. Sterret till you in the carriage. Then you gonna take it off and go to a safe place."

Charlie sighed. If it was necessary to evade the Home Guard, then he would have no choice but to go along with the scheme. He held up the dress in front of him, white cotton with a blue floral design, and shook his head. He stepped into the garment, and Ruthie helped to pull it up over his shoulders.

Even as thin as he was, his shoulders were too broad to allow the dress to close in the back. "We puts a shawl over you," Lizzie patted his arm reassuringly.

Once the broad straw hat was situated on his head, and Lizzie was satisfied that it sufficiently shielded his face, she went to retrieve the shawl. Charlie stood in the hallway waiting, and a glimpse in the mirror revealed the most ridiculous sight.

Lizzie draped the shawl over him and led him down the stairs to the front door. Once there, she paused with her hand on the knob. Her face, as black as molasses, peered up at him solemnly. "God bless you and keep you safe," she offered in parting.

"Thank you," Charlie replied, touched by the sincerity in her eyes.

As Charlie descended the porch stairs, he lifted the skirt with one hand and held the rail with the other, hoping that at distance his discomfort beneath the layers of fabric was not readily apparent. How did women function all day while smothered in such restrictive clothing?

Once within the enclosed carriage, Charlie was relieved to find Abigail waiting with her father. He would have regretted leaving without the opportunity to tell her good-bye. She sat next to her father on the bench facing him, and Charlie realized this was the first time he had seen her face by the light of day. Her dark brown hair was pinned up beneath a bonnet adorned with flowers, accentuating the curves of her cheeks and her small shell ears.

"Where is Mrs. Sterret?" Charlie wondered, certain she would not have actively participated in this deception.

"She left early this morning to visit a friend in Centreville," Irving Sterret replied. "She took Harris with her. He'll be very disappointed to learn that you've gone."

"How did the Marshal know I was here?" Charlie worried.

"Joe Goldsborough said that they were still looking for you, and he'd had a report of someone lurking in the attic window several nights in a row. I'm guessing they've been watching the house for a while. I pray to God they aren't following us now," he added, his eyes looking past Charlie through the rear window of the carriage to the road behind him.

Abigail leaned forward, her hands clasped together in her lap. "We're taking you to the miller's cottage. Mr. and Mrs. Allen are very kind, and I'm sure they'll allow you to stay and work with them."

"I'm introducing you as a distant cousin, John Harris," Irving explained. "I'm going to tell them that you've been ill, and you're looking for work now. They may suspect something, but they won't ask questions, and I believe they can be trusted."

Chapter Ten

M r. Sterret instructed Abel to pull the carriage off the road as it passed through a wooded area. Hidden within the shelter of the trees, Charlie removed his disguise while Irving stood watch to intervene if there should be any curious or concerned passersby.

Once free of the cumbersome garment, Charlie paused to turn his face to the sky. Through the canopy above, a thin shaft of sunlight pierced the green shadows. It was the first time in weeks he had felt the sun's golden warmth upon his cheeks. The breeze ruffled his hair, and the air smelled of blossoms and new growth. He breathed deeply, relieved to be out of doors again.

Reluctantly, he climbed back into the carriage, every fiber of his being loathing the confinement. He offered the dress and bonnet to Abigail, noting the amused smile on her face as she accepted it. Having seen his reflection in the mirror, he knew what a comical sight he had been.

"If the Home Guard had stopped the carriage, I don't think I could have convinced them I was your mother," Charlie teased. The sound of her laughter was like music to his ears.

"If I'd married a woman who looked like *that*," Mr. Sterret joined in the joke, "I think I'd deserve to be locked away."

Their laughter renewed, and Charlie saw that Abel had twisted around on the driver's bench to peer inside with curiosity. He waved him on, enjoying the full smile which graced Abigail's delicate features. He realized that he had never seen her smile before; he only hoped he would be able to again.

The atmosphere of levity faded as they turned onto the public road. Approaching them at a leisurely pace was a mounted soldier. Within the carriage, the fugitive and his rescuers held their breath until the blue belly had passed them by without as much as a glance.

"I don't think we need to be too concerned," Irving said, although Charlie noted that the tension in his voice contradicted his assertion. "For all they know, you've headed south. The Home Guard has other problems to worry about. Since they searched Bloomingdale without finding anything suspicious, I imagine they'll turn their attention to other things."

Abigail relaxed at her father's assurances, however false they may have been. She leaned back against the leather seat, her mouth lifting slightly at the corners as she said, "When Marshal Goldsborough said that someone had reported seeing a figure in the attic, Daddy was very convincing as he replied, 'The slaves have been telling me for years that the place was haunted. I thought it was superstitious nonsense, but I think I'd rather have a ghost in the house than an escaped prisoner. You're welcome to search the place.' If I hadn't known better, I would have thought he didn't know a thing about you."

Mr. Sterret's eyes crinkled in the corners as he smiled in reply, "I've never been very good at deception, so I was terrified it would be obvious that I knew more than I was telling."

"I can't help but wonder," Charlie mused, "who reported seeing someone in the attic, and how did they know that it wasn't a member of the family or a slave? Are you sure no one else knew I was there, and that those who do can be trusted?"

Both Irving and Abigail considered the possibility

thoughtfully. Irving's brows drew together as he replied, "I trust Lizzie implicitly. As for the others, I don't believe they would betray me."

"Other than Abel, who else knows where you are taking me today?" Charlie worried.

"No one else," Irving answered. "I only told Lizzie I was taking you to another location. I'll give Abel strict orders not to tell anyone—not even his father—where you are. If the information leaks, we'll know where it came from."

Seeing the fear which had crept back into Abigail's eyes, Charlie regretted voicing his concern in front of her. "It could have been a guard posted to keep watch," he reminded her. "Perhaps they saw me moving about the room without a candle and it seemed unusual. I did need to stretch my legs sometimes."

"No use speculating," Irving patted his daughter's hand. "There are any number of possibilities. But I don't think anyone would consider the miller's house. He should be just fine there."

"I want to thank you again for the risk you've taken on my account," Charlie extended his hand gratefully.

Irving gripped it warmly. "I'm grateful I've been given the opportunity to bless and not harm. There's enough of that in the world today. I'll be back to check on you from time to time, and there's nothing unusual about that since you're my cousin."

"I guess I get to call you Johnny again," Abigail added softly, a measure of regret in her voice.

She wasn't the only one who would miss their midnight conversations, but it was hardly appropriate for Charlie to say so. He hoped that when Mr. Irving came to visit, Abigail would be with him.

"Here we are," Irving announced as the carriage rolled to a stop in front of a modest brick cottage built in the tradition of a Cape Cod, the cedar shingles extending from the roofline to the front porch. On the other side of the dirt lane stood the three story mill, the large wooden wheel rotating as the water's current turned it.

Irving was the first to emerge from the carriage, followed by Charlie, who held Abigail's hand as she stepped down. He held onto her perhaps a second longer than necessary, and her eyes fluttered up to meet his, clouded with emotion.

The door of the cabin swung open and a red-haired woman emerged, an infant perched on her plump hip, with a line of children following at her heels like a flock of ducklings behind a mother duck. In a simple homespun dress, with an apron tied around her thick waist, she was a striking contrast to Abigail in her white dress patterned with green oak leaves, the skirt embellished with three tiers of flounces and a wide hoop beneath.

"Nancy," Irving greeted her warmly, "how are you this morning?"

"I'm right as rain," she replied with a wide grin. "Miss Abigail, it's a pleasure to see you today!"

The door of the cabin, left ajar by the last child to exit, swung open yet again and a dog sped across the lawn toward them, ears back and tongue lolling. She ran three circles around Abigail, barking excitedly, before plopping onto her haunches and looking up at the young mistress adoringly.

"Sophie!" Abigail exclaimed, leaning down to scratch the brindle terrier behind both ears with obvious affection.

Charlie could only shake his head. Another of Miss

Abigail's pets.

Irving stepped forward, "Nancy, I'd like to introduce John Harris. He's a distant cousin of mine who's just recently come in to town. He's been recovering from an illness, but he's gaining strength every day. I was hoping I could rely upon your and Philip's hospitality to take him in for a while. In return for bed and meals, John can help Philip at the mill, and with whatever other work you may need."

"Of course, of course," the mother clucked, stepping toward Charlie with a welcoming smile. "It's a pleasure to meet you," Nancy said as she took in his scrawny physique and weak color. "We'll get you filled out in no time!" she promised.

"Thank you, ma'am," Charlie offered a wan smile. "I'm sorry to impose." He feared he was more trouble than he was worth, first to Henry and Eli, then the Sterrets, and now this kind family.

"Not at all," Nancy countered. "Philip's at the mill, if you'd like to introduce John to him. I've got to get to back to the stove," she suddenly remembered, turning abruptly on her heel and bustling back into the house.

"I'll go with you," Abigail offered, casting a sideways look at Charlie as if regretting that it was her place to remain with the women and children.

Charlie followed Irving into the mill, a three story structure which housed the automated gristmill. A broad-shouldered man with a thick beard was tying off sacks of freshly ground flour. Philip Allen turned at the sound of their arrival and greeted Irving, who proceeded to explain to him as he had to his wife that Charlie was a cousin in need of place to stay and work.

As warm and hospitable as Nancy had been, Mr. Allen

assured Irving that John would be a welcome guest in their home. "With our passel of young ones," he chuckled, a deep and hearty sound, "we could use some help with the vegetable garden and grounds. Awfully hard for Nancy to do it all with the babies clinging to her skirts."

"I'm happy to help however I can," Charlie promised.

It was difficult to peg the Allens' ages. Nancy had red hair, pulled up in a bun which may have been tidy at the beginning of the morning but now looked as if the baby had loosened a fistful at her neck. Her face was smooth, with only laugh lines to testify to her good humor. Philip, on the other hand, appeared older, with gray taking over his beard and heavy creases at the corner of his eyes.

Charlie pushed down a wave of resentment at his dependency, and instead remembered his vow to survive. *This* was how he must survive. He would pretend to be a distant cousin of the Harris sisters and play nursemaid, gardener, and miller, if necessary. Somehow, he had to find a way back home.

~

Abigail lay awake that night, watching the sky overhead through the lace curtains covering the window. The moon had waned, and the stars were hidden behind the clouds. Sleeplessly, she stared out at the shifting patterns of darkness and light as the clouds scudded across the sky, pushed by an easterly wind.

The summer scents of magnolia and jasmine drifted through the open window, and Abigail sighed restlessly. She blamed it on habit, this wakefulness in the middle of the night. But she couldn't get Charlie out of her mind.

His brief moment of humor in the carriage, after he had removed her mother's dress, had given her insight into another side of him. A side which she hadn't even imagined existed. The light which glimmered in his eyes for the merest second, the smile which had transformed his features, had been a glimpse into the man he had been before the war had changed him.

Abigail wished she could have known that man; but just as much, she wanted to learn about who he had become. Her father had stated his intention to visit often, and she hoped that she would be able to come with him. On the way home, Mr. Sterret had also mentioned that he planned to deliver financial assistance to the Allens while Charlie remained with them.

No one knew how long this arrangement would last. Not only was there the risk of discovery, but it was anyone's guess as to how much longer the war would last, and when it ended, what the penalty would be for those who had sided with the rebellion.

There were a few who still held on to the hope that the Confederacy had a chance of winning their sovereignty, but most knew that they were just holding on for as long as they could. Since Charlie's arrival, Abigail had taken an interest in reading the newspapers, and rumor had it that the financial state of the Confederacy was not stable. Their army was low on manpower, and drafting was causing the same dissent in the South as it was in the North.

Slavery, and the subject of emancipation, seemed to be often in the news. Last fall, with his Emancipation Proclamation, Lincoln had freed the slaves within the states of the rebellion but had allowed the practice to continue within the Border States which had stayed—even if against their will—within the Union.

Having grown up in Maryland, Abigail was as used to the presence of slaves as she was to the arguments for abolition. As a girl, she had heard about such local figures as Harriet Tubman, "Moses," as some called her, who had led many slaves to freedom in Canada. Frederick Douglass had begun his life in Talbot County, on the Eastern Shore, and was later educated in Baltimore and became a unique voice for anti-slavery. Although Abigail had certainly never read any of his works, she was at least familiar with his name when he was mentioned or quoted in the papers.

She read both views, North and South, and found herself growing increasingly confused and curious. One day she went down to the kitchen to talk to Lizzie, who was one of the handful of slaves whom she knew personally. Most of them worked out in the fields and on the grounds, and had no interaction with her at all.

"Lizzie," she said, pulling out a chair at the table as the cook prepared vegetables for dinner, "do you wish you were free?" Abigail situated Sprightly in her lap, the calico purring loudly.

Lizzie looked at her as if she had lost her mind. "You wish you was a slave?" she countered. "If you gots to choose, what you think you say?" Her dark eyebrows were poised high over her eyes, wrinkling the mahogany skin of her forehead. "And don't you get no fur in my dinner!"

Abigail felt foolish for having posed such an obvious and clearly hurtful question. "I'm sorry, Lizzie. I didn't mean to offend you. I never thought about any of this much before, but lately I've been reading the newspapers—States Rights and Unionist—and I'm trying to sort it out."

"Ain't easy sortin' life out, honey," Lizzie patted her hand gently. "I ain't upset with you. You ain't in control of things no more than I is."

"Some people say the purpose of this war is to end slavery," Abigail mused, retrieving a handkerchief from her pocket and dabbing gently at her face. With the fire in the stove always burning, the kitchen was a regular inferno throughout the summer months.

"I 'spect it depends on who you ask," Lizzie replied. "I's been cook here for Missus Sallie and Mary for more years than I can say. I's met all sorts of people, and I's been treated all kinds of ways. Some of these Yankees what tryin' to free slaves treat me like I's nothin'; and then some of these men who wants to keep things the way they is, acts like I's a person much as they is. It ain't so simple as some folks tries to make it out."

"My aunts are kind to you, aren't they?" Abigail worried.

"Most everybody here at Bloomingdale kind to me," Lizzie assured her with a fond smile.

"How many slaves live here? I don't even know," the young woman admitted sheepishly.

Lizzie wrinkled her brow thoughtfully, "Now, I ain't so sure 'bout numbers. But the quarter gots sixteen windows, and each family gots its own. So, with babies bein' born or folks dyin', it more or less on any day."

"There's a convention meeting to vote on a new state constitution that would free the slaves," Abigail revealed. "Queen Anne's County voted against it, but I guess there were enough Unionists in Maryland who voted for it to pass. In addition to freeing slaves, it would disallow southern sympathizers to vote, and restructure the General Assembly in such a way that it would exclude them as well. It hasn't been ratified yet, but if it is…"

"You seem awful interested in pol'tics all the sudden. Ain't got nothing to do with no certain somebody, I reckon?" Lizzie asked with a sly wink.

Abigail blushed. "No! I mean, yes I suppose, but... It's just a very relevant issue that affects all of us, and—"

Lizzie chuckled. "Chile, ain't you got no white folks you can talk with bout pol'tics?"

"If you're freed, you wouldn't leave us, would you?" Abigail cut to the heart of her concern. In many ways, odd as it was, Lizzie had taken the place of a mother in her heart.

"If I can, I happy to stay put," Lizzie assured her. "Now, I needs to make the crust for this chicken pot pie, and I can't have no cat fur floatin' round my kitchen."

"*He* treated you well, didn't he?" Abigail queried as she came to her feet, afraid to mention Charlie's name, but certain Lizzie would know of whom she spoke.

"He did," Lizzie affirmed. "Now git on out of here with that animal."

Cradling Sprightly against her chest, Abigail complied. "A little cat fur never hurt anyone," she couldn't resist teasing Lizzie as she went. Her pink cotton dress was coated in a layer of black, brown, and white fur, and she grinned as the cook pursed her lips and shook her head at the sight.

Exiting through the rear door, Abigail walked across the sprawling green lawn to the bench where she often retreated to think. Before Charlie came to Bloomingdale, she had only thought about the war in terms of how it affected her and the people she knew, like Jane and Clara. Now she found herself thinking about it in much broader terms.

If the slaves were freed, it would be a miracle for Lizzie and her son Billy, and for Ruth, Esther, Abel and Washington. But what would it mean for Bloomingdale, since their plantation was dependent upon slave labor to grow the wheat and corn, and to manage the sheep, hogs, turkeys and chickens? Then there was her family. They lived on the fat of Bloomingdale.

And what would become of all the sons of Maryland who had joined the Confederacy? This was their home as much as those who had volunteered or been strong-armed into the Union Army. She had heard reports of some southern sympathizers being banished to the other side of the Potomac after their arrest.

If Charlie was discovered, would he be put in jail or sent back to the south as an exile? And what penalty would her father face for harboring him?

With a burdened sigh, Abigail closed her eyes and let the gentle breeze stir her long hair, hanging loosely around her shoulders. A shout startled her from her quiet reverie, and jerking her head toward the sound, she noticed the slave quarter.

She had seen it many times before, of course, but today she looked at it with new eyes. This was the home of sixteen slave families, including Lizzie and Billy. Lifting Sprightly, Abigail stood, her feet carrying her toward the stark brick building, not even as large as the barn. She knew better than to go inside, or even get too close, but she observed in detail from a safe distance.

It could have been worse, she was certain. Still, to imagine sixteen families living within that one structure troubled her. What sort of floor did they have? What kind of beds?

Turning to look over her shoulder, Abigail saw Bloomingdale in a new light. It was a beautiful structure, elegant and elaborate, with more than ample space for its few occupants. Perhaps Charlie was right about her. She *was* both spoiled and sheltered.

Chapter Eleven

It was a peaceful life, not unlike Laurel Hill before the war. Charlie enjoyed tending Nancy's vegetable garden and seeing to the chickens and hogs the Allens kept. When needed, he assisted Philip with packaging the flour and loading it onto the wagon for transport. The automated gristmill was an ingenious invention from a century before which dramatically minimized the amount of labor involved in the process of converting grain into flour.

The grain was transported mechanically to the upper floor to be cleaned, sent down to the hopper to be ground, then back up to be spread and cooled, before passing through the bolting hopper as fine flour. Powered by a water wheel, the process was completed from beginning to end without the need for human hands. The finished flour was then packaged into barrels or bags to be stored or sold.

Owned by the Harris sisters, the mill was often referred to as the "Sallie Harris Mill," such was the impression that old Miss Sallie had left upon the area. Her vivacious personality and winsome ways had apparently left a trail of broken hearts in her wake. Although she was now an old woman, retired to the old wing of Bloomingdale with her sister, her legacy lived on.

Mr. Allen never invited Charlie to assist with making deliveries, and he could only assume Philip suspected there was more to Charlie's story than he had been told. Even so, the Allens welcomed Charlie warmly into their home. He was given a crudely constructed bed with a tick mattress in a room shared with the two boys, Henry and Thomas. No more than five and six years old, the boys were the oldest of the brood and assumed a protective role with their three younger sisters.

Ada, Helen and Susan were all in diapers, and followed Nancy's every step like a puppy underfoot of its master. Sweet and pretty, the girls were well behaved, but easily upset and prone to tears. As precious as they were, Charlie was relieved that his time with them was limited.

He tried to find tasks that the boys could help him with, weeding the garden and gathering vegetables, or feeding the chickens and hogs. Their father was busy managing the mill, and their mother was in a constant flurry of activity —cooking, cleaning, and changing diapers. Thomas and Henry needed a man to take them under his wing and teach them the value of work. They were good boys, eager to please and quick to learn.

Between their hero worship, the hospitality of the Allens, and the open sky overhead with sunshine warm against his skin, Charlie found a measure of peace returning to him. Every day the regrets and atrocities of the past slipped just a little bit farther behind him, shadowed over by the passage of time and the mending of his soul.

Perhaps if he had abandoned following the newspapers, this state of being would have continued longer. But as he read the reports of the second battle at Cold Harbor, the past drew near once again.

There had been another great victory for the Confederacy. They had fortified their position well and were able to defend themselves against the Union onslaught. Only ten miles from the Confederate capital of Richmond, Virginia, it was an essential win. The cost in lives, however, both gray and blue, had been high.

Charlie had been with General Stonewall Jackson at a battle fought in the same area in June of 1862, sometimes referred to as the Battle of Gaines' Mill. His memories carried him back to it.

They had won then, too, saving Richmond and sending Major General George McClellan into retreat. Charlie's regiment had been called in as reinforcements, traveling by rail from the Shenandoah Valley where they had just recently fought at the battle of Harrisonburg. General Stonewall Jackson's men were to crush the left flank of McClellan's forces. If McClellan had realized the advantage he held in superior numbers, the outcome would have been quite different. Luckily, McClellan believed that the Confederate Army outnumbered his and refused the suggestions to attack.

Lee's offensive appeared to be successful and the Rebels were winning ground until they were thwarted by swampy terrain. Major General Longstreet arrived to discover the difficulty, and postponed further attacks until Jackson could arrive. Unfortunately, he was delayed by a civilian who led them down a road where their way was obstructed by felled trees left by the retreating Union army. Sharpshooters had positioned themselves to take advantage of their quandary, and forced Stonewall Jackson's men to take another route, thus slowing their progress further.

When they did finally enter the fray, Charlie's regiment was able to hold off the assault by Federal infantry until the Baltimore Light Artillery could be positioned to scatter the Federal troops. The following day they participated in another attack, capturing guns, weapons and prisoners.

When McClellan led his men into retreat and abandoned the march on Richmond, the Rebel soldiers had felt a great surge of hope. Maybe, by divine orchestration, they could win their sovereignty despite the crushing odds.

Now two years later, in almost the same location, history had repeated itself. The Union was badly beaten, but the war was still far from won. How many more lives would Lincoln, Davis, Grant and Lee require before they were ready to make peace?

Sometimes he wondered if they had considered the account they would have to give one day, on the other side of heaven, for all the lives they had taken. With far less blood on his hands than these two presidents or generals, Charlie felt the weight of guilt and sorrow rest heavy on his shoulders.

The first time he had been called upon to take action was at the Battle of First Manassas, Virginia, in July of 1861. He had been wholly unprepared for all the war would entail. Whatever he had imagined it would be, it was a thousand times worse. The blinding haze of smoke from the gunpowder of a thousand firing guns, the deafening sound of the concussive explosions as these weapons released their ammunition, and the horrifying sight of the damage inflicted on both sides of the line.

The newspaper reported that after Grant led his men into senseless death at the Battle of Cold Harbor, some were referring to him as the "fumbling butcher." As far as Charlie was concerned, they were all butchers, down to the man: Every soldier who carried a gun; every commanding officer who relayed the orders; every general who issued them; and every politician who talked about the war as if it were a game of chess. Each and every one of them had to live with their actions here on earth, but also be prepared to stand before the Creator and explain why they had seen fit to kill their fellow man.

Charlie closed his eyes as the guilt crowded out any vestige of peace. Not only would they be demanded to give account for those lives they had taken, but for those they had maimed and impaired as well.

~

Abigail inhaled the sweet smells of the summer morning. Leaning against the second story porch railing, she gazed out at the sky, a canvas painted with sweeping brushes of mauve, tangerine, and gold. Against the brilliantly glowing background, the clouds were dark smudges of purple as the sun made its glorious entrance into the day.

She found her thoughts returning to the painting she had noticed the previous night, while passing through the main hallway. Abigail had seen it thousands of times, but something had compelled her to pause below the painting of the Great Aunts Sallie and Mary. She had studied it as if for the first time, as if the secrets of the old ladies might be revealed within their likeness.

The bloom of youth had still been upon their cheeks at the time of their sitting, their blue eyes sparkling like jewels as they smiled down sweetly from the timeless image, adorned in dresses of black velvet with pearls around their slender necks. Hair pinned up atop their heads in the fashion of the day, they were undeniably beauties.

The artist had skillfully captured the personalities of his subjects, depicting Aunt Sallie with a subtly flirtatious smile and a twinkle of mischief in her eyes, while Aunt Mary's likeness conveyed a more meek and sweet temperament.

As she watched the constantly changing colors of the sunrise, Abigail pondered the mystery which was her aunts. They'd had their pick of almost every gentleman in the area. They'd strung quite a few of them along, encouraging the attention only to rebuff their suitors one and all. Abigail wondered if their games hadn't backfired on them. Perhaps they had played the coquette with a man they loved, only to have him turn his attentions to a young woman who didn't toy with suitors the way a cat plays with a mouse.

She could only speculate, but Abigail could easily imagine Sallie reveling in all the male attention she received, not considering the effect her games had on the men who genuinely loved her until one day she was spurned by the one man she had deeper affections for. Being the more dominant sister, it was possible that Sallie had convinced Mary to follow her into bitter seclusion.

Of course, these were only speculations. But it was curious that two such renowned belles should both spend their lives as spinsters, hidden away in the older, simpler part of the house they owned while Abigail and her family enjoyed the lavish wing of Bloomingdale.

"I think I'm going to pay the Aunts a visit," Abigail announced, turning to face Harris, sitting behind her on the white painted boards of the porch floor in a gray suit, straddling a box of slides between his legs, and holding them up to the light to reveal the picture.

Harris had received the slides as a gift from his tutor, Mr. Reynolds, on the last day of school. Abigail suspected the tutor was as relieved to see the year end as his student.

His freckled nose wrinkled in confusion. "Why do you want to visit them?"

"I imagine they're lonely, and since we live here, we ought to visit them from time to time."

Harris shook his head decidedly. "I think they want to be

left alone. I'm not going."

"Suit yourself," Abigail smiled indulgently at her younger brother as she walked past.

"Can we visit Johnny today?" Harris tilted his head up to peer at her curiously.

"Let's ask Papa," she replied, admitting to herself that she would very much like to know how Charlie was getting along at his new location.

Access to the old wing was gained through a narrow hallway off the dining room, and Abigail felt strange as she passed from the familiar part of the house into the Aunts' domain. Even the smell was different, a combination of dust and dried roses.

Knocking gently on the door to the main room, she hesitated, waiting for the signal to enter.

"Come in," a quavering, high-pitched voice called out.

Aunt Mary was seated near the fireplace, its grate covered over with an ornamental screen for the summer, deeply absorbed in the book in her hands. Sallie occupied the sofa, her fingers nimbly worked the yarn and knitting needle in her lap. Both women wore gray muslin gowns, simply cut, without any embellishment or ornamentation.

Neither of the elderly aunts looked up at Abigail. They must have presumed she was either Esther or Ruthie, seeing to their daily duties.

"Excuse me," Abigail ventured quietly.

Suddenly both sets of eyes were upon her, studying her with a combination of curiosity and irritation.

"Yes?" Sallie's silvery white eyebrows arched.

"I hope I'm not interrupting, I just thought that perhaps you would like some company," Abigail explained. The women stared at her expressionlessly. For a moment, Abigail feared Harris' assessment was correct.

"How can we help you, child?" Mary queried gently.

"What is it you want?" Sallie demanded imperiously, quickly overriding any hint of generosity her sister may have implied.

Abigail swallowed nervously. "I don't want anything! In fact, I'd like to thank you for allowing me and my family to live at Bloomingdale. I was only hoping to get to know you better."

"Have a seat, dear," Mary gestured to the empty cushion next to her sister on the worn damask sofa. Abigail cast a nervous glance at Sallie, moving slowly toward the indicated place as she waited for affirmation from the oldest of the two aunts.

"I don't bite," Sallie assured her, although her words were clipped and her tone lacked warmth.

Obediently, Abigail plopped down onto the faded bronze cushion. The ceilings in this wing of the house were low, the fireplace much smaller and the mantle plain. Everything was constructed for utility, and while it was certainly an improvement over the rustic cabin which had preceded it, the later structure Thomas Seth had built was intended to impress.

"What is your age?" Sallie inquired, gnarled hands resting on the half-finished knitting in her lap.

"I'm twenty-three, ma'am," Abigail answered.

"That was a good age," Sallie reflected with a nod. "Do you

132

have any suitors?"

"No," Abigail felt an inexplicable blush creep into her face.

The sudden color in her cheeks was not overlooked by Aunt Mary, who offered a sympathetic smile, but said nothing.

"Hmm. Well, no one stays twenty-three forever, I can promise that," Sallie mused bitterly. "I'd find one sooner rather than later, if I were you."

"Yes ma'am," Abigail answered obediently. If it wouldn't have been impertinent for her to ask the aunts how and why they had missed out on the blessings of matrimony, she would have.

There was little of the lovely young ladies in the paintings to be found in the elderly women who now carried the names of Sallie and Mary Harris. There was barely a trace of their former selves discernable in the shape of Mary's jawline and the curve of Sallie's nose, but they were wrinkled and distorted relics of the beauties they had once been. If anyone knew just how fleeting youth was, it was these spinster sisters.

The lull in the conversation lengthened, and Abigail realized they were waiting for her to take the lead as she had been the one to initiate the visit. Grasping for any topic, no matter how trite or petty, Abigail's mind raced to find a suitable question.

Her eyes fell on the knitting in the lap of Sallie's gray dress. "You're fingers move so fast, they're a blur. What are you making?"

"Socks," Sallie answered.

"For the soldiers?" Abigail presumed.

"They need socks; I need something to do," the old woman replied, her silvery gray hair glinting in the sunlight passing through the window behind her.

"Our boys are having a time of it," Mary shook her head sadly. "They're fighting their hearts out, but I'm afraid it isn't enough."

Confused, Abigail's brows furrowed as she clarified, "You mean'—"

Sallie flashed her sister a scathing look. "Let's steer away from politics, dear. No need to bore our young visitor with that."

Reminding herself that curiosity killed the cat, Abigail bit her tongue to keep from probing deeper into what was obviously forbidden territory.

Mary shrugged delicately, her thin lips pursing in subtle rebellion, a spider's web of wrinkles fanning out from the corners of her mouth.

"Do you knit?" Sallie queried, an obvious attempt to redirect the conversation.

"Some," Abigail admitted, more curious about the old spinsters than ever before.

"I'm not as gifted as Sallie," Mary contributed, "but I do what I can."

"What are you reading?" Abigail decided to shift her focus back to the aunt with a sweeter, and more forthcoming, nature.

"The Bible," Mary answered, patting the leather bound volume with a wrinkled hand, spotted with age. "The Apostle Paul had a lot of interesting things to say," she continued. "He was a very outspoken man."

"Jesus, too," Sallie corrected her sister piously. "I would say he was the most important voice in the Bible."

"Yes, of course," Mary huffed, "but I'm reading the book of Galatians at the moment, which was written by Paul."

"Sometimes she reads aloud to me while I knit," Sallie commented. "Helps pass the time."

"Yes, I'm sure it does," Abigail said, feeling as if the visit had run its awkward course. "I'm afraid I should be getting back now, but thank you for..." she hesitated, catching herself in a near lie. She had almost finished "a lovely visit," but that would not be entirely true. "Thank you for having me."

"Honesty is a virtue," Sallie smiled knowingly. "Come back again, dear. I like you."

Mary nodded in agreement. "Please do visit us again. We're out of practice, but we did enjoy your company."

Abigail gained her feet, promising, "I'll come again. Thank you for the invitation."

As she made her way back to the new wing of Bloomingdale which served as home for herself and her family, Abigail had to smile. They were a curious old pair, even more curious than she had first presumed.

Chapter Twelve

A fter lunch, I'm taking Harris to visit Johnny at the Allens, if you'd like to come," Irving extended the invitation to Margaret and Abigail as they sat at the table enjoying the midday meal.

"I still don't understand how you said this fellow is related," Margaret commented, lifting a crystal glass of water to her lips and drinking delicately.

"He's a distant relation on my father's side," Irving replied, eyes focused on the knife in his hands as he buttered a flaky biscuit.

"Hmm… So he says. I fail to see why it's your responsibility to see him housed and fed. I swear, you don't know if he's merely claiming to be a relative to take advantage of us. And what's worse, you wouldn't care if he was," Mrs. Sterret finished irritably.

"Charity is a virtue, my dear, not a sin," Irving reminded her gently, resting his hand over hers.

Margaret sighed. "Common sense is also a virtue, I believe."

"Then I take it you won't be coming along?" Irving asked innocently, casting a sly wink in Abigail's direction.

"I should say not," Margaret affirmed, dabbing at her lips with a linen napkin.

Sometimes Abigail wondered how her father never ran out of patience for her mother. In a lavender day dress, her dark hair pulled back into a chignon and covered over with a snood, Margaret was a lovely woman. But Irving wasn't the type of man to be captured by beauty, and the love he demonstrated for her was deeper than could be affected by mere looks.

What secret virtues did her mother possess that had so completely taken her father's heart? Or was he simply a man of committed resolve, determined to love to the end no matter how challenging the vow was to keep?

"I'll come," Abigail offered nonchalantly. "I'd like to check on Sophie and see how she's getting along."

Margaret shook her head disapprovingly. "I've never known a woman of breeding to be so enamored with common, domestic animals. It's strange, you know," she pointed out for the hundredth time, elegant brows raised in condemnation. "One day I hope you'll be married, and most men are not going to tolerate that kind of eccentricity."

Abigail sighed. She wished she could wink and go on unperturbed as her father did, but Margaret's constant nagging was as wearisome as a dripping faucet. "Well then, I shall have to marry one that will," she retorted, cringing inwardly as she saw the warning glance her father shot her across the table.

"Abigail Sterret, I will not allow such impertinence. Between your sharp tongue and your fondness for barn cats and sheep dogs, you'll be hard pressed to find a husband at all," her mother snapped.

Pressing her lips together in a firm line, Abigail swallowed down the retort that burned on her tongue. Out of respect for her father, she would not demonstrate further disrespect to her mother.

"Yes ma'am," she offered with as much sincerity as she could muster.

Privately, her thoughts turned to William Wilberforce, that eccentric man who had established the first society for the prevention of cruelty to animals in England. She had read about his collection of owls, hares, cats and dogs which inhabited his house, and how he spoke up on the street to men whipping their horses in the pouring rain. He was a great man of unusual kindness and personal courage, who not only was unusually fond of common animals but was an advocate for abolishing the slave trade in England when it was a very unpopular position.

As strange a fellow as he had been, Wilberforce had found a wife who was fully devoted to him. If it would not have been considered insolent to say so, Abigail would have reminded her mother of this.

"Don't return a harsh word with a harsh word," her father chastised in the carriage as they made their way to the Allens. "Haven't you heard, 'a kind word turns away wrath?'"

"I'm not sure that philosophy works on Mother," Abigail admitted. "She prods you into harsh replies, than faults you for them. And if you say nothing, she beats your spirit down with her tongue-lashings."

Irving took his daughter's hand in his tenderly. "We are each responsible only for our own actions and for our responses to other's actions. You cannot change her, but you should not allow her to change you."

"Yes sir," Abigail replied, recognizing the wisdom of his advice even if it sounded impossible to implement.

Next to their father on the seat of the open carriage, Harris offered a sympathetic look of commiseration. Abigail acknowledged it with a solemn nod. They were all three in the same boat with Margaret Sterret.

Upon reaching the miller's house, Abigail was amused and delighted to find Charlie standing beneath a cherry tree with little Henry standing on his shoulders. The child was picking cherries and dropping them into a basket held by his brother Thomas, who was sitting on a lower branch.

At the sound of their approach, the clopping of the horse's hooves and the crunching of the carriage wheels on the dry earth, Charlie turned. His face had darkened into a healthy tan from his work in the sun, and the combination of exercise and Nancy's cooking had worked their magic. He looked healthy and robust, and if possible, even more handsome than Abigail remembered.

An easy smile lit his features as Charlie recognized his visitors. Lowering Henry from his shoulders to the ground, he hoisted Thomas down from his perch as well, tousling his hair. Handing the older of the two boys the basket of cherries, he sent the children into the house to deliver them to Nancy and announce the arrival of the Sterrets.

"You're looking well!" Irving declared approvingly. Abigail silently concurred.

"Thank you, sir," Charlie replied, his demeanor equally improved by the fresh air and honest labor. "It's good to see you today. And you, Miss Sterret," he turned to include her, his eyes taking in her pink checkered dress and flowing curls. To Harris, he grinned, "And always a pleasure to see my young friend," he winked.

Harris grinned. "I hardly recognized you! Last time I saw you in the cellar, you looked like you had one foot in the grave!"

"Well, I did for a while, remember?" Charlie joked. Harris

chuckled, remembering how Charlie had posed as his grandfather's ghost in the attic.

To Irving, Charlie asked, "Have you had any more visits from the Provost Marshal or Home Guard?"

"No," Mr. Sterret assured Charlie. "But I'll only drop by here once a month to prevent drawing attention. If you have any needs, Philip can deliver a message to me at the house."

Charlie nodded, and Abigail noted the discomfort that crept into his casual stance. "Thank you, sir," he replied stiffly.

Irving acknowledged his gratitude with a silent nod.

The door of the cottage burst open and the boys emerged with the two older girls toddling along behind. Nancy carried the infant on her hip as she came out to greet them.

"Hello, hello!" she called cheerfully. Her ginger hair glowed like flames in the sunlight.

"Good afternoon, Mrs. Allen," Irving replied warmly, as if they were friends and equals. "She gets bigger every time I see her!" he observed of the child in her arms.

The girl instinctively encircled her mother's neck, burying her face into her plump chest. "She'll be a year old next week," Nancy kissed the top of the baby's head, covered with a fine layer of peach fuzz as red as her mother's hair. "Ada Mae, are you being shy? Can't you say hello to Mr. Sterret?"

Blue eyes peeked out from under Nancy's chin. Her lower lip protruded, and she quickly inserted a thumb into her mouth and buried her face again.

"I think Ada Mae needs a nap," Charlie laughed.

"These kids have taken such a liking to our guest, they've

started calling him Uncle Johnny," Nancy grinned at the young man.

Abigail observed the way Henry held onto Charlie's hand.

"Well, that is good to hear!" Irving grinned. "If you'll excuse me, I'm going to go talk with Philip for a bit."

"Nancy, if Miss Abigail doesn't mind, we can take the children to the creek so you can put Ada down for her nap and get some work done in peace. Or, take a nap yourself," Charlie offered.

"I wouldn't mind," Abigail quickly assured both Charlie and the children's mother.

"I'll keep an eye on the boys," Harris declared sincerely, as if he were much older than they.

Nancy smiled. "How could I say no?" To the children, she ordered, "Now you mind Uncle Johnny, Miss Abigail and Mr. Harris, you hear?"

"Yes ma'am," the little angels chorused.

"Where's Sophie?" Abigail wondered.

"Chasing rabbits, if I had to guess," Nancy replied, and Abigail cringed inwardly at the prospect.

"Can we go, Mama?" Thomas asked eagerly, poised to bolt as soon as permission was granted.

At her nod, he set off at a run, Harris and Henry hot on his heels. Susan scampered after the boys, while Helen, the younger of the two, looked up at Abigail with big eyes and asked, "Carry me?"

Scooping up the sweet child, Abigail situated the toddler on her hip, glancing sideways at Charlie as they followed after the children toward the creek.

~

There was a little pool which eddied around in a slow circle at the edge of the creek, at a safe enough distance from the mill that the children were allowed to use it as a wading spot. They ran eagerly to the bank, pausing only long enough to kick off shoes and socks, and to cuff pants legs or lift skirts before plunging into the cool water.

Just a few feet from this wading pool, a willow tree as old as the creek itself spread out its leafy limbs in a majestic sweeping umbrella around its massive trunk. Beneath its green canopy was situated a patio set which Charlie understood had once graced the porch at Bloomingdale. Wrought iron, with a pattern of climbing roses comprising the seat and back of the chairs as well as the circular table between them, they showed rust in several places.

"Helen likes to sit here and look for four leaf clover," Charlie said as he lowered himself into one of the chairs. "She's nervous about the water."

"I see," Abigail replied, seating the child in a patch of clover, where she immediately set to work entertaining herself. "You seem to be doing quite well here," she commented, her tone both pleased and amused.

Charlie smiled. "It's unexpected," he admitted. "I never imagined that I'd enjoy playing nursemaid and gardener. But here I am."

"Life is full of surprises," she returned. Charlie noticed the way her eyes took in the details of his face and form. He was certainly aware of the beautiful young woman she was.

"I'm happy to see you doing so well," Abigail continued. "Harris is right. You looked like you already had one foot in the grave when we first found you."

"Well, for the moment anyway, both feet are firmly planted on the grass," Charlie responded gratefully.

A shriek followed by a splash and a giggle caught their attention, and they turned to watch the children frolicking in the shallow water.

"If you weren't here, I'd kick off my shoes and join them," Charlie confessed, enjoying the antics of the children as much as the amusement and pleasure on Abigail's face as she observed them.

"It's ironic," she said thoughtfully. "I'm actually jealous of the miller's children when I'm the great-niece of the Harris sisters of Bloomingdale. While I spent my childhood in a nursery, they're free to romp and play in the wild."

Free... Such a relative term, Charlie realized. To prisoners or slaves, they would be considered free. Yet she was trapped by propriety and social position, while he was restricted to the Allens' property and his false identity.

In the thicket nearby, a loud rustling was quickly followed by intense barking. Charlie startled as Abigail sprang to her feet.

"What's wrong?" he worried.

"Sophie's chasing a rabbit!" she exclaimed, her skirts rustling as she ran toward the sound.

Charlie furrowed his brows. "She's a dog," he stated the obvious, confused by her apparent concern.

He followed her to the place where Sophie sat with a rabbit just old enough to leave its mother's den dangling from her mouth. "Drop it!" Abigail ordered firmly. The dog immediately obeyed. The fragile bunny sat stunned, wide eyes blinking in fright.

Tenderly, Abigail cradled the little creature in her hands and examined it thoroughly. "You'll be all right," she said to the animal as she carried it a ways from the dog and released it back into the woods.

"It's just a rabbit," Charlie informed her, baffled by her behavior. "If it survives the summer, it's only going to end up being snared for the stewpot."

He regretted the words, however truthful, as a range of emotions played across her lovely face: disappointment in him, embarrassment, and finally anger. Her cheeks flushed and her brows narrowed darkly.

"And to the Yankees, you're just a Rebel."

"You're not equating me to a mere animal, are you?" he demanded, his temper flaring.

She sighed, her expression pitying. "Of course not. *Are not two sparrows sold for a cent? And yet not one of them falls to the ground apart from your Father. But the very hairs of your head are all numbered. So do not fear; you are more valuable than sparrows.*'"

An arrow of guilt pierced Charlie's heart as images of those he'd slain in battle rose up before him. The first time he'd taken a life, the horror had felt like an ice-cold bath tossed over him. But he'd quickly adapted to the work of a soldier, killing men with as little remorse as if they were rabbits. Or sparrows.

In war, the cost of lives was high but their value was low.

Still, there was a vast difference between a rabbit and a

human being. "You do eat meat, don't you?" he questioned.

Abigail motioned Sophie to follow her as they returned to their place beneath the willow tree. "I do," she conceded. "You may find me sentimental, and perhaps I am, but I believe that life should not be taken without purpose. If that rabbit serves as a meal for you and the Allen family when it is fat, it's a very different thing than for Sophie to kill it for sport."

Charlie considered her philosophy silently. He'd never thought about it in quite those terms before. That the value of a life could be cheapened by the means of its death.

"You were right when you called me sheltered and spoiled," Abigail continued sheepishly, presenting him with her profile as she spoke. Her eyes were trained on the children splashing in the creek. "I don't know any more about what you've been through than they do. But," she turned to face him, "I'd like to know, if you're willing to tell me."

The sincerity in her almond eyes took his breath away. Moved by her compassion, Charlie felt ashamed of the way he had spoken to her. "That was my bitterness speaking," he admitted with a ragged sigh. "I'm glad you have no experience with the atrocity of war. Your heart is still pure and your conscience clean."

She studied him intently, her eyes searching his so deeply that he was compelled to look away. "Will you tell me?" she whispered.

To his chagrin, tears blurred his eyes. Blinking them away, Charlie answered somberly, "I read in the paper yesterday that General Johnson had intended to liberate the prisoners at Point Lookout, to arm them and march to Washington as a part of General Early's offensive. A deserter leaked the information and the plan was aborted, although Major Gilmor had led his men bravely to the Point with the belief that they would be raiding the prison camp." Charlie shook his head, grieved to think of all the men left behind while he sat in the sunshine with a beautiful woman by his side.

"I don't know if his plan would have worked," Charlie admitted. "The prison is surrounded on three sides by water, guarded by patrols on land and a battleship in the bay. It would not have been an easy feat to accomplish. But the report is that the General had heard about the condition of his men and couldn't bear to leave them like that."

"What is their condition?" Abigail wondered. The breeze stirred the flounces of excess fabric on the hem of her dress and the long chestnut locks of her hair which fell down her back. He feared that to tell her would take away a piece of her innocence.

"You couldn't begin to imagine," he answered hoarsely as the past crowded into the present.

"You looked half-starved," she recalled. "Your clothes were worn thin, useless against the cold. You looked and smelled like you hadn't been given an opportunity to attend to your hygiene in quite some time," she added, without a hint of humor in her expression.

Charlie nodded slowly, admitting the accuracy of her observations. He longed to share the burden with her, but feared it would be wrong to place that weight upon her slight shoulders.

As if reading his thoughts, she challenged, "Don't mistake my kindness for weakness."

The words pressed against his throat, and he let them tumble out in a torrent of hurtful memories. "They called it the bull pen, because it was no better than a corral for cattle. Summer and winter, we slept outside in the elements, crowding into the tents for shelter from the rain. But there was no relief from the cold. Sometimes as many as three men were forced to share one ragged, lice-infested blanket..."

He closed his eyes, rubbing his temples as the degradation of the experience returned full force. "We caught and fried rats for meat," he admitted, ashamed. "Every day there were multiple deaths from disease and starvation. And cruelty... We meant less to those guards than your rabbit meant to Sophie."

"How did you escape?" Abigail's voice was raspy, and tears of sympathy glistened in her eyes.

Leaning forward, elbows resting on his knees, Charlie hung his head as he answered, "There were some whose kindness moved them to courage. They risked their lives to free me, though I have no idea why. If they came to harm because of me, I'll never forgive myself."

The soft warmth of her hand upon his shoulder brought a new tide of emotion. "No one can take the gift of their sacrifice away from them. Not even you," Abigail informed him softly.

Charlie searched the depths of her almond eyes, and he saw the same strength which showed in the firm angle of her delicate jaw. Both she and her father had chosen to rescue him, fully knowing what the consequences could be.

It was a gift, freely given, not to be diminished by his own misgivings and fear of unworthiness.

Chapter Thirteen

Abigail's thoughts were a maelstrom of confusion. Looking at her reflection in the mirror, Abigail positioned a straw bonnet over her dark hair and secured it with a hat pin. It was high time she went to visit Clara, and the opportunity to refresh her thoughts away from Bloomingdale was welcome indeed.

As Abel drove her to Centreville, her thoughts turned round and round in rhythm with the wheels of the carriage. Sooner or later, there would be a day of reckoning. She feared Charlie's presence would be discovered by a Union spy and he would be thrown into jail, and possibly she and her father with him. Or perhaps the war would finally draw to an end and a new set of circumstances would arise. If the Confederacy lost the war—and that seemed most likely—what would the punishment be for those who had opposed the Federal Government?

Would Charlie choose to return to the south once the fighting was over, and even if he wanted to stay, would he be allowed? He certainly couldn't hide out so close to his home and family forever without making them aware of his presence.

The more time Abigail spent with him, and the more he shared of himself and his past with her, the more such thoughts plagued her. Charlie Turner had become a central figure in her life, and as much as she hated to admit it, he was also gaining a unique place of affection in her emotions. But to allow these feelings to continue unchecked was to invite heartache.

If she didn't talk to another woman about her feelings,

Abigail feared she would explode. Of course, she couldn't reveal his true identity to Clara and Jane. She would have to continue the ruse that he was Johnny Harris, a distant relation. But she could admit that he was a Rebel deserter, as it was this fact which complicated the situation for them.

The storefronts on Commerce Street flashed past on her right, then the imposing white brick building of the courthouse on her left, and as she approached Turners Lane, Abigail's mind raced faster still. She had sworn not tell anyone else about his presence, but if she didn't talk about these new and frightening feelings, she would lose her mind!

Abigail had sent a note to Jane the day previous to meet her at Laurel Hill. Her intention at the time had merely been to distract herself from the silly romantic ideas which plagued her mind. But the notions had persisted until she knew that the only way to regain control of herself was to air these thoughts to trusted friends.

"Missus Clara and Miss Jane waitin' for you on the back porch," the slave woman who answered the door informed her. Abigail followed her thin form through the narrow hallway to the rear exit. Compared to the spacious grand hall of Bloomingdale, the passage seemed cramped and stifling. The summer heat was oppressive, and there wasn't enough of a cross breeze to bring relief within the house.

"Miss Ab'gail Sterret here, ma'am," the slave announced as she led Abigail through the open door to the covered porch which overlooked the orchard, flower gardens, and family cemetery.

"Thank you, Phoebe," Clara smiled, standing to welcome Abigail.

"Oh! Look at how she's grown!" Abigail exclaimed as she

noticed baby Henrietta resting in a basket on a nest of folded linens.

Clara beamed. "I swear I say the same thing every morning," she laughed. "She's three months old already. I just can't imagine how I ever lived without her!"

Abigail peered down into the sweet little face, like a delicate china doll with pale skin and a dark fringe of eyelashes fanning out over her cheeks. Sweat dampened her nose and upper lip, and the thin layer of dark hair which covered her head. Even so small, the child still bore a resemblance to her Uncle Charlie.

"She's an angel," Jane observed, joining them. "Sweet as I've ever seen."

A male voice startled them from behind as Jeremiah chuckled, "You would think they'd never seen a baby before!"

The three women turned at the sound, Clara bestowing a loving smile on her husband as she replied, "Our baby is just exceptionally precious, dear."

He stepped onto the porch, removing his felt hat as he brushed his bearded face against his wife's cheek in a brief kiss. "Yes, I'd say she is," he affirmed. Turning to the other women, he smiled a greeting. "Miss Jane, Miss Abigail."

He angled his left hand behind his back as he leaned in close to Clara, positioning the hook which he had attached to his prosthesis safely away from the women. Jeremiah's plaid shirt was drenched through with sweat from working in the fields. He scratched at his dark beard with his right hand as he said, "I need to get back to work, but I just wanted to stop in and say hello to you both."

"It's good to see you, Jeremiah," Jane smiled at her brother-in-law.

"How are you?" Abigail asked as naturally as possible. It felt wrong not to tell Jeremiah that his brother was living only a few miles away.

"Let me get you a glass of lemonade before you go," Clara squeezed her husband's arm gently as she rushed to pour him a glass from the pitcher resting on the table beside the wicker divan.

"Thank you, darling," he said as he accepted the glass, draining it in matter of seconds. Droplets clung to his mustache as he smiled, wiping the sweat from his brow with the back of his sleeve before replacing the hat to his head. "Wish I could stay, but there's work to be done," he said, glancing down reluctantly one last time at his sleeping daughter before he returned to his work in the fields.

"He works so hard," Clara commented softly as her eyes followed her husband's retreating back. "Without his brother and the two slaves who joined the army, there's always more work to be done than there is time."

"Still no word from Charlie?" Jane asked as she turned to sit on the wicker divan, tucking her yellow skirts in close to allow room for Abigail to join her.

Clara settled into the rocking chair, creaking slowly back and forth, the edges of her blue plaid skirt swaying gently. She shook her head sadly, her auburn brows drawing together in concern. "The patrols haven't located him, dead or alive, and if he tries to send us a communication it would surely be intercepted."

"I'm sure he's found a safe place to wait out the war," Jane assured her sister. "He'll find a way to let the family know he's safe when the time is right."

Abigail chimed in quickly, "I'm sure Jane's right, Clara. You know what they say, no news is good news."

"I'm sure you're right," Clara sighed. "I only hope that Francis can hold on until the prodigal son returns. The work and the worry are taking a heavy toll on him," she said of her father-in-law.

Abigail bit her lip, wishing she could confess that Charlie was safe, but knowing she must not give away his location to anyone. "He's probably found someone sympathetic to the cause to hide him until it's safe," she suggested. Leaning forward she whispered, "Can you keep a secret?"

The two women glanced at one another curiously, nodding their promise as they listened eagerly for Abigail's disclosure.

"We're hiding a Rebel deserter at Bloomingdale," she confessed, watching Clara and Jane's eyes grow wide with surprise.

"You are?" Clara exclaimed in a hushed voice. "Who is he?"

"A distant relative, Johnny Harris. My mother and aunts don't know he's a Rebel deserter, only that he was sick and came looking for work," Abigail replied quietly. "You can't tell anyone!" she repeated sternly.

"No, of course not," Jane promised.

"Perhaps he knows where Charlie is?" a spark of hope lit in Clara's eyes. "The patrols said he was traveling with at least one other companion."

"I can ask him," Abigail offered, uncomfortable with the lie.

Jane studied her intently. "How old is this deserter?"

Feeling the flush on her cheeks deepen, Abigail answered, "He's young."

"And handsome," Jane added, her eyes knowing.

Clara's jaw dropped. "Abigail Sterret! Tell me you haven't fallen for a deserter!" she exclaimed, clearly appalled by the idea.

Hanging her head, Abigail brushed a wayward tear from her eye. "What can I do?" she asked, her voice breaking.

Next to her on the divan, Jane reached over to rest a hand over hers. "Guard your heart," she answered certainly. "But without love, what is there to make life worth living?"

Abigail studied her friend's solemn face as she asked, "Will you marry Judson, then?"

Jane sighed as she admitted, "I'm thinking about it."

~

Charlie watched as Philip Allen effortlessly tossed fifty pound bags of flour onto the wagon as if they were loaves of bread, one after the other without so much as a grunt. Meanwhile Charlie labored to hoist one onto his shoulder and shift it onto the wagon bed alongside the others.

Although his strength was slowly coming back to him, Charlie could never be as burly as Phillip Allen. He just wasn't built that way. Phillip was broad through the shoulders, heavy through the midsection, and had biceps as round as tree trunks. He boasted a full, thick beard and his meaty forearms were covered with a layer of dark hair.

Philip Allen was a bear of a man, yet with his wife and children he was a lamb. He treated Nancy as if she were made of glass, although she was a woman who could never be described as delicate. Plump and large-boned, she was neither graceful nor refined, yet it was obvious to anyone who spent time with the Allens that she was cherished and treasured by her husband.

With his five children, the big man was soft-spoken and gentle. The little ones curled up against his massive chest, cradled tenderly in his rough and callused hands. Watching them, Charlie felt an odd and unfamiliar tug at his heart. A longing perhaps for the bygone days of his childhood, when his mother was alive, his father was still young and robust, and he and his brother Jeremiah were the best of friends, enacting Lewis and Clark adventures in their own woods around Laurel Hill.

Philip didn't talk very much, but his actions spoke louder than words and when he did speak, Philip made his few words count. It therefore wasn't surprising, in light of Philip's quiet nature, that he didn't ask Charlie questions about either his past or his political affiliations.

Nancy, however, was as garrulous as her husband was reserved. She was seldom silent, always singing, humming, or chattering with her small children. Charlie sensed her desire to know more about him, but she kept her curiosity in check— which seemed to Charlie a surefire sign that the couple suspected he had secrets to hide.

After Abigail's visit the day previous, Nancy did indulge her curiosity in one personal area. "You and Miss Sterret seem well acquainted," she observed, her voice casual even as her eyes carefully gauged his response.

"Not really," Charlie was quick to deny the assessment. "Miss Abigail is a very kind and affable young lady. Easy to get to know, comfortable to be with."

Appearing unconvinced, Nancy merely smiled. "Miss Abigail is a sweet soul," she affirmed.

Charlie let it go at that, quickly changing the subject. "I'll stack some firewood for you before supper," he'd offered, adding, "I noticed you were low." And with that, Charlie had ducked outside and set to work transferring the split logs from the shed to the front porch.

Today as he worked alongside Philip loading flour onto the wagon, Charlie's mind slowly turned over the time he had spent with Abigail Sterret. It seemed as though he *was* quickly becoming well acquainted with the young woman, growing closer to her every time they met. Society's expectations of what was considered proper had been bypassed by the manner of their unusual meeting. Shallow pleasantries and superficial chit-chat seemed foolish considering the nature of their friendship. And Abigail's compassionate nature and open manner made it easy to confide in her.

The wagon was loaded, and Philip offered a nod which Charlie translated as gratitude for assistance with loading the sacks of flour. "Be back by supper," the miller said as he climbed up onto the buckboard and snapped the reins.

Charlie wished he could go with Philip to the Centreville wharf where he was making his delivery. It had been years since Charlie had seen the Corsica River, the dock teeming with steamers and cargo ships transporting goods to Baltimore and Annapolis, and before the war, to points further south along the Chesapeake Bay in Virginia.

Retrieving a scythe from the barn, Charlie walked to the hayfield where he began cutting the tall grass to feed the Allens' two horses and dairy cow through the winter. Under the summer sun, the hay would continue to grow until fall when he could harvest it again, bundling the shorn grass to feed the animals when it became too cold for them to graze in the pasture.

The smell of the freshly cut hay was sweet, reminding Charlie of the many summers he had spent at Laurel Hill. Sometimes his longing for home was almost unbearable.

The war must end sooner or later, though what would become of the nation when it ended was anyone's guess. Such bitter division could not be easily mended.

Under the command of the newly appointed commander-in-chief, Lieutenant General Ulysses S. Grant, the Union army had not retreated after their loss at the Battle of Cold Harbor, as Charlie had presumed they would. Instead they had rallied their forces and continued south to Petersburg.

Most of the supply routes to the Army of Northern Virginia had already been cut off, and Petersburg was the last outpost leading to Richmond, the capital of the Confederate States where Jefferson Davis resided in the southern White House. By surrounding Petersburg, Grant could effectively shut down the entire Confederacy.

Without supplies, the Rebels would lose not only the strength but the spirit to fight. This then was the beginning of the end—the long awaited end. Though not as Charlie and so many others had hoped it would be.

Recognizing the critical position Petersburg played to the South, a ten mile trench line had been dug around the city in 1862 to protect it from Federal onslaught. Fifty-five gun batteries were placed along the trench line, with walls reaching up to forty feet high.

On June 15, twenty thousand Union soldiers attacked the

eastern portion of this defense line. General Beauregard immediately sent for reinforcements, and from their entrenched position the Confederates were able to keep the Federals at bay. Realizing that the manned earthworks gave the Rebels a defensive advantage, Grant had settled in to lay siege on the city. Taking possession of the James and Appomattox Rivers, the Union army could receive daily shipments of supplies.

Establishing a base in City Point for more than 90,000 troops, Grant's intention was clear. He was going to starve the Rebels out.

Charlie was certain that both sides knew the game was almost played out. But the South had fought too hard for too long to just give up. They would fight until they could fight no more, and while Charlie admired their tenacity and resolve, it seemed like such a waste of human life—on both sides of the battle lines.

Perhaps to surrender before it was absolutely necessary was to render meaningless all the lives which had been lost for the Southern cause. They had to fight to the end to make the fight seem worthwhile.

Last night after reading over the paper, Philip had contributed his opinion: "No matter which side wins the war, the nation has lost. When her sons spill their brother's blood, she is broken."

The words resonated deep within Charlie. They cut like a sharp knife into his heart. *"When her sons spill their brother's blood..."*

It was meant to be a metaphor, speaking of the sons of freedom as a family of brothers. But the statement held a deeply personal meaning to Charlie.

"She is broken." Not only was the nation broken by this internal feuding, but thousands of families had been split down the middle.

"Broken." Charlie dropped the scythe to the ground, watching as the uncut grass around it swished over the blade as if startled. Leaning forward, he rested his elbows on his thighs, a primal cry breaking free from his lips as a sob rose up from deep within him.

Could any of them be made whole again?

Chapter Fourteen

The sky was the slate gray of twilight, with the moon a silver crescent suspended high above the fields and trees. Charlie pulled the cottage door closed silently behind him, sinking down on the steps to stare out at the expanse of open space above him.

Already the August humidity was oppressive, the air thick with moisture in his lungs, making his clothes cling damply to his skin. Running a hand through his sweaty hair, Charlie leaned back against the porch railing. The smell of the corn and wheat fields surrounding him was comforting, and the rustling of the wind as it stirred the growing plants and the shuffling of the deer as they awoke early to steal an ear or two was soothing music to his ears.

Rubbing his eyes, Charlie sighed heavily. It was a peaceful life he had here, serene and simple. During the day hours while he worked beneath the sun, it was easy to find internal peace in the rhythm of his labors. But at night, he could only sleep for a few hours before he was awakened by nightmares filled with raging violence, blinding gun smoke, and the horrible screams of the wounded and dying.

He had to find a way to live with his past. He could no more bring back to life those he had slain, or heal the skin and bones of those he had shot or stabbed with his bayonet, than he could stop the morning sun from rising.

Charlie was only a small part of the elemental world that surrounded him, the sky and fields and grazing deer, no matter how consuming these thoughts and feelings were to him. He was of no more significance than a speck of sand on the surface of the earth. No matter what regrets he carried, the war would rage on and the earth would continue to turn on its axis.

It was his task to find a way to live with himself.

But the past was only an aspect of his suffering. It haunted him to know that the events which plagued his nightmares were still being played out daily for many soldiers.

The siege on Petersburg continued, with no end in sight. Seven hospitals had been built in City Point, near Petersburg, to care for the Federal wounded as the two armies engaged in deadly trench warfare. Unable to breach the Confederate line of defense, they had dug their own trenches and settled in for the long haul.

Everyone was ready for the war to end. A regiment of soldiers from Pennsylvania, formerly coal miners, hoped to speed the inevitable defeat of the Rebels along by digging a five hundred foot tunnel underneath the Confederate fort, Elliot's Salient, and packing it with four tons of black powder. Their intention was to blow the enemy to kingdom come, one brigade going to the right and one to the left of the resulting crater, opening a way to the Jerusalem Plank Road, and from there, into the city of Petersburg.

General Burnside approved this scheme, and began training a division of colored troops to lead the assault. But at the last minute, General Meade ordered white troops to replace the colored troops, for fear of political consequences, and untrained men were sent in after the explosion. Additionally, the footbridges which should have been placed over the trenches to allow for quick movement were missing.

When the mine exploded, they successfully killed the South

Carolina men residing ignorantly above it, but a clear line into Petersburg did not open for them. Like a bear stung by a bee, the enraged Rebels fought ferociously as the untrained Federals units charged into the crater they had made and were trapped.

Major General William Mahone quickly organized the Confederate units and launched a counterattack, effectively sealing the breach in their defenses. Burnside ordered the colored troops into the fray, and they too went down into the crater and became easy targets for the Rebels shooting from the rim above them.

When the smoke cleared, only 1,800 Southern soldiers were killed, wounded or captured, compared to the 4,000 Northern men. And the stalemate continued, with only the promise of more fighting to come.

Charlie's attention was brought back to the present as something brushed against his leg. Looking down into the shadows, he saw a cat staring up at him with large green eyes. Rubbing its whiskered face against his knee, the cat arched its back, lifting its front paws into the air as it leaned into him.

With a sigh, Charlie reached down and scratched the cat behind its ears as if it were a dog. Abigail's young face, eyes wide and sincere, floated before Charlie's vision. He'd never been one to take to felines before, but he scooped the cat up and sat it on his lap. It placed its paws on his shoulder and rubbed its whiskered face against his cheek, purring loudly.

Perhaps the time away from the battlefield and the prison camp, as well as the influence of his beautiful rescuer, were changing him more than he realized. The anger and bitterness he had felt for so long were giving way to grief at the hatred at work in the world, and regret for the hand he had played in aiding it.

He had joined the Confederacy in the belief that he could

make the world a better place by fighting against tyranny. The words Ben Franklin had proposed for the Great Seal when the United States was being forged in 1776 had seemed to speak to him: *"Rebellion to Tyranny is Obedience to God."* Although it had not been accepted for the Great Seal, the motto had been so liked by Thomas Jefferson that he had appropriated it for his own personal seal.

It was a worthy ideal, but now it seemed clear that Charlie's sacrifice was as useless as every other Rebel's sacrifice who had been, was being, or would be killed or wounded in the war. They were fighting a losing battle this time, having won their freedom from England first in the Revolutionary War, then again in 1812, only to lose it internally to a government which had grown beyond its original intent.

Though the states who had chosen to stay within the Union did not realize it, this loss would affect them too. The federal government, having achieved new power, would only continue to grow. The liberty of her citizens would diminish a little at a time until the republic which had been born in 1776 would be no more than a fond memory, usurped by a dictatorial form of government which would mandate both personal and religious matters. The *"land of the free and the home of the brave"* was moving toward a climactic and tragic end.

William Turner, Charlie and Jeremiah's grandfather, had fought in the war of 1812 to preserve the independence of the United States from England, proudly preserving a free country for their children and their children's children.

What would the current generation have to say to their grandchildren about the way they had chosen to shape the nation?

The cat circled around Charlie's lap until it had curled into a ball against his belly, rumbling in contentment. Charlie stroked it absently, enjoying the softness of its fur. If the leaders of this country had valued the lives of its citizens the way Miss Abigail valued cats and rabbits, they would have worked much harder to find a solution to their disagreements before it ever came to war.

There had been a great number of legislators who promoted compromise for many years before the war erupted. Charlie wondered if those who had rejected these proposals now regretted it as they read over the casualties printed in the daily paper. Had a different path been possible for the North and the South to work out their differences peaceably instead of resorting to violence?

But even if these men wished they had accepted a compromise, they had no more power to reverse their decisions than Charlie did. The past was set in stone, and could never be sponged away no matter how many tears were shed. They each had made their choices one day at a time, none of them able to see into the future and predict what the consequences would be.

His choices had led him here, to this time and place, on the porch of the miller's cottage with a cat in his lap. To the casual onlooker, it was a picture of tranquility. But no one could see the wounds which had been carved deep into his soul, leaving scars which would remain forever.

~

It had been over a month since Abigail had seen Charlie. When he emerged from the mill with Philip, his white teeth flashing in a smile of greeting, her breath caught in her chest. If the twinkle in his eye was any indication, he was equally pleased to see her.

All traces of his imprisonment and gunshot wound had

165

disappeared, and Charlie looked as strong and healthy as if it had never happened. His plaid cotton shirt stretched taut over his broad shoulders and muscled chest, and the line of his tanned jaw was lean and strong over his collar.

"Mr. Sterret," Charlie acknowledged her father first, his eyes sliding back to and locking with Abigail's. "Miss Abigail." He glanced behind her to the carriage, noting the absence of her younger brother. "Where is Harris today?"

"I'm afraid he is being punished for misbehavior and was not allowed to join us today," Irving explained.

Chuckling, Charlie replied, "I suppose I shouldn't be surprised."

Irving sighed and shook his head. "Certainly not. That boy finds new ways to cause trouble every day."

"He's rather ingenious at it," Abigail added, with obvious affection.

"Please tell Harris I missed him," Charlie replied. "And tell him to stay out of trouble so he can come along next time."

"I certainly will. Perhaps it will serve as an incentive," Irving grinned, turning to greet Philip with a firm handshake. "I take it all is going well here?"

"Yes sir," the big man nodded. "Still pleased with young Johnny there."

"Good to hear," Mr. Sterret beamed approvingly.

"I'm guessing you'd like to take a walk now," Philip said to Charlie, his thick eyebrows lifting as he grinned knowingly at Abigail. "I don't mind if her father doesn't."

As if seeing the obvious for the first time, Irving's forehead wrinkled under his brown bowler. Uncertainty glimmered briefly in his expression as he studied the two young people. Abigail glanced down at the dirt road under her feet, feeling the heat of embarrassment upon her cheeks.

"Yes, Abigail may take a short walk with you," her father granted his permission, but she could hear the underlying warning in his voice. She wondered if it was merely because of Charlie's unique situation, or if he would be wary of any man who made her blush so easily.

"Thank you, sir," Charlie replied stiffly. "We'll just walk to the willow tree, by the creek, and come directly back," he promised.

Irving nodded, and Abigail felt her heart skip a beat as Charlie stepped forward, his expression inviting her to follow him. He waited until she was abreast of him to continue, Abigail lifting her full skirts as she accompanied him to the patio set beneath the willow tree.

"You look as lovely as ever," he said finally, breaking the awkward silence which had lengthened between them.

"Thank you," she replied, a little breathlessly. "You're looking well."

Abigail had carefully chosen her dress that morning with the knowledge that she would be seeing Charlie. Remembering that she had worn the pink checkered dress the last time, and the white linen with green oak leaves the time before, she had selected a lilac dress accented with pale blue flowers. She had been told many times that these colors complimented her complexion.

"I've missed you since leaving Bloomingdale," he admitted, the shyness which crept into his ruggedly handsome face making it even more difficult for Abigail to catch her breath in the tightly laced corset.

"Our conversations, I mean. I've missed our conversations," he added, clearly unsure how to proceed with her since Philip had made their mutual attraction an open matter.

"I-I've been reading the newspapers since you left," Abigail stammered, just as unsettled as Charlie by this unexpected turn in their relationship. "Trying to follow what's happening."

"Did you read about the Battle of the Crater?" he asked, his demeanor immediately relaxing. Steering the conversation away from personal matters seemed to put him at ease, which relieved Abigail's jitters as well.

"I did," she said. "It's all so horrible. I can't even begin to imagine the scenes described in the paper the way you can, and it still leaves me feeling sick," Abigail admitted.

Reaching the willow tree, Charlie held the back of the chair in a gentlemanly fashion as Abigail lowered herself into the wrought iron seat. Running a hand through his sandy hair, Charlie took a seat across from her, his blue eyes meeting hers solemnly.

"The Confederacy is standing their ground admirably, but I don't think even Lee can find a way out of this one. The Federals are advancing south, cutting off the Rebels' supply lines while they have access to endless supplies and reinforcements. If the Rebels don't find a way to push the Federals back soon, they're not going to be able to hold out for much longer."

"So you think the war is as good as lost?" Abigail queried, feeling mixed emotions at the possibility.

"I do," he admitted with a ragged sigh. "We put up a good fight, but we're outnumbered, plain and simple. And we don't have the resources the North does, the armories and the iron works. If we could have successfully enlisted the aid of European countries, I think we'd have had a fair chance. But when Lincoln issued the Emancipation Proclamation, he made it impossible for France or England to come to our aid without endorsing slavery. So he was able to prevent outside help for us while inspiring more volunteers for the North, all with one executive order."

Abigail leaned forward, searching his face intently as she asked a question which had been lying heavy upon her heart. "Is the war about slavery? Some say it is, while others say it isn't. And if it is... what do you think about it as a 'domestic institution'?"

Charlie offered a half smile, affection and admiration evident in his eyes. "You are an unusual woman, Abigail Sterret. I never imagined having this sort of conversation with such a beautiful woman. I can't tell you how much I've missed our late night conversations... But to get to your question about slavery and the war, I would say the answer is both yes and no.

"The South is fighting for the freedom to make its own laws and institutions, one of which is the right to own slaves. But they're also protesting the imbalance of representation in Washington, and the unfair tariffs placed on Southern exports. They're demanding to be treated as an equally valuable part of the United States, even though they are agricultural and may appear backward and simple to the industrial North."

Attempting to pretend that his statement hadn't affected her pulse, Abigail persisted, "But what do you think about slavery, as a moral and ethical issue?"

"Ah, that is the big question, isn't it?" he replied. His gaze shifted away from her, and though he appeared to be studying the currents of the rushing creek as it flowed past, Abigail sensed that his thoughts were far away.

"I guess I never thought about it much before the war," Charlie admitted. "It was just the way things were done. Now... Now I owe my life to two Negro men, and I can't endorse an institution which deprives them of their basic human rights."

"Were they the ones who helped you to escape from Point Lookout?" Abigail wondered.

He nodded. "They were slaves at Laurel Hill. When they were sent to guard the Confederate prisoners, they devised a scheme to set me free." Charlie blinked away tears, his throat constricting as he said, "I don't know what made them believe I was worth the risk."

Abigail considered this new information silently. Perhaps this was why he had felt his life wasn't worth saving when she first brought him to Bloomingdale, because he had fought for a government which perpetuated slavery when it was the slaves who had set him free.

"So you think that perhaps this is a 'just war' then, for the North?" she wrinkled her brows in confusion.

Charlie snorted derisively. "Hardly. I believe the Quakers and Friends who organized the Underground Railroad were genuine philanthropists acting on behalf of a moral cause. But politicians exploit causes. They manipulate the public with causes. If Lincoln cared so much about black lives that he was willing to sacrifice thousands upon thousands of white lives for them, and to allow the nation he claims to love to be rent in two over the matter, he would be a great enigma to me.

"No," he continued adamantly, "I believe he uses the ethical question of slavery to perpetuate the conflict and to inspire volunteers to fight to hold together his empire—the Union. If he cared so much for the lives of slaves, I would ask why he didn't care equally for the lives of American citizens."

"You don't think he's a genuine abolitionist?" Abigail pressed, intrigued by his argument.

He shrugged. "He may not believe in holding Negroes as slaves, but in 1858 he made a statement in a debate against Stephen Douglas that he did not believe in the equality of the races, nor in granting Negroes the rights of equal citizens to vote, hold office, intermarry with whites, etc. His solution to the problem of the freed Negroes was to send them to Central America. In fact, Lincoln suggested a constitutional amendment authorizing Congress to pay for colonization. True abolitionists, like Frederick Douglass and William Lloyd Garrison, were enraged by the idea. And once it was no longer politically expedient, he never mentioned it again, signing the Emancipation Proclamation as a war effort instead."

"But you think the slaves should be set free?" Abigail thought of Lizzie and her son Billy, and of Esther and Ruth and Abel. She pictured the primitive slave quarter in her mind, set against the elegant backdrop of Bloomingdale.

Charlie considered his answer carefully before he replied. "I do, but I don't think it had to happen like this."

Chapter Fifteen

It felt good to be on horseback again. The rhythmic motion of the animal beneath him, its raw power and restrained strength reminded Charlie of a time when he had been free. The wind cooled his sweat-dampened skin and ruffled his hair as he raced the bay mare along the grassy strip between fields of corn. Reaching the forest, he slowed the mare, Nellie, to a walk. Philip had mentioned a need for fresh meat, and Charlie had volunteered to go out at first light to hunt for venison. He'd been eager to do whatever he could to repay this family's kindness to him.

The early morning light had yet to penetrate the darkness within the woods, overshadowed by a thick canopy of green summer leaves. He maneuvered between the columns of trees, circling around shrubs and undergrowth, leaning forward into Nellie's neck as they passed under low lying branches. Charlie glanced over his shoulder more than once, an eerie feeling of being watched plaguing him.

He knew it was nothing but foolishness, yet he couldn't resist the urge to peer around for Union patrols. The last time he had been in the woods, he and Wilson had been fleeing for their lives. One of them had died there; one of them had survived.

Abigail had found him, just hours from death, and saved his life. And somewhere between the cellar, the attic, and the miller's cottage, he'd fallen in love with her. He'd had no intention of ever making a declaration of any sort. He'd assumed that he would simply continue to enjoy her friendship until circumstances allowed him to return home. Charlie had no idea what would happen after that. He couldn't bring himself to think beyond his homecoming.

He hadn't realized that his affections for Miss Abigail were so readily apparent that Philip should notice them. More shocking still, Abigail had not seemed either surprised or offended by the idea, but instead had seemed pleased to join him for a walk with this understanding between them. Charlie had been so taken by the warmth in her almond eyes and the flush upon her cheeks that he had let himself voice his joy at sharing the moment with her.

Now he felt like a fool. Not only was he a Rebel in a Union occupied area, he was an escaped prisoner of war, and worse, a deserter. He was unsure what part, if any, of Laurel Hill would be his inheritance. He was as good as a nameless pauper, a fugitive hiding from the authorities.

Why should Irving Sterret ever sanction a relationship between his daughter and Charlie Turner?

Halting the mare, Charlie tethered her to a tree branch and continued farther into the forest on foot. Reaching a grove of shrubs, he settled down to wait for a white-tailed deer to wander past. An odd and momentary twinge of regret that he should have to take down the unsuspecting creature struck him.

Such thoughts had never entered his mind before, but now Charlie felt a kinship with the deer. He felt as if he were wandering through his days, waiting for a predator to strike. This peaceful life of Johnny Harris could only last so long. It was only a matter of time before something or someone brought it to an abrupt end.

September had arrived just as hot and humid as August.

Little else in the world seemed to be changing, but just as Charlie knew that fall was around the corner, he knew also that the end of the war, and the Confederacy, was looming ahead.

Since July, General Sherman had been trying to take Atlanta. After intense trench warfare and hand-to hand combat failed to defeat the Confederate forces surrounding the city, Sherman had placed Atlanta under siege. CSA General John Bell Hood found that his supply lines had been severed by a broad flanking maneuver which captured railroad tracks from Macon to Lovejoy's Station. Hood had little choice but to withdraw his troops from Atlanta, destroying supply depots and munitions as he left to ensure they did not fall into Union hands.

On September second, Mayor James Calhoun surrendered the city. By the seventh of the month, General Sherman had established his headquarters there.

In Virginia, Grant was still trying to take Petersburg. The stubborn Southerners refused to yield, proving once again that the North had underestimated them. In a daring raid, brought on by hunger pangs resulting from the seizure of supply lines, the Rebels managed to steal three thousand head of cattle from behind Union lines. Charlie suspected that to those Rebels, beef steaks had never tasted so good. Not only was it a refreshing addition to their limited diet, it was seasoned with the sweet saltiness of revenge.

Of course, the Union newspapers were publicizing the fall of Atlanta and the desperate actions of General Hood as he evacuated with his troops. With the Presidential election only two months away, this victory would undoubtedly influence the votes.

Running against Lincoln was the former Union General McClellan, who was running on a peace platform, promoting a truce with the Confederacy. Any hope of his election was now overwhelmed by the desire for a conclusive military victory.

In Maryland, the State Constitutional Convention had begun drafting a new constitution in April, finally completing this new plan of government in September. The three primary changes proposed to the state constitution involved the immediate end to slavery within Maryland; a formal acknowledgement that the federal government superseded the authority of the state; and finally, it disallowed anyone who had shown southern sympathy to vote or hold office.

If this constitution was approved, and the Union would ensure that it was, the Maryland Charlie had grown up in would be gone forever.

The end to slavery would mean freedom for Henry and his wife, Phoebe, and for their son, Joe. It would give new opportunity to Eli and the other slaves at Laurel Hill. But what would it mean for the Turners? How would it affect the big plantations like Bloomingdale, which relied heavily on slave labor?

Fighting a sinking feeling of hopelessness, Charlie tried to remain alert to the world around him, listening for the telltale rustling of leaves and watching for the flash of that flag-like white tail. He blinked, then steadied himself, attempting to direct his senses to the world around him.

But the chaos in his head would not relent. It seemed as if everything that mattered most in life was destined to slip through his fingers. Like a fistful of sand, no matter how hard he tried, Charlie couldn't keep the fine grains contained within his hand. His dream of a wife and children, now embodied by Abigail, seemed impossible. His relationship with his brother was forever altered, and even if he could return home, Laurel Hill would never be the thriving farm it had been before the war.

Perhaps life had always been a gamble, a complex series of risks, a mad shuffle of hope mingled with desperate fear. Now that the varnish of life had been stripped away, the vulnerability was exposed in its fullness. Not just for Charlie, but for everyone within the state of Maryland and throughout the states of the Confederacy. Anyone whose livelihood had been built upon the southern way of life would have to find new ways to survive in this uncertain and changing world.

A movement from the corner of his eye snagged Charlie's attention, and he trained his sights upon a large buck as it sauntered confidently into the clearing. His heavy rack of antlers was held high, his neck graceful and muscular, and his eyes bright and clear.

Aiming for the heart, Charlie squeezed the trigger. The report of the gunshot sounded through the forest, ricocheting off the trees and echoing through the surrounding fields. A spot of red darkened the tan coat above the buck's shoulder, sending him bolting forward in a futile flight for survival. Charlie raced in pursuit, carefully taking a second shot when the opportunity afforded, and watching with mingled pride and regret as the majestic animal buckled to his knees.

~

Abigail stared somberly through the glass panes of her bedroom window. The vibrant fall leaves of scarlet, ochre, and gold contrasted against the gray November sky. In her lap, Sprightly dozed, purring in contentment as Abigail rubbed her velvety ears with thumb and forefinger. It was difficult to say which of them found more solace in the companionship of the other.

Her father had taken Harris with him to visit Charlie, and for the second time, Abigail had been left behind. When Philip had brought attention to the mutual attraction between the two young people, he had never intended to bring heartache to them. But it was, nonetheless, what had resulted.

Irving had been oblivious to the depth of friendship growing between his daughter and the fugitive he had taken in. On the ride home from the miller's cottage after Philip had brought it to his attention, Mr. Sterret had chewed nervously on his fingernail for several minutes before leaning forward, resting his elbows on his knees, and studying Abigail with an expression of earnest concern.

"So there is an understanding between you?" he began gingerly, his forehead wrinkling with discomfort at having to initiate this conversation.

"No," Abigail replied, perhaps too quickly. "I mean, there's no verbal understanding," she clarified, her voice sounding high pitched to her own ears.

"But there is a tacit understanding," Irving presumed, leaning back against the leather seat in consternation.

Abigail twisted her hands together nervously in the lap of her lilac dress. "I thought you liked him."

"I do… I mean, I don't really know a lot about him, but I have no reason to dislike him. As a person, anyway. But as a suitor for my daughter—that's an entirely different matter!"

Biting her lip, Abigail blinked back hot tears. "All my life, I've never met anyone I cared for. Not a man, I mean. Why does it have to be so complicated?"

Irving sighed, leaning forward again to take her hand. "I'm sorry, my dear, that I can't give you a simpler world. I have no grudge against Charlie, nor any fault I hold against him. It's just that due to the nature of who he is, and the present political climate, I think it wise for you to take some time away from him. You may find that these feelings pass. And if not, well, there's no use in cultivating them when no one knows what the end of the war will bring, nor when it will occur."

A knot grew in Abigail's throat. She had never disobeyed her father before, and she couldn't argue the wisdom of his counsel, but a painful ache grew in her chest as she nodded in understanding.

"I'm sorry," Irving's voice was raspy as he shared in his daughter's suffering. "I only want what's best for you."

Believing the truth of his words, Abigail whispered, "I know, Papa." There was nothing more to say.

Now, two months later, her feelings for Charlie had not grown cold with lack of encouragement. If anything, the longer they were separated, the more she longed to see him again.

The world had changed since last they had spoken, and she longed to discuss these changes with him. A new constitution had been voted upon by the people of Maryland in October. Although the majority of those who voted at their usual polling places were against it, the soldiers in the field were allowed to vote, tipping the scales just enough to secure ratification.

Not only did this new constitution disenfranchise southern sympathizers, it required an oath of allegiance to run for any political office. It also redistributed the representation of the General Assembly to the number of white inhabitants in a given county, meaning that those with large slave populations (which were generally those who had supported secession) were limited in their influence within the state government.

But perhaps most importantly, this new state constitution emancipated all slaves within Maryland effective November 1, 1864. While it did not grant the Negroes equal rights as citizens, it made them free men and women. The resulting problem was that they now were responsible for providing for themselves and their families the shelter and food which their masters had previously supplied.

Some chose to leave and experience the fullness of their newfound freedom, but many chose to remain where they were and receive wages for the work they had been doing all along. For the farms and plantations, this loss of labor force as well as the sudden financial burden of paying the remaining "servants" took its toll. It seemed almost an intended punishment for their Southern way of life and political leanings.

For those former slaves who wished to build a new life, few whites in the vicinity wished to hire them. In fact, many local farmers had sent to Germany for laborers to replace the Negroes who were reveling in their newfound freedom. The face of the landscape was changing, too, as small houses emerged in little clearings where the freedmen built their own communities.

The celebration which marked their release from bondage was soon overshadowed by the realities of fending for themselves in a world which was still largely hostile to them. In addition, freedom brought with it responsibilities for which the former slaves were unprepared due to their inexperience and lack of education. For most slaves, remaining in a type of bondage, clinging to the interdependent relationship they shared with their former masters, was the safest and most certain path to survival.

As she had promised, Lizzie the cook stayed at Bloomingdale after her emancipation. Many of the older Negroes and mothers had chosen to remain, while the younger men were eager to chase their dreams without consideration of the risks involved. To Abigail's relief, Abel had chosen to stay, as he was the only one who knew Charlie's current location. Esther and Ruthie had also remained.

Washington had left, but returned within less than two weeks, his head hanging. The life of a freedman was not what he had imagined it would be.

Most of those who were eager to build new lives were the field slaves, who had the most physically demanding work and were at the mercy of the elements of nature. They were also the most crucial to the production of crops, and their absence created a predicament for the plantation's field overseer, as well as its financial manager, and of course, for its owners.

Abigail heaved a burdened sigh. The future looked every bit as somber as the gray skies beyond her bedroom window.

As if this new constitution wasn't bad enough, Abraham Lincoln had been elected to a second term as President. Although it had been unlikely that McClellan would win after the fall of Atlanta, Abigail had nurtured a secret hope that he would be elected, and that despite having rejected his party's platform of peace, McClellan could then be persuaded to negotiate a truce with the Confederacy.

"I don't understand," Abigail had admitted when informed that Lincoln had been reelected by a landslide. "Has any United States President ever been responsible for so much blood shed?"

Her father had eased himself down into the armchair in the library, his pipe gripped between his teeth. Running a hand over his balding head, Irving had admitted, "No, I don't believe so. Certainly never of its own citizens. I keep thinking about King David, the warrior king, who was told by God that he couldn't build the temple because he had too much blood on his hands." He shook his head. "Now we are guaranteed the end of the war will only come with more death."

"Why don't more people want peace? How can mothers and wives be willing to keep sending their sons and husbands into battle, knowing the high likelihood that they will never return?" Abigail demanded, angry that the killing must go on.

Irving tapped his pipe against his chin and pressed his lips together as he considered his answer. "There are many who want peace, Abby. If mothers and wives could have voted, there may have been a different result. In any case, none of the states of the rebellion were involved in this election; many states allowed their soldiers to vote from the field, and Lincoln has gained the favor of the bloodthirsty; and if the Democratic party hadn't been so divided and indecisive about their platform, they may have been able to run a ticket which could have defeated Lincoln. Maybe, but with the fall of Atlanta, and the ongoing siege at Petersburg, most of the Republicans want a clear and decisive victory. Why call for truce when you can win the war?"

"I'm glad the slaves are free, Papa, even though I know it will hurt Bloomingdale, the Aunts, and possibly us. But I don't see how anything good can come from the way it's been achieved."

Nodding in agreement, Irving said, "The damage done by the war is irreparable. The nation is scarred forever. But perhaps in the wake of its destruction, peace and compromise will be more highly prized. Even though Lincoln solidly won his reelection, there is still no unity in the Union. There are War Democrats who want the fighting to continue; Peace Democrats who don't; Moderate Democrats who want to negotiate peace with a Union victory; and Radical Democrats who want peace without Union control. And some Republicans want the Union restored without the end of slavery, and some insist upon it. There will be plenty of need for compromise even once the war is ended."

"Do you think there could ever be another such war between the states?" Abigail was horrified at the prospect.

"Not in your lifetime, my dear," Irving answered thoughtfully. "But once those of us who have seen firsthand the devastation of a civil war are gone, it's possible that the next generation may repeat our mistakes."

Abigail longed to talk to Charlie about all of these matters, to hear what he thought about the way things were unfolding. She wondered if he understood why she hadn't been to visit, and if he missed their conversations as much as she did.

A brisk fall wind set the colorful fall leaves into motion, the trees swaying and bending in a sort of dance. Staring out her window, Abigail reflected on how much her life had changed since the spring when she had found the nearly dead Rebel soldier in the woods. Never had she imagined that one day she would find herself pining for even the briefest of time with him.

She missed the sound of his voice, watching the emotions play across his handsome face in a series of open expressions, the way Charlie's eyes softened when he was moved by something she had said. He was an attractive man, and there was no denying that he could melt her heart with his dashing grin. But what Abigail missed above all was the openness of the friendship they shared, the honesty of their exchanges. It was the genuine depth of their interactions, charged with an undercurrent of something indescribable which promised so much more, that made their relationship different from any other she had known.

If she missed him so, when she had only known him for a few short months, how much more must Charlie's family miss him? Jeremiah and Charlie had been very close growing up, from what Abigail had heard. They had remained not only close as brothers but friends, right up until the war pulled them in different directions. She could only imagine the grief the Turners felt at being separated from Charlie for so long, especially now when they knew nothing about his wellbeing or his whereabouts.

Charlie too must be suffering as he was so close and yet still so far away from them, even more so as the holidays loomed ahead.

Abigail wished there was something she could do to bring comfort and joy to Charlie and his family. Perhaps her father could be convinced to arrange an opportunity for the brothers to reunite. And surely he would allow her to be present to witness such a special moment.

A flicker of a smile touched her lips. Irving was a tender-hearted man with a soft spot for his daughter. If she committed herself to the cause and presented her case with both wisdom and persistence, she was confident that her father could be persuaded.

Chapter Sixteen

Atlanta, Georgia had burned. Although General Sherman denied giving orders to set it on fire, every city through which his men marched had been razed. If he was not issuing the orders, he was giving tacit consent by turning his head while the torch was being set.

Since the city had fallen under attack in July, the damages had been adding up a little at a time. Parts of Atlanta had been destroyed during the fighting to build fortifications or to open fields of fire between the entrenched soldiers. Additionally, Sherman had bombarded the city for five weeks without regard to the civilian life within. Many women and children from surrounding areas had taken refuge at Atlanta, only to once again fall under attack.

When Confederate General John Bell Hood was forced to evacuate the city, he took as many supplies and munitions as possible with him. Those left behind he ordered burned so that they could not be used by the enemy, including a train consisting of five engines and eighty-one boxcars. While its eruption was undoubtedly a significant explosion which caused damage to surrounding buildings, the destruction was nonetheless isolated to the localized area.

When Sherman's men pulled out of Atlanta on November 16, the southern city was a smoldering blaze. It was reported that all he had authorized was the destruction of certain military targets. His men, however, had followed the precedent Sherman had set for taking a merciless approach to all Confederates, whether military or civilian, and set fire to private residences as well.

When a former captain of the CSA, Robert Cobb Kennedy, was caught conspiring a plan to burn New York in retaliation, he was imprisoned with the intention that he would face trial and be hung for his proposed crime. Yet General Sherman and his troops were allowed to march through the south, leaving a trail of smoke and rubble.

Charlie clenched his fists as he read over the newspaper reports. It was in times like these that he wished he could return to military service and be given the opportunity to send that villain and butcher Sherman to his grave. The south was wearied and nearly beaten, and both sides knew it. This was nothing but a vindictive and hateful crime under the guise of a military campaign.

The irony of the North claiming to be the moral and philanthropic party in this war while they endorsed and supported the widespread and wholesale destruction of property held by innocent civilians was not lost on Charlie. They might believe that right and wrong were determined by the one with the most muscle and the deadliest weapon, but one day they would stand before God right next to the slave owners and have to offer justification for their actions.

What God would answer to all of them, Charlie wasn't sure. None of them in this bloody war were blameless.

It was easy to cultivate hatred for the military enemy, to allow him to become a personal enemy. The boys in blue condemned and despised the men in gray, and likewise the Rebels loathed the Yankees. And this hatred, not for a political affiliation or a domestic institution but for the person who held it, was what moved men like Sherman to such acts of indiscriminate violence.

No, Charlie was grateful that both he and Jeremiah were out of uniform, spared from committing further sins in the name of following orders or under the excuse of war. Even though his own anger flared and his sense of justice was provoked when he read the reports of Sherman's path of thievery and devastation through Georgia, Charlie was thankful to be well out of it. He wanted no more blood on his conscience. He wanted his hands to be instruments of life as he cultivated the gardens and fields, and mechanisms of kindness as he helped to care for the Allens' children.

Whatever atrocities the Union Army now committed, Jeremiah at least was exempt from participation and from any corresponding guilt. Charlie ached to see his brother and father again, to stand at the bottom of the hill and look up at the white edifice of Laurel Hill standing tall and proud as ever. He missed home so painfully that at times he considered traveling under the cover of night to knock upon the door. But his fear of the Home Guard's night patrols and the risk of recapture held him back.

And then there was Abigail. For the last two months when Mr. Sterret came to visit, he had brought only Harris with him. Nothing had been verbalized, but it was plain enough to see that Irving did not wish to encourage a relationship between Charlie and his daughter. And while he couldn't blame Mr. Sterret, and in fact agreed that it was probably in Abigail's best interest to forget about him, Charlie felt as if he'd been given a glimpse of the sun only to be relegated once again to the darkness of the cellar.

Philip blamed himself, though without knowing the truth of Charlie's identity, he had no way of knowing what an undesirable suitor "Johnny" was. As it was Irving who had brought Charlie there and who was supporting him financially, it was reasonable to assume that Mr. Sterret would approve a union between them, even if he suspected there was more to the story.

Her absence on the visit immediately following their disclosure was suspect, though it was possible she had genuinely been unable to come. The second time, it was obvious that she had been instructed not to come.

"I'm sorry," Philip had said, resting a beefy hand on Charlie's shoulder. "I guess I should've kept my mouth shut."

"Well, I was a fool if I didn't think she could do better than me," Charlie had replied bitterly. "No one to blame but myself."

"Not sure I'd agree with any of that," the big man had countered as he stroked his bushy brown beard. "Character's worth more than money or property. And love is one of those rare, but priceless things that money can't buy. Give it time. If God wills, you'll be together."

"If God wills..." Charlie grumbled. Why should God waste a moment's thought on him?

~

A white dog with patches of black raced through the shorn cornfields, a young Negro boy pumping his thin legs behind him in a futile attempt to catch up. The dog flew over the ground with amazing speed and agility, puffs of white steam issuing from his nose as he soared over the frozen earth in long powerful strides. The barren trees, denuded of their leaves, and the leaden sky beyond them were somber and lifeless, adding to the startling contrast of motion as the dog and boy sped by.

Within the enclosed carriage rolling up Turners Lane to Laurel Hill, Abigail smiled. It must be Rags, the puppy she had given Clara from Sophie and Sam's first and only litter. Clara had asked for the puppy, but it had soon become apparent that it was intended as a gift for the boy, whom she had entrusted with the animal's care and training.

An evergreen wreath adorned with a crimson ribbon hung on the front door, overshadowed by the white portico. With Christmas only weeks away, many of the houses throughout Centreville were dressed with festive boughs and ribbons, or fruit displays of pears, oranges, and pineapple over the doors. Even the white-washed brick courthouse wore cheery decorations along the wrought iron railing which graced the narrow balcony over its doorway.

As Abigail stepped down from the carriage, the dog bounded around the corner of the house, running toward her at full speed. On his heels was the boy, panting breathlessly and gripping his sides. "Rags, sit!" he ordered in a voice surprisingly deep and stern for such a thin boy.

The dog immediately dropped his haunches to the ground, tongue lolling out of the corner of his mouth, which was fixed in a toothy grin. His square jaw and barrel chest reminded Abigail of Sam, and she patted him on the head. "Good dog," she said.

"What is your name?" she asked the child, unable to remember though she had been told before.

"Silas," he replied, showing his teeth in a dimpled grin which immediately melted Abigail's heart. She observed that the child was dressed in a new wool coat which fitted him so perfectly that it had to have been purchased with him in mind.

It made Abigail wonder if the "servants" at Bloomingdale, especially the children, were adequately dressed for the winter weather.

"You've done an excellent job training Rags," she praised. "I'm sure Missus Clara is very proud of you."

If possible, Silas' grin grew even wider. "Thank you, ma'am," he ducked his head, but not before she saw the pleasure shining in his eyes.

The front door of Laurel Hill opened and the slave woman, Phoebe, welcomed Abigail in out of the cold. Removing her coat and scarf, she surrendered them to Phoebe just as Jane appeared in the doorway of the parlor.

"Abigail!" she exclaimed, her eyes twinkling. There was a flush in her cheeks which wasn't just from sitting too close to the fireplace.

"Jane! You look wonderful," Abigail replied, noting the way her burgundy frock complimented her auburn hair, and the vitality which had returned to her cheeks.

Standing behind her sister, Clara greeted Abigail with a plump baby girl perched on her hip.

"This can't be Henrietta!" Abigail exclaimed, marveling at how the infant had grown since her last visit. Her dark hair was thickening, curling around her ears and the lacy neckline of her white dress. She looked up at Abigail and smiled, revealing four tiny teeth. The likeness to her uncle was undeniable.

In a high collared dress of emerald green, Clara was the picture of health and contentment. "She's growing into quite the young lady," she laughed, and in her arms Henrietta waved her chubby hands gleefully and emitted a high pitched squeal of delight.

The sisters invited Abigail into the parlor, and she was grateful to take the offered chair nearest to the blazing logs in the fireplace. As hot as Maryland could get in the summer, it was just as cold in the winter.

"How are you all faring here at Laurel Hill since all of the changes have been implemented?" Abigail wondered.

"Times are hard," Clara admitted. "But they're hard for everyone. Paper money is so scarce, I've heard that many of the shops in town have printed their own due bills and are encouraging barter and trade for payment rather than credit. Without Charlie, Eli, and Henry we weren't able to plant as much as usual, and the harvest yielded less than what we really need to pay our debt and wages. Francis had planned to offer share-cropping as an option for male slaves, so we will try that method next year."

"Doesn't she sound just like a planter's wife?" Jane teased. "I'm not sure I'll ever be able to worry about crops and harvest the way you do." She smoothed the burgundy satin of her dress as if brushing away the soil from the fields.

"Give it time. You'll learn," Clara encouraged.

Abigail's jaw dropped as she faced Jane. "Does that mean...?"

A sheepish grin spread slowly across Jane's face. "I've accepted Judson's proposal of marriage," she affirmed, joy sparkling in her eyes.

"Maybe *you* should find a one-armed planter," Clara giggled to Abigail, "since that seems to have worked out well for us."

Ignoring this comment, Abigail flew to Jane's side, taking her hands and pulling her to her feet. "Congratulations!"

When Jane's fiancé Louis had been killed at Antietam, Jane had gone from a vibrant belle to a mere shadow of herself overnight—dressed from head to toe in the black of mourning, thin, pale, and withdrawn. To see her so alive again, brave enough to love and to hope, brought tears of joy to Abigail's eyes.

"I'm so happy for you, Jane!" she exclaimed, hugging her friend as she celebrated this new season in Jane's life. "Have you set a date?"

"June," the young woman answered, joy and longing mingling in the one word. "Judson says the war will be over by then."

"I hope it will," Clara chimed in, "and nothing will overshadow your happiness!"

Abigail felt as if she would burst with excitement. Not only was Jane to be married, but she had a wonderful surprise for them. She hated keeping secrets, especially happy ones, and she could hardly keep from blurting out the news.

With restraint, she said, "I'm delighted! And that means we have even more to celebrate this Christmas. I would love to have you both, and your escorts," she grinned meaningfully at Jane, "attend a holiday supper at Bloomingdale on December twenty-second."

"That would be wonderful!" Clara grinned broadly. "I suppose Mamie and Phoebe could watch my little angel for the evening," she added thoughtfully, kissing the top of Henrietta's silky head.

"Thank you for the invitation," Jane beamed. "I'll speak to Judson."

It had taken all her powers of persuasion, but Abigail had at last succeeded in convincing her father to facilitate reuniting the Turner brothers. She couldn't wait to give this moment as a gift to Charlie and to Clara's husband. They hadn't seen one another in years, since the outbreak of the war as she understood it, and they would surely be overjoyed to be together again under the same roof.

Abigail's mother would be in Baltimore the week before Christmas visiting friends and shopping. It was the perfect opportunity to host the reunion supper without her ever needing to know a thing.

Mr. Sterret had been concerned about the risk of exposure. If any of the slaves, other than those already in on the secret, learned Charlie's identity, it would place all of them in danger. And they would be extending their trust to Judson, as well.

"Not to mention," he'd removed his glasses, his forehead furrowing as his brown eyes bore into hers, "I thought I had made it clear that I did not wish to encourage your feelings for the boy by spending time with him."

"But Papa," Abigail had protested, "we won't be alone together! And I'm sure he'll be visiting with his brother most of the time and forget I'm even there. You and I have the opportunity to give Jeremiah and Charlie one of the most special Christmas gifts they'll ever receive. It would be a pity to deprive them of it merely because it would place Charlie and me in the same room!" she insisted earnestly.

Just as she had anticipated, her father had seen the wisdom of her argument and relented. He was at heart as compassionate as the daughter he had raised.

Thanksgiving had passed with little for Abigail to feel she had to be thankful for, but today her cup of blessings was full and running over. The announcement of Jane's engagement was only one more thing she had to be grateful for.

That moment, when Charlie entered the room and the brothers recognized one another, was one Abigail waited eagerly to see. She imagined them laughing and crying simultaneously as they embraced one another, rejoicing that they had both survived the war and were together again.

And of course, Abigail yearned to see Charlie. He wouldn't have any fine clothing to wear, and she hoped he didn't decline his invitation for that reason. He probably assumed he would eat in the kitchen with Lizzie and the servants. Whatever he was wearing, it was the welcoming smile on his face which Abigail longed to see again, and that telltale softness in his blue eyes when he looked at her, melting her insides.

Loud barking outside the parlor window startled Abigail and made baby Henrietta to cry. As Clara bounced the little girl on her hip, shushing her gently, Abigail peered through the window to watch as Silas brought the dog back under his authority.

Not only was Silas wearing a new wool coat, she noticed, but a knit hat, scarf and gloves. As she observed him, a new mission of mercy formed in her mind. A smile curved her lips as she imagined what her father would have to say about it.

She was going to ensure that every one of the men, women, and children sleeping in that brick slave quarters at Bloomingdale had adequate clothing and blankets for the winter—whatever it required of her to make that happen.

Chapter Seventeen

On the distant horizon a pink smudge was visible through the trees as the sun sank into the western sky, but the thick gray clouds overhead hid any colorful displays which might otherwise have been visible. Charlie rode on the back of the Allens' mare, Nellie, the cold seeping through his boots and wool socks to his toes as he made his way down the lane to the public road. Memories of the previous winter, spent as a prisoner at Point Lookout, made him grateful for the heavy coat and hat he wore.

This was the first time since being delivered to the Allens that he had ventured further than the nearby woods to hunt. Abigail had sent him a personal invitation to celebrate a Christmas supper at Bloomingdale, imploring him to attend as well as to spend the night. She didn't want to risk him travelling back to the Allens after dark.

Although her mother was out of town, he would still have to exercise discretion. While it wasn't unusual for the Sterrets to entertain guests during the holidays, if he was stopped by patrols, it was possible that they could recognize him and take him into custody.

He wondered if Mr. Sterret intended to welcome him into the formal dining room and assume that there was no one to question his identity with Margaret being in Baltimore. It hardly mattered. Charlie would have gladly accepted bread and soup in the kitchen if it had been accompanied by Abigail's company.

Prior to the war, he would have attended supper at Bloomingdale dressed in a fine black suit with a white linen shirt, black silk tie, and polished leather shoes. Instead he was wearing the only clothes he owned, which were the costume of a common laborer. Such trivial details no longer mattered to Charlie, and he assumed they didn't matter to Abigail either.

He was surprised her father had permitted him to come at all, and wondered what manner of persuasion Abigail had used to convince him. Mr. Sterret must have decided that there would be enough others present to keep Charlie and his daughter from having a moment alone together.

While Charlie regretted that he would be unable to steer her under the mistletoe in a shadowed hallway, he was grateful just for the opportunity to see her.

By the time he arrived at Bloomingdale, the sky was charcoal gray and the bare trees appeared as hulking figures with skeletal limbs. Abel must have been watching for his approach, as he promptly appeared to stable the mare and deliver a message.

"Merry Christmas, suh. Miss Lizzie waitin' on you in the kitchen," the Negro directed him.

"Thank you, Abel. Merry Christmas to you," Charlie replied. He was not to go through the front door, then.

He knocked once on the kitchen door and it promptly opened. Lizzie appeared, her dark face split in a wide, welcoming smile. She was shorter than he had remembered, petite and thin, with angled features and bird-like limbs. A white turban was wrapped around her head, and a white apron was tied around her tiny waist over a gray cotton dress.

"Johnny!" she winked, reaching up to pat his shoulder

affectionately. "It sure good to see you again—'specially lookin' so fat and saucy!" she exclaimed.

"Like a Thanksgiving turkey or a Christmas ham?" he winked.

Lizzie chuckled, taking him by the wrist and leading him into her kitchen. "Just like I said, fat and saucy!" She gestured to a chair at the table. "I's glad to see Mrs. Allen's cooking agrees with you, but ain't no one can whip up a Christmas dinner like Lizzie can!"

"Am I eating alone?" he wondered, struck by a pang of sharp disappointment.

"Don't be silly—I be with you!" she assured him, then burst into a fit of laughter at her own joke. "Don't you worry none. Miss Abigail, Harris, and Mr. Sterret gonna eat with you. They just needs a minute longer to get things ready."

Relieved, Charlie shook his head. "I would have been honored to eat with you, Miss Lizzie. I was just a little worried you might get confused about where to aim that butcher knife!" he teased.

She rested a bony hand on his shoulder, smiling broadly. "I only used my knife on you once, and that was to pry that bullet out of your side. I hardly gonna undo my good work!"

"That's good to know," Charlie grinned. Then sobering, he rested a hand over hers. "Thank you, by the way, for all you did to save my life and bring me back to health. I'm grateful."

"You welcome, son," she answered fondly.

Suddenly the inside entrance to the kitchen burst open, and Abigail bustled inside, the wide bell skirts of her burgundy taffeta gown swishing. Her hair was done up in a mass of pinned curls and braids atop her head, her slender neck accentuated by the low neckline of the dress, which stopped just shy of revealing her shoulders.

"Charlie, you're here!" she exclaimed, her lovely face expressing her joy at seeing him again.

Charlie wanted to hug her, but feared it would be considered inappropriate. Instead he reached for her hands, squeezing them warmly, but resisting the urge to linger. "Miss Abigail..." his voice was low and husky.

He took in the fullness of her festive gown, the small puffed sleeves adorned with black satin bows, the narrow cut of the waistline opening into a full hoop skirt. A strand of pearls with a garnet pendant encircled her neck, and matching earrings dangled from her earlobes. "You look beautiful," he announced sincerely.

"I's still here," Lizzie reminded him, jabbing him in the ribs with a sharp elbow, "Ain't planning on goin' nowhere neither."

Abigail giggled nervously, and Charlie could only grin wolfishly. It was probably a good thing they weren't alone.

"It's wonderful to see you," he finally offered, reaching unconsciously for the hand he had just released. It was cool within the warmth of his own, her skin as soft as rose petals.

"I'm so glad you're here," she returned, gazing up at him through dark eyelashes. "I have a surprise for you," she confessed, her eyes sparkling with excitement and affection.

"A surprise?" Charlie repeated, curious what it might be.

"You'll never guess!" she assured him, tightening her grip on his hand as she led him from the kitchen into the hallway, Lizzie on his heels.

He glanced back at her, eyebrows raised in question.

"I ain't tellin' you!" Lizzie retorted.

Charlie could hear voices in the dining room. Harris cried excitedly: "Hush! They're coming!"

"Who's coming?" a masculine voice queried skeptically.

As the door opened and he followed Abigail into the room, Charlie stopped short. Sitting at the oval dining table laid out with festive china, linen napkins, and crystal wine goblets, was not only Mr. Sterret and Harris, but two couples dressed in their holiday finery.

His eyes swung around the table, moving from face to face. Jane Collins. Judson Shephard. His sister-in-law, Clara...

Finally his eyes collided with the very last person he had expected to encounter. "*Jeremiah?*" Charlie's voice broke at the sight of his brother, and he stepped forward uncertainly.

Jeremiah's eyes widened in shock. His mouth slid open and he stared in disbelief. "Charlie?"

~

Abigail stood at Charlie's side, waiting for the brothers to embrace. But instead they studied one another warily, like two bulls sizing up their opponent.

Instead of the joy she had expected to replace the shock on Jeremiah's face, his expression hardened and his eyes blazed with rage. Holding up his prosthetic rubber hand, he thrust it at Charlie, demanding, "*How could you do this to me?*"

Clara pushed back her chair and sprang to her feet, resting a restraining hand upon her husband's good arm. Her eyes met

Abigail's with mixed apology and alarm, and Abigail realized that while Clara was distraught by Jeremiah's response, she wasn't surprised by it.

"I'm sorry," Charlie stepped forward, his expression tortured. "I didn't think—" he began, but his brother cut him off.

Jeremiah glowered at his younger brother as he fumed, "You saw me. You recognized me. You took aim, and then you fired. *Do not dare lie to those present that it was an accident!*"

Abigail recoiled, covering her mouth in horror. She turned to Charlie, waiting for him to deny the charge and defend himself, but instead he wore an expression of profound brokenness.

His shoulders sagged and his eyes glittered with pain. "Jeremiah, I… didn't think it through," he muttered, his voice small and defeated.

"*You* are the one who shot him?" Abigail stepped forward to search Charlie's eyes, her mind spinning. He looked away, unable to meet her gaze.

Abigail felt something fragile, deep within her heart, shatter into a million jagged pieces. Never would she have imagined Charlie was capable of such a thing.

"I don't understand," she whispered, her voice pleading him to offer an explanation which would allow her to forgive him.

"It's not what you think," he finally allowed his blue eyes to lock with hers. In their depths, she could see the intensity of his regret and suffering.

This was why he didn't believe he was worth saving.

Abigail laid her hand gently upon his arm, leaning in close to him. She wanted to understand. She wanted him to exonerate himself.

But Jeremiah stepped between them gruffly. Abigail struggled to maintain her balance, her wide hoop skirt swaying wildly, and her ankle turning in her high heeled boots. Clara sprang forward and caught her elbow, steadying her.

Thrusting the prosthesis in Charlie's face, Jeremiah stormed, "*This* is what you did to me! My hand was shot to pieces! I spent days waiting for medical attention, wondering if I would bleed to death or die from infection first. When they finally sent me to a man who called himself a surgeon, there was nothing he could do but saw it off and dump it into a bucket with the other dismembered hands and feet!" He was shaking, his face mottled red beneath his dark beard.

Abigail's stomach turned at the graphic account of what Jeremiah had endured. Clara had gone to Gettysburg after the battle to find her husband. What had she witnessed while she was there?

Charlie's eyes pooled, the tears trailing down his face. "I'm sorry," he whispered raggedly. "I'm so sorry..." His voice cracked.

Jeremiah stared at him coldly, unmoved by his tearful apology. "Some things are beyond forgiveness," he stated.

Charlie brushed the tears from his eyes, spinning on his heels as he turned and fled down the hallway.

Abigail ignored her father's voice behind her as she took pursuit after him. "Charlie!" she cried breathlessly, her corset squeezing the air from her lungs. "*Charlie, wait!*" Her feet wobbled on the narrow heels of her boots as she ran.

By the time she reached the kitchen, the door to the yard was ajar and an ice cold wind slapped her across her face.

Following behind her, Lizzie grabbed her arm.

"Let him go," she advised. "For now, let him go."

Abigail turned into the Negro woman's embraced and wept.

"Did you hear?" she asked Lizzie.

"I heard, honey." She stroked Abigail's head as if she were a child. "I heard it, but I still don't believe it," she admitted, clucking her tongue in disbelief.

"How could he shoot his own brother?" Abigail cried, remembering how she had grieved when her sister, Jeanine, had died.

Lizzie shook her head. "I don't know, chile, but somethin' about this just don't seem right."

~

Charlie dug his heels into the mare's flanks. Her hooves beat a staccato rhythm as she galloped down the dirt lane. Hot tears blurred Charlie's eyes, the cold air stinging his face like needles. Searing pain ripped his chest from the inside out, his heart aching with unbearable self-loathing and regret.

Ever since their encounter at Gettysburg, Charlie had been dreading the day when he would stand face to face with Jeremiah. Still he had harbored the tenuous hope that if he was given the chance to explain his actions, made in the heat of battle, Jeremiah would understand and forgive him.

He had known, deep down, that it was impossible. But he couldn't move on until he had tried.

Charlie had presumed he would choose the moment of their meeting, but instead it had been thrust upon both him and his brother with impartial surprise. Perhaps if Jeremiah had been warned, had expected to see him, his reaction would not have been so explosive.

Then again, perhaps the details surrounding their reunion wouldn't have changed anything. It was not a trifling incident which Charlie was asking him to forgive.

He had done far worse than merely cost Jeremiah his hand. It was worse even than placing his life in danger. Charlie had broken his trust, brutally severing the bond of friendship which had held them together all of their lives. It wasn't just Jeremiah's hand which was buried in a ditch in Pennsylvania, but something far more valuable even if less tangible.

Did his father know that it was he who was responsible for pulling the trigger that day, rendering Jeremiah an amputee? The possibility triggered an even deeper stab of guilt and isolation. Profound, raw pain throbbed in his chest.

Slowing the mare to a walk, Charlie guided her onto the public road. He did not dare bring attention to himself if there were patrols riding on such a bitter night.

The thought of returning to the Allens and continuing to take advantage of their hospitality didn't seem right. Up until now, Charlie had allowed himself to believe that he could excuse the choice he had made. Now he saw clearly that he was undeserving of any further kindness from Philip and Nancy, from Irving, and especially from Abigail.

How could he ever face any of them again now that his darkest secret had been exposed?

Rather than placing Mr. Sterret and the Allens in the difficult position of having to decide if they should allow him to stay or if they must send him on his way, Charlie would make the decision for them. He would sleep in the barn, so as not to disturb his gracious hosts, and at dawn's first blush he would relieve them of his presence. In the morning, by the light of day and the feeble warmth of the sun, he would embark upon another journey.

As he began to consider his next destination, the answer seemed clear. Charlie could not right the wrongs of his past, but one thing he could do: he could register at the nearest Confederate enlistment office and report for duty. At least he would not have to live with the stigma of being a deserter all of his life.

He did not fear the repercussions formerly associated with desertion, such as execution by gunshot or hanging. The CSA was in such desperate need of men that they would welcome him back with open arms, without asking as much as a question. Although Charlie thought it would be pertinent to question his sanity. Why would any man return to the battlefield in the final days of a war, and on the losing side, no less?

He did not agree with what the Confederacy had come to stand for: the continuation of slavery. But he did hold fast to the belief that the states should retain a level of sovereignty which the Federal Government was attempting to deprive them of, and which would only lead to continued growth in the scope of authority which the federal government held over them.

It was possible that he was signing his own death warrant. But at least he could die as a man fighting for a cause he believed in rather than hiding like a coward. Should he survive to the end of the war, he would be honorably discharged instead of being remembered by future generations as a deserter.

And if he should die, the world would go on as it had before, oblivious to the sudden silence of one more voice.

Chapter Eighteen

Rubbing his eyes, Charlie sat up in the pile of hay, wondering what time it was. Sleep had eluded him for most of the night, only to claim him in anxious exhaustion in the wee hours of the morning. Now the sun had cleared the horizon, and below the hayloft where he had slept, footsteps indicated that he had missed his opportunity to slip away before the Allens awakened.

He could hear Philip calling his name, having noticed his absence from the cottage but finding the mare stabled. Charlie hoped he would not think to check the hayloft. After all, why should the man expect his guest to be hiding with the barn cats instead of sleeping in his own warm bed?

When several moments of silence was followed by the thud of the cottage door, Charlie crept down the ladder and peered from the shadows of the barn across the sunlit yard. Seeing no one, he spun around, darted through the rear door, and sprinted toward the tree line.

When no shouts or calls followed him, Charlie assumed he had not been spotted bolting for the woods. The naked limbs offered little camouflage and Charlie set off at a trot, veering away from the road and the house. His breath made puffs of steam as he ran, the cold causing his lungs to ache. But at least the exertion set his blood to pumping and warmed him to his extremities.

Reaching a creek, he paused to drink from it like a dog, kneeling to lap from the shallow water as it flowed past. A thin layer of ice had formed along the bank where the current was slower, and Charlie had no desire to place his bare hands in the water.

He drank enough to slake his thirst, but also to fill his belly. He had no food with him, and no idea when he might have opportunity to eat again. But Charlie had survived both the harsh winter weather and starvation at Point Lookout, and he drew on that knowledge to sustain him. He could survive it again.

His plan was to head south to Virginia, and from there to find a means across the bay and on to Richmond. There he could report for active duty and receive information on where to rejoin the Second Maryland Infantry.

It was too cold to travel at night, so he would have to hope and pray that not only Irving Sterret and Philip Allen wouldn't sound the alarm, but that his brother would remain silent as to his whereabouts as well. With Christmas just days away, and with the frigid temperatures, it was doubtful that the patrols would be eager to search field and forest without good cause.

If he stayed clear of main roads and skirted farms and towns, and if he kept a steady pace, he hoped to reach Virginia in less than a week. He would have to find shelter to sleep at night, as well as forage for something to eat, being mindful not to bring attention to himself. The last thing he wanted was to end up in enemy hands a second time.

Pushing all other thoughts from his mind, Charlie focused on one thing only: moving forward and avoiding capture.

~

Abigail awoke with a start. *Charlie.*

She felt heartsick just thinking of him. Her mind couldn't

quite accept what he had claimed to be true. He had shot his own brother. Intentionally.

Tears seeped from her eyes and she wiped them away impatiently. Abigail had been certain she had cried herself dry the night before as she tossed and turned sleeplessly in her bed, recounting every second of the exchange between the brothers. Yet somehow more tears still came.

Rolling onto her side, she tucked her hands under her cheek and closed her eyes. Sprightly, on the pillow next to her, nuzzled her gently.

The combined hurt and rage which had contorted Jeremiah's expression as he thrust the prosthesis at Charlie rose before her.

"How could you do this to me?"

Abigail's eyes ached from crying, yet still more tears came.

"Jeremiah, I... didn't think it through," Charlie had replied, his eyes haunted with grief and regret.

What did he mean, he hadn't thought it through? She couldn't make sense of it. A soft sob escaped her lips. Charlie hadn't even tried to deny it.

She tried to remember the images he had described of war, the gun smoke and the noise. Perhaps Charlie had been caught up in the heat of battle, carried away with the passions of a soldier, and was unable to disengage from it when confronted with his brother. After all, they were fighting against one another, Rebels and Federals.

"Somethin' about this just don't seem right," Lizzie had declared. Charlie had admitted to committing the crime, yet he was clearly as broken over it as Jeremiah.

And even if only to herself, Abigail had to admit that part of her pain stemmed from his hasty departure. He had left without even trying to make her understand. They had grown so close, had shared so much of their deepest selves, and when she needed him to open up to her the most he had disappeared into the night.

Not only had she longed to hear him offer an explanation which could make sense of the matter, Abigail wanted to wrap her arms around him and ease the suffering she saw in his blue eyes. He had deprived her of both the chance to understand his choice and the opportunity to love him despite it.

The sound of footsteps in the hallway drew her attention, and Abigail burrowed further into her wool coverlet. She had no intention of taking breakfast this morning.

But instead of turning the knob to her bedroom door, Esther rapped her knuckles on the door of Mr. and Mrs. Sterret's room.

"Sir, you's got a visitor downstairs," the young woman called through the door. "Mr. Allen here to see you."

Irving's reply was muffled. Abigail sat up straight, throwing the warm blankets off her as she grabbed her robe and quickly slipped her arms into it, cinching the waist. There was only one reason she could imagine for Mr. Allen to be at Bloomingdale so early. Something had happened to Charlie.

Her door opened simultaneously with her father's, and they exchanged worried glances before bolting down the stairs to the library where Philip was waiting.

"What is it, Philip?" Irving demanded without preamble, his thin hair tumbling over his creased forehead.

Abigail bit her lip, her hands knotted together as she waited for his answer.

"Is Johnny here?" the big miller asked by reply.

The look on their faces was answer enough. Philip continued, "I found Nellie in the barn this morning, but Johnny's nowhere to be found."

Covering her mouth, Abigail closed her eyes. He had left. Without telling her good-bye or giving any indication of where he intended to go. He was gone.

~

By nightfall Charlie had reached the Wye River. He had recently passed a farm, circling wide around it, and he determined to wait until the lights at the farmhouse were extinguished before taking refuge in the barn. It was a dark and moonless night, and his toes were stiff from the cold. The horses and dairy cow within the barn would produce some heat, and it would be a relief just to be out of the wind.

Crouching down at the base of a tree, Charlie huddled into his coat. The tree provided something of a break from the bitter gale, and after hours of steady walking, Charlie's hunger and weariness won out. He dozed, head nodding forward onto his chest.

The subdued sound of voices awakened him. Startled, Charlie almost gave his position away. He blinked, clearing the fog of sleep from his eyes and his mind. About a hundred yards away from him, at the river's edge, four men were unloading the contents of a wagon onto a schooner by the light of a single lantern, speaking to one another in hushed tones.

Although the Eastern Shore had been seized by Union forces, Charlie knew that many southern sympathizers had continued to support the Confederacy in covert ways. Blockade runners continued to transport supplies to Richmond, despite the

Union Navy's attempt to control the Chesapeake Bay and all her tributary waterways. The brave captains of schooners and steamships ran their contraband cargo under cover of night, slipping silently under the noses of the Union blockaders.

The only reason for these men to be here on the Wye River at this hour, silently transferring goods onto a schooner on a cloudless night, Charlie reasoned, was that they were Confederate blockade runners. His heart began to pound against his ribs as he slowly came to his feet. If he was wrong, he would pay dearly for the mistake.

He stepped forward cautiously, his breath surrounding him in a cloud of steam. A twig snapped under his boot and he froze, his heart thumping wildly. The men made no indication that they had heard it, continuing their task with brisk and purposeful movements.

Charlie took another tentative step forward, and another. A jab of pain in his back drew him up sharply as the barrel of a gun pressed hard against his shoulder blade. A voice growled low in his ear, "Don't take one more step, mister."

Lifting his hands in the air, Charlie whispered, "I'm on your side."

"And which side is that?" the man behind him demanded warily.

Charlie hesitated before answering, "Freedom from tyranny."

"How can I trust you?" The pressure of the cold steel against his back eased ever so slightly.

Taking a deep breath, Charlie replied, "My name is Charlie Turner. I fought with the Second Maryland Infantry. I was taken prisoner at Gettysburg and held at Point Lookout until my escape. I came home to see my family, and now I'm on way back to Richmond." He waited, praying he hadn't just gambled his own freedom away.

"Charlie!" The gun fell away as the assailant stepped around Charlie to face him. "Is that really you? I thought you were dead!"

Relief sluiced through Charlie. He strained to recognize the man's features in the darkness.

"It's Bucky! Bucky Wallace! You remember me?" the young man laughed.

Charlie nodded, chuckling now. "How could I ever forget?" Bucky had given him a bloody nose when they were boys attending grammar school together. They had run in the same social circles right up until the war had broken out. "I thought your family had sided with the Union?"

Bucky grinned, placing one hand on his hip and pushing the brim of his hat back jauntily with the other. "There's more than one way to skin a cat," he laughed.

Charlie cringed. How Abigail must hate that phrase.

"We're good law abiding citizens," Bucky elaborated, "by day. But we still know who we are. We fight in our way. Doesn't seem like we can bust through the blockade, so we just work around it. Our boys need uniforms, weapons, and food supplies, so we make sure they get it."

Bucky's family owned a mercantile located at the Centreville Wharf, on the Corsica River. They had access to a wide assortment of resources and contacts. Charlie grinned. No one would have suspected.

"You order supplies for your store, then ship them on to

Richmond? Doesn't that get expensive?" he wondered.

"Oh, we're not alone. Some fund our work, others contribute to it. You'd be surprised how many silent sympathizers there still are. We just picked up a load of flour, salted pork, and warm socks made from fine merino wool from a local plantation. Further down the river, we'll pick up some gunpowder and ammunition. Then we'll slip out into the Eastern Bay and from there, enter the Chesapeake and follow it down to the James River. For every blockade runner who gets caught, there's at least twenty more who don't.

"The Union Navy is so smug. They underestimate both our commitment to the cause and our seafaring skills. Just because they can't navigate on a pitch black night doesn't mean us Eastern Shore boys can't!" Bucky boasted.

Merino wool... Something tugged at Charlie's memory, but he couldn't place it.

"Come say hello to the rest of the boys," Bucky waved Charlie to follow as he headed down to the bank of the river where the other three men were still loading the schooner. "We can see you get to Richmond, Charlie. You can count on that!" he declared.

Charlie recognized two of the other three, and they welcomed him with thumps on the back and smart salutes. "How'd you ever get away from Point Lookout?" Bucky asked, after he had recounted Charlie's brief report to the rest of the men.

"Some good friends happened to cross paths with me, and they made sure I had what I needed to make an escape."

"Pretty risky. Must've been very good friends," Bucky commented.

Charlie could only nod. "Yeah. They were."

~

It was Christmas Eve. Abigail's burgundy taffeta ball gown was draped over the chair, and Ruthie would be coming soon to see her dressed and style her hair. But Abigail was in no mood for festive parties. She would resort to that most overused of feminine excuses and claim it was a headache which had eclipsed her holiday spirit.

Her father would know the truth and be understanding. And Lizzie, of course. The last thing Abigail wanted was to pretend that all was right in her world, to paste a false smile upon her face and dance with men too old to be off fighting, or those who had returned because of injuries.

It would have been a dismal enough evening, celebrating one more Christmas Eve with the nation at war, the fourth Christmas of families being divided and the country which called itself "United" destroying itself from within. But her mother had insisted that Bloomingdale must hold its annual ball as it always had, no matter what else was happening in the world.

It seemed wrong to sip punch from a crystal glass, to nibble at petit fours and heap a plate with honeyed ham and sweet potato biscuits when so many men and boys, North and South, would bring in the holiday huddled next to a campfire with nothing but stale military rations.

Abigail wondered where Charlie was at that very moment, and if he was warm and well fed. She sighed, sinking further into the pillows. Sprightly, her dear calico, licked her nose sympathetically. Immediately after the midday meal, Abigail had retreated to her bed, and she was only waiting for Ruthie now so that she could send her away.

Days of crying had left her eyes so puffy that no amount of cool compresses or herbal treatments could soothe her swollen face. In all honesty, she did have a headache from the countless hours she'd spent sobbing into her pillow.

Margaret had returned from Baltimore only an hour ago and had yet to see her only daughter. She would surely be disappointed with what she found. But Abigail's appearance would make it easy enough to beg off in the name of illness.

When Ruthie entered the room, she pretended not to notice Abigail's pathetic state. "Come over here, Miss Ab'gail and we get you dressed," she said, producing the corset, cage hoop, and crinolines from the wardrobe which would be worn under the ball gown.

"I'm not well," Abigail sniffled, wishing she was better at hiding her emotions. "I don't think I'm up to it tonight. Please tell Mama that I've got a headache and need to rest."

Ruthie pressed her lips together as if she wanted to say something, but instead she merely nodded and quietly left the room. Abigail lay back, pressing her cheek into Sprightly's soft fur. What had Ruthie been thinking that she didn't feel she could express?

Abigail had heard stories of slave families being separated either intentionally or merely as a business transaction, husbands and wives torn apart without any recourse, children taken from parents... Had Ruthie ever been in love?

Reminding herself that she wasn't the only one who had suffered a broken heart, Abigail sat up and straightened her shoulders. Black attire had become an accustomed sight as the number of mourning widows, mothers, and sisters steadily increased. She remembered Jane, draped with a heavy crepe veil, her eyes red rimmed and hollow, after her fiancé had been killed at Antietam.

No, Abigail had no right to feel sorry for herself. While she had no intention of attending the Christmas Eve ball, she could at least pull herself together and consider the needs of others. Even if she had no way to relieve either her own heartache or Charlie's, perhaps she could ease the suffering of others.

Aunt Sallie and Aunt Mary had never attended the party since the Sterrets had come to live with them. Abigail had been meaning to pay them a visit, but had been preoccupied with planning the reunion of the Turner brothers. Now was as good a time as any to approach them about her concerns for the former slaves. The worse they could do is laugh at her, and then she would simply have to think of another way to procure blankets and coats.

Her thoughts returned to Charlie on this cold December night. *Lord, wherever he is, keep him safe and warm.*

Chapter Nineteen

Unable to argue with Abigail's claim that she was not herself, Margaret had given her a hug and tucked her in.

"I hope you're better in the morning, dear. I have a wonderful surprise for you," her mother had smiled.

Abigail forced a return smile. It was probably new leather boots, or a lace collar or some other such item which would have once delighted her, but now seemed trivial. Unfortunately, Abigail knew that she would feel no better come Christmas morning.

She had sent word to Clara and Jane about Charlie's disappearance, and assumed that they too would not be present at the Bloomingdale Christmas Eve Ball. None of them would enjoy this holiday, and she felt partially responsible. If she had just left well enough alone and let things work themselves out in time, perhaps Charlie and Jeremiah would have met when they were ready to face one another.

She'd had only the best of intentions. How could she have known it would end so badly?

Curling into a ball, Abigail pulled Sprightly against her chest and took comfort in the responding purr the animal produced. Her green eyes met Abigail's with love shining in them, reminding her that sometimes her good intentions ended well. All she could ever do was try.

Abigail closed her eyes, biding her time until the family had descended to the hall below and the guests had begun to arrive. To avoid discovery, she would use the slave staircase at the rear of the house and slip down to the kitchen, and from there make her way to the old wing of the house.

The sound of the knob turning again caused her eyes to open, and she wasn't surprised to see her brother approaching the bedside. Wearing a black suit and tie, Harris looked like a little gentleman, hair combed neatly to the side. Compassion and understanding were evident in his solemn expression as he eased himself onto the edge of the coverlet.

"Are you going to be all right, Abby?"

She had only seen him once in the two days since Jeremiah had revealed Charlie's dark secret. She had kept mostly to herself, and neither her father nor brother seemed to know what to say about the situation. They had both expressed condolences for her heartache as well as shock at the disclosure, but neither had condemned Charlie or treated her for the fool she feared she was.

"I don't know," she whispered, reaching for his hand. "I guess I'll have to find a way."

"He loved you, you know," Harris stated. "Charlie. He loved you. I saw it in his face. And I know he admitted to shooting Mr. Turner, but you and I both knew him well enough to say he was a kind man, a good man. There's more to this story, Abby. Maybe one day we'll know what it is."

Abigail squeezed her brother's hand, offering him a smile. He sounded so much older than his years. "Thank you, Harris. I hope you're right."

Harris turned the key to the oil lamp before he left her, the flame springing to life and chasing back the deepening shadows.

A fire crackled in the fireplace, warding off the wintry chill. Abigail sat up in bed, tucking her knees up to her chest as she considered her brother's words.

She hoped and prayed that one day she would see Charlie again, and that when she did, he would reveal the missing piece of the story. She did believe he had genuinely loved her, and even though this revelation had triggered doubts and questions as to his character and integrity, it couldn't diminish the bond which had been forged between them.

Bowing her head, Abigail prayed earnestly, *Lord, as long as Charlie's alive there's still hope that he will forgive himself and that the relationship between the brothers can be restored. Keep him safe and bring him back to us. And soften Jeremiah's heart...*

Leaving the security and comfort of her bed, Abigail slipped back into her day dress and boots. Twisting her hair up and pinning it into place, she glanced in the mirror. Between her puffy eyes, hasty hair styling, and plain dress, she certainly hoped she didn't encounter any of the party guests on her way to the old wing.

Lizzie's eyes widened with surprise when Abigail appeared in the kitchen via the narrow back staircase.

"I thought you's sleepin' off a headache. You want somethin' to eat?"

Breathing in the tempting smells of a Christmas feast, Abigail hesitated. "Not right now. I'm actually going to visit the aunts."

Dark eyebrows lifted in curiosity. "Ain't none of my business, but seems awful odd that you goin' to see them tonight. You up to something?"

"It's always a possibility," Abigail winked, finding a smile. She hoped that Lizzie would be pleased when she learned what Abigail aimed to do. But she wasn't ready to tell her. If the aunts not only refused to help but forbid Abigail's interference, it would be better if Lizzie didn't know. And with Esther, Ruthie, and several other women helping in the kitchen tonight, it wasn't the time.

"Should I wish you luck?" the Negro cook wondered, placing a hand on her narrow hip.

Abigail nodded. "You definitely should."

"All right, well let me know when you's ready to eat," Lizzie replied, her eyes lingering curiously over Abigail's features.

Nodding, Abigail left the kitchen and followed the hallway to the door which led to the Aunts' wing of the house. She knocked tentatively, hoping they wouldn't be angry with her for suggesting that they weren't taking adequate care of their slaves. *Former* slaves.

At the call to enter, she slowly opened the door. At the sight of her, a strange expression crept over the faces of the elderly women. Guilt?

Aunt Sallie quickly rolled her sewing project into a ball and placed it in the basket on the sofa beside her. "Why, it's Miss Abigail come to pay us a call!" Her silver eyebrows arched in surprise.

Aunt Mary's hands were folded primly on her lap, absent of either a book or sewing. Although Abigail noted that she too had a basket positioned next to her on the decorative side table next to her armchair. Had she tucked her sewing away as well?

Aunt Mary wore a smile of delight, but her expression

quickly clouded. "Is everything all right, dear? It's Christmas Eve... Why aren't you dressed for the party?"

"Have a seat," Aunt Sallie directed Abigail to join her on the sofa, moving the sewing kit to the floor at her feet. "Tell us what's happening. You look like you've been crying for a solid week."

"Not quite," Abigail sighed as she situated her skirts around her on the bronze damask sofa. "For two days," she admitted.

"What's his name?" Mary queried, her eyes gentle with compassion.

"How did you know it was a man?" Abigail wondered.

Sallie huffed. "Is it?" At Abigail's nod, she added, "We were young, once. We remember. What else would you have to be so upset about at?"

Abigail shrugged, unable to argue. "His name is Charlie."

"What did he do?" Sallie demanded sharply, her wrinkled face narrowing in disapproval for whatever the young man had done to make Abigail so unhappy.

"Well, I-I didn't come to talk to you about that," Abigail confessed.

"What then?" Mary encouraged her kindly.

"I, well I..." Abigail hadn't expected the conversation to go quite this way. She had planned to make small talk first and then ease into her request.

"Best to say it plainly," Sallie declared, skepticism moving into her eyes.

Abigail remembered that upon their first meeting, she had

implied that Abigail had to come to visit them only because she wanted something from them.

She swallowed down the guilt and took a deep breath. She had to tread carefully. "I grew up in Baltimore, and then of course, my family moved here. To Bloomingdale. Ever since I can remember, we had slaves and never... never once did I wonder how they lived or what they had until just recently. I guess with them just being freed and all, it made me think about what life was like for them." She paused, gauging the aunts' reaction to her narrative.

"You still haven't gotten directly to your request," Sallie stated observantly.

"I—I just was hoping that they had everything they needed to be warm," her eyes slipped to the fire blazing in the fireplace and the blankets folded neatly on the settee in case they should be needed. "I don't know what they already have," she finished, feeling suddenly very foolish.

"Ah," was all Mary had to say on the matter, but she seemed pleased.

Sallie eyed her curiously. "That was unexpected, I'll admit. I supposed you wanted something for yourself, or for your Charlie. Well, I can honestly tell you that I don't know what the slaves have or need either. Why don't you ask Lizzie to make a list and I'll be sure everything is provided for them. How does that sound?"

"Really?" Abigail could hardly believe her ears.

"I guess we just never thought about it before, either," Mary admitted, appearing slightly ashamed. "We always left that sort of thing to the overseer."

"Well, I'm not going to invite them in to sit by the fire,"

Sallie cautioned Abigail not to get too carried away with her philanthropic mission. "But I don't want anyone freezing on my land when I have the power to prevent it."

"Thank you, Aunt Sallie, Aunt Mary," Abigail said to each of them in turn, grateful for their willingness.

"Actually, I do have one condition," Sallie added, her blue eyes twinkling and a half smile touching her lips. "I want to know what this Charlie did to make you cry for two days."

Surprised by this sudden turn of events, Abigail hesitated. She could hardly tell them the truth in its entirety. But she owed them some explanation. "He didn't do anything to *me*," she began, searching for a way to word how Charlie's choices had affected her. "He had unfinished business with his family, and he… had a conflict with his brother that led him to leave suddenly. Without any word to me about where he's going. I don't know if he's all right, or if I'll ever hear from him again…" Traitorous tears formed yet again in her eyes. "I'm afraid he may never come back."

"Oh, my dear girl," Mary offered gently.

Sallie pursed her lips, wrinkles cutting deep grooves into her thin skin. "Do you think I'm senile and I can't see there's more to this than your telling?" she demanded.

Cheeks flushing, Abigail answered, "Of course not!"

"Then strip the varnish off the tale and tell us the plain truth," the elderly woman snorted.

"Oh, I…" Abigail stammered anxiously.

"Trust us, Miss Abigail," Mary added. "We can keep a secret if we need to," her eyes slid to her sister's and something passed between them.

The aunts stared at Abigail expectantly, waiting for her to elaborate upon her story.

With a deep breath, unable to avoid reply, Abigail began with the most questionable part of the unvarnished tale. "He's a rebel soldier." The aunts merely exchanged glances again and nodded for her to continue. "His brother fought with the Union, and they met at Gettysburg. I didn't know until the other night that it was Charlie who had shot his brother and cost him his arm. His brother hasn't forgiven him, and accused Charlie of shooting him intentionally. He didn't deny it... And then he just left. No one knows where he is now, and I'm afraid that he misinterpreted my shock and surprise for something worse. I mean, I think it's horrible, but... I wish he would have tried to explain. I know him well enough to believe he would never hurt his brother on purpose," she finished, her voice impassioned.

"Well." Sallie declared.

"I'd certainly be curious to know what really happened," Mary commented, "if he were my beau."

"It's war!" her sister retorted. "They were at war against one another and Charlie had to shoot him. Plain and simple."

"Well, his brother didn't see it that way," Abigail sighed, dabbing at her eyes.

"No, I suppose not," Mary agreed. "It becomes very personal when it's your arm that's getting amputated."

"Can't let personal emotions interfere with military decisions," Sallie countered. "Once you've chosen your position, you have to stand by it." She dipped her chin in a decisive nod, as if giving her approval for Charlie's actions.

Abigail hadn't considered this perspective, and wasn't sure she was completely convinced. But it did give her something new to think about.

She noticed the aunts exchanging meaningful glances yet again. Sallie nodded, almost imperceptibly, and Mary leaned forward in her chair. "If you write him a letter, we can try to find a way to get it to him," she offered. Her silver hair was pulled up in the back, with ringlets framing her face, in a style reminiscent of the styles of her youth. Mary wore her hair in a similar fashion, as if they had made special pains for Christmas Eve.

Confused—and more than a little curious—Abigail wrinkled her brows. "But I don't know where he is."

"Don't ask questions, dear," Sallie responded conclusively. "Just write the letter and let us see what we can do."

"Now, go ahead and get that list from Lizzie," Mary encouraged, as if dismissing Abigail.

"Would it be all right if I helped distribute the items when they arrive?" Abigail asked hopefully, fully expecting to be told that such behavior was unacceptable for a woman of her social standing.

Instead Sallie replied vaguely, "We'll get back to you on that."

Chapter Twenty

The river, black as ink, slapped against the hull of the schooner. With only the light of the stars overhead in the velvety darkness, the craft slipped through the water as silently as a ghost.

"It's not as easy as it once was," Bucky spoke in a voice that was just above a whisper. "The Union Navy has doubled up on their efforts to enforce the blockade. But mostly they're on the lookout for runners coming up from Bermuda and the Bahamas, carrying goods from England. If it wasn't for their willingness to sell us munitions and supplies, and to buy Southern cotton and tobacco, the Confederacy wouldn't have been able to hold out this long."

"Ironic," Charlie commented, thinking of how hard they had fought to get out from under the control of England, only to now have England aid the South in its attempt to be freed from its own government.

"Life and politics, everything ebbs and flows like the tides," Bucky replied philosophically.

Many were of the opinion that Lincoln's Emancipation Proclamation had not been inspired by the president's desire to see the slaves freed, but was a political strategy to leverage slavery as a preventive measure to keep England and France from allying with the Confederate States. As both countries had previously outlawed the practice, the proclamation formally shifted the focus of the war to slavery and by aligning with the

South, these European countries would have had to condone the institution.

Initially, the North's official position had been that secession was not constitutionally legal, and the wayward states must be brought back into the Union by force. Slavery had been a background issue of the war, but this maneuver pushed it to the forefront.

"We'll lay low," his old friend said quietly, "hiding out in coves during the day and traveling at night. With the hull painted gray and the mast shortened for speed, we can sail undetected for miles. We should arrive in Richmond within three days," Bucky pulled the collar of his coat closer around his neck. A knit hat covered his head and a scarf encircled his neck, but out on the water on a moonless night in December, the cold was bitter.

"Three days sounds good to me," Charlie said, stamping his feet to chase away the numbness creeping into his toes.

In the silence that followed, his thoughts wandered back to the ebb and flow of international relations. At the very outbreak of the war, there had been a possibility of England siding with the South when two Confederate diplomats were taken prisoner aboard the British mail packet boat, RMS Trent, intercepted by the United States Navy. The British government had been infuriated by this violation of neutral rights and demanded an apology, as well as the immediate release of the two prisoners.

Fearing that England would side with the Confederacy, which had just soundly beaten the Union Army at First Manassas, President Lincoln had released the envoys. A formal apology was never offered, but Mason and Slidell were allowed to complete their voyage to England. Their petition for support and diplomatic recognition, however, was denied.

"We can run up a British flag if we need to, and we have special coal, anthracite, which produces barely any smoke," the captain of the blockade runner added. "Lucky thing you ran into us."

Charlie folded his arms, trying to ward off the chill which had long since penetrated his coat. Was is just "luck" which had brought him this far or something—or *Someone*—more? Shaking his head at the notion, unable to believe that Providence would take special pains to protect anyone, least of all him, he dismissed the idea.

"You can go below and rest if you want," Bucky glanced over at him, noticing the shiver which had begun to set in after hours outside in the frigid temperatures. "It's warmer down there too, with the lantern burning."

Grateful for the suggestion, Charlie lowered himself through the hatch into the hold below. A lantern hung from a hook in the ceiling, swaying gently as the schooner sailed down the Wye River. He cast about for a place to rest, and spotting a pile of folded blankets, he moved toward them. Sacks of flour were stacked against crates and barrels, and Charlie hunkered down, resting his head against one and spreading the blanket over himself.

The rocking motion seemed unnatural at first, but as Charlie adjusted to the subtle movement of the floor beneath him, it lulled him into a deep and dreamless sleep. When he awoke, three of the other men were sprawled across the floor of the hold, and he assumed that the fourth stood guard on the deck.

Easing his aching muscles into a stretch, Charlie slowly sat up. It was then that the label on the sack of flour he had used as a pillow caught his eye. In the fog of weariness the night before, he hadn't noticed the design printed on it.

"*Mount Mill, 1665,*" it read, with a semi-circle pattern of wheat stalks framing the words and date.

Charlie had seen these sacks on a daily basis while living with the Allens at the old miller's cottage. Mount Mill was the original name of the Bloomingdale plantation until the Harris sisters had rechristened it. That it was flour ground at Bloomingdale was no question.

What Charlie wished he knew was if Philip and Irving were aware it was being sent south to aid the Rebels, and if Sallie and Mary Harris had any knowledge of its presence aboard the blockade runner.

Bucky had mentioned socks knit from merino wool... which was one of the products Bloomingdale was known for. Interesting, indeed. It wouldn't surprise him a bit if he learned that the Harris sisters were southern sympathizers. After all, their plantation embodied the Southern way of living.

Of course, flour and socks were far from solid proof. But they did make for a powerful suggestion.

Bucky Wallace and his crew took turns throughout the day resting, with one man always remaining on guard. Darkness fell early due to the season, and they waited until the hour was late and the Union blockaders would be sleeping with one only or two lookouts of their own.

As they sailed down the Chesapeake into the waters between the eastern and western shores of Virginia, the dangers increased. Charlie remained on deck with the crew, who were prohibited from smoking, using any form of light, or talking above a whisper when absolutely necessary.

One of the crew members tapped Charlie on the shoulder and pointed into the darkness. Charlie squinted, trying to determine what he was seeing. Slowly the shape of a hulking ironclad ship of the Union Navy came into focus. His heart hammered in his chest as they sailed silently past without notice.

They continued unmolested and sometime later, the blockade runner left the bay and entered Hampton Roads, veering northwest into the James River. After several hours of sailing, they found a secluded area near the mouth of the Chickahominy River to anchor before the sun rose. Charlie volunteered to take the first shift standing guard.

There was less to fear now that they were in Rebel territory, but the waterways were still under scrutiny by the Federal government who considered all waters and soil to be under their jurisdiction. The day passed without incident, and several hours after nightfall they resumed their voyage.

The James River wound its way through Virginia in a series of turns and switchbacks, and only by careful navigation did the schooner not run aground on the shoals or strike rocks hidden in the rapids. Straining to see into the black shadows ahead, Charlie felt his pulse race as he gripped the rail with white knuckles.

He could see why Bucky and his crew thrilled at the challenge and adventure of running the blockade. Nothing he had done before compared with the excitement he felt as the wind whipped the sails overhead and the shoreline slipped past like a charcoal smudge in the darkness.

As they approached the port of Richmond, Bucky ran up the Confederate flag and casually moored the schooner alongside the pier. They were quickly met by several uniformed officers who verified Bucky's identity and purpose. The schooner was searched, its crew remaining under supervision on deck until approval was given.

Charlie helped unload the cargo, finding among the contraband a satchel of mail to be delivered to the Richmond Post Office for delivery. He had a fleeting thought that perhaps he could find a way to smuggle a letter home to Jeremiah, but just as quickly as the thought came, he dismissed it. What could he possibly say to convince his brother to forgive him?

"I've got to conclude some business," Bucky informed him, and Charlie wondered what sort of profit he yielded from the items he delivered, including those which had been donated. The Confederacy was desperate for supplies and would likely pay handsomely for what they could get their hands on. "But you're welcome to stay with me and my crew till morning. There's a family, hospitable and loyal to the cause, who'll put us up until we're ready to head back. We'll just need a military escort to confirm our stay."

As they traveled through the streets of Richmond, the street lamps illuminating the brick sidewalks and elegant residences, Charlie caught a glimpse of something in the distance. A light flickering on an island in the James River. Belle Isle, if he had to guess.

To his companions, he asked, "Is that the Prisoner of War camp at Belle Isle?"

"It is," one affirmed, scrubbing his face wearily as he sank back into the leather seat of the carriage.

"How are the prisoners there treated?" Charlie wondered, fearing he already knew the answer.

With a gruff chuckle, Bucky replied, "Lincoln must not be too worried about them. If the Rebels can't keep their own boys fed and clothed, he can't expect them to spare much on their enemies."

A sick twist in his gut accompanied the callous remark. Charlie closed his eyes, memories of the deprivations he had faced at Point Lookout pressing close. These men, these prisoners, were considered "enemies," yet they were brothers, cousins, and uncles of those who refused to spare their resources. And all because they had chosen an opposing political view. If he had believed his own mistreatment at Point Lookout was wrong, then the neglect of the prisoners at Belle Isle was just as much so.

Last March there had been an attempted raid on Richmond with the intent to set the prisoners of Belle Isle free. An advance force was sent by river, while another traveled by land, with the plan that they should converge in Richmond and take her. However, when Kilpatrick's men arrived on foot, Dahlgreen's forces had not yet reached the city via the James River. Kilpatrick was unable to attack alone, and was under pursuit by Confederate Calvary.

Dahlgreen was unable to breach Richmond's defenses and in his retreat, was ambushed and killed. On his body a most interesting and inflammatory document was found. It was an official Union order to not only burn Richmond, but to assassinate Jefferson Davis along with the members of his cabinet.

Naturally, President Lincoln, General Meade, and Brigadier General Kilpatrick all denied the document's authenticity. But the possibility of a war of extermination did not soften the hearts of the Southerners toward their Northern brethren.

Charlie sighed heavily, an exhaustion both physical and spiritual descending upon him with the weight of a thousand tons. He leaned forward, resting his elbows on his knees, as he covered his face.

"You aren't going soft, are you?" Bucky queried, gripping his shoulder. "You're on your way to kill those sons of b—"

"I know," Charlie sat up, shaking free of Bucky's grip. "But a lot of those boys are our friends and family. I'm fighting an ideology—tyranny and oppression—not the men who conform to it. I hate the thought of our government growing out of control, but I refuse to hate the men who defend that government."

"It's hard when the family's divided," Bucky agreed quietly. "At least you know Jeremiah's home. He got busted up at Gettysburg, but I'm guessing you already heard about that."

Charlie nodded.

"You were there, too. Weren't you?"

Charlie offered another silent nod.

"Well, you have to stand for something, and when you do, sometimes it means you have to stand against those you love," Bucky commented, shrugging his big shoulders.

"What do you stand for?" Charlie challenged, his eyes penetrating the shadows.

A half-smile curved Bucky's lips as he answered, "Myself, first and foremost. And freedom after that."

"At least you're honest," Charlie shook his head, confident that Bucky and his family were making a fortune exploiting the war's peculiar circumstances.

He was relieved when they arrived at their destination, a stately brick edifice of the Georgian period with a wide sweeping portico over the front door. The carriage was driven around the corner, past the main entrance, and down the lane into the carriage house.

There the blockade runners were met by a Negro man who directed them to their room, which was not within the mansion they had passed, but in the second level of the carriage house.

Spies were everywhere, Charlie reminded himself. Even among those who masqueraded as friends. It was wise for these men of the Chesapeake to remain discreet than to risk discovery and land in a cell at Fort McHenry.

Easing down onto his cot, Charlie stretched out his legs and pulled the homespun wool blanket over himself. Tomorrow he would report to the recruitment office and resume his life as a soldier.

Within a matter of hours, Charlie was standing before an officer of the Confederate States Army, explaining who he was, where he had been, and why he was now returning to service. Sitting behind his desk in a crisp gray uniform with brass buttons displaying an eagle with the shield of the U.S., a branch and arrows held in its talons, the officer stroked his gray beard as he studied Charlie with interest.

"We need more men like you," the distinguished older gentleman replied, "courageous and dedicated to the cause of freedom!" He flipped through the pages of a notebook in search of the information he sought. When he found it, he lifted his eyes to Charlie's with something akin to regret in them.

"The Second Maryland Infantry has suffered great losses. Those who remain have been attached to McComb's Tennessee Brigade. At Petersburg," the officer added, letting the words sink in.

Charlie nodded solemnly, then offered a smart salute.

It was the worst possible assignment a soldier of the Confederacy could imagine at this time. But he hadn't returned with hopes of an easy mission or opportunities for glory. He was rejoining his regiment, or what was left of them, to stand beside his former comrades as they endured another demoralizing defeat.

He doubted anyone still held out hope that the South would win. General Sherman had reached Savannah, Georgia at the beginning of the month, and on the twenty-first of December, the Governor had surrendered the city.

General Hardee, CSA, had declined Sherman's invitation to lay down his arms and instead escaped across the Savannah River. Sherman had been reinforced by the Navy and resupplied with guns and artillery. Thus empowered, he made his threat clear to Hardee. If he was not allowed to take the city, he would do to it what had been done to Atlanta.

In exchange for a promise of safety, the Governor gave Sherman the keys to the city. In turn, Sherman presented Lincoln with the Southern city as an early Christmas present, along with the guns, ammunition, and twenty-five thousand bales of cotton that accompanied it.

Georgia was effectively subdued. The Confederacy was worn down, the number of desertions increasing as men returned home to care for families or simply gave up on the cause, feeling its demands were too high considering the all but certain outcome.

The war was almost lost, and Charlie was simply there to see it through to the bitter end.

Chapter Twenty-One

Whether we like it or not," Aunt Sallie began her diatribe, staring down her nose imperiously at Abigail as she spoke, "there are, and always have been, distinctions of class in society. And to put it plainly, different classes live in different ways. You may accompany your father as he distributes coats and blankets and such to the slaves, but I absolutely do not want you to get it into your head that we should make improvements to the slave quarter, or build each family its own cabin, or any other similar idea. If any such notion enters your mind, please do not tell me about it.

"I have already spoken with the overseer and extracted a promise that he will ensure the existing building is solid and tight, and that the slaves are well supplied with firewood for the winter. Lizzie will see that they are properly fed. And I believe that more than fulfills any obligations I—," she glanced over at her sister, "*we*—have for them."

Aunt Mary nodded, her hands knotted in her lap as she leaned forward earnestly, the delicate skin at the corners of her eyes crinkling. "You are very kind-hearted, Abigail, which is an admirable quality. Just don't let yourself get carried away and try to move faster than the world around you is willing to change. It will only lead to disappointment, or possibly worse. Everything has its own time."

Aunt Sallie harrumphed emphatically. "Stuff and nonsense. I just want the girl to be reasonable, that's all."

"Yes ma'am," Abigail offered an obedient nod to both women, grateful for their generosity. She had noticed that they referred to the Negros as "slaves," although this was no longer legally accurate. But she was hardly going to correct them.

"Thank you for your kindness," Abigail smiled as she came to her feet, eager to seek out her father and arrange the delivery.

"Did you bring a letter for your beau?" Sallie wondered, glancing down to see if she held an envelope in her hand.

Abigail extracted it from the pocket of her skirt, staring down at it uncertainly. She had penned four different attempts, only for three of them to land in the wastebasket. The last she had deemed as acceptable, and by that point her hand was cramped and ink stained from the effort.

She bit her lip as she presented it to Aunt Sallie. "I did. I wasn't sure exactly what to say… If he replies, will his letter find its way back to me?" Abigail suddenly worried.

"It should. It will just take time, dear. I certainly wouldn't hold your breath waiting for it," Sallie replied cryptically.

More curious than ever, Abigail handed over the letter, sending a silent prayer with it.

She hoped that somehow the missive found its way to Charlie, wherever he might be. The Aunts had many connections, and they seemed confident that they could find him. However, they refused to tell her how, or if they would divulge his location to her once he was located. Abigail shifted from one foot to the other, trying to hold back the flood of questions which swirled in her mind.

When and if it did find him, she prayed that Charlie was in a frame of mind to be receptive to both her confirmation of continuing affection and her curiosity as to what had actually taken place. Abigail had expressed in the letters which she ultimately discarded, just how hurt she had been by his rash departure and his failure to offer any light on the situation for her. But she felt it was selfish to add to his burdens. For now, all he needed to know was that she still cared about him.

"Go ahead dear," Mary encouraged, "I believe your father is waiting for you in the library," she smiled.

"Thank you!" Abigail clapped her hands together, excited for this opportunity to make some small impact on those less fortunate.

She found her father sitting at his desk in the library, as Aunt Mary had said. "Go and get your coat," he smiled. "Everything is ready."

Abigail hadn't said anything to her father prior to gaining approval from the aunts for fear of his disapproval. She didn't want him to feel that she was imposing on the aunts after they had already shown her family great kindness.

But the smile on her father's lined face was anything but disapproving. She ran toward him, and he stood to receive her hug as she flew at him. "Thank you, Papa!" she cried.

He held her at arm's length, his brown eyes searching hers. "You make me proud," he said. "I feared that you were pining over your broken heart and instead you were plotting acts of charity." A sheen of moisture glistened in his eyes. "I'm truly sorry for how it's all played out, Abby."

Nodding, Abigail swallowed down the lump which had lodged in her throat. "I know, Papa," she whispered. "The Aunts said they would try to find him and get a letter to him." She noticed the flicker of surprise in Irving's eyes. "They are quite the pair, aren't they? They were rather mysterious about the whole thing… I didn't ask any questions, but—"

"Good," her father interrupted, tweaking her nose as he used to when she was a little girl, "then don't ask me either. Now run and get your coat. We have work to do."

As Abigail ran to fetch her coat, her mind raced. All the unanswered questions and evasion almost seemed like answers in themselves. She felt as if there were pieces of a puzzle that were slowly drifting into place, only she couldn't be quite sure that she was fitting them together properly.

Grabbing her coat from the hook in her room, she shrugged into it quickly. Made of cashmere and wool, it was red with black piping at the edges. It buttoned up the snug-fitting front, then flared out at the waist over the width of her skirt, with a black bow decorating the waistline in the back. She hastily tied the ribbons of the matching red hat under her chin as skipped down the steps.

"Mr Wayne is waiting outside for us. He said it was best to keep the situation very organized," her father cautioned. Mr. Wayne had been the overseer at Bloomingdale for at least two decades. "And Harris will be joining us shortly. He's currently tidying the playroom."

"Good afternoon, sir, ma'am," Mr. Wayne tipped his hat in greeting. Unlike Mr. Sterret, the overseer lacked a bearing of education and refinement. He had a gruff quality to his voice, and his face was leathery and creased with wrinkles from hours spent beneath the sun.

Rough around the edges, some might describe him, but Abigail sensed that he could simply be described as "rough." There was nothing in his demeanor which inspired Abigail to believe that Mr. Wayne saw the Negroes as anything other than intelligent animals designed for hard labor. Perhaps she was being hasty in her judgment of Mr. Wayne, but Abigail knew that the idea prevailed in many places, and it wouldn't have surprised her to find it in the man charged to keep them submissive and productive.

He removed the cigar clenched between his teeth as he said, "I've divided the coats into three piles: men, women, and children. I think it'd be best if Miss Abigail saw to the children."

Suspecting that Mr. Wayne thought her naïvely sympathetic for convincing the Harris sisters to provide new coats for the former slaves, Abigail nodded dutifully as she offered him a sweet smile. He wouldn't be the only one around Bloomingdale to think so. After all, she did have a reputation for carrying around a lame cat she had rescued. But, Abigail decided, there were worse things that one could be known for than kindness.

Some of the Negro workers stood awkwardly around the entrance of the brick building which served as their home, waiting for the signal that they could claim a coat of their own. When Mr. Wayne beckoned them forward, barking instructions as to how they should line up, more men, women and children slowly appeared through the doorway. In all, Abigail guessed there must have been a hundred of them.

She couldn't imagine the responsibility of caring for all the needs—food, clothing, and health—of so many people. The mere thought of it was daunting.

Leaning close, Mr. Wayne advised, "Give the children their coats a little big so they can get a few years' wear out of them. If what they're wearing is too small, but in decent condition, save it for a smaller child."

Abigail observed the number of children forming a crooked line and had to concede to the wisdom of Mr. Wayne's suggestion. Sizing up the first child who stepped up boldly to accept his Christmas coat, Abigail began sorting through the crate. Selecting two options, she stepped forward to hold the first coat up to him for comparison.

"I ain't never had a brand new coat of mine own," the boy, who had to be about the same age as Harris, confided as he reached out gingerly to touch the softness of the new wool. The article of clothing which currently served the purpose of a coat hardly deserved the name. Threadbare and worn at the elbows, it had long outlived its usefulness.

"Well, try this one on for size," Abigail smiled even as his confession pierced her heart. "If it's just a bit big, it might fit you for a year or two."

White teeth gleamed against his dark skin as he grinned, obediently removing the old garment and slipping his arms into the new coat. The joy and satisfaction on his face brought a sheen of tears to Abigail's eyes. "I gets to keep it—till I get too big? Then I gets a new coat?" He asked in unbelieving wonder.

"If I have anything to do with it," she winked in reply. "It fits you well. Warmer?"

He grinned and nodded, running his hands down the front of the brown wool proudly.

"Thank you, ma'am," he beamed, stepping away for the next child to move forward.

A little girl, just a slip of a thing, stood nervously with her older brother, his hand resting reassuringly on her shoulder. She stared up at Abigail with round black eyes. "You gots the prettiest coat I ever seen. Can I gets one like that?"

"Well, why don't we see what we have in here that would fit you," Abigail replied, chagrined that she had worn such a flamboyant display of her wealth without giving it a second thought. She did have another coat of dove gray which she could have worn if she'd taken a moment to think about it. It was usually reserved for more somber occasions.

Rummaging through the crate, she realized that all the coats were simply cut, either black or brown, and none were even remotely pretty. Regretfully, Abigail lifted out a black coat which appeared to be about the right size for the little girl whose hair was braided close to her scalp in a series of rows.

"How about this one?" Abigail presented the item apprehensively, fearful the girl would be insulted.

But the child only smiled. "It's still got all its buttons!" she observed, accepting it gratefully. "It's so thick and soft!" she added as she clutched it against her chest.

"Put it on," her brother encouraged, and Abigail turned her attention to him. His wrists protruded from the sleeves of his coat and he had strained to pull it across his chest in order to fasten the two remaining buttons. Even if it had fit him, it looked as if it had seen more than its share of winters.

Abigail had just retrieved a garment for the boy when a female voice called her name in her ear. Turning, Abigail found Esther standing behind her, wearing a new black coat that was clearly made for function and not fashion. The Negro woman's arms were folded across it proudly, just the same. "I just want to say thank you, Miss Ab'gail," Esther said, "My brother and sister ain't never had warm coats before. And I ain't never had one this new!" she grinned.

"You are more than welcome," Abigail answered, ashamed that for so long she had lived in luxury so close to people who lived in deprivation. How could she never have seen it before?

"Look Esther!" the little girl spun in a circle to show off her new garment, "See my new coat! We match!"

Esther bent over to kiss her sister's cheek. "We sure do!"

"Hey Rufus," Harris appeared by Abigail's side, greeting Esther's brother as if they were friends. Beside him stood the boy to whom she had given the first coat, and it took her a moment to recognize him as Lizzie's son, Billy.

"Billy and me can help pass out coats," Harris offered, looking up at her as if he genuinely saw nothing wrong with his proposition.

Kneeling down, Abigail put her arm around his shoulders and whispered in his ear, "I don't think it's a good idea for Billy to give them out. It might not seem fair to the others."

Understanding dawned in his eyes and Harris nodded. "All right. Well, can we go play then?"

"No," Abigail answered, shaking her head. "You may help me while Billy runs off to play."

"I gots to hand out these coats," Harris told Billy, "and then I can play." Billy nodded, and he and Rufus ran off together. Esther took her sister by the hand and led the little girl back into the cabin.

Abigail gave her brother a reproving stare. "Do not talk like that, Harris Sterret. You know better."

Unrepentant, Harris grinned up at her, his front teeth having grown in overly large and crooked. "It don't hurt nothing to talk like Billy when I'm with him."

Cringing, Abigail corrected, "It *doesn't* hurt *anything*. And yes it does. It sounds awful."

Harris only shrugged, clearly unaffected by his sister's

correction. Abigail sighed. She hoped her father would be able to take him in hand before he was old enough to get into real trouble.

As he joined her in distributing winter coats to the former slaves, she observed that Harris knew many of the children by name and that he treated them as if they were no different than he. In a rapidly changing time, Harris would adapt easily to the new world order being ushered in by the Lincoln administration. The Senate had already passed the Thirteenth Amendment in April of 1864; the House would vote on it in January of 1865. It was more than likely that it would be approved, and slavery would be constitutionally abolished throughout all of the United States.

Later that afternoon, as she warmed herself by the fire in the library, Abigail mentioned these thoughts to her father.

Sitting at his desk, Irving sipped at a steaming cup of coffee before he replied. "There are some things which have changed forever. No matter what happens now, the North and South will never be unified in spirit. The cost of this war has driven a deeper, more permanent, stake of division between them. This bloody time in history will be remembered by the South for generations to come with bitterness and hostility. For Negroes and abolitionists, it will be held as a great victory, turning the tide for freedom. Eventually Negroes will gain the full rights of citizenship."

"Do you really think so?" Abigail could hardly imagine it. "Do you think they should?" she wondered.

Irving ran a hand over his balding head thoughtfully. "Honestly, I don't know. If they're educated, I suppose there's no harm in it. But Lincoln, his administration, and all the abolitionists in the world can't make the world a fair place of equality for all. You simply can't legislate heart change. Look to the west—we're pushing out the Indians as second class humans unworthy of the land they've held for centuries, subjecting them to our government's rules and restrictions. If Lincoln believed— truly believed—in the equality of all, he wouldn't conquer these natives and steal their land. But that's not a politically expedient position.

"Even for these former slaves, and for their children, there will always be class distinctions. You can declare a people free, you can even make them citizens, but you cannot change either the way others view them or the way they view themselves. Some things will never change, Abby, no matter who holds the office of President. There will always be rich and poor, greater and lesser citizens. "

Abigail studied the depth of wisdom and sadness in her father's eyes, the skin around them creased with lines and wrinkles acquired through the years which had taught him these lessons. She met his gaze steadily as she answered, "But we should try to change them anyway, shouldn't we?"

He offered a half-smile of mingled pride and regret. "You can try, my dear girl, but you must know that change always comes at a price, particularly for those who attempt to usher it in."

"Papa, which side of this war do you stand on? I feel so confused..." Abigail sank down into the plush cushion of a delicately carved mahogany chair. "I hate to see our way of life end... yet I feel the hope of the freedmen to shake off the past and build something new."

Her father sighed wearily. "It's not easy taking sides. I still stand by the rights of the states to choose their own laws. One thing this war has changed is the role of the Federal Government.

It's gained new power through this struggle. Yet I see the plight of the Negroes and am moved by compassion for them. Anyway, I think slavery would have come to a natural end in its own time if Lincoln had been willing to let the Confederacy go their own way.

"But he believed in the Union at all costs. And so here we are."

Abigail felt the turmoil and conflict within her own heart, pulling her in opposing directions, and she wished that there was a different solution available than taking sides. Soon the war would be over, the South conquered, and they would all have to learn to work together again, rebuilding the brokenness into something new.

Remembering the gratitude in Esther's eyes, and the awe and pleasure in her little sister's as she accepted her new coat, Abigail leaned forward and spoke earnestly. "We can't change the world, Papa, but we can make a difference in our own small, but meaningful way—as we did today. Our dear aunts may not wish to know it, but my work has just begun."

Irving chuckled. "Don't you think they already know? Never underestimate those two, Abby. Innocent as doves but cunning as wolves, they are," he revealed.

Chapter Twenty-Two

Charlie's breath formed a cloud of vapor around his face as he exhaled. He rubbed a hand over his thickening beard, grateful for the warmth it provided. In his newly issued gray uniform, he huddled next to his compatriots in the frozen mud which filled the trenches.

This fighting was unlike any he had known before.

He had fought with the First and Second Maryland Infantry in numerous battles, but all in the traditional Napoleonic style. It took bravery to lift your head above the protective earthworks to fire at the enemy, and blazing courage to run full on, charging the enemy with bayonet attached to the muzzle of your musket. But this trench warfare was a matter of perseverance.

It was a unique and dreadful kind of misery all its own. Both sides, Federal and Rebel, had dug miles of deep ditches into the ground by moonlight, under fire by enemy cannons and sharp shooters. Around these, engineers had overseen the construction of a complex series of defensive fortifications and obstructions.

The dirt removed from the earth by spade and shovel was piled into an embankment, supported by a sort of retaining wall constructed of logs. This revetment provided a defensive barrier for artillery units and sharp shooters to fire at the enemy trenches, which were dreadfully close in parallel lines.

Between them stretched an open field where once a forest

had stood. Its trees had fallen prey to the construction of military fortifications, forts, winter shelters for the soldiers, and firewood. This expanse also opened up a direct line of fire between the trenches.

To deter the enemy from thoughts of a frontal onslaught, a series of obstructions littered the field. A line of spikes cut from the felled trees wound in a sharp line in front of the trenches, in which the soldiers huddled, despite the bitter cold. Beyond this "abatis," another layer of barricades had been constructed, the logs tied together in a series of X shapes to form a long and jagged fence called a "chevaux de frise," which posed a deadly threat to cavalry units on horseback. The stumps which littered the field were also used as an obstruction, wires connecting them to trip any spies which might brave the distance, as well as an assaulting army.

The lengths which had been taken to defend these trenches were partially to blame for the stalement which had now lasted for over six months. No one was willing to budge.

The Rebels were outnumbered, at least two to one, but they held their ground as tenaciously as ever. Grant was determined to wear them down and cut off supply lines to the south. He'd been making steady progress since the initial attack on Petersburg in June of 1864. But despite the efforts of Generals Meade and Grant, they had yet to break through the Confederate lines to take the city.

Little by little they had continued to take possession of supply lines, capturing many of the surrounding roads and railways. Still, Lee remained unyielding as he dug his heels in and defended the city. It was all that stood between the Union Army and the Confederate capital of Richmond. When Petersburg fell, the Confederacy fell.

Charlie had arrived during a lull in the fighting. The last Union offensive had been back in October, when Federal forces had marched west in attempt to take the Boydton Plank Road. A counterattack near Burgess' Mill had pushed the Yankees into retreat and the Rebels had regained control of the road.

His regiment had been reduced to a battalion from the losses sustained in previous battles. They were now attached to McComb's Tennessee Brigade, which was part of A.P Hill's Third Army Corps, Heth's Division. With their new Southern brothers, they sat like gophers in the earth while on duty, retreating to their crude and cramped cabins to rest when permitted.

Due to the scarcity of wood, the shelters built to protect them from the elements were barely tall enough for a man to stand in, and would have been considered small if inhibited by only one man. Four men slept in Charlie's cabin, each assigned to a crudely built bunk more adapted for elves than for men. When he stretched out fully, his feet hung over the end of the bed. But he was off the ground, out of the wind, and the cabin afforded the surprising luxury of a small, brick-lined fireplace complete with chimney.

It was a small space to share with three men, and Charlie considered himself lucky to have been assigned such decent fellows. His cell-mates in this frozen hell were Isaac Roberts, William Prentiss, and Norwood Goldsborough. Roberts had been with the Maryland Infantry since the beginning, and had welcomed Charlie back with a back-pounding hug. Sharing such confined quarters, and under such stressful circumstances, Charlie quickly got to know Prentiss and Goldsborough.

Roberts and Goldsborough were from the Eastern Shore; Prentiss came from Baltimore, but they didn't hold it against him.

"You know one of the good things about trenches in the winter time?" Roberts asked him as they huddled together for warmth in the ditch which had become a second home to them. The coldness of the ground beneath them penetrated through their britches into their skin, and the frigid air found its way into their bones.

"I don't. Why don't you tell me?" Charlie burrowed deeper into his wool coat. Above, the sun was a pale, flat disk in a sky as gray as gunmetal.

"No mosquitoes," Roberts grinned.

"And," Prentiss added, "you don't have to worry about sinking up to your ankles in mud. It's frozen."

"Don't forget the most important benefit," Goldsborough chimed in. "You can't smell Prentiss and Roberts."

The men laughed, and Charlie reminded himself that the trenches must have been a nightmare through the summer months. They weren't exactly a paradise in the winter.

One other advantage of the miserably cold temperatures was that the enemy was less likely to stage an attack. Though, the very improbability made it a possibility. It was the surprise attacks which were often the most successful, which was why they must remain on guard and be prepared at all times.

Soldiering was a rough way of life, and the men dealt with it as best they could. Humor and bravado were the first line of defense. When one had to adapt, he found a way to do it. Charlie realized that he had grown soft during his time away from the army. He'd become used to sleeping in a real bed and eating a woman's cooking. The Allens had been good to him.

Any weight he had gained during his desertion would quickly shed away as he returned to a military diet. The daily rations they were allotted were one point of beef or one-third pound of bacon, one pound of flour or cornmeal, sixteen ounces of rice, and small quantities of vinegar, salt, coffee, sugar, and soap. The overall shortage of food drove the price of groceries up in Petersburg, but when desperate for fresh vegetables or fruit to add to their diet, the men found a way to pool their resources. Using their fireplace, they prepared and cooked such meals for themselves as they were capable.

As little as it sometimes seemed, it was more than he'd subsisted on at Point Lookout. Charlie would never view hardship in the same light again after that experience. Remembering what the prisoners there would have done for the rations he now enjoyed prompted him to consume whatever he was given with gratitude.

"Who's going with me into the city tonight?" Goldsborough asked the group of men huddled around him. "I got wind of another party."

The socialites of Petersburg and Richmond, who had hosted grand galas and balls prior to the siege, continued their festivities as best they could. Dressed in their finest, with music and dancing, these parties were a distraction from the war for local citizens and soldiers alike. Called "Starvation Parties" for the lack of food, these occasions provided not only much desired diversion, but opportunities to meet and interact with women.

"You can count me in," Prentiss grinned. He'd met a young woman at the last such Starvation Party who seemed to be quite taken with him. Many of the soldiers were taking advantage of the high emotions surrounding the siege, and the war in general, to marry in and around the Petersburg area. Some took their vows more seriously than others, intending to keep them if ever the war ended. Others saw it as a temporary relief to the loneliness of a soldier's life.

"I know I can't count on Roberts," Goldsborough leaned into the man beside him, nudging him with his shoulder. "He'll be lying on his cot staring at that picture of Harriet till he falls asleep."

"That's because he's a faithful husband," Prentiss replied. "Nothing wrong with that."

"What about you, Turner? You comin'?"

"No, I think I'll keep Roberts company."

"You got a girl somewhere?" Goldsborough guessed.

Abigail's face appeared before Charlie's eyes as he had seen her for the last time. Her hair elaborately pinned up, her slender neck encircled by a strand of pearls, her figure emphasized by the burgundy gown she wore.

He felt a sharp stab of loss as he remembered the stricken look on her face when Jeremiah had revealed the awful truth about his amputated arm. "*You are the one who shot him?*" she'd whispered in shock and disbelief, the hope in her eyes begging him to tell her that she'd misunderstood.

"I did have a girl," Charlie admitted regretfully. "But I'm afraid I've lost her. And no one else will do."

~

The white house on the hill came into view as the carriage turned the corner onto Turners Lane. The fields lay dormant, waiting for spring. The whole world, it seemed, was gray and silent. Waiting.

A curtain moved in a second story window, catching Abigail's eye. Clara's face appeared, and she held up her hand in greeting.

Clara was descending the stairs as Abigail was ushered through the door by the black woman, Phoebe. Sweeping Abigail up in a warm embrace as soon as she reached the bottom step, Clara exclaimed, "I'm so glad to see you, Abigail! I've been wanting to visit, but Henrietta's been sick with a cough for the last two weeks now. I just put her down for a nap, so your timing is perfect."

"I wanted to say how sorry I am," Abigail began, her eyes filling with tears.

Taking Abigail by the elbow as she brushed the tears from her cheeks, Clara steered her into the parlor. "Have a seat and Phoebe will bring tea and refreshments. There's nothing to blame yourself for."

As Phoebe retreated to the kitchen, Clara ushered Abigail into the parlor, directing her to the place beside her on the settee.

Abigail gripped Clara's arm. "I never imagined there was such enmity between Jeremiah and Charlie. I only knew that Jeremiah was concerned about his brother's safety and whereabouts, and Charlie often spoke of his brother with fondness... And I thought it would be a wonderful Christmas present to reunite them. If I'd known it would cause such a dreadful scene to bring them together in the same room, I never would have!"

Clara squeezed Abigail's hand firmly. "You did nothing wrong, my dear. Your intentions were pure. As you said yourself, you didn't know."

"I'm just so terribly sorry," Abigail repeated, remembering afresh both the raw emotions and the staggering secret which had been revealed the night she had intended to be so special.

Clara held up a finger, signaling that she wished for Abigail to wait until after the tea had been delivered. Phoebe's footsteps could be heard in the hallway, then she reappeared with a tray bearing a blue and white china teapot, two cups and saucers, and a plate of cookies.

"Thank you, Phoebe," Clara smiled graciously. "It's a bit cold today. Would you mind closing the door when you leave? And please let me know if Henrietta wakes up."

"Yes ma'am," Phoebe nodded, doing as directed. A fire blazed in the fireplace, and she sealed in the heat as she closed the door.

Clara leaned forward, whispering, "No one here knows," as soon as the door had latched behind the Negro woman. "And I think it best to keep it that way for now."

"But you knew, didn't you?" Abigail asked, recalling Clara's reaction to what should have been appalling news.

"I did," she admitted. "Jeremiah was so broken after Gettysburg. It was more than just the war, or the loss of his hand... He seemed burdened. He finally told me one night that he had seen Charlie on the battlefield. That his brother had recognized him, then took aim and fired. The bullet struck his hand, but an equally painful wound struck his heart."

"Charlie loves Jeremiah! I know it!" Abigail rushed to defend him. "There must be some other explanation!"

Clara lifted one shoulder in a delicate shrug, sighing heavily as she answered, "He had the opportunity to deny it, and didn't. You were there."

"But I know him!" Abigail insisted. "He loves his brother! He would never have intentionally hurt Jeremiah!"

"Your secret is out now, Abigail. I know who the Rebel

deserter is that you fell in love with," Clara reminded her gently. "It's written all over your face: you're still in love with him. And I don't fault you for it. I don't know what happened that day any more than you do. It seems as if Charlie did in fact shoot Jeremiah, and perhaps we'll never know why. What was it he said? He didn't think it through."

He *had* said that. Charlie *had* admitted it. He'd apologized for it, clearly heartbroken and repentant. And his brother had declared that "*Some things are beyond forgiveness.*" Perhaps if Jeremiah had responded differently, Charlie could have explained what had really led him to fire his gun that fateful day in Gettysburg.

"I wish I could have been there," Abigail sighed raggedly. "I wish I could know what really transpired."

Shaking her head certainly, Clara countered, "No. You don't. I saw the aftermath, and it was more dreadful than anything you could imagine. It was appalling..." her eyes clouded as she returned to that place in her memory. Her eyes glistened as she continued, "It's barbaric and inhumane, war. There's nothing gallant or noble about what it does to a man. Not just the body, but the spirit. I'm not demeaning the convictions which lead a man to fight, nor the courage it takes to follow through in a field of battle. But the effects, on all involved, are ghastly and devastating.

"Gettysburg was Jeremiah's one and only battle. For Charlie, he had been living with war for years. I know what that one battle did to my husband's mind and soul. I cannot comprehend how it might have changed Charlie."

Abigail choked back angry tears. "I never knew him before the war—only after it. And he is a good man! Yes, he carries scars upon his heart and soul, but he is not some mindless killer who would shoot his brother if he had another option. Perhaps he feared being shot first, and it was a measure of self-defense."

"You misunderstand me," Clara rested her hand upon Abigail's, sitting next to her on the settee. "I don't think that at all. I'm only saying that when a heart is broken, when a spirit is broken, it never heals back the same. Like a bone that's been shattered and cannot grow whole again. It's never the same. Charlie had grown accustomed to the demands and ravages of war. Perhaps it was a matter of instinct and training."

"Perhaps," Abigail answered slowly, considering Aunt Sallie's explanation: *They were at war against one another and Charlie had to shoot him. Plain and simple.*" This was a war which would be remembered as brother against brother, father against son, cousins and friends against same.

Between strangers, war may be a detached fight against opposing ideals. But between brothers, every choice has a deep and penetrating impact. To harm an unnamed man is not the same as to inflict harm on a man whose face is as familiar as your own. Try as they might, personal emotions could never be separated from military action involving friends or family.

"All I can know with certainty," Abigail decided, "is that Charlie loves his brother. And I hope that one day Jeremiah can find it in his heart to forgive him, regardless of what prompted him to that particular course of action."

"Me too," Clara agreed. "For all our sakes."

"Do you think he can?"

"I don't know," Clara answered honestly. "He loved his brother deeply. Charlie was his best friend. When love is betrayed, it can easily turn to hatred. With time, I hope Jeremiah can see beyond his own pain to understand that life is short and forgiveness is essential. It would be a shame to wait to forgive until it's too late."

Abigail heard what Clara didn't say. No one knew where Charlie was or if he was safe. He could have been recaptured by the Home Guard and thrown into prison; he could have returned to the battlefield; or he could be hiding out somewhere in the deadly cold without provisions. One thing they had all learned from the last three years was that there was a very thin and precarious line separating life from death. Life was a precious and fragile gift, and time with those you love should never be taken for granted.

"If you hear anything from him, will you let me know?" Clara asked, clearly thinking along the same lines as Abigail.

"I will. But I don't know that I shall hear from him. When Charlie left Bloomingdale he was so upset, he left without speaking to me. And I haven't heard from him since. I'm afraid I was so shocked by the discovery that I may have given the impression I don't want to hear from him again. But I do! I desperately want to hear from him again."

"All we can do is pray," Clara said quietly. "I've seen God do amazing things in the past. He can do so much more than we can think or imagine. We have to entrust Charlie and all of these things to His care."

"You must have been beside yourself when Jeremiah was wounded at Gettysburg. How did you survive?"

"It took me some time to accept the wise counsel I was given, but I learned that when I surrendered all of my life—everything and everyone I loved—to Providence, my burdens were lightened. We don't have to carry them on our own. And there's so much more that God can do than we can. It's the simplest and most difficult decision you'll ever make: to face your trials alone or surrender all to God."

"I can try," Abigail leaned back wearily against the cushions behind her. She thought that she trusted God, but as she listened to Clara's advice, she realized she hadn't fully yielded to Him this situation which was closest to her heart.

"None of us relinquishes our independence easily," Clara reminded her. "It's a matter of knowing that you're surrendering it to One who can be trusted to always have your best interest at heart, and to never leave you nor forsake you."

Chapter Twenty-Three

Winter dragged on. Charlie alternated between confidence in his decision to return to his post and absolute certainty in the error of it. If anything, he wished he'd waited until spring to report for duty. Nothing of any military importance was likely to occur until then. He could have at least waited out the winter months someplace warm.

But remembering the events which had forced his hand, Charlie knew he'd had nowhere to sit out the cold. He'd left Bloomingdale that December night knowing there was nowhere for him to go but back into the Army of the Confederate States. And so, here he was.

By February, he'd fallen into the routine of a hardened soldier and his uniform hung loosely on his frame. Goldsborough, Roberts, and Prentiss had become like brothers to him. He regarded them with affection even though they aggravated and annoyed him. The confined space did little to help matters.

Having known Wilson, they were sorry to hear about his manner of death. To have come so close to home and freedom, only to die, seemed worse than perishing on the battlefield. Remembering his comradery with Wilson, and his grief upon Wilson's death, Charlie exerted great effort to remain patient with his cabin-mates when their irritating habits frayed at his nerves.

It was more than likely that they would not all four survive to the end of the war. He would never lose sight of that heartbreaking reality again. All of their days were numbered, and some were given more than others.

Sometimes it took all of his will power to refrain from biting words when Goldsborough, on the bunk above him, picked his nose and dropped the findings onto Charlie's cot below. Or when Roberts' snoring rattled the roof and kept him awake at night.

Prentiss had once inserted acorns into Roberts' nostrils as a desperate measure to silence him. The strategy had been successful until Roberts woke up and discovered the "treatment." He went into a fury and promised to burn every meal he cooked if it ever happened again. That threat was enough to ensure he was left undisturbed.

One evening as they passed the time playing cards, gambling with "chips" made of stones or flattened bullets, which represented their daily rations, Prentiss confided that he had a brother fighting for the Union.

"Clifton could be just across the way there, in the enemy trenches, and yet we're as far away as if there were an ocean between us," he mused. "I haven't seen him since the war began, when we chose our different paths. I'm sure we've fought on the same field of battle, but never had the misfortune to meet. And I don't know what we'd do if we did."

"I don't know either," Goldsborough affirmed. "I've got family on both sides of the line, too. Sooner or later, we're bound to cross paths."

"In Gettysburg," Charlie said quietly, these men having fought with him there, "I saw my brother. As the wind shifted and I recognized his face through the gun smoke, I thought of all the bodies which littered the hill that day, their lives snuffed out like a candle in the wind. I had one desire, and that was for him to make it safely home."

"What did you do?" Roberts leaned in, sensing the gravity of the confession which was to follow.

"I shot him," Charlie breathed out, closing his eyes. "I took aim at his left hand, supporting the barrel of his musket, and I shot him." He pressed his thumbs into his eyes to stop the flow of tears as he remembered the tortured anger on his brother's face when he'd demanded, *"How could you do this to me?"*

Charlie knew these men would understand. "I knew it would get him out of the war. I didn't realize just how devastating the battle would be, and how long it would take for the wounded to be treated afterward."

"Do you know if he survived?" Prentiss wondered, his eyes sympathetic.

"He did," Charlie affirmed, and every one of them sighed with relief. "But he hates me for it now. He thinks I wanted to hurt him. I saw him when I was in Maryland, and the look in his eyes..." Charlie couldn't continue, his throat swelling with grief.

Roberts, sitting cross-legged on the floor next to him, reached over to squeeze his shoulder. "One day maybe he'll understand. Have you considered writing a letter? I know a blockade runner who brings me letters from Harriet. We could try to get it to him."

"I'm no good at putting my thoughts to paper," Charlie confessed.

"Neither am I," Prentiss raked a hand through his hair as he leaned back against the bunk behind him. "I've thought of writing Clifton, but even if I had a way to get it to him, I don't know what I'd say."

"I've learned that when mending rifts, there's a simple statement which carries great power: *I love you*. It doesn't mean you think you were wrong, or that you're sorry for whatever you've done. It just means that all of that doesn't matter," Roberts offered, reaching instinctively for the picture of his wife, which he carried in his chest pocket.

"Maybe you should have Roberts write it," Goldsborough suggested.

"I'd be happy to help," Roberts replied. "I carry a letter in my shirt every time we go into battle, for Harriet. I consider it my final farewell. If I'm killed, I hope that whoever takes my body will see it delivered to her."

"You're such a romantic," Prentiss laughed. "Which may be why you're horrible at poker. Your face says everything."

Roberts grimaced as he lay his cards on the table. "I'm out."

Goldsborough grinned. He won nine out of ten games. Charlie suspected he cheated, though he wasn't sure and didn't really care. It was a way to pass time.

It seemed all there was to life now was passing time. Either in the trenches or the cabin. The second hand on the clock moved slower than the heartbeat of a dying man, the minutes and the hours and the days all merging into one long spell of waiting.

There had been one break in the monotony at the beginning of February when Union cavalry, flanked by two protective units, had attacked a supply route. The fighting had lasted three days, and although the advance was stopped, the Federals lengthened their siege works to the Vaughn Road crossing of Hatcher's Run. Although the Confederates were able to keep the Boydton Plank Road open for supply wagons, they were forced to extend their thinning lines.

Since then, there had been no movement from the Yankees. They were biding their time, well fed as supplies streamed in from the James River to City Point. Rumor had it that their intention with this latest offensive was to capture and destroy any Rebel supply wagons found traveling the Boydton Plank Road. They had encountered few. Unable to fight the Rebs into submission, they would wear them down and starve them out.

Charlie watched as Goldsborough shuffled the deck and dealt the cards. As Marylanders in the Confederate Army, they were each in a unique position in this war. The boys of the Deep South found it easy to hate the Yankees invading their home states, and who could blame them for it? But it wasn't so simple for the Maryland soldiers. Many of those Yankee invaders were their kin.

How could Charlie ever convince Jeremiah that he had intentionally wounded him for the greater purpose of saving his life—that it had been *love* which had prompted him to the pull the trigger? Even to him, it sounded suspect.

Amid the horror of the battle, it had seemed an act of mercy to take his hand to spare his life. Charlie's only motive had been to get Jeremiah off the battlefield and into the safety of the medical tents before his unit charged up the hill and the work of butchery ensued full-scale, the grass scattered with men whose eyes fixed vacantly upon the sky.

But as the lead penetrated his brother's hand, mangling it into a mass of shattered bone and bleeding flesh, a sickening wave of regret had washed over Charlie. He'd had only seconds to react to the sight of his brother, and even the most sincere remorse couldn't reverse the course of action he'd chosen. It was done, and they both would have to find a way to live with it.

~

Sam pressed his wet nose into Abigail's hand, bringing it to her attention that her hand had stilled. She resumed scratching him behind the ears and stroking his black, silky coat. "Sorry boy. You've been neglected lately haven't you? I'm sorry about that. Spring will be here soon, and we can resume our walks."

"You know he just a dog, right? He don't know what you sayin'," Lizzie shook her head, pressing chicken wings and thighs into a bowl of flour as she prepared the family's supper.

"He understands, don't you boy?" Abigail leaned down and the dog licked her chin in reply.

"You is the craziest white woman I ever met," Lizzie declared, shaking her head again, her turban wobbling precariously. "If you mama knew I let that animal in my kitchen while I's making supper, she won't be none too happy. If she knew you lettin' that animal lick you face, she have a conniption!"

"Oh, there's a long list of things Mama doesn't like," Abigail replied with a sigh. "If I were to write a list of all of them, there wouldn't be enough paper and ink in the world."

"Don't disrespect you mama," the cook chided. "Bible says, '*Honor your mother and father.*'"

"Yes ma'am," Abigail replied reflexively. Then realizing that she had deferred to a Negro, she glanced up at Lizzie and grinned. "Mama wouldn't like that either."

Chuckling, Lizzie dropped the chicken into a frying pan of sizzling butter and lard. Affection sparkled in her eyes. "No, I reckon she wouldn't."

Sam rested his chin on Abigail's lap, where Sprightly resided. He gave the cat a lick, leaving a trail of slobber on her fur. The calico laid back her ears and swatted at him.

Unperturbed, he licked her again.

Abigail rubbed Sprightly's head to calm her, reminding the cat, "Look at those jaws. He could do worse than kiss you."

"You ever hear from Charlie?" Lizzie wondered.

An ache throbbed in her chest as Abigail answered, "No, and I don't know that I ever shall."

"I sure hope he doin' all right, wherever he be," the little woman clucked. "That poor boy been through too much."

Keep him safe, dear Lord, Abigail prayed as Clara had admonished her to do when worry began to prey like vultures on her mind. *Please let him receive my letter and write back to me.*

As Lizzie used tongs to turn the chicken in the pan, frying it evenly on both sides, Abigail listened to the sounds of the dear woman's cooking, of the fire crackling in the cast iron stove, and the purring of her sweet companion. Sam leaned against her, his warmth comforting, his brown eyes gazing up at her adoringly.

Outside, the rain fell in steady torrents. For weeks the sky had wept, and the mood couldn't have been more somber for President Lincoln's second inauguration in Washington D.C., scheduled for tomorrow. Those who attended would have to wade through the mud to hear him.

The Thirteenth Amendment to the Constitution had been approved by both House and Senate, and when put before the people, it had been ratified by eighteen states before the end of February. Throughout the nation, the Negro peoples were once and for all legally free. They were not citizens, and they did not have the full rights of citizens, but at least they were no longer slaves and could begin to take hold of their own destinies.

There had not yet been a conclusive end to the war, though

it drew nearer every day. General Sherman had captured Columbia, the capital of South Carolina, and like Atlanta, left it ablaze. He then led his army into North Carolina.

Generals Grant and Meade still held their ground against General Lee at Petersburg. From what Abigail understood, it was impossible for the Rebels to continue holding their position for much longer. They must either bend or break.

The day after Lincoln had been sworn in for another term as President of the Dis-United States, Abigail found her father sitting in the library reading the newspaper with a peculiar expression on his face. His forehead was wrinkled into a series of creases, and his brows drew together fiercely.

"Something wrong?" she worried.

Irving glanced up as she lowered herself onto a plush armchair next to his desk. In front of the fireplace, Harris had taken up residence and was playing a game of jacks.

"No, no…. Just trying to decide what I think of Lincoln's inaugural speech. Listen to this: '*On the occasion corresponding to this four years ago all thoughts were anxiously directed to an impending civil war. All dreaded it, all sought to avert it. While the inaugural address was being delivered from this place, devoted altogether to saving the Union without war, insurgent agents were in the city seeking to destroy it without war— seeking to dissolve the Union and divide effects by negotiation. Both parties deprecated war, but one of them would make war rather than let the nation survive, and the other would accept war rather than let it perish, and the war came.*'

"It sounds like he blames the war entirely on those parties who wished to secede from the Union peaceably and takes no responsibility for rallying volunteers to invade those states, which is what I would argue prompted the war. If he hadn't taken such harsh action, many men who loved their flag would not have felt compelled to take up arms against it," Irving stated.

"I always found the slogan, 'Union At All Costs' to be rather ironic," Abigail admitted. "It certainly sounds like tyranny to demand that a state which voluntarily joined the Union has no right to leave it. How can you have Union without unity?"

"Quite," Irving agreed. "And he goes on... Let me see. Here it is: '*Neither party expected for the war the magnitude or the duration which it has already attained. Neither anticipated that the cause of the conflict might cease with or even before the conflict itself should cease. Each looked for an easier triumph, and a result less fundamental and astounding. Both read the same Bible and pray to the same God, and each invokes His aid against the other. It may seem strange that any men should dare to ask a just God's assistance in wringing their bread from the sweat of other men's faces, but let us judge not, that we be not judged. The prayers of both could not be answered. That of neither has been answered fully. The Almighty has His own purposes.*'"

Abigail tapped her chin thoughtfully. "I've often thought the same thing. Both North and South believe that God is on their side and pray for Him to give them the victory. Which side do you think God is on, Papa?"

"Abby, I'll have to be honest and say neither. I don't believe God endorses slavery; nor does he endorse tyranny. Neither side in this war is without fault. Though if you were to listen to Lincoln, he entirely blames the South. He evens use Scripture to point the finger. '"*Woe unto the world because of offenses; for it must needs be that offenses come, but woe to that man by whom the offense cometh.*" *If we shall suppose that American slavery is one of those offenses which, in the providence of God, must needs come, but which, having continued through His appointed time, He now wills to remove, and that He gives to both North and South this terrible war as the woe due to those by whom the offense came, shall we discern therein any departure from those divine attributes which the believers in a living God always ascribe to Him?'"*

"The offense he speaks of is slavery, and the war is God's judgment for it?" Abigail tried to understand the President's perspective.

"So he thinks. Although I'd like to see him take some responsibility for his part in it. There could have been a peaceable parting of the states prior to the war, and slavery would have ended in its own due time. Even so, if another man had been elected, we might even now be negotiating terms of peace with the South rather than continuing in madness and butchery. For Abraham Lincoln to deny his own hand in the deaths of the thousands of American citizens who have perished in the course of these last four years is blindness and denial. His predecessor, Buchanan, was of the opinion that secession was illegal—but going to war to prevent it was equally so. Another man might have chosen a different—and less destructive—path for America in this time of controversy. No, his hands are not clean.

"He concludes this speech, or sermon if you will, by saying: *'Fondly do we hope, fervently do we pray, that this mighty scourge of war may speedily pass away. Yet, if God wills that it continue until all the wealth piled by the bondsman's two hundred and fifty years of unrequited toil shall be sunk, and until every drop of blood drawn with the lash shall be paid by another drawn with the sword, as was said three thousand years ago, so still it must be said "the judgments of the Lord are true and righteous altogether."*

"'With malice toward none, with charity for all, with

firmness in the right as God gives us to see the right, let us strive on to finish the work we are in, to bind up the nation's wounds, to care for him who shall have borne the battle and for his widow and his orphan, to do all which may achieve and cherish a just and lasting peace among ourselves and with all nations.'"

Abigail had to concur with her father's aggravated huff. "He gave Sherman a free hand to plunder his way through Georgia and South Carolina, then has the nerve to say, '*With malice toward none, with charity toward all.*' Sherman made his intention clear when he said, 'I will make Georgia howl,' and he was referring to all the residents of that state, not just those enlisted in the military. No, Lincoln has made his purpose clear from the beginning, and it is to hold together his Union no matter the cost to the American people. I'm sorry to say that it's merely more political jargon disguised in spiritual language."

"You don't think he believes what he says?" Harris interjected from his position on the floor, marbles and jacks surrounding him on the carpeted floor.

Having forgotten her little brother was there listening, Abigail was quick to affirm, "I suspect he does. He must believe that he is doing what is right for the country and that is the will of God for him to pursue the war."

Irving added solemnly, "Son, it is a weakness of mankind to convince himself that his motives are pure and then to find evidence to support it, rather to examine his own heart first to find if there might be lurking selfish purposes. At one time or another, we're all guilty of it. Even me."

"Did you ever consider joining the war?" Harris wondered. "Which side would you have joined?"

Irving rested his elbow on the desktop, his expression thoughtful. "I did consider it. I would have joined the

Confederacy, I think. But I am the manager of a plantation which has built its success on the back of slavery. I did not enlist because I am a father, and more gifted with words than with weapons. When I search my own heart, I'm glad I never did take up arms on either side. I regret that slavery has been a source of benefit to many, including myself, and yet I cannot stand on the side of tyranny either. Though both sides seek to spiritualize this conflict, it's a clash of sections and cultures, with both sides having valid claims as well as selfish motives."

"I would have joined the Rebels," Harris stated certainly. "Like Charlie."

"As many young and impetuous boys did," Irving replied sadly, "only to learn afterwards of their mortality. Life is short, my son. It is a precious gift that too many have squandered in the name of a cause, for the sake of excitement or adventure. I've heard that Lincoln ensured the safety of his own son, while willingly sacrificing the sons of those whom he was elected to protect. This war has left many orphaned and widowed, and I'm glad that you and I are both here safely in the library now. Whatever good this war may have brought, it's responsible for just as much evil. And I for one do not believe that God has smiled down upon it."

"Nor do I," Abigail whispered, the image of a man in rags lying face down upon the ground coming to mind. A man whose ribs threatened to pierce his skin, whose eyes were glazed over from starvation, and whose skin was sallow from malnutrition. Blood ran from the wound in his side, which would have proven mortal had not Lizzie intervened. If it was wrong to treat the Negroes with brutality, then what justified the Union's treatment of their Rebel prisoners?

Chapter Twenty-Four

As the calendar turned from February to March, the soldiers awaited spring with mingled dread and eagerness. The months of inactivity had made them restless and itching for a fight; yet a spirit of defeat hung over the Confederacy. On a daily basis men stole away from camp to return home, quitting the war. The desertions were so many that there was no way to stem the tide.

Charlie sat with his battalion in the trenches, feeling the whisper of warmth in the breeze that blew over them. Soon the daffodils and crocus would begin to bloom, and the grass to green over beneath the sun. With these heralds of spring would come either an enemy onslaught or the call to attack. Either way, their lives would once again hang in the balance.

Completing their morning roll call and drill, the Second Maryland settled down into the ditches to protect their territory should the Yankees choose to attack. Goldsborough puffed a cigarette beside Charlie, his bearded face obscured by a cloud of smoke. On his other side, Prentiss yawned expansively. Roberts studied the sky, predicting that the gray clouds overhead would blow over and the day would remain dry.

Suddenly Goldsborough leapt to his feet. "Be right back!" he called, resting his musket in the crook of his arm as he trotted toward the latrines.

"What do you think those Bluebelllies are planning for us?" Roberts wondered. "The weather is about to turn. They have plenty of men and munitions. One of these days, they're going to ambush us."

"That's why we're here," Prentiss reminded them. "It takes two of them to lick one of us, so don't let their numbers scare you. We've been outnumbered since the beginning, and we've given 'em hell for four years."

"Scholars from Massachusetts are no match for Eastern Shore boys who grew up with a gun in their hands," Charlie agreed.

They all knew that the days of the Confederacy were numbered. But they clung to their bravado, refusing to cower even in the face of almost certain defeat.

After a time, Goldsborough returned to his position in the trenches with a groan.

"You all right?" Charlie asked him, as disorders of the bowels were a common plague among the soldiers

"Not sure," Goldsborough answered. Within fifteen minutes, he was running back to the latrines.

"Looks like he's caught the quickstep," Prentiss observed. The doctors called it the flux or dysentery, but the men who had to make a bolt for the latrines had a different name for it.

When Goldsborough returned the second time, he declared, "I'm going to the medical tent for dogwood bark tea if I have to get up one more time." His color was pale.

No one replied. The flux could come and go, or it could take a man with it.

They weren't surprised when he didn't return to the trenches after his next urgent call. Charlie hoped the tea and a day's rest would help. He bowed his head and offered up a quick prayer to heaven.

When they were released from trench duty and given leave to return to their cabins to make dinner, they found their friend sleeping on his cot. As it was Charlie's turn to cook, he quietly set about preparing the evening meal, hoping Goldsborough would awaken with renewed health and vigor.

"I'm heading out to the Post Office," Roberts informed them. Although he only received letters from his wife at distant intervals, he checked in with the Post Office almost daily.

Charlie grunted in reply as Prentiss returned from the well with a bucket of water for him to mix with the cornmeal and salt, then fry in reserved bacon grease. He'd also managed to get his hands on some dried beans which he set to boil with the rice over the fire.

Prentiss napped while Charlie stirred the pot. Goldsborough moaned in his sleep once or twice, but otherwise seemed to be resting peacefully.

The meal was almost ready by the time Roberts returned. "Guess who got a letter today?" he said as he thrust an envelope under Charlie's nose.

Disbelieving, Charlie took the envelope and stared at the feminine script. "Charles Turner of Laurel Hill, Queen Anne's County, Maryland," it said. Abigail clearly had no idea where he was… which made him all the more curious how the letter had found him. Someone had obviously known where to send it.

The envelope was discolored and wrinkled, and as he unfolded the letter within, he noted that it was dated at the beginning of January. It had taken that long for it to find its way to him.

His heart thumped in his chest as he read, her delicate

penmanship making it easy for him to hear the words in her own sweet voice.

"Dear Charlie," she began, *"I am writing this letter in hopes that by some miracle it will find you, wherever you may be. I pray daily for your safety and wellbeing, and that we shall one day meet again. My wonderfully planned present went horribly awry, and although I was certainly shocked by the outcome of the meeting, I am mostly perplexed. Knowing you as I believe I do, I am confident that there is more to this story than I have heard. And I hope one day that you will share it with me, trusting in the friendship we share. My affections for you remain unchanged, and I shall carry in my heart forever the memories of the time we shared. Though I have no reason to expect a reply, for you may never read these words, I shall wait and pray to receive one just the same. I will never forget you. You have changed my life. Affectionately Yours, Abigail Sterret."*

He had thought he'd lost her. After learning he was responsible for Jeremiah's wound, which might have proven fatal at Gettysburg and had resulted in the amputation of his hand, how could he expect her to feel the same way toward him?

Yet despite the evidence, Abigail had chosen to believe the best in him. Without any real reason—as he had admitted to the crime—she had trusted in his character when drawing her conclusions.

If she could do that, why couldn't Jeremiah? It said more about Abigail's character than his own. She always saw the good in everyone, her natural instinct to cherish and nurture. He should have known that Abigail would never cast him aside without confirmation that he was deserving of it.

Charlie's eyes grew damp. He should send the reply she prayed for. If he didn't, he may never have the chance to tell her what she meant to him. As Roberts had reminded him, a soldier's life was uncertain, and it was wise to share what was in one's heart while there was still time.

"Your girl?" Roberts assumed.

Charlie looked up to see that Roberts had rescued the fried bread from the pan before it was burned. He nodded in reply, his heart warmed by the knowledge of her continued affection.

"She still loves you?" Roberts grinned, sharing in Charlie's joy and relief.

"Miraculously, it seems she does," Charlie replied, feeling renewed hope spark within him.

Prentiss wakened from his nap, wrinkling his nose as he demanded, "What's that smell?"

Goldsborough groaned, clutching his stomach. Blood and refuse stained his cot.

Roberts, Prentiss and Charlie exchanged worried glances. The bloody flux was nothing to be trifled with. Immediately they sprang into action.

"Grab the ends of his blanket," Charlie ordered Roberts as he grabbed the top corners of the blanket. Together they lifted Goldsborough from his cot on the makeshift stretcher.

Prentiss ran to the door, throwing it open for them. "I'll run ahead to prepare a wagon."

Once they reached the medical tent, there was no need to convince the nurses that Goldsborough was in dire straits and required hospitalization. They worked swiftly and efficiently to shift him from his blanket onto a stretcher and lift him into the wagon to be transported to Chimborazo Hospital in Richmond.

Charlie, Prentiss and Roberts returned solemnly to their cabin. The pot of beans and rice left on the fire had simmered over, and what was left in the bottom was charred. Silently they went to work stripping Goldsborough's cot to boil the sheets, mopping the floor, and scrubbing the cast iron pot.

On his first day of leave after Goldsborough had been taken to the hospital, five days since the dysentery had claimed him, Charlie donned his coat and turned to his friends. "I'm going into Richmond. Who wants to go with me?"

"I'll go," Roberts answered as Prentiss reached for his coat. Together the three men slipped out into the brisk dawn and began the thirty mile hike toward Richmond. Encountering a dairy farmer transporting fresh milk in glass jugs, they hitched a ride with him and reached the city one hour after sunup.

Arriving at the hospital, they reported to the front desk to ask where Goldsborough could be found and if he could receive visitors.

The young woman leafed through the papers on her desk which cataloged the patients and their locations. As she looked up at the three soldiers in front of her, regret moved into her eyes. "I'm so sorry. He was moved two days ago to the morgue. He's likely already been buried at Oakwood Cemetery. I am truly sorry."

Charlie nodded in gratitude for both her compassion and the information. Another friend, gone. Illness had taken twice as many lives as the Yankees. Shoving his hands deep in his pockets, Charlie felt the heaviness of grief settle in his chest. There was no point in tears. When the fighting resumed, which was likely to be any day now, more men would cross that invisible threshold which led from life into death.

The Second Maryland had already gone from 325 men

down to barely one hundred. It was quite possible that all three of them could be lying alongside Goldsborough at Oakwood before the month ended, sacrificed on the altar of "the cause."

"Hey Roberts," Charlie said after they had walked for a while in somber silence, "I've got two letters I think I'd like to write. Will you help me?"

~

"Miss Ab'gail, you gots visitors, ma'am," Esther ducked her head into the library to inform her. "They's just now climbing down from they carriage."

Setting the book she had been reading aside, Abigail peered through the window at the two women whose approach Esther had observed. She recognized Clara, but was unsure of the second woman's identity. Delicate, with her dark hair covered in a snood at the nape of her neck, she might have been mistaken for a girl if it had not been for the womanly figure her striped dress revealed.

"Thank you, Esther. You may bring them into the drawing room. I'll wait there. And then fetch tea and refreshments, please."

"Yes ma'am," the young Negro woman answered dutifully.

Relocating to the drawing room across the hall, a more feminine space where Abigail usually entertained her visitors, she noted with appreciation that a fire already blazed in the fireplace. Although the calendar predicted the approach of spring, the weather had yet to comply.

Within moments, Esther led the visitors into the drawing room. "Mrs. Turner and Mrs. Wright," she announced.

Abigail rose to her feet, greeting Clara with an affectionate hug and a kiss on her cheek. She offered her hand in welcome to Mrs. Wright, whom she felt looked vaguely familiar. Remarkably petite, Mrs. Wright was memorable for her diminutive size as well as the lively spark which danced in her eyes.

"I know where he is!" Clara exclaimed, gripping Abigail's hand in wild excitement.

"Who? Charlie?" Abigail's heart sprang to life, pounding against her ribcage within the whale-bone corset.

"Yes! He's gone back into the army!" Clara's eyes were wide as she whispered the answer, still holding tight to Abigail's hand.

"But how did you find out?" Abigail asked in bewilderment.

Clara turned to her companion, "This is Mariah Wright. Her husband serves in the Second Maryland Infantry, and he manages to get letters home to her now and then. Well, he happened to mention in his most recent missive that he had been greatly surprised by the return of a certain Charles Turner, who had been taken captive at Gettysburg and quite suddenly reappeared in their midst again."

"Where?" Abigail breathed the question.

Mariah lifted her delicate chin to meet Abigail's gaze. "They're in Petersburg."

Abigail's head began to spin. She stumbled over to the armchair and lowered herself into it.

Clara and Mariah had just settled onto the settee when Esther appeared with a tray. The women remained silent until the Negro woman had departed and they were alone.

In a whisper, Clara confessed, "I hope you didn't mind my bringing Mariah into our secret, but I knew you would want to know right away. She had just arrived at my house with the news, when I straightaway begged her to come here to tell you."

"No, I don't mind at all," Abigail managed to reply.

"I brought the letter, if you'd like to read it… just that part, I mean," Mariah added with a hint of a blush.

Not wanting to intrude on the personal contents of the letter, Abigail read only the paragraph which Mariah pointed to as she placed the letter in Abigail's trembling hands.

It was simply written, much as Clara had explained upon her arrival. Private Charles Turner had returned to their ranks at the beginning of January. The last Mariah's husband had heard, Turner had been taken prisoner at Gettysburg and he was grateful to see him alive again. That was it.

But now at least Abigail knew where he was. In Petersburg, where a siege had been in play for almost a year.

"Do you know… do they have food enough, and are they all right?" Abigail worried.

Mariah bit her lip as she answered, "I don't know for sure. George doesn't share with me of the dangers or deprivations he faces. He doesn't want me to worry. I'm always only grateful to get a letter, to know he's still alive and thinking of me." Her dark eyes grew shadowed within her small, pale face.

"Yes," Abigail nodded, realizing the full implications of Charlie's return to the battlefield. Turning to Clara, she asked, "Jeremiah doesn't know?"

"Not yet," she said quietly. "I only just found out myself."

Her gaze shifting back to Mariah, Abigail queried, "How

does your husband send letters across enemy lines?"

"Blockade runners," the Confederate soldier's wife explained. "They carry supplies and letters under cover of night to Richmond. It's risky. More now than ever. But there are far more silent sympathizers on the shore than you might realize."

"Are you going to send a reply?"

"I am. Would you like to pen a letter before I leave today?" Mariah offered. "There's never any guarantee it will be delivered. But we can try."

"Yes, I would!" Abigail exclaimed. She could only assume that the letter she had given the aunts had never reached its intended recipient. After all, they hadn't known he had returned to military service.

"If you don't mind, I'll do it right now," she said, springing to her feet. Her guests nodded in understanding, and Abigail hastily ran across the hall to the library. Taking her father's chair behind the desk, she reached for paper and pen. She would have preferred to use her own stationary, but she didn't have the patience to run up to her room to retrieve it.

Her heart was full of conflicting emotions. Abigail could hardly steady her hand to pen the words. Her emotions spilled out in a mad rush of relief and worry, and all she could think to do was reassure Charlie of her love and beg him to come home to her alive.

Everyone said that the war was almost over. Yet even if they lived to see the end of it, what would happen to men like George Wright and Charlie Turner who had committed treason against their country? Would they even be permitted to return home?

If they were banished to the south, Abigail knew she would

want to go with him, just as Mariah would follow her husband. She would gladly be a poor man's wife in a demoralized and beaten land rather than to remain where she was in the lap of luxury, alone.

If Charlie were to be killed, Abigail doubted she would recover as Jane had, whose marriage to Judson Shepherd was scheduled to take place in just a few short months. But perhaps one had to find new strength when the occasion called for it. The war had left many widows who were forced to face the morning alone, to walk through the day with their shoulders straight, and to lie down with nothing but memories and heartache when the night had fallen.

War was a lesson in endurance.

What adversities was Charlie facing, even in this very moment? Returning the nib of her pen to paper, Abigail let her prayers be for his strength, his wisdom, and his safety.

She willed, as so many other women like her, that her love and prayers would somehow be enough to keep him alive and bring him back to her. Yet deep down, knowing it wasn't.

Chapter Twenty-Five

"Please tell me you're not going to feed that animal?" Prentiss raised an eyebrow in disbelief. "He looks like he eats better than we do."

With the warmer temperatures, the men had abandoned the cabin to take their meals outside. The air smelled of fresh growth, the grass was beginning to push through, and green leaves were budding on the trees.

Charlie ignored Prentiss, kneeling down with a bit of beef to tempt the large, cream colored tomcat which had wandered near their cabin. The feline did appear to have consumed a fair number of rodents in his day.

"I thought you didn't like cats," Roberts reminded him.

"When did I say that?"

"Back when you first enlisted. I distinctly remember."

Charlie remembered the incident Roberts spoke of. There had been a stray wandering near their tent, and he had shooed it away with a few distasteful remarks about its species.

He didn't deny it. "Well, a man can change his mind."

"A man only changes his mind about cats when a woman's involved," Roberts grinned. Prentiss chuckled.

"Here you go, Tom," Charlie said as the cat sniffed his offering cautiously. Placing it on the ground, he let the cat decide if it was safe to consume. He watched as the tidbit quickly disappeared.

"You know, once you feed that thing, he's never going to leave," Prentiss taunted. "Is he our new mascot?"

"Why not?" Charlie sat down, leaning against the log walls of the cabin as he took another bite of beef and rice. The cat sauntered up to him and lowered himself onto his haunches, waiting for another handout. Charlie complied.

"You gonna ask her to marry you?" Roberts pressed.

Charlie sighed. "I would. But what do I have to offer her? My brother has the family farm. We're about to lose the war, and I'm not sure what to expect after that. What will any of us have?"

No one replied. No one knew the answer.

Only a few days before, General Lee had ordered one last desperate attack in the hope that it would thwart General Grant's plans to assault them by weakening the Union lines. Fort Stedman was the target, a fortification that was closest to Confederate lines and without heavy obstructions surrounding it. Behind it, a supply depot on the U.S. Military Railroad was less than a mile away. Once the fort and its artillery were captured, a lead party could clear the lines and make way for a main attack ending at City Point. Not only was it Grant's headquarters, but perhaps more importantly, it was the main supply base for the Union army.

Although the attack had begun well, a series of misfortunes interfered with the execution of the plan, and ultimately it proved a disheartening defeat. Losses were estimated at four thousand, while the Union suffered only a little over a thousand. In addition to the invaluable loss of men, which the Confederacy could not afford to spare, they had also lost hard-won ground.

The end drew ever nearer.

The Confederacy had put up a valiant effort, fighting more courageously than the Federals had ever imagined. They had believed they could put down the rebellion in a few short months, but time and again the South had bested them, despite the odds. Now, finally, they had run out of men and supplies. They were humbled. And they must either keep fighting until there was no one left to fight, or submit that they had in fact been beaten.

Surrender. The word tasted bitter on the tongue of every Johnny Reb who had fought beneath the banner of freedom: the infamous battle flag which bore the "Southern Cross." They had fought long and hard for their independence, only to see it slip through their fingers.

In February, three representatives of the Confederacy, Vice President Alexander Stephens, Senator Robert Hunter, and Assistant Secretary of War John Campbell, had met with President Lincoln and Secretary of State William Seward aboard the steamboat *River Queen* at Hampton Roads. This Peace Conference proved fruitless as Lincoln still refused to consider granting Southern Independence.

The argument was that if peace was achieved through any form of compromise, it would wreck the good accomplished by the Thirteenth Amendment. The Emancipation Proclamation was issued under war powers; and the states could individually refuse to ratify the Amendment. If the slaves were to remain free, the Confederacy would have to be brought under subjection.

Such ideas were troubling for Charlie, and for many like him, who wished to see the Southern States free from tyranny but also wished to see the Negro people set free. Why must it be one or the other? Could not both be accomplished?

It seemed to Charlie that if men like Lincoln and Davis were to taste the wretchedness of battle, to see its effects firsthand, they might be more willing to compromise their hard-nosed positions. If they were far-sighted men, they might look into the future and see that the south had already been forever changed. It could never return to its former ways as if the disruption and destruction of the war hadn't occurred. If given independence, they would eventually be forced to recognize that the antiquated practice of slavery must come to end. And they would end it of their own volition.

At least, this was Charlie's opinion. Unfortunately, the only one who might put some stock in his point of view was Tom, the cat, and only because he had a vested interest in Charlie's rations.

Scratching the feline behind his ears, Charlie said quietly, "We'll soon all be soldiers of a defeated cause and a conquered army. What will be done to us? Sent to prison? Exiled? We gambled and we lost. But the nation, the Union, has lost too. My father once compared the Southern states to a wife who wished to be freed of a controlling husband. If he brings her back by force, he still has not earned her loyalty or her affection. All he has is a resentful woman under his roof."

"Well said," Roberts agreed gravely. "How can the nation ever be unified after this?"

"What about our families?" Prentiss added quietly. "Can they ever be unified after this? I have this foolish dream that one day I'll be able to live under the same roof as Clifton. But how can we forget that we spent these years in brutal opposition to one another?"

Leaning forward, Charlie rested his head in his hands.

"Only by understanding that we love them more than any country or cause. If we can only make them understand…"

~

With a shawl draped around her shoulders, and her calico cat Sprightly cradled in her arms, Abigail descended the front steps of Bloomingdale to enjoy a beautiful, clear spring day. Finally the cold snap had broken, and the sky stretched out overhead as blue as a robin's egg. The sun was warm against her cheeks, and she inhaled the smells of fresh growth as her feet trod over the new grass.

Sam ran circles around her, barking joyfully. His black coat gleamed in the sunshine. Sprightly flattened her ears in annoyance at the dog's antics, and Abigail laughed at both her beloved pets.

It felt wonderful to be out of the house and to witness nature's rebirth after lying dormant through the gray, stark months of winter. Somehow, every year, it felt like a miracle.

Abigail's step was light as she followed Sam across the lawn, with no particular destination in mind. She had spent the morning in her room in prayer, as she had learned to do in recent days, and she felt the peace which often accompanied it. Her wide bell skirt of checked pink cotton swayed as she walked, the wind stirring the tassels of her knit shawl and the tendrils of loose hair which hung down her back.

Suddenly Sam stopped, sniffing the air as if something on the breeze had caught his attention. He looked back at Abigail, then bolted forward toward the slave quarter.

A strange feeling twisted in Abigail's gut. She knew she should not follow him, that she was not allowed to be near the brick building which housed the slaves—former slaves. But curiosity compelled her forward.

No, it was more than mere curiosity. She trusted Sam's instincts. Dread grew within her as she followed him, pausing to scan about her for watching eyes.

No one appeared to be about. But it was possible that someone inside could spy her trespassing into forbidden territory through a window, and a knot of fear tangled with the growing dread.

A whimper could be heard on the other side of the building. Was it Sam... or was it the sound of human suffering? Forgetting that she could be in dire trouble if she were caught, Abigail ran around the corner of the slave quarter.

She stopped short at the sight which met her eyes, her skirt bouncing wildly back and forth as she stood suddenly still, staring.

The Staffordshire terrier lay on the ground beside a boy with skin dark as night, thin and half-naked, his back and legs caked with dried blood. He was more of a youth than boy, she observed as she stepped toward him, his eyes studying her warily.

"What happened to you?" she whispered, stepping closer.

He raised his eyebrows in disgust, managing to wield his reply with sarcasm despite his exhaustion. "What you think happen? You think I did it to myself?"

It was then Abigail noticed the manacles which bound his wrists to the wall. Her stomach churned. "You... were beaten?" she asked what seemed an obvious question, but she could not grasp the reality of it.

"Ain't that what it look like?" the boy glared.

"Who did this to you?" she demanded, anger surging through her veins, replacing the shock and horror she had felt upon first discovering him.

He looked at her like she must be daft. "Mr. Wayne, who you think?"

Her hands curled into fists. She began to tremble with rage and indignation. "Why did he beat you?"

He huffed. "Say I ain't work fast enough. Beat me last night, left me outside with no supper and going to come back and see if I's ready to work faster t'morrow."

"How often does something like this happen?"

"How of'en you think?" he challenged.

Abigail couldn't blame him for the resentment and hate which charged his words and filled his face. She was privileged, sheltered, white. Pressing her lips together in a firm line, Abigail blinked back the tears which burned her eyes.

"What's your name?" she asked gently, hoping to convey that she was not what he believed her to be. She did not condone such cruelty, and she would not stand silently by and allow it to continue.

"Why? You gonna tell Massuh I was sassin' you?"

Abigail could read the distrust in his eyes. What reason did he have to trust anyone with white skin? Hot shame flooded her.

"I'll be back," she whispered firmly, "with someone to tend your wounds. I will do all I can to ensure that this sort of thing does not happen again. I'm so—" she choked on the words, feeling as if she was somehow responsible simply for the color of her skin and for living on this plantation. "I'm so sorry."

The boy regarded her with disdain. "You ain't know this go on? And now you gonna stop it?" He huffed again.

Abigail did not answer. She was too ashamed.

She turned on her heel and ran back to the house, entering through the rear door which led to the old wing. She did not pause to knock upon the door which led to the aunt's parlor, but burst into the room in a mad rush.

The old women stared at her, mouths ajar.

"What on earth?" Aunt Sallie demanded.

"Do you know that Mr. Wayne is still beating our workers?" Abigail gasped out.

"Have a seat dear," Sallie ordered. "And calm yourself."

Reluctantly, Abigail obeyed. But she pinned her great-aunt with a piercing stare.

"I know that when it is necessary for the sake of order and discipline, the overseer will use a whip to bring the Negroes into line. Why do you ask?"

"Because I've just seen a boy outside the quarter who's been cruelly beaten because Mr. Wayne did not believe he was working fast enough. It was not the hand of discipline, ma'am, that wielded the whip, but one of brutality and evil. That boy was beaten last night, left outside without food and water overnight and throughout the day, without any care given to his wounds. It's unforgivable!" Abigail's voice quavered with conviction.

Her whole body trembled as she continued her impassioned tirade. "The Bible says that *God created man in His own image; in the image of God He created him; male and female He created them.* It does not say there is more or less of His image in one race than another. All human beings have the same dignity and worth, and I am appalled that such events should occur at a place which I call home!" The pitch of her voice increased which each word that passed her lips.

"I won't ask how you came to see this," Sallie began, her voice thoughtful. "I've heard of slaves being whipped, but I've never been exposed to the sight of it. As slavery has come to an end, I suppose such a form of discipline should also."

"We've always been removed from such goings on," Mary admitted, her hands folded in her lap and her gray eyes damp with regret. "There's always been a way things were done. We never really questioned it."

"I can't stand by silently," Abigail declared in a rush. "Please allow me to send Lizzie to tend the boy's wounds. And please—*please!*—don't allow such treatment to continue here! I only hope my father is as unaware of these whippings as you and I were. But he will be informed, and I will beg him also to see that things are changed."

"Now, now," Sallie's silver brows drew together sharply. "I'll advise you to proceed with caution and respect. We've been very tolerant of your histrionics, but I will not have you telling us what will be done. You may submit your opinions to us trusting in our affection for you, but do not overstep your place."

"Yes ma'am," Abigail replied contritely. On her lap, Sprightly meowed and Aunt Mary gasped in surprise.

"Is that a cat you're holding?" Sallie's voice cracked in startled amazement. "In my parlor?"

"I'm sorry, I forgot I had her with me. She's lame, and I take her outside with me for walks," Abigail explained.

"Will wonders never cease?" Sallie muttered under her breath, shaking her head in disbelief. "You are a most unusual girl."

"I admire your spirit and your heart," Mary interjected, a smile curving her wrinkled lips. "Now run and get Lizzie. And we'll deal with Mr. Wayne."

"Thank you!" Abigail sprang to her feet, thankful that her confidence in the aunts hadn't been misplaced.

"Please send your father to see us, once you've spoken to Lizzie," Sallie added.

Abigail ran to do as she had been told. Her father was startled by her sudden appearance in the library, where he was bent over a ledger. "Please go and see the aunts right away," she gasped out. "I'm going to help Lizzie bind the wounds of a boy beaten by Mr. Wayne. I've told the aunts, and they've summoned you."

Coming to his feet, a peculiar smile shaped Irving's face. His forehead wrinkled as he said, "You are determined to right all the wrongs of the world, aren't you my dear?"

"Whenever I can," Abigail affirmed, spinning on her heel to hurry after Lizzie.

When she reached the quarter, she found Lizzie kneeling beside the youth. Sam remained by his side, comforting the boy with his presence. Lizzie could not free his wrists from the irons, as only Mr. Wayne had the key, but she put salve on the skin to ease the wounds caused by chafing against metal.

Ruth had come with her, carrying a bucket of water, and together they dampened cloths and tenderly ministered to the angry welts which crisscrossed the boy's thin back. Abigail pressed her fist to her lips, tears moistening her cheeks.

"My name's Mark," the boy told her, grimacing as the raw

cuts began to bleed afresh. "You did what you said, bringin' help. But I sure hope you ain't bringin' more trouble on your head and mine."

"I hope so, too," Lizzie agreed. "But I reckon that Mr. Wayne done met his match," she gave Abigail an approving nod.

That evening, after supper, Abigail sought out her father. He was smoking his pipe in the library and appeared to have been waiting for her. He indicated for her to take a seat.

"How could you let this happen here?" she demanded without prelude, still standing. "You cannot tell me you did not know."

"Please sit down, Abigail," Irving instructed. He looked tired.

Abigail lowered herself onto the armchair which faced his desk, her eyes begging him to offer an explanation she could believe.

He sighed, leaning back in his chair. She waited for him to speak, watching as he puffed thoughtfully on his pipe.

"I suppose you have more courage than I do," he finally admitted, rubbing his balding head. "I came here from Baltimore to manage the *finances* for the estate. It wasn't my place to tell anyone how to manage the slaves any more than it was my place to tell them how to manage the fields or the livestock. I knew that overseers were often harsh, but I turned a blind eye to it, pretending that because it wasn't something I witnessed or condoned, I didn't have to confront it. I was wrong. And I'm proud of you for taking a stand today."

While she could understand her father's predicament, she was thankful he didn't try to shrug off his failure to act.

"Will things change?" she wondered, remembering Mark's fear that she had only made things worse for him.

"The Aunts have assured me that Mr. Wayne would be called to a meeting with them this evening. He is probably in the old wing right now, hearing that he must change his ways as overseer if he intends to stay on. If he values his job, things will change."

Chapter Twenty-Six

As Charlie regained consciousness, he pushed himself up onto his elbows. Looking around, he saw that the fighting had ended, but the field of budding spring grass was littered with blue and gray uniforms.

Tentatively, Charlie reached up to touch the left side of his head. It was sticky with drying blood. Pushing himself upright, he saw a puddle of red where he had lain. He felt light-headed and weak, but he was alive. A cursory examination indicated that he had sustained no further injuries.

The attack they had been anticipating had finally come, and with a vengeance. The fighting had begun five days ago, at Lewis' Farm, then White Oak Road, Dinwiddie Courthouse, and yesterday, at Five Forks. General Grant, empowered by their continued success, had ordered the Union Army to a general assault at dawn that morning, April second, which would end the ten month stalemate at Petersburg.

Despite being weakened by illness and desertion, the Rebels forces which remained had fought tenaciously. And even though the field where he lay was quiet now, Charlie knew the day's fighting was far from over.

The Second Maryland Infantry, attached to McComb's Tennessee Brigade, Heth's Division, had defended the earthworks between Indian Town Creek and Burgess Mill. They had held the line valiantly until they were overwhelmed by Wright's seven brigades. The attackers pushed through and quickly took Fort Davis, but McComb's men counterattacked and were able to reclaim it. Their victory, however, was short lived as within twenty minutes, it had fallen back into the hands of Wright's men.

It was in the course of this fierce attack that Charlie had felt a sharp sting bite into his left temple, followed by a rush of warmth over his cheek and ear. Around him, the bayonets glinted in the early morning light and the air grew thick with the gun smoke. The frightening cry, which they called the Rebel Yell, echoed in his ears, along with the grunts and groans of men straining against one another in combat.

He felt the earth tilt beneath his feet as his vision began to fade, and as he staggered forward, he could only think, "Don't fall on your bayonet." And he pushed the musket away from himself as he toppled to the ground, landing face down on the muddy field.

Perhaps it had been a mercy that he had appeared to be dead to the Union soldiers who had swept over Heth's division. The bruises and aches throughout Charlie's body indicated that the attackers had trampled over him as they continued their charge. He moaned as he shifted into a sitting position, observing the carnage around him.

To his right, a corpse stared vacantly into the sky, eyes open, his face torn by a bayonet and his chest ripped open by the force of a musket ball. To his left, a similar sight greeted him. And in the midst of these men rendered forever silent, the wounded hobbled and limped toward the medical tents visible on the far end of the field. To one side were the Confederates; to the other, the Union.

Charlie closed his eyes. Not only had the effort of sitting up made his head swim, he felt a deepening ache grow in his chest at the carnage which surrounded him. Some of these men lying dead upon the ground in Federal blue, he was responsible for killing. In the heat of battle, there was a vicious law at work within each man, a heart pounding rhythm of survival and a warrior's thirst for the blood of his enemy.

It was only in the aftermath, in the pathetic display of human wreckage and busted limbs, that reason returned. And with it, grief and horror at the desecration and waste of life.

If indeed there was sacred value to human life, then who would carry the burden of guilt for so many deaths on this one day, in this one place? If all the souls which had been severed from their physical bodies in the course of the last four years were to cry out as one voice, what horrible earth-shaking sound would they make?

Who decided that when war was declared, one life mattered less than another? That a Yankee's life meant less than a Rebel's, or a Southerner's less than a Northerner's... or that a white life meant less than a black? If Abigail's beliefs were true and sound, and God had breathed life into all mankind from His own divine being, then were they not all equally sacred? And was God even now weeping in the heavens as He looked down at the violence men enacted against one another?

Charlie was jarred from these musings as he heard a sound of movement nearby. Looking up he saw a Yankee soldier with a canteen walking toward him. He offered it without regard for Charlie's gray uniform.

Charlie accepted the water with a nod of thanks.

Nearby, he heard a familiar voice speak. It was Prentiss, lying wounded on the ground. "Excuse me," he was asking of another Union officer bearing a canteen, "is the Sixth Maryland nearby?"

The soldier knelt down in front of Prentiss to give him a drink. "Yes. We belong to that regiment. Why do you ask?"

"Then you should know my brother," Prentiss replied, wincing in pain. His leg was badly injured where he had been struck by a shell fragment above his right knee.

"What's his name?" the Marylander inquired.

"Captain Clifton K. Prentiss," William Prentiss answered hopefully.

The two Yankees exchanged glances. "We know him. He's our major now. He was wounded today, and is lying just over there."

"I would like to see him, please."

Patting his shoulder kindly, the young man promised, "I'll send word of your request."

Charlie and Prentiss waited until the answer came. The Major's message was: "I want to see no man who fired on my country's flag."

The crestfallen expression on Prentiss' face must have moved the young Colonel, for he called to some orderlies nearby to carry William on a stretcher over to where his brother rested beneath a tree. Charlie watched as his friend was placed alongside his brother, who appeared weak and wore a large bloodstain upon his chest.

The Union major glared at his Confederate brother, but William only offered a smile in return. And even at a distance, Charlie could see the quiver of softening in Clifton's expression just before he reached out his hand. As the brothers grasped one another, the past was forgiven and tears love and regret rolled down their cheeks.

Wiping roughly at his own damp cheeks, Charlie gained his feet. He swayed slowly, then straightening himself, began making his way over and around the dead and wounded who lay in his path, to the far side of the field. He had no intention of being taken prisoner again.

He thought of the letter he had written with Roberts' help and hoped that it had made it into the right hands, and would somehow find its way back to Laurel Hill. One day, he hoped, he could find a way as William had to thaw the ice around his brother's heart.

Arriving at the medical tents, Charlie stared at the mayhem. Those with the more severe wounds were still waiting on the field to be carried in for treatment. Still, the tents were filled with men like Charlie, who were well enough to transport themselves. The nurses and orderlies were working quickly to evaluate the needs and manage the high volume of injured.

Charlie waited outside the tents for over an hour with a growing number of wounded before he was finally examined. A young man knelt down in front of him and gave him a quick look over.

"Only your head?" he verified.

"Yes," Charlie affirmed. "I think so."

The nurse's sleeves were cuffed to his elbows, and like his shirt front, were stained with blood. He dabbed at the side of Charlie's head with a damp cloth to ascertain the extent of his injury.

"You got lucky," he said. "Bullet grazed you." He reached into the basket resting beside him and retrieved iodine and a swab. Once he had applied the brown liquid to the wound, he procured a flask of whiskey from the basket. "I'll need to give you a few stitches," he explained.

Charlie took a swig and ground his teeth together while the needle moved in and out of his skin. Once the cut had been sewn, the young man obtained a roll of linen bandages, wrapping it slowly around Charlie's head.

Then writing Charlie's name, rank, and injury in a ledger he carried, the nurse announced, "Heth's division has retreated to Sutherland's Station, last I heard. You should try to catch up with them. We need every able-bodied man we can find," he thumped Charlie on the shoulder before he turned to the next patient.

Thus dismissed, Charlie went in search of nourishment, finding only water and a bit of hard tack. A wagon load of men who were deemed fit to return to duty were assembling and Charlie was sent to join them.

By the time he had been reunited with his division, it was late in the afternoon. He was relieved to learn that Roberts was still alive and well, and was quick to assure everyone that his own injury wasn't as bad as it looked with his head swathed in bandages. Unfortunately, most of their battalion had not been so fortunate. Their numbers had been tragically reduced.

Lieutenant General A.P. Hill, commander of the Third Army Corps, had also lost his life that morning, shot by Union stragglers while he was en route to Heth's headquarters.

Their situation was dire. General Lee had resigned to losing Richmond and Petersburg and sent word to President Davis that he and the cabinet should evacuate and take the Richmond train to Danville, Virginia. The Confederate Army would retreat under cover of night, crossing over the Appomattox River by various routes and assembling at the small town called Amelia Court House.

Unfortunately, Brigadier General Miles had pursued Charlie's division to Sutherland's Station, where they had gathered to defend the South Side Railroad. Heth managed to regroup four brigades to fight, but the weary Rebels were no match for their attackers and were forced into another retreat. Charlie was kept to the rear of the lines due to his injury, and he was grateful for the reprieve.

Miles captured nearly a thousand Rebel prisoners before they slipped away, reducing their numbers yet again. As far as Charlie could tell, the war was already over. Lee just wasn't ready to admit it yet. More men would have to die.

~

"*Abigail!*"

Sitting up in bed, Abigail blinked. It was her father's voice calling to her through the closed door.

Springing from the bed, she slipped her silk kimono over her nightdress and cinched the waist. Opening the door, she saw her father holding a newspaper in his hand.

"What's happened?" Her blood turned to ice even as her heart slammed heavily against her ribs. "Is it Charlie?"

"Richmond and Petersburg have fallen. His name isn't listed among the casualties, but that's no guarantee. Get dressed and come down to the library and you can read the report for yourself."

Nodding, Abigail closed the door and quickly donned a day dress. Twisting her hair up into a chignon, she pierced it with a handful of hairpins then covered it with a snood, hoping it would suffice for the time being. Then racing down the stairs, she hurried into the library.

Her father sat at his desk, bent over the paper, his expression grieved. He puffed his pipe slowly as he read the account. Acknowledging her arrival, he surrendered the paper. Abigail pulled up an armchair beside him and began reading over the account.

It was a crushing military victory for the Union, which of course meant that there had been a great loss of life sustained by the Rebel army. President Davis had fled Richmond, and after its capture, President Lincoln had toured the city and the Confederate White House, even going so far as to take a seat behind Davis' desk.

The capital of the Confederacy had been taken, large portions of it set ablaze. Lee's army had retreated during the night, sparing the heavy bombardments which the city might have sustained if it had not been surrendered.

"How much longer can they hold out?" Abigail whispered, praying that Charlie would not be killed now in the final hours of the war. It was tragedy enough that men should die such violent deaths at the hands of their own countrymen, but somehow it seemed even more horrible that they must die in this way when peace seemed just on the horizon.

"Not much longer," Irving sighed.

The list of dead and wounded was long, but incomplete as always. And in an effort to invalidate the sovereignty of the Confederacy, the newspapers were forbidden to use the acronym C.S.A. behind the names of Rebel soldiers reported. As Abigail scanned over the list, she recognized the names of several men she knew from the Eastern Shore.

It was no longer a question of *if* they would know someone who was killed, but rather a question of *whom* it was they had lost. She shook her head as she read the name George Wright, hoping against hope that it was another man with the same name—as it was very common name—and not Mariah's husband.

"I'll be glad to see it end, I just wish it didn't have to come like this," Abigail admitted.

"What's this?" Margaret appeared in the doorway, immaculately stylish as always. "What's happened?" she asked as she joined Abigail on the settee, her gray skirts rustling.

Irving recounted the news report to his wife. She shook her head sadly. "We'll all be glad when it's over. Even the South. No one wants to see this butchery continue. It's so wearisome and heart-breaking with everyone walking around in mourning. It almost makes me feel guilty when I wear lively colors. Especially today... I just couldn't," she smoothed a hand over the somber fabric.

Abigail paused, feeling guilty for having forgotten. Today marked the ninth anniversary of Jeanine's death. Had it really been so long since her sister had died?

"Jeanine," Irving said quietly. "We all miss her." Abigail suspected that he too had forgotten, distracted by the war news.

Margaret nodded quietly, and Abigail was relieved that they weren't reprimanded for not having remembered. Reaching over, she took her mother's hand and gave it a gentle squeeze. It was in moments like this she remembered that her mother had been a different person before Jeanine's death. Losing a child had been more than Margaret was able to bear.

Her mother offered her a sad smile, and Abigail wondered why it was that some were made gentler with grief, while others felt they must harden to keep from letting those they loved too close. It would not make another loss any easier to endure, it only hurt the ones she feared losing.

Harris had been only a child when Jeanine passed. He could not share in their grief, for to him Jeanine was only the name of a young girl in a portrait on the drawing room mantle. He had no actual memories of her, only stories recounted on days like this, when the buried recollections were resurfaced and shared as a tribute to a life which had ended far too early.

Even for Abigail, sometimes it seemed that Jeanine was no more than the stories told and retold each year as the time passed and the distance between the events and the present lengthened. It was unsettling to think that a lifetime could fade away like mist, remembered only by those who had known you. And once they too were gone, it was as if you had never been.

But the very transience of life was in part what made it so precious. Every day must be wisely spent, for no one knew when it would be the last. Every breath was a gift.

Please keep Charlie safe, she prayed. *Bring him back to those of us who love him. Remind Jeremiah, as I have been reminded today, of the frailty of life. And let that reality prompt him to forgive while there's still time.*

Chapter Twenty-Seven

The air was thick with emotion, and a silence appropriate to the solemnity of the occasion had fallen over all present. Charlie's throat constricted with grief and humbled pride as he joined the procession in the official surrender ceremony. There were only about forty men remaining of the Second Maryland Infantry to lay down their weapons in this symbolic act of capitulation.

While Charlie had suspected that this day would come, like so many others, he had clung to an irrational hope that this conflict would have a more positive outcome. But the odds had not been in their favor and the unrelenting Union would see it no other way.

The retreat from Petersburg to Amelia Courthouse had not been unhindered. The Army of Northern Virginia was weakened and on the run, and Grant was determined to press the advantage. Wagons of provisions had been burned; artillery captured; and more men lost in a series of small skirmishes as well as larger engagements.

The Second Maryland had been fortunate enough to be spared from the fighting. Charlie was grateful, as he wasn't sure he had much more fight left in him.

The final breaking point had been a series of battles which erupted around Saylor's Creek, and the systematic destruction of more trains carrying rations for the war-weary soldiers. Almost eight thousand men were killed, wounded, or captured. The army had lost about a fifth of its remaining forces. Those who remained were exhausted and without supplies.

General Lee, upon seeing the survivors fleeing the battlefield, had thought the whole of his army had dissolved. And while there remained men of courage still ready to fight, they were at such a disadvantage that Lee was forced to confront the moment he had once said he would rather die than see.

For the sake of his faithful men who still followed him, for the sake of the South he loved, he must meet his adversary in humiliation and admit defeat.

On April 7th, Grant had initiated communication with General Lee, stating that surely now he must see *"the hopelessness of further resistance"* and surrender in order to prevent *"further effusion of blood."* He invited Lee to meet with him to this end, but Lee did not believe that the time had come for such drastic measures, although he admitted interest in knowing what the terms of peace might be.

The following day Grant made it clear that the Confederate officers and men must lay down their weapons and concede; Lee refused to meet unless it was to discuss terms of peace, and not absolute surrender.

But by April 9th, Lee realized that he had no other recourse and a meeting was arranged in Appomattox Court House at the home of Wilmer McLean, an unfortunate soul whose life had been disrupted with the first battle of the war at Bull Run, and who had moved one hundred and twenty miles away in the hope of escaping further involvement. It was Palm Sunday.

Feeling deeply the gravity of the moment, General Lee had dressed in a fresh uniform with a red silk sash tied about his waist, and a jeweled sword with which he had been gifted while abroad. His celebrated foe arrived mud-spattered, in a uniform which could hardly distinguish him from a private. It was rumored that Grant sported a headache that morning, though if his reputation held true, it was more likely a hangover.

A ceasefire was called while the generals discussed the terms of surrender. Grant's proposal was generous, and without much alternative, Lee felt that he must accept. And so, the Army of Northern Virginia—the most powerful of the Confederate Armies—agreed to lay down their weapons in exchange for a full pardon.

They were to be paroled and allowed to return to their homes with any private property they had with them, including horses. Officers were allowed to retain their side arms, and perhaps most generous of all, the hungry men would be fed from Union rations.

Charlie's parole form was tucked into the pocket of his shirt beneath his coat. It would allow him to travel safely home, without fear of arrest or harassment. A printing press had been set up at a nearby tavern, Clover Hill, and was in continuous use until such time as every one of the over twenty-eight hundred Rebels were given their paroles.

This was not the official end of the war, but all present knew that it marked the end. There were still Confederate forces fighting elsewhere, but they would soon follow General Lee's example and military resistance would cease. How they would all come together again as one nation, Charlie could not begin to imagine. But he was encouraged by the kindness they had been shown in the terms of surrender.

Now, three days later in a formal act of submission, the Confederate Army made their way down the muddy road to lay down their muskets, pistols, flags and drums, which had been such a part of their lives for the last four years. Charlie's heart was heavy. Beside him, Roberts' shoulders slumped in dejection. Their feet dragged slowly as they approached the army in blue gathered to witness this final disgrace.

Just then the bugle sounded and the Union soldiers of each regiment shifted their weapons from "order arms" to "carry," in an unexpected salute. Instead of jeering their defeated countrymen, they honored their valiant fight. Tears sprang to Charlie's eyes.

In response, the surrendering men were given the order to return the salute, in a corresponding show of honor to their conquerors. The only sounds to be heard in the silence were those of the shifting arms. The atmosphere of mourning and reverence was not unlike a funeral procession, and Charlie felt a stab of grief as the flag he had followed so many times into battle was folded and laid upon the ground.

With the same discipline they had followed to this point, the Confederate soldiers executed the manual of arms procedures for stacking their weapons. With military precision, they arranged their rifles in groups of four, bayonets interlocked and pointing to the sky. The finality of the action resonated within Charlie as he stacked his musket for the very last time.

For him, at least, the war was finally over.

~

Something had happened. As Abigail rode through Centreville in the carriage, en route to Laurel Hill to visit Clara, the streets were teeming with people who seemed to be in a state of high agitation. Some laughed while others cried; some rang bells and waved American flags, while others stared at copies of the newspaper with faces ashen white.

As she neared the Courthouse Green, Abigail called to Abel

to stop the carriage. Climbing down, she approached an older woman sitting on a bench, a newspaper resting in her lap, while the tears streamed down her face.

"Excuse me, ma'am," Abigail said gently as she sat down beside her. "Can you tell me what has happened?"

"Lee surrendered." Her voice was hollow with disbelief and sorrow.

Abigail exhaled slowly, trying to grasp the full ramifications of this simple reply. *General Lee had surrendered the Army of Northern Virginia.* The gaiety around her swirled into a hazy blur. The Southern Cause was lost; but the killing could finally come to an end.

"What—" She paused, her voice coming out in a breathless squeak. "What of the Rebels? What will happen to them now?"

"Paroled. Sent home," the woman replied, her gazed fixed blankly ahead of her.

Abigail's heaviness lifted. *Charlie could finally come home!*

"You are not pleased by this news?" she observed.

Fresh tears trailed down the woman's lined face. "My boy was killed one day too early," she said. "One day…"

"I'm so sorry," Abigail rested her hand over the grieving mother's. "I'm truly sorry."

With a nod, the woman stood, clutched the newspaper against her chest, and disappeared into the riotous crowd. On the corner, a young boy was hawking newspapers. Abigail stopped to purchase a copy before continuing on her way.

Upon arriving at Laurel Hill, she rushed up the walk to the door. It immediately swung open, but it was not the dark face of

Phoebe who greeted her, but Clara herself.

"You've heard?" she asked Abigail, her face flushed and her eyes bright.

"I have." Abigail followed her into the house. "Just now, as I came into town."

"Jeremiah and Mr. Turner are on the back porch," Clara took Abigail's hand and led her into the parlor. "They are both just sitting there, speechless! I don't think either one of them knows quite what to think."

"Did you hear that the Rebels have been paroled, free to return to their homes?" Abigail wondered if Charlie would dare after the last meeting with his brother.

"I have... but there's no guarantee we'll ever see Charlie again," Clara said aloud what Abigail feared most.

She blinked away tears at the thought. "I saw George Wright listed dead after the battle of Petersburg. It wasn't...?"

"It was," Clara affirmed.

"Poor Mariah." The surrender had come too late for her as well.

"What is the response in town?" Clara wondered.

"I would say both jubilation and mourning," Abigail answered. "I should go. Your husband will not be in the mood to entertain today. Besides, although I'm sure my father has already heard, I'd like to take this paper home to him."

"I'm sorry you took the trouble to come only to turn around. Would you like something to eat or drink before you go?" Clara offered.

"No, but thank you," Abigail assured her. She paused, then faced Clara certainly. "He will come home, Clara. Charlie *will* come home. I know it."

"I hope you're right. I'm not sure which brother needs it more than the other."

"We must pray that God will move in both their hearts. If I should hear from him, I'll let you know, and—"

"If I do, I promise to send word to you immediately," Clara promised, pulling her into a tight embrace.

~

The morning of April 13th, a handful of men from the Second Maryland Infantry began their journey home. Many chose to stay in Virginia rather than returning to their home state, invaded and overrun with Unionists.

Those who felt the pull to return home, regardless of what they may find there, bade farewell to their officers and to the men of the Tennessee Brigade with whom they had made friends. The air of tragedy which had hovered over them the day before was replaced by eagerness. Many had left wives, children, or sweethearts behind, whom they had not seen since entering service.

Charlie knew that he could not return to Laurel Hill, but he longed for the Eastern Shore. Roberts kindly invited him to remain at his house in Queenstown until he was able to make other arrangements.

"Won't your wife mind?" Charlie worried.

"I'm sure she'll just be glad to see me home safely," Roberts assured him with a smile, his spirits much higher now that a homecoming was on the horizon. "She's staying with her parents, but I should think they wouldn't mind putting you up for a bit."

For Charlie, thoughts of the Eastern Shore were bittersweet. It was the only place he had ever called home. And Abigail was there, waiting for him. Although she had sworn her affection was not diminished by the knowledge of Charlie's greatest mistake, he dreaded further conversation on the subject and could not shake the horrible weight of unworthiness which rested heavily on his shoulders.

And what of Jeremiah? Could he one day achieve the same peace which William Prentiss had made with his brother, Clifton?

There were almost three hundred miles separating him from his brother. Charlie would take the time to think. And pray.

While they traveled through Virginia, they were treated kindly by residents who offered whatever food and lodging they could spare. Many times as they walked along the roads, carriages or wagons stopped to offer transportation for as far as they were going.

The spring breeze that stirred Charlie's hair beneath his kepi hat reminded him of last April, when he had made his way from Southern Maryland to the Eastern Shore by water, and then on foot. Had it only been one year ago? So much had happened. So much had changed.

Reaching up to touch the scab which marked his temple where the bullet had blazed a trail along his scalp, Charlie thought how lucky he was to be alive. He could have died a thousand times over since enlisting in the Confederate Army in the spring of 1861. Last year, he had come close.

When so many had died, it felt like a privilege to be among those left standing. Although he may not have a warm reception to return to as Roberts anticipated, as least he was alive. He had no idea how Irving Sterret would feel about Charlie's interest in his daughter, whatever Abigail may desire. But as long as he could put one foot in front of the other, he would not give up hope.

"I'll never forget the first day I saw her," Roberts was reminiscing as they made their way down a winding dirt road bordered by fields where farmers were at work with their plough. "Harriet was the prettiest thing I'd ever seen in a pink dress with a white lace collar, and I told myself right then that I would find a way to win her heart."

Charlie half-listened as Roberts reminisced about the bygone days when he had courted his wife. They both knew that he was a different man now after four years of living as a bachelor, under military discipline, learning to kill fellow human beings as if they were crows in the field. Not a one of these veterans returning from war was the same man he had been the day he left. Beneath Roberts' ramblings, Charlie sensed both his eagerness and his apprehensions. Four years was a long time away from one's wife.

They spent their second night on the road in a barn, offered by a farmer who served them supper on the front porch. "My son's on his way home," the lady of the house had told them. "And I hope someone will give him a meal and a roof over his head."

Charlie and Roberts rose at dawn to continue on their way. They had walked for nearly two hours when they passed a roadside pub which smelled of biscuits, sausage, and gravy. As they neared the building, they heard a commotion within, though it did not seem of a violent nature.

Cautiously entering, Charlie scanned the room. It was a newspaper which seemed to be the cause of the hubbub. Approaching the proprietor, Charlie asked if the gentleman accepted Confederate dollars and if they could take breakfast there.

Once seated, they turned to the table beside them to ask what news had brought such excitement. Charlie imagined another Rebel army had surrendered, or in defiance, another battle had been fought.

A man with a bristly beard which reached the top button of his shirt and sported eyebrows equally notable, took in their Rebel uniforms and announced victoriously, "The tyrant is dead!"

"What? *Lincoln*?" Roberts exclaimed.

"How did he die?" Charlie asked, wondering if the strain of the last five years had contributed to his sudden death.

"Murdered," the grizzly Virginian replied. "Assassinated at Ford's Theatre while watching a play."

The fellow beside him, thin as a reed and apparently less prone to growing facial hair, was happy to supply the details. "Shot in the back of the head by an actor, who jumped down onto the stage after he'd done it and shouted, '*Sic semper tyrannis!*'" He raised his fist in the air as he quoted.

"Thus ever to tyrants!" his friend translated with equal fervor. Charlie had heard it before, as it was the motto of that state.

"Was he caught?" Roberts leaned forward, and Charlie waited to hear the answer. It was a shocking act of daring and foolishness. The likelihood of the assassin precluding capture and subsequent hanging was slim.

"Not yet," the big bearded fellow grinned. "He didn't act alone. Another assassin attacked Secretary Seward at the same time. Slashed his throat. Don't know if he'll pull through."

How ironic that only five days after Lee's surrender, as the bloody war finally ground to a halt and the Union was restored, President Lincoln should be shot. It was miraculous that it hadn't happened sooner. And as tragic as the news was, it came as no surprise.

If you wished to disrupt a government, killing its leaders was usually an effective method. The Union had intended to assassinate Jefferson Davis and all of his cabinet members in March of 1864 with just such a hope. However, the messenger delivering the signed orders, Ulric Dahlgren, was killed outside of Richmond and the plot came to an end. It was since referred to as "the Dahlgreen Affair," and was denied by the North as a fraud.

"The President's been killed," Charlie repeated, still trying to grasp the implications. The Vice-President would have to be inaugurated into office. The Union government would be reeling from the blow for a while, just as the war came to an end and the decision was being made how to deal with the secessionist states.

The burly fellow slammed his fist upon the table, his eyes blazing. "Justice has been served, I'd say. And not too soon, either."

His companion added with a nod of agreement, " *'Whoever sheds man's blood, by man his blood shall be shed; for in the image of God He made man.'* Genesis 6:9."

Whether or not the assassination had been an act of God's judgment, Charlie couldn't begin to presume. While some would make Abraham Lincoln a saint—and now a martyr—for freeing the slaves, he would also be remembered by posterity as the president who held the Union together at the cost of six hundred thousand of its own citizens. Some might say he left a legacy of freedom; others might call it a legacy of blood.

Chapter Twenty-Eight

I sn't it cowardly to shoot someone in the back of the head?" Harris asked as the family sat around the supper table. "The President couldn't see it coming, and he didn't have any way to defend himself."

"Yes, Harris, it is cowardly," Irving affirmed. "I suppose John Wilkes Booth thought it was the only way to do it, since the President is usually so well guarded. He waited until he had his opportunity and he took it. But when he pulled the trigger, he signed his own death warrant."

Ten thousand federal troops, in addition to detectives and police, had been sent to track down the President's assassin. It was a mystery how he had managed to avoid capture as long as he had, but after twelve days on the run, Booth had been captured.

He and an accomplice had fled as far as Virginia before they were apprehended. Union troops surrounded the farmhouse in which the men were hiding and set it afire. Although his accomplice surrendered, Booth remained inside and in the course of events, was shot in the neck. He lived only a few short hours more, and his last words were: "*Useless, useless.*"

"I don't understand why he waited until the South had lost the war to kill Lincoln," Abigail admitted. "What good could it do? It might have made some difference to the outcome earlier in the war; but now all it can do is deepen the North's animosity for the South."

"I suppose it was a crime of passion," Margaret commented, lifting her delicate shoulder in a half-shrug. "Driven by anger and hatred, spurred by the surrender, he lost his sense of reason and acted upon his feelings."

"Do you think Booth wanted to kill Lincoln because he voiced his support for Negro suffrage?" Abigail speculated.

"Very likely," her father affirmed.

"What's suffrage?" Harris asked. "Wait! I know! It means the right to vote!"

"Very good, darling," Margaret offered her son a doting smile across the table.

"What do you think, Mama? Should they be able to vote?" the boy asked as he scooped another heap of mashed potatoes into his mouth.

"That's not for me to say," she replied stiffly. "And please use your manners."

"Well, I think that they should have the full rights of citizenship," Abigail interjected. "If they are to be free, and to live here among us where they have served and put down roots, they have as much right to be involved in the government as anyone else."

"I wouldn't offer that opinion too loudly," Irving cautioned. "It certainly isn't popular around here."

"And look where it got the President," Abigail's mother reminded her sternly.

"They say this actor, John Wilkes Booth, was the mastermind of the plot and had two other men working with him," Irving commented. "They had planned to kill the President, Vice President, Secretary of State, and General Grant all in the same evening. They thought if they disrupted the government, it would give the Confederacy time to regroup. Booth, however, was the only one who succeeded in his mission."

"Why?" Harris wondered. Abigail noticed that her twelve year old brother's freckles were returning with the spring sunshine. She was saddened to remember that he was the same age as the President's youngest surviving son, Tad Lincoln.

"Well, they say that General Grant was invited to attend the play with Lincoln, but he declined. Otherwise, I suppose Booth would have shot him too. Seward was attacked in his home, recovering from a carriage accident, and they suspect it was the metal brace on his jaw which protected him from a fatal blow. And Johnson's would-be attacker went to the hotel where he was staying, but paused at the bar long enough to get drunk and lose his nerve. And so there you have it," Irving finished.

"What's the platform called that the coffin lies upon?" Harris scrunched his eyebrows as he tried to remember the story his father had read about the President's body lying in state in the rotunda of the Capitol before it was boarded onto a train named the Lincoln Special, which bore a picture of the President upon the front of its engine.

"A catafalque," Irving supplied.

"I wish we could have gone to Washington D.C. to see his coffin," Harris sulked, his curiosity having prompted him to ask his father numerous times before the President's funeral train had carried him away.

"As we were not among his supporters in life, I hardly think it fitting to gawk upon his death," Irving reminded him.

The President's funeral procession would carry his body

over a thousand and a half miles, visiting many of the cities Lincoln had traveled as president-elect. With him on board the train was the coffin of his son Willie, who had died at the White House in 1862 of Typhoid Fever. When the train reached its final destination in Springfield, Illinois, father and son would be buried together in his hometown.

At each stop, the American people would have the opportunity to pay homage to their fallen leader. In some places, the coffin would be opened and thousands could pass by and view the President lying in eternal repose. As the route would carry him only through pro-Union cities of the North, and his casket would remain guarded, there was little risk of the body suffering desecration or disrespect.

"I suppose it's safe to admit it now, since the rebellion has crumbled," Margaret commented, having previously shushed her husband any time he made an admission of his political standing. "But with his assassination, it may be even more dangerous to say so," she reconsidered.

"Perhaps so," Irving acknowledged, patting her hand reassuringly. "We will use caution."

Abigail wondered how many citizens would flock to pay their respects out of morbid curiosity, as Harris had expressed. Even so, thousands upon thousands would stand in line to view the martyred president. There was something about sudden tragedy which inspired the living to immortalize the deceased as a saint, scrubbing away any faults or flaws they had previously observed. Death had a peculiar way of transforming sinners into saints.

After supper, Abigail moved to the front porch with Harris, bringing Sprightly with her to enjoy the last few hours of the day. The sprawling lawn surrounding Bloomingdale was a thick green carpet from recent rains, and flowers were erupting everywhere with fragrant and colorful beauty. Sam bounded around in the yard chasing squirrels which scampered up tree trunks and scolded him from the safety of their perch above.

Since learning of Lee's surrender, Abigail's feet had led her down the lane to the public road more than once, her foolish imagination conjuring fantasies in which she spotted Charlie walking toward her. He was on his way to Bloomingdale, and when he spotted her, Charlie would break into a run, his arms outspread to pull her into an impassioned embrace.

It was romantic nonsense, she knew. But still, every time she passed a window her eyes drifted toward the lane lined with poplars in wishful thinking. Even now, she watched the drive with hope that he would suddenly appear.

Beside her on the wicker divan, Harris was unusually quiet. "What's on your mind?" Abigail prodded her younger brother from his reflection.

Eyes fixed on the horizon, Harris' eyelashes gleamed golden in the evening sunshine. "I know we're living in a dark time in history," he began thoughtfully, "but it's an exciting time too. I'm still young enough to accept the changes that are coming, even to want them. I want Billy and Rufus and all of them to be free, to be citizens, to be able to vote. We have an opportunity to do something that matters, to advocate for them during this time of change.

"I'm sorry for the deaths of the soldiers—all of them—and for Lincoln's death too. But maybe the future will hold something better. And maybe we can have a hand in it," he finished.

Abigail's jaw dropped open. "I believe that if your tutor were here right now, he would be even more impressed by that speech than I am! I must admit I wasn't expecting anything so profound!"

"Well, please don't tell Mr. Reynolds. It would ruin my reputation as a hellion and he'll expect better work from me." Harris' capricious grin quickly turned serious as he added, "I learned that from you, Abby. From watching you insist on the Negroes having warm clothes and being treated fairly."

Eyes misting, Abigail reached over to squeeze her brother's hand. "Thank you, Harris. That means a great deal to me."

~

"*Halt!*" a voice called out harshly from behind the Confederate soldiers as they walked along the muddy road.

Turning, Charlie wasn't surprised to see that it was an officer of the Home Guard.

"Do you have papers with you?" the Union soldier demanded.

Charlie and Roberts procured their parole passes. The officer perused the documents leisurely before returning them. "Was your pre-war residence in Maryland?" he questioned.

"Yes sir," they both answered with as much respect as they could muster.

"Then you'll have twelve hours to report to the provost marshal when you reach your destination. He will want your name and your current address. And as soon as you're settled, you must replace those secessionist uniforms with civilian clothing. That's the law," he pronounced unapologetically.

Offering their nod of obedience, they continued on their way. They walked in silence for a time, waiting until they were out of earshot of the bluecoat.

"I suppose we're lucky they let us return at all," Roberts sighed. "I remember the night I left home, confident that I was going to make a contribution to preserving independence," he scoffed. "Now look at us: the cocksure rebels returning in defeat."

"At least we can say we stood up for a cause we believed in. We didn't cave or cower. We stood strong to the end," Charlie replied. "In that much, our consciences are clean."

"At least in that much," Roberts agreed.

"I guess it was just as well that Maryland wasn't allowed to secede," Charlie mused. "Who knows what her fate might have been, or what might have happened to our homes and families. I can honestly say I doubt there is a single soul who could have predicted how this struggle would have ended.

"I for one thought we'd fight a few battles, make a show of strength, and prove that the Confederacy should be permitted her sovereignty. In my mind, it would all be settled within a year and then somehow my life would return to the way it was before. I guess we were all naïve fools."

"I can promise I never thought it'd be four years before I saw my wife again!" Roberts agreed. "I can't say I would have joined if I had known what the war would demand from me. But it's all done now. I'm glad to be done with the military—the training, the fighting, the killing. I'll be happy to settle into a peaceful life and raise a family. A quiet life sounds like paradise to me now!"

"Will you return to your living as a clock maker?" Charlie wondered.

Roberts shrugged. "I have no idea how I will be received in

town. I'll have to wait and see. We lived above my shop before the war. Now, I have nothing."

Charlie nodded. They were all beginning again with nothing. He had no intention of imposing upon Harriet's parents for more than a few nights. As soon as he could find a paying job, he would see what accommodations he could secure for himself. Even if it meant mucking stalls and sleeping in a hayloft.

Before reaching Queenstown, the returning soldiers stopped to bathe in a creek, rinsing the sweat and grime from their bodies and clothes as best they could. Using the grooming kits they had carried with them in the war, they shaved their stubbled beards and trimmed their hair. They wanted to be as presentable as possible under the circumstances.

They were stopped again by a Union soldier upon reaching the small town. After reviewing their parole passes, the mustached soldier's eyes widened and he exclaimed, "Isaac Roberts! Is that you? Welcome home!" He extended his hand and gripped Roberts in a firm handshake.

"Thank you, Porter," Roberts' eyes grew damp. "It's good to be home."

"Have you been informed of the requirements?"

"I have. I'll report to the provost marshal once I've had a meal and changed my clothes," Roberts assured him.

"Where are you headed now?" the Union soldier and a former friend, inquired cordially.

"To see Harriet. I've just now arrived from the front," Roberts replied, his eagerness evident in his wide smile.

"I see," Porter answered hesitantly. "Well, I wish you the

best of luck," he tipped his blue kepi hat and strolled away. Rather briskly, it seemed to Charlie.

Roberts glanced nervously down the street at his in-laws' house. Life had not stood still while he was away.

As they approached the clapboard house, Charlie saw a woman sitting on the porch in a rocking chair. She cradled an infant in her arms, her full skirt of pale pink cotton swaying around her ankles as she moved to and fro.

"Harriet?" Roberts' voice broke as he ascended the stairs in his worn gray uniform. He removed his hat and stared down at her with joy and adoration.

Charlie waited on the sidewalk. He could see why Harriet had stolen Roberts' heart so completely. She was lovely.

Harriet wore her blond hair pulled back from her face, and she stared up at Roberts with wide blue eyes. "Isaac?" she whispered in disbelief, slowly coming to her feet.

"I'm home," he reached for her hand. "I'm here with you at last."

He glanced down at the child in her arms with questioning eyes. "Has little Millie had a baby?"

Harriet exhaled slowly. "No, this isn't my sister's baby... She's mine."

Charlie winced at the pain which registered on Roberts' face. He released his wife's hand and staggered back as if he had been struck. "Yours?"

"You were gone for so long!" Harriet's eyes pooled and tears began to run down her delicate features to drip onto the soft wool blanket swaddling the babe in her arms. "I was so alone, Isaac. You have to understand! I didn't know if you would ever come back."

"But you couldn't wait?" Roberts' voice was strained as he forced the words out. "Who...?"

She had the decency to look ashamed. Harriet bit her lip, glancing over at Charlie in embarrassment. "Remember that you had asked Jack to look after me while you were away?"

Roberts nodded, his lips compressing in a desperate attempt to control the mixed rage and grief which boiled inside him.

"We fell in love," she whispered. "I'm sorry. So sorry."

"My best friend," Roberts shook his head, closing his eyes against the pain of looking at her with another man's child in her arms. "Why didn't you or Jack tell me before I came home? You wrote to me..." his voice broke.

"I didn't want to be cruel," Harriet answered, but the regret in her eyes said she realized now she had been exactly that. "I'm so sorry, Isaac. I'd like to secure a divorce with you and marry Jack as soon as possible. He's the father of my child now."

She reached for him, but Roberts stepped away from her. "You were what kept me alive, Harriet. How could you do this to me?"

"I still love you, Isaac," her voice was husky with emotion and beneath her golden eyelashes, her blue eyes were sincere. "I didn't want for it to happen this way. I was weak. I didn't know how to be alone. One day, I hope you can forgive me."

Roberts' face was stony as he stared down at her. Then, turning on his heel without another word, he strode down the steps to where Charlie waited on the sidewalk. With nothing else to do, they returned the way they had come, exiting town.

Charlie remained in step with Roberts. He could only

imagine the emotions which roiled inside his friend. While he was grateful to be with Roberts in his hour of loss, Charlie was sorry to have been witness to such a personal moment of humiliation and heartbreak.

When they had reached the public road and were out of view of the townsfolk, Roberts allowed the tears to course down his cheeks. His jaw was clenched, and Charlie could hear the force of his teeth grinding against one another. At his side, his fists were clenched. Charlie wished there was something he could say to ease his friend's suffering. But he knew there wasn't. This was a wound Roberts would carry with him for the rest of his life.

Chapter Twenty-Nine

When I was in Maryland after I escaped Point Lookout, I stayed with a miller's family. Unless you know of another place to go, we could inquire if they would let us stay in their barn. I can't promise anything, as I don't know how Phillip Allen feels about me now. I'm assuming he's learned that I shot my brother, and he may turn us away," Charlie admitted.

"We could camp out in the woods," Roberts muttered, his shoulders slumped.

"If we have to, we could," Charlie agreed. "But if we offer to work for them, maybe we could be fed real food for a while, even if it's just their scraps."

Roberts shrugged. He was so despondent that Charlie felt he must take charge of their welfare until the jilted man could find a reason to live again. All those letters Harriet had sent him… and all the while she was involved with the very man Roberts had entrusted with her welfare.

As they traversed the road which led to Mount Mill, they were forced to pass by Bloomingdale. Charlie's eyes swept the miles of green lawn which surrounded it and the lane lined with poplars. The last time he had seen it, the grass had been brown and withered and the trees had been like hulking gray giants in the darkness of the December night. Now spring had brought it back to life. The grass was a thick green carpet, and on the outspread limbs of the trees, leaves fluttered in the breeze.

It was an impressive mansion, with its two story white portico and dentil trim contrasting against the red brick. Set in the middle of the great expanse of lawn, it was the picture of elegance and grandeur. But for Charlie, its appeal was the woman who lived within it: Abigail, with her dark, flowing hair and her sweet smile, her gentleness and her strength. She had said that her affections for him were unchanged. That was the flag of hope he carried, giving him a reason to put one foot in front of the other.

Charlie had nothing to offer her but his love. But for a woman like Abigail, Charlie suspected that would be enough. They could always move south if need be, live as tenant farmers until they could buy their own land. Or like so many others, they could travel west to build a new life there. Either way, they wouldn't have much, but what did they really need but one another?

Of course, Mr. and Mrs. Sterret might not see it that way. And that was the one obstacle Charlie feared they might not be able to overcome.

As they turned down the winding drive leading to the Allens' cottage, Charlie felt a twist of anxiety in his gut. He remembered Philip and Nancy with fondness and hoped that had not been turned against him. He realized now that he had left without giving anyone a chance to either ask questions or offer understanding. In his shame and anger, he had simply run away.

"So you don't know how you'll be received?" Roberts asked, as if sensing Charlie's growing apprehension.

"No, I don't. It might be best if you wait in the yard while I knock on the door. They won't be unkind; I'm just not sure that they will be welcoming."

Roberts nodded. His homecoming certainly hadn't been as

welcoming as he had hoped.

As Charlie stepped up onto the porch of the miller's cottage, he drew in a deep breath. For the thousandth time, he wished that he had simply drawn back into the woods that day in Gettysburg and left his brother's fate to God.

Before he had lifted his knuckles to the door, it swung open and Nancy stared at him with open mouthed shock. Her red hair was pinned back, but was just as tousled as he remembered. "Johnny!" she exclaimed, pulling him into a surprisingly strong embrace and transferring the flour which dusted her plump cheek onto his.

He'd forgotten entirely that he had gone by a different name while staying with them. "Mrs. Allen!" he exclaimed.

Suddenly he was pounced upon by two small boys. "Henry! Thomas!" he scooped them up and hugged them tightly.

The little girls, Ada, Helen, and Susan, gathered behind their mother's skirt and peered up at him with shy smiles. Charlie tipped his hat at them. "Ladies," he winked, and was rewarded with high-pitched giggles.

"Come in! Come in!" Nancy shooed her children away from the entryway and invited Charlie inside.

He paused. "I'm afraid that first I need to tell you three things. First off, I have a friend here with me," he glanced back at Roberts, who tipped his gray hat in greeting.

"Well, bring him in too!" Nancy insisted, waving Roberts forward.

"First, please let me finish," Charlie said, not wanting to take advantage of her hospitality. "My name isn't Johnny—"

"Well, I know about all that," she interrupted. She reached

out to take hold of his arm. "I heard the whole story, and it doesn't change a thing. So don't worry about it one bit. We can talk later, if you wish. But for now, please come inside. And your friend too."

Charlie felt relief sluice through him as he nodded for Roberts to join him. They were overwhelmed by the children, who bombarded them with questions while Mrs. Allen set to work preparing a feast. Philip was on a delivery, but was expected home for supper.

When he returned, his welcome was as warm and genuine as his wife's had been. "You've come back to us!" the big man boomed joyfully.

"Only for a while," Charlie assured him, "until other arrangements can be made."

"Nonsense! Stay as long as you wish—both of you!" Philip insisted. Charlie was deeply touched by their generosity, especially as the couple was not exactly well off.

"Thank you," Charlie gripped his hand warmly. "Thank you."

Roberts stepped forward and offered his hand in appreciation as well. "Thank you for your kindness. As soon as I can, I plan to find employment and secure housing. Until then, I am indebted."

"Nonsense," Nancy huffed as she pulled a pan of cornbread from the oven. "I'd throw him out on his duff if he didn't take you both in." She tossed Charlie a wink and grinned.

Even Roberts couldn't suppress a chuckle. Philip grinned and nodded in acceptance of Roberts' gratitude.

As they gathered around the table, Charlie observed

Roberts' expression as he took in the bounty set before them. Honey glazed ham, smoked venison, sweet potatoes, squash, green beans, cornbread, and sourdough biscuits weighed down the roughly hewn table. Nancy had cooked for them as if they were her own sons returning from the war.

Charlie blinked back tears as Roberts stared in awe, his stomach rumbling loudly. Charlie had enjoyed a reprieve from the simplicity of military rations, but for Roberts, this was the first time in four years that he had enjoyed such a meal. They ate until they were stuffed, which was far less than it would have been if their stomachs hadn't shrunk from want of proper meals.

While staying with the Allens before, Charlie had shared a room with the boys. But tonight Henry and Thomas were instructed to sleep on the floor in their sisters' room for the sake of their guests. Charlie had maintained that they would be just as happy to sleep in the barn, but neither Nancy nor Philip would hear a word of it.

Roberts insisted on taking the floor, leaving the tick mattress to Charlie. After they had lain down for the night and the oil lamp had been extinguished, Roberts spoke quietly into the darkness.

"I'm glad you brought us here. They're good people. I don't know what I would have done."

"They are good people... I'm awfully sorry about your wife. You didn't deserve that." Charlie wished he could give this Jack a good thrashing for his part in it.

"I guess four years is a long time to wait," Roberts replied quietly. "She was so young, and we hadn't been married very long before I left. I thought Jack could keep an eye on her, keep her safe. I suppose it was just too much temptation."

"What has Jack been doing while you were away—other than seducing your wife?"

"Staying out of the war, running the family business. I guess everyone in town knew what was going on, and Porter didn't know how to warn me. I guess it's just as well I didn't know any sooner. I might not have been able to endure the war if I hadn't believed I had a reason to survive."

Charlie had to agree. Perhaps Harriet had been wise to spare Roberts the heartbreak while he was fighting for his life. "True enough. And now you're here. You never know what your future may hold."

"No," Roberts agreed, though his voice was heavy with resignation. "I don't."

~

Abigail turned at the sound of hoof beats on the lane. Sam, who had been lazing in the sun at her feet, lifted his head at the sound. On her elbow, a basket dangled with the cat Sprightly nestled inside.

She had been staring into the distance, watching the workers as they watered the plants in the cornfields. She envied their purpose and activity. Here she stood, with nothing more to do than watch.

Turning to glance down the lane, Abigail saw a single rider on horseback. She peered from under the brim of her straw hat as he rode toward the house. The sun was high overhead, and she blinked against its brightness as she studied the young man curiously. He wore a brown bowler, which cast his face in shadows, and a tweed coat covered his plaid shirt. He was likely a farmer or laborer coming in search of work. Ruthie or Esther would fetch her father from the library to see what he wanted and determine what should be done with him.

Abigail turned back to the fields which spread out for miles before her, the cornstalks not yet reaching the knees of the dark-skinned men and woman who walked down the long rows. The sun was warm, but a breeze blew over the workers to cool them in their labors. Above, the sky was cerulean blue dotted with downy clouds.

Feeling eyes upon her, Abigail glanced over her shoulder at the young man. The breeze kicked up and set her dark hair whipping like a mane around her shoulders. She pulled the curls back from her face, observing that he had dismounted and was standing beside his horse, watching her.

It couldn't be! She took a few hesitating steps forward, straining to make out his features beneath the shadow of his hat. But there was something about the way he stood that touched a chord in her heart. She placed the basket on the ground.

"Charlie?" Abigail whispered hopefully, her steps quickening.

That was all the encouragement he needed. He removed his hat and ran toward her, meeting her halfway. Just as in her fantasies, his arms were outstretched and the tenderness in his eyes said more than words ever could. Charlie enfolded Abigail in an embrace, his arms strong around her waist as he pressed her against him.

Her arms encircled his neck, and she buried her face into his shoulder. She could hardly believe he was real, solid beneath her touch. Sam bounded around them in circles, barking in elation.

"Abigail," Charlie breathed her name into her ear, his voice raw with emotion. The smoothness of his cheek against hers was the sweetest sensation she had ever known. Such a small and innocent contact, and yet there was something intimate about the touch of his skin against her own. Abigail sighed as she pressed into him.

"You came back!" she whispered. "I'm so glad you came back!"

"I've been aching to see you again," he confessed, drawing back to study her face, his hands gripping hers.

Abigail studied the planes of his face, the blue of his eyes, the sandy hair which tumbled over his forehead. A dark scab at his temple caught her eye and she gasped. "Are you all right?"

Charlie nodded. "They say a miss is as good as a mile. The bullet grazed me, that's all." He leaned down to rub Sam's head, the dog's tail wagging wildly in excitement.

"I'm so glad you're safe!" she clung to his hands tightly. Her chest was so full of joy that she could hardly breathe.

"Abigail, I'm so sorry I left in such a hurry that night... Did you receive my reply to your letter?"

She shook her head, wishing that she had. "Actually, I sent you two. What did you say?"

"Well, I hope we'll have plenty of time to talk later. Is your father angry with me?" he worried.

"No. I mean, we would like to know more about what happened. But we trust you to be able to explain," she gazed up at him, hoping he could see the truth shining in her eyes.

A half smile shaped his lips. He was so handsome, so dear to her, and the warmth of his hands over hers was so sweet, that she felt dizzy with happiness.

"Thank you for believing in me, Abigail. You and your

father have shown me more kindness than I can ever repay." He lifted her hand to his lips and kissed it. She felt herself go weak in the knees.

She was quickly revived as she heard the front door of Bloomingdale slam closed. Charlie promptly dropped her hand and took a hasty step to widen the distance between them.

"Charlie!" Irving cried as he ran toward them. Harris followed on his heels.

Mr. Sterret gripped Charlie in a firm handshake, then pulled him into a hug. "It's a relief to see you again!" he admitted. "We've been worrying about you since the day you left. Very thankful that you've made it safely back to us!"

"I'm grateful to be here," Charlie admitted, leaning down to hug Harris as well.

"We've missed you!" the boy declared.

"Thank you for your warm welcome," Charlie appeared genuinely moved.

"Where are you staying?" Irving wondered.

"With the Allens," Charlie replied. "Only until I can find employment. I have a fellow soldier who's returned with me, and he is staying there for the time being as well."

"Will you visit Laurel Hill?" Irving asked tentatively.

Charlie sighed wearily. "I'm torn. I long for home more than I can say, and I miss my father dearly. But I fear my presence would not be well received. You were there the last time my brother and I met. It didn't go well."

"No, it didn't," Irving agreed. "But you can't give up."

Abigail regretted her father's arrival if only because it had prompted Charlie to release her hand. But she was thankful for the rapport between the two men she loved most, and for the affirmation her father offered the man she hoped to marry.

Charlie breathed heavily, straightening his shoulders as he closed his eyes to bolster his courage. "I want to explain to you all why I did what I did. I'm sorry I ran away that night instead of facing you, but I feared Jeremiah had turned you against me. I was so burdened with my own guilt, I couldn't bear to face your judgment."

Irving gripped his shoulder. "We didn't judge then, and we don't now."

"We've never lost faith in you," Harris insisted with boyish devotion.

Charlie tousled the lad's hair as he smiled his gratitude. Then his eyes sought Abigail's as he continued with his confession. "I knew that if Jeremiah were wounded, he would be moved away from the front lines to safety. Not only that, but he would be discharged and sent home. I did it to protect him from more serious harm. I had only seconds to act, and no time to think before I did. I saw my brother, and I knew I had the power to send him home. So I aimed and pulled the trigger. But once I did…" he bit his lip as tears glistened in his eyes. "I felt sick with regret."

Abigail exhaled in relief and sympathy. What a horrible thing all these men had been through.

"I knew it!" Harris exclaimed jubilantly.

Irving squeezed Charlie's shoulder in acceptance of his confession. "Sometimes our intentions are better than the actions they prompt. Explain this to your brother. Make him hear you."

"He's only so angry because he loves you so much," Abigail added, remembering her conversation with Clara.

"He has every right to be angry with me," Charlie admitted, staring down at the ground beneath his feet. "And no reason to forgive."

"You are his brother and you acted out of love," Abigail insisted. "That is reason enough."

Irving nodded in agreement. "Don't give up. Never give up."

"Thank you, sir. For everything." Charlie's voice was thick with emotion.

"You're welcome. Now, why don't you take my daughter for a walk while I inform Lizzie that she has a guest for supper," Irving replied. "Harris, come with me."

"What about Mrs. Sterret?" Charlie worried. "I'm not sure that she'll be pleased to entertain a Rebel soldier."

With a twinkle in his eye, Irving retorted, "I'm guessing she's going to have to get to know you sooner or later. It might as well be sooner."

Abigail's heart leapt at her father's words of approval. She glanced over at Charlie and saw the embarrassment and pleasure on his face at Mr. Sterret's words.

"Now, go on," Irving shooed them off, grinning as he walked around the perimeter of the house to the kitchen entrance. Harris followed him reluctantly.

"Your father is an exceptional man," Charlie commented, offering Abigail his elbow.

Slipping her hand through the crook of his arm, Abigail

agreed.

"I don't have anything to offer you," he began softly, ashamed.

Sensing what he was going to say, Abigail's pulse quickened and her cheeks flushed.

"I only know that I can't live without you. If your parents would give their blessing, I can't promise to support you in the style you are accustomed. We would have to start over. Go south or west, and build a simple life together. It won't be easy..." his voice trailed off, and his feet slowed to stop.

Turning to face her, Charlie gently cupped her cheek in his hand. "You deserve so much more than I can ever give you. I fear I don't even have the right to ask."

There was a depth of pain in his blue eyes that pierced Abigail to her soul. The devotion in his expression, the sweetness of the way he cherished her, were the greatest gifts she could imagine a man bestowing on a woman.

Covering his hand with her own, she whispered, "I would follow you to the ends of the earth, Charlie Turner. I could never be happy without you, and that's the truth."

His handsome face was transformed with joy at her words. Grabbing her hand, he pulled Abigail into the shade of a towering oak, guarding them from prying eyes within the house. Feeling the scratchy bark against her back, Abigail tilted her chin upwards as her arms wound around his neck and pulled him close.

He kissed her as if she were his greatest treasure, with exquisite tenderness and respect. Abigail wove her fingers into his hair, feeling the strength of his passion and restraint as he deepened the kiss.

She had no idea what her future might hold, but as long as Charlie was in it, she could face it with hope.

Chapter Thirty

"Why do I get the peculiar feeling that I've been left out of something?" Margaret demanded after Charlie had taken his leave.

She had handled herself well throughout supper, suppressing any curiosity she may have felt and putting on the face of a gracious hostess. But now that their guest had departed, Margaret wanted answers.

She pinned her husband with an inquisitive stare. "It appears that you, Abigail, and even Harris, have made this young man's acquaintance before. And yet I have never even heard of him!"

If Irving had introduced Charlie as Johnny Harris, she might have remembered that he was the young man Irving had arranged to work with Philip Allen at the mill. But he had introduced their unexpected guest by his actual name, Charlie Turner, and although Mrs. Sterret had certainly heard of him, she did not have an association with him.

"Yes, we've had the opportunity to interact," Abigail replied vaguely as her father shifted his feet uncomfortably.

It had been apparent to anyone with eyes that there was more than mere friendship between the two young people. Margaret raised her delicate eyebrows. "That was obvious," she huffed. "What I would like to know is how you and your brother came to be so familiar with him, when I do not recall ever being in his company." She leveled her gaze at Abigail's father, who had suddenly become fascinated with a spot on the Persian carpet.

"Irving Harris, I demand an explanation. I do not like being left in the dark," she insisted. Her wide lavender skirts swayed as she took a step toward her husband, forcing him to meet her gaze.

Abigail watched her father nervously as he considered his options. Guilt was written plainly on his features, as well as wariness of confessing the truth. He finally sighed, his shoulders sagging, and gestured for them all to join him in the drawing room. "Let's sit down," he said, and Abigail and Harris glanced at one another anxiously.

When they were all seated in the drawing room, Margaret folded her hands in her lap and stated, "I'm dying of curiosity. Please put me out of my misery."

"Last spring there was a wounded soldier found on the grounds of Bloomingdale. We took him in and brought him back to health," Abigail's father began matter-of-factly.

"I never knew about this!" Margaret exclaimed.

"Yes, well it was a secret," Irving confessed, "because he was a *Rebel* soldier."

"*What?* I declare, Irving Harris, I don't know what you were thinking!"

"The aunts knew and gave their permission," he was quick to inform her. "We only kept him here until he was well enough to be relocated to Mount Mill."

"Ah. So that was the distant relation who showed up needing a job," Margaret recalled, shaking her head as the pieces fell into place in her mind.

"I didn't realize the aunts knew?" Abigail interjected.

"It wouldn't have been right to put Bloomingdale as risk without their knowledge," Irving answered. "I felt that they must know."

"So, am I to understand that everyone knew but me?" Margaret appeared genuinely injured.

"I found him, Mama," Abigail tried to explain, "and I could hardly leave him to die. And I told Papa, but Harris found him accidently."

Margaret nodded slowly, as if trying to comprehend why she should have been excluded.

"Darling, you would hardly have been agreeable if you had known," Irving said quietly, "and the boy needed looking after."

"I see. And now which one of you would like to explain what is going on between this Rebel and my daughter?" Her eyebrows arched in challenge.

"Mama, the war is as good as over and it won't matter anymore that he was a Rebel. Charlie's a good man, and..." Abigail wanted to say that she loved him, but she lost her nerve, and her gaze slipped to her hands knotted in her lap.

"And I suppose that you approve of this romance," Margaret turned accusing eyes to her husband, "since you invited him to eat with us this evening."

"It is character that matters most, my dear," he replied in a soothing voice. "Charlie's honest, hard-working, and he genuinely loves our daughter. I see no reason not to approve."

Abigail offered her father a grateful smile, but her mother

was not to be so easily put off.

"Who exactly is this young man, and how does he intend to provide for Abigail?" Margaret demanded.

"His father owns Laurel Hill, in Centreville." Irving hesitated, "He hasn't asked for her hand yet, as he doesn't quite have all of his affairs in order. He has only just returned from the war."

"I should hope he hasn't asked for her hand yet," Margaret sighed. "And until he has his affairs in order and can answer that question satisfactorily, I don't think we can even consider it."

Abigail leaned forward, hoping she understand what her mother wasn't saying. "But if he *could* answer the question to your satisfaction, you *would* consider it? Even though he's a Rebel?"

Margaret's eyes were tender as she reached for her daughter's hand, sitting next to her on the settee. "I want your happiness, above all else. And if he is the means to your happiness, than I would agree. *If, and only if,* he can adequately support you. Besides, when the war is over once and for all, there are going to be an awful lot of Rebels returning home and trying to settle back in. If the Federal government isn't going to hold it against them, I see no reason why I should."

"Oh Mama!" Abigail blinked back tears of gratitude. "I never thought you'd even consider it!"

"Well, it's pleasant to know that I'm not always so predictable," Mrs. Sterret retorted with a smile.

~

The sight of the house caused an ache to throb in Charlie's

chest. The white structure stood just as he remembered it, just as it had through all the years of his life. From his vantage point beside the barn, he could see the family graveyard in the rear, where his mother was buried, and beyond it, the peach orchard.

He was home, and yet he felt every bit like an intruder. In order to avoid meeting anyone he knew until he was ready, Charlie had bypassed the town of Centreville and arrived at Laurel Hill by following a course through the woods and fields. And now that he had reached home, he had no idea how to proceed.

When the prodigal son returned home, his father had been quick to forgive his sins and call for a celebration dinner. But Charlie's sins were far worse than the prodigal's; and even the prodigal's brother hadn't rejoiced at his return.

Charlie feared that no one would welcome him with open arms. And the thought was like a knife in the heart. This was the place which he held most dear, and these were the people whom he loved the best.

He stood outside, gazing with longing at his family home as if he were an outsider and not a son of Francis Turner. But his life's choice had made him an outcast. First he'd enlisted with the Rebels, then he had shot his brother. If his father knew, it had probably broken his heart. He would never let Charlie step foot into the house again.

Scrubbing his face with his hands, Charlie took a deep breath and offered up a prayer for wisdom. What should he do now that at long last he stood upon the grounds of Laurel Hill?

Just then he heard barking and turned to see a big black and white dog approaching him cautiously. Charlie reached out his hand for the animal to sniff and spoke gently to assure it he was no threat. Just then, a young Negro appeared around the corner of the barn behind the dog. He was tall and lanky, but still recognizable. Silas had been just a boy when Charlie had left for the war. Now he was more of a young man than a child.

"Hello. What can I do for you?" Silas asked, signaling the dog to sit by his feet.

Charlie studied Silas' face for signs of recognition. Seeing none, a plan formed in his mind. "Is Mister Jeremiah in?"

"Yes sir," the Negro lad replied.

"Can you please tell him that there is a drifter here to see him, looking for a job?"

Silas' dark eyebrows narrowed suspiciously, but he nodded and ran off in the direction of the house, his dog following on his heels.

Charlie retreated into the shade of the barn, concealed from view until he chose to reveal himself. His heart began to pound against his chest and his palms were slick with sweat. Remembering the last meeting he'd had with Jeremiah left him shaken. Why had he dared to come here?

Through the crack between the hinges of the barn door, Charlie watched his brother's purposeful approach. In place of his left hand, a hook protruded from his sleeve. His dark beard was tinged with gray, and his hairline was thinner than Charlie remembered it.

Jeremiah's eyes scanned the area, looking for the drifter who had summoned him from his midday meal. He called out, "Hello?" as he neared the barn. He paused at the entrance to allow his eyes time to adjust to the dim lighting within.

"Jeremiah," Charlie said softly as he stepped forward, removing his hat and crumpling it against his side.

For a brief second, he thought it was joy which flickered in his brother's eyes. But perhaps he had only imagined it.

"What are you doing here?" Jeremiah demanded, his voice harsh and far from welcoming.

Cursing himself for his foolish hope, Charlie stilled. Would enough time ever pass for Jeremiah to forgive him? *"Explain to your brother. Make him hear you,"* he heard Irving Sterret's words echo in his ears.

He had to try.

"You have every right to hate me," he began, faltering at the steely contempt which stared back at him from his brother's eyes. "And I will leave after I've spoken my piece."

"Then make it quick," Jeremiah snapped.

"I only wanted to send you home," Charlie tried to find the words, but the fury and hatred which confronted him muddled his thoughts. "I knew you would be discharged, and—"

Jeremiah closed the distance between them, his hook raised in the air. "This was your way of doing me a favor?" His voice shook as he stared at the metal apparatus which had replaced his hand. "I'm sorry if I can't thank you for it."

"Better your hand than your life," Charlie countered, his voice pleading for understanding.

"You nearly *took* my life," Jeremiah hissed angrily. "I was lucky to survive, and no thanks to you!"

"I'm sorry, Jeremiah! I've regretted it a million times over, but I can't take it back. All I can do is try to make you understand that I did it because I love you. I wanted to get you out of the war, and it was the only way I knew how!"

Jeremiah's eyes narrowed to slits and his eyebrows furrowed into one long, jagged line. "You really expect me to believe that? Do you have any idea how ludicrous that sounds? You shot me, for God's sake!" He held up his hand. "They had to saw my hand off, it was so badly shattered from your act of kindness!" His right hand fisted against his thigh.

"I'm sorry, Jeremiah, I just—"

"You've said your piece. Now leave," Jeremiah said coldly, turning on his heel and striding away.

~

A breeze blew through the open window, stirring the curtains and bringing with it the fragrance of flowers blossoming in the yard. Abigail faced her great-aunts across the narrow space of the sitting room, her mind racing with questions.

"I was very surprised to learn that you knew about our Rebel soldier," she began tentatively. "I was under the impression that it was a secret."

"Well, it was!" Aunt Sallie exclaimed. "Only your father, you, and Mary and I knew about it. Well, and a few of the slaves knew too, of course. But that was all."

"I suppose you didn't want me to realize that you supported the Southern cause in whatever capacity you could," Abigail continued carefully, not wanting to offend her aunts when she was very grateful for their kindness.

"The fewer people who know a secret, the more likely it is to be kept," Mary replied.

"Then you knew who I had fallen in love with," Abigail concluded.

"Of course we did. But we didn't know he'd gone back to fight in Petersburg. It took quite a while for us to figure out where to send your letter," Sallie grinned at her own cunning.

"How did you find out?" Abigail wondered.

"You don't need to know all our secrets," Sallie retorted, her silver eyebrows arching proudly. "Let's just say we learned from a mutual friend."

"I see," Abigail answered thoughtfully.

"All our efforts have availed to nothing," Mary sighed. "Three more Confederate generals have surrendered. The war is as good as over, and everything will change."

"Did you hear that Jefferson Davis has been locked away at Fort Monroe?" Abigail asked, having read in the paper that he'd been captured in Georgia after President Johnson placed a large bounty on his head.

"We did. And that poor woman, Mary Surratt, has been arrested along with eight other alleged conspirators of the plot to kill Lincoln. I hate the thought of a woman being hanged, and I certainly hope that President Johnson will not let it come to that!" Sallie proclaimed.

"I declare the whole world has gone mad," Mary sighed. "You heard about the Paca murders, I presume?"

Abigail had heard. Two men had been killed while digging post holes for fencing. The property in question had been Edward T. Paca's portion of the estate on Wye Island, but when he joined the Confederate Army, his land was confiscated and sold at auction. His uncle, William Paca, was the purchaser.

Edward's brother, John, and another uncle, Alfred Jones, resented this situation and set about fencing in a portion of the confiscated property. William and his three sons brought shotguns to the site and demanded that the fencing operation cease immediately. In the ensuing altercation, both John and Alfred Jones were shot and killed.

"Yes, I think everyone has heard. In fact, there's such an uproar over the murders that troops have been sent into Centreville to maintain peace. They've set up quarters at the courthouse, just as they did before the war," Abigail related. "I know that the returning Rebels aren't being tried for treason, only the leaders of the Confederacy, but there's still so much conflict and hard feelings. Even among family members. I worry about the men who return being able to reestablish their trades and find employment."

"Anyone in particular you're worried about?" Sallie feigned innocence, but her expression was knowing. At the corners of her mouth, her paper thin skin crinkled as she smiled.

"Well, I did have a certain young man in mind," Abigail admitted sheepishly.

"What are his plans for the future? And shall I presume that whatever these plans are, they include you?" Sallie queried.

Abigail blushed. "He hasn't *exactly* asked me to marry him yet, but we have an understanding. He wants my parents' blessing, of course, and they cannot grant it until they know how he will support me."

Mary nodded, her white hair gleaming in the afternoon sunshine. "Fair enough."

"Yes, I do understand, and quite agree..." Abigail sighed. "I know that practical matters such as housing and money do matter in the long run—"

"I should say so!" Sallie interrupted.

"Only I wouldn't care if we did go west and live in a log cabin," Abigail finished passionately.

"Oh my! I hope it's not as desperate as that!" Mary exclaimed.

"I have an idea," Sallie's eyes brightened, "but I need to know more about Charlie's life before the war. Tell me what you know about him."

"He grew up on his family's farm, Laurel Hill, in Centreville. He's the younger of two brothers. He's at odds with his family now, but even so, I'm sure his older brother is set to inherit the farm."

Mary and Sallie's eyes met in silent communication. "So, you would say he is accustomed to hard work out of doors? And is familiar with managing sla—laborers? And in a manner you agree with?"

Abigail wrinkled her brows, not understanding where this line of questioning was leading. "Yes, on all counts, I would say."

"Well then, I think I will have to talk to my estate manager about hiring this young man. As it turns out, we are not very pleased with our current overseer. Despite repeated reminders, Mr. Wayne seems unable to remember that we live in a new era and our workers are to be treated with a certain amount of respect. It sounds to me like this Charlie Turner might be the perfect solution," Sallie concluded.

"You would offer him a job here, at Bloomingdale?" Abigail could hardly believe her ears. Her mother would certainly not refuse Charlie if he was employed at Bloomingdale!

"Your father spoke highly of him, and Philip Allen seemed

pleased with his work at the mill. I am in need of a man with a strong work ethic, moral character, and both wisdom and compassion in leadership. And if he has personal motivation to seeing Bloomingdale thrive, all the better," the elder of the two aunts proclaimed.

Abigail flew from her seat and paused to kiss first Aunt Sallie's cheek, and then Aunt Mary's. "Oh, I just can't find the words to thank you!" she cried, tears of joy blurring her vision.

Chapter Thirty-One

It sure is good to see you 'round here again. Even better to have you comin' in through the front door," Lizzie called as she appeared around the corner of the house.

Charlie startled at the sound of her voice, looking up in surprise. "Thank you. I much prefer it myself!" he replied. "They let you out of the kitchen?" he teased.

The little black woman grinned. "Only to go to the smokehouse. You stayin' for supper?"

"I'm not sure," Charlie admitted. "But I certainly wouldn't turn down an invitation."

Lizzie chuckled. "I'll make extra, just in case."

The front door swung open, and Ruthie stepped out onto the landing. "Come on in, and I'll tell Mr. Sterret you're here," she stated.

"If I can, I'll drop by the kitchen for a visit later," Charlie called to Lizzie. She waved and grinned in reply.

Charlie had an uneasy feeling that Ruthie had been watching for his arrival, and had been instructed to intercept him before he met with Abigail. Based on all the information he had gleaned on the lady of the house, he had feared Margaret Sterret would not be as accepting of him as her husband was.

Overhearing his arrival, Irving emerged from the library with a welcoming handshake. "Ah, Charlie! Come have a seat. I need to talk with you."

Despite the warmth of the greeting, Charlie apprehension deepened. If Abigail's mother had put her foot down firmly against him, he had no hope of ever winning Abigail's hand.

"As you know, I am here in the role of manager for Misses Sallie and Mary Harris," Irving began.

Charlie's worry now had confusion for its companion. He offered a polite nod in response.

"I have been asked by the owners of Bloomingdale to offer you the position of overseer here," Mr. Sterret stated bluntly, grinning at Charlie's apparent consternation.

He had braced himself to be asked not to return to Bloomingdale, and instead was being offered a position. Charlie's mind couldn't quite process the unexpected turn of events.

"I'm not sure I understand," he admitted, flabbergasted.

Irving's forehead creased as he broke into an even wider grin. "Life is full of surprises, my boy! Now, let me explain. For some time now, the Harris sisters have had concerns over the way that their current overseer has been treating the laborers. It was our Abigail who brought some of the these situations to their attention, and although Mr. Wayne has been given very clear instructions as to what is expected of him, he is unable to change his opinion of how the Negroes under him should be managed.

"When Abigail mentioned to her great-aunts that you were unsure what you would do with your life since returning from the war, and even mentioned the possibility of moving west and living in a log cabin, they thought that it would be the perfect solution for you to replace Mr. Wayne. You have experience with farming, and anything you need to know about the plantation here, you can learn. You obviously worked with slaves at Laurel Hill, and you have a good rapport with Lizzie and Ruthie, which bodes well for your management of our workers.

"And," Irving chuckled, clearly pleased as punch with the idea, "the best part is that Abigail can continue to live at Bloomingdale with her family."

Charlie's head was spinning. It was the absolute last thing he had ever expected. Any niggling concerns he might have about accepting the position were not worthy of consideration in the face of what he was being offered. Not just employment, but a career which would keep him close to home, and would gain him the approval he needed to marry Abigail. How could he refuse?

"Life is indeed full of surprises!" Charlie leaned back in the plush armchair and ran his hand through hair absently. "Of course, I'm honored to be offered the job and I'd be a fool not to accept! But I must admit that I don't feel adequate to the task. I'm certainly willing to learn as long you and the Harris sisters know that Bloomingdale far exceeds anything I've been accustomed to at Laurel Hill."

"Of course," Irving brushed away his concerns. "It's a man's character and his willingness to learn what he doesn't know that make him fit for a job. Now, let's discuss your salary."

Charlie listened to the generous amount the Harris sisters were prepared to offer him, along with room and board, and he feared that it was all a dream from which he would awake to find himself in the trenches of Petersburg again. He blinked, trying to grasp the reality of the moment.

"Where do I sign?" he laughed, giddy with shock and

pleasure.

When he had finished the legalities with Mr. Sterret, Charlie was sent to the drawing room to wait for Abigail. Ruthie went to fetch her from upstairs, where Charlie assumed she had been waiting in her bedroom for word that the business had been settled.

She breezed into the drawing room, her wide skirts swaying. "Isn't it wonderful!" she reached for his hands as he stood and leaned in to plant a kiss on his cheek. Charlie was both delighted and surprised by the forward gesture.

"You're assuming I accepted the job offer," he couldn't help but tease her.

Her face drained of color and her mouth dropped open. Immediately Charlie regretted the joke, and drew her close to him again. "Of course I accepted! I'd do anything if it meant I could be with you!"

Abigail sighed in relief as she sagged against him. Suddenly, she planted her hands on his shoulders and stepped back. "That was a cruel prank, Charles Turner! Don't you dare ever trick me like that again!"

"Yes ma'am," Charlie chuckled, enjoying the spark in her eyes. "Will you kiss me again?"

She giggled and stood on tip-toe to kiss his cheek again. Charlie would have much preferred to take her in his arms and kiss her thoroughly, but he didn't dare do so in the drawing room.

"Does this mean that your mother approves?" Charlie asked as they seated themselves chastely apart from one another, she on the settee and he in an armchair facing her.

Her face lit up as she answered, "I could hardly believe my ears, but she said that as long as you have a means of supporting me, she would give her blessing. And then the Aunts offered you a job here!"

Never in his life had Charlie felt simultaneously so unworthy and so privileged as he did in this moment, beholding the unabashed love which Abigail had for him sparkling in her eyes.

"It seems almost too good to be true," Charlie admitted. "Life has been a struggle for so long, it's difficult to believe there can be better times ahead. But I'm hopeful. And I'm grateful. Both to God and to you," he added sincerely. "The day you found me, you did more than just save my life. You brought me back to life."

The blush which warmed Abigail's cheeks and the tenderness in her eyes brought a smile to his face. "You know I think that your aunts were afraid I was going to take you to live in the western wilderness with me," he admitted, "and that's the only reason they offered me the job."

Abigail giggled. "That may be part of the reason. But they wouldn't have offered it if they didn't believe you would be capable of doing it well."

"I am a bit nervous. Laurel Hill is a farm of less than two hundred acres; Bloomingdale is two thousand! I've worked with slaves, but to manage an entire crew of free Negro workers is an entirely different matter."

"But that is precisely why you are the right person for the job," Abigail insisted. "You worked with the slaves at Laurel Hill almost like equals, and you're lack of experience will allow you to develop your own ways without influence from the past. That was Mr. Wayne's downfall. He wasn't willing to accept that times have changed."

Charlie paused to consider her words. Perhaps this was an opportunity for him to take the blessing he'd been given by Eli and Henry and pass it along to the Negro men and women who worked at Bloomingdale. They had chosen to see him not as a white master to be punished for his superior position, but as an equal, a friend in need. They had risked everything to save him.

He was surprised to find that the memory of their sacrifice brought tears to his eyes.

"What is it?" Abigail leaned forward in concern.

"You may remember that when I was at Point Lookout Prison, Negro troops were brought in to guard us. Many of them saw it as an opportunity to take revenge. But two of the men who grew up as slaves at Laurel Hill were assigned there, and it was these guards who devised a means for me to escape. I hope and pray that they were never associated with my absence and punished for it. I owe them a debt I can never repay."

"I know how you can repay that debt," Abigail suggested softly. "We can work together to improve the living arrangements for the Negroes here, and I would like to open a school and teach the children how to read and write. Not only will it enrich their lives, but it will give them more choices for the future. Just because they are not white doesn't mean they should be made to work in the fields."

Charlie nodded in agreement. "In the South, the Freedman's Bureau is working to set up schools. Since Maryland was an anomaly, a slave state that remained in the Union, there aren't programs in place to educate our former slaves. But we could undertake it here, at Bloomingdale. As long as your aunts approve."

"I think they will... They are trying to move into the present, but they still carry some of the ideas from the past."

"The past can be hard to leave behind," Charlie sighed heavily. "I went to Laurel Hill to see Jeremiah. He is no closer to forgiving me than he was in December."

"Did you try to explain?"

"I tried. But he's still not ready to hear me. I'm afraid he's going to hate me until the day he dies," Charlie's voice was raspy with emotion.

~

Abigail couldn't bear to see the pain behind Charlie's eyes. The very next afternoon, she asked Abel to take her to Laurel Hill.

"Did you know that Charlie has been here and spoken with Jeremiah?" she asked Clara as soon as they were settled in the parlor. The small room was charming and quaint, and made the drawing room of Bloomingdale seem unnecessarily extravagant.

"What?" Clara exclaimed. "I had no idea! He never said anything."

On the floor, little Henrietta sat surrounded by wooden blocks and a rag doll. Her smile revealed four perfect little teeth and a sparkle of mischief in her eyes. Her dark hair was wispy, but long enough to be coerced into two little bows on either side of her head. Abigail still thought she resembled her uncle.

"I don't know the details," Abigail lowered her voice to a whisper and leaned in close to Clara, afraid that someone might overhear. "Only that Charlie came to see him and Jeremiah did not respond well."

"Did you ever learn more about what happened?" Jeremiah's wife wondered, her brows drawing together in curiosity.

"I admit it sounds strange to say that Charlie shot his brother as an act of love, but that's what it was," Abigail began.

"What do you mean?" Clara demanded.

"He shot Jeremiah in the hand knowing that the injury would spare him the fight to come, and that it would see him sent home. He did it to get Jeremiah away from the battlefield."

Clara's eyes clouded. "But... I was there to see the aftermath of the battle. It was more horrible and gruesome than anything I could have imagined. Jeremiah had to wait days for treatment, and he could have died of any number of things while he waited for medical help. By the time I arrived, he had endured the amputation of his hand and was just as emotionally scarred as he was physically."

In her jade muslin dress, with her auburn hair pinned back from her face, Clara was such a picture of femininity and grace, it was difficult for Abigail to imagine her amid the atrocities she described.

"I know," Abigail grasped Clara's hand, begging her to understand. "But Charlie didn't know just how devastating that battle would be. He had no way of knowing how long the wounded would wait for treatment. It was a rash decision, and perhaps born of his own desire to be out of the war, he did the one thing he knew would honorably discharge Jeremiah. It was a mistake, and one he's regretted dearly. But at least his motives were pure."

Stunned, Clara could only stare at Abigail. "I admit, that is a bizarre explanation. No wonder Jeremiah had difficulty understanding."

"Charlie's deeply grieved. He loves his brother as much now as he did before the war. Is there nothing we can do to see them reconciled?" Abigail pleaded.

Clara's expression grew thoughtful. "I love my husband dearly, as you know, but I am not ignorant of his faults. His pride can sometimes cloud his judgment. When I went to Gettysburg to find him, he was ashamed of his disability and lashed out angrily at me. After all I had been through to be by his side, I did not react kindly to his ingratitude. I don't know what might have happened if it hadn't been for the chaplain of his regiment, who was able to talk sense into my hard-headed man.

"Jeremiah still corresponds with him. I believe the last I heard, Chaplain Davies had been wounded at Harpers Ferry and was sent home to recover. He lives in Chestertown. If he is well enough to travel, I'm sure he would be willing to come to our aid."

"Will you write to this chaplain?"

"I certainly will. But where should I invite him to meet with the Turner brothers? If I invite Chaplain Davies to Laurel Hill, I'm afraid my father-in-law may overhear and I don't think it's good for his health to witness such a scene. And I don't believe I could persuade Jeremiah to return to Bloomingdale under any pretense."

The women lapsed into thoughtful silence. On the floor, little Henrietta in her starched white dress entertained herself with gurgles and coos as she played with her toys.

"I have an idea!" Abigail suddenly cried out. "Jeremiah wouldn't suspect anything if you invited him to visit Mariah with you. And if I invited Charlie to pay his respects to the widow of

Private Wright, he wouldn't have any reason to decline. Do you think Mariah would mind hosting this meeting when it's certain to be charged with raging emotions?"

"I don't know," Clara answered slowly. "But it's a good idea. I'll call on her tomorrow and inquire. And I'll send you a note with her reply."

"And you think this chaplain can get through to Jeremiah?"

"If anyone can, it's him. We shall have to pray, and pray hard!"

When Abigail returned home, she reported immediately to the library to inform her father of their plan.

Irving was sitting behind his desk, puffing on his pipe as he perused the pages of a newspaper. "Do you think it wise to interfere again, Abby?" he asked skeptically.

"I must do something, Papa. I love him too much not to try."

"Well then, we will hope for the best," he replied, pausing to take another puff from the briarwood pipe. He held up the newspaper. "The war is officially over. The last Army of the Confederate States, led by General Smith, has surrendered in Texas. It is time to for us all to learn how to live in peace."

"Has Mr. Wayne been released of his duties?" Abigail queried.

"Yes, he has. I gave him the opportunity to stay on for two weeks and train Charlie, but he did exactly as I knew he would. He exploded with rage, delivered a great tirade, packed his bags and left in a huff. And I tipped my hat and said to his back, 'Good riddance, sir.'"

Abigail covered her mouth as a laugh escaped. It wasn't

often her father was so saucy.

"Out with the old, and in with the new," he grinned. Abigail suspected that his eagerness was only partially due to his affection for Charlie. The greater part of his joy was in having secured a way for her to remain at home.

"Will you have Charlie move into the overseer's cabin? And how will he know what to do without Mr. Wayne to explain?"

"I believe it best for him to be in the cabin for the time being. At such time that his status here changes, I'll be happy to welcome him into the big house. But for the sake of propriety, I think it wise to have him take up residence in the cabin. He's free to eat with us, should he wish. And as for his knowing what to do, between myself and the men who have worked this plantation all their lives, I'm sure we can have him up and running in no time."

Abigail gazed fondly at her father's creased face and balding head. "Thank you, Papa, for all you've done. For Charlie and for me. I'm so very grateful."

"I'm proud of you, darling," he answered, his expression softening. "You've grown into a brave and compassionate young woman. What more could a father ask for?"

Biting her lip, Abigail decided she may as well reveal her scheme to her father and ask him to have it approved by the aunts. "I hope that you will continue to support my efforts to make changes for the Negroes, and to help them in their newfound freedom."

He sighed, slumping back in his leather chair. "What are you planning now?"

"I'd like to begin teaching the children to read and write.

The adults, too, if they're interested. I would like to teach them how to take responsibility for their lives and their wages, and to learn how to care for themselves so that they aren't dependent on a master to care for them. What good is their freedom if nothing changes?"

"Hmm." Irving straightened, his expression growing serious as he leaned forward and rested his elbows on the sleek surface of the mahogany desk. "There is a tension, you understand, for those of us who own or manage a plantation. We need men and women to work the fields, to bring in the harvest, to tend to the livestock. If you create discontentment in their lives, give them false hope that they can find employment in other avenues, won't they be eager to leave us in search of better things that they aren't likely to find?"

Abigail considered her father's concerns and answered carefully. "I don't want to give them false hope. But I don't think it's fair for them to believe that they have no other options. And their freedom has no meaning if they don't learn how to think for themselves, to manage their money and resources for themselves. As free men and women, they can live fuller lives if they know how to read and write."

Mr. Sterret released a resigned sigh. "I'll talk to the aunts about it. But don't try to overwhelm them with too much change all at once. I have this sinking feeling that you have other schemes cooking on the back burner?"

"Until the world is perfect, there will always be room for improvement," Abigail retorted.

Chapter Thirty-Two

Beneath the shade of an oak which had seen close to a hundred years come and go, Abigail sat with a handful of eager children holding slates and chalk. The evening breeze was refreshing as the June day was hot and humid. The round, gray trunk of the oak tree was their schoolhouse, and its leafy canopy their roof.

The dark-skinned girls and boys sat with their legs folded beneath them, their eyes riveted upon Abigail as she demonstrated the shapes of the letters on her slate and encouraged them to repeat it on their own. She had no experience teaching children how to read or write, and was quite overwhelmed with the prospect. Harris had offered to be her assistant, and he moved from one child to the next, surveying their work and offering praise or correction.

Harris' tutor, Mr. Reynolds, had been kind enough to contribute a primer, and Abigail used it as a guide for introducing the alphabet and its corresponding sounds. Once her students had acquired a basic knowledge, she hoped to convince her aunts to purchase primers for each of them.

The children were curious and regarded the opportunity as the privilege it was, comprehending that they were being offered something which had previously been forbidden to their parents. There was, however, a certain amount of confusion over the value and necessity of the squiggles drawn on Abigail's slate, and the funny sounds which she claimed went with them. In a world which revolved around the four seasons, planting and harvest times, and was deeply rooted in the elemental aspects of nature, the alphabet and phonetics seemed impractical and unnecessary.

But Abigail hoped and prayed that in time they would grasp that through an understanding of reading and writing, new doors would be opened for them. Not only in terms of employment, but in the way reading could enrich their lives and touch their imaginations. At the end of each session, Abigail had the children set their slates aside and listen as she read a story from a book to demonstrate the secret worlds hidden within what appeared to be a lifeless compilation of paper.

She knew that the war had begun and continued for many reasons, noble and ignoble, but when Abigail watched the way Rufus stuck his tongue out in concentration as he drew his letters, Abigail was grateful that at least something good had come from it. When she gazed out at her Negro students, their full attention focused on her teaching, she had hope that they would know a better world than their parents and grandparents had. Not without challenges and resistance, of course, but at least this was the beginning of a pivotal movement to change the social order. And she was honored to play even a small part in it.

It was easier for her to embrace the disintegration of culturally accepted barriers than for her parents or her aunts. While they were moving with the tide, there was still a part of them that was moored in the past, where the lines between the races were definitively drawn. As Abigail spent time with the Negro children, she had trouble understanding where the discrimination originated.

The little girls and boys she taught demonstrated intelligence, kindness, and fear: all of the basic elements of humanity. The only apparent differences she could see were in their skin color and in their education and life experiences. One could be overlooked; the other could be changed.

Charlie had moved into the overseer's cabin and was immersed in an education of his own. Mr. Sterret, along with the Negroes who had worked there for years, were attempting to teach him all that was required to run a plantation like Bloomingdale. Every evening at supper, he reported to Abigail and her family what he had learned. He seemed exhausted and a bit overwhelmed, but invigorated by the challenge.

Sometimes it was easy to forget that he was but an employee and she was only the daughter of an employee at Bloomingdale. They had no ownership or personal investment in it. When the aunts passed, their cousin, Severn Teackle Wallis, was set to inherit. And Abigail didn't resent this arrangement any more than her father did. They were appreciative of whatever opportunities they were given.

They owed much to the generosity of Sallie and Mary Harris. They lived as though they were one of the elite, benefiting from the wealth and social standing of the aunts. And now, because of the position the aunts had given Charlie, Abigail could marry the man she loved without fear of alienating her mother or moving across the continent.

Irving and Margaret had informed Charlie that they would give their blessing if he would work for the Harris sisters for half a year before formally asking for Abigail's hand. She hoped that they would not demand a long engagement. Her mind was already spinning with dreams of a wedding in the spring of 1866, right here at Bloomingdale.

When she had first found the emaciated Rebel soldier with a bullet hole in his gut, Abigail had never imagined the way he would change her life; or for that matter, the way that she would change his. She believed Providence had a hand in bringing them together, intending for them to both challenge and bless one another. Charlie had been so bitter after his experiences in the war and at Point Lookout Prison. And with little wonder.

It was interesting to learn that the commander of a Union Prisoner of War camp in Andersonville, Georgia had been arrested and was to be tried for murder and conspiring to impair the lives of Union prisoners. Abigail had heard horrible things about the way Union prisoners had been treated there, the overcrowding, starvation, and cruelty. Yet those who mistreated the Rebels prisoners were apparently without reprimand.

In fact, Abigail's father had brought it to her attention that Resolution 97 was passed by congress in January of that same year which stated: *"Rebel prisoners in our hands are to be subjected to a treatment finding its parallels only in the conduct of savage tribes and resulting in the death of multitudes by the slow but designed process of starvation and by mortal diseases occasioned by insufficient and unhealthy food and wanton exposure of their persons to the inclemency of the weather...."*

As always, the rules were made by those who wielded the power, and justice and mercy were not always traits of the victors.

It was only natural that Charlie should be so embittered after all he had experienced. But the scars he had incurred in the prison camp and on the battlefield were beginning to show signs of healing. Still, Abigail knew that they had a long road ahead. His wounds ran deep, and it would take time and the grace of God to see them healed.

The festering wound she worried might cripple him forever was one he had in many ways inflicted upon himself. Mariah had agreed to host the meeting, and Chaplain Davies had replied that he would do whatever he could to promote reconciliation between the brothers. The date had been set, and as they waited for the hour to come, Abigail and Clara dedicated themselves to prayer for God to soften Jeremiah's heart and to give Charlie the words he needed to reach his brother.

Abigail found hope in remembering this verse: *"For with God, nothing shall be impossible."*

A surprising incident had occurred as evidence of this truth just two days before. Charlie had related to Abigail that Washington, the stable master, had come to him with his head hanging low and asked for a word.

"What is it?" Charlie had wondered, as the man's behavior was uncharacteristically humble and contrite.

"I needs to ask you forgiveness," the big Negro man had said, still staring at his feet.

"What have you done?"

"When you was here, sir, back when you was wounded and hidin' in the attic, I gave you 'way to the authorities. I saws that Rebel uniform, and I thought you was like them men what want us to stay in slavery. So I thought I'd get you put in jail. And now I knows you, sir, and I's sorry for what I done. You ain't like that at all. You been real good to us, and I just wants to say I sorry." The stable master had ventured a tentative glance upward to gauge Charlie's reaction.

"Ah. I wondered how the provost marshall knew to look here. Well, that's one mystery solved," he'd replied. "It takes courage to admit when you're wrong, Washington. I thank you for trusting me enough to confess, as I never would have known otherwise. Don't worry about it. I've made enough mistakes in my life to have no right to hold yours over your head. Let's forget it ever happened," Charlie told him, extending his hand.

Washington's face had split with a wide grin as he took Charlie's hand and shook it firmly. "Yes sir!"

The black man had paused then, his brows drawing together as he asked, "How come they didn't find you?"

Charlie had answered, "Let's just say I found a way to blend into the woodwork."

Abigail wasn't surprised to learn that the informant had been Washington. What surprised her was that he had chosen to apologize when no one knew he was the one to blame. It was proof of the respect Charlie was earning from the Negroes at Bloomingdale, and just one more reason for her to love him.

~

Charlie glanced over at Abigail beside him in the open carriage. Her profile was set against the afternoon sky, preoccupied and thoughtful. She wore a straw hat with blue and green flowers, which complimented her white dress accented with green oak leaves. She was so beautiful that sometimes Charlie could hardly keep his eyes off her.

Now, however, he studied her with curiosity. She seemed unusually pensive. What was Abigail thinking that her jaw was set so firmly, and her lips pressed together so tightly? Perhaps she was thinking about the Widow Mariah Wright, whom they were calling on to offer their condolences. Her husband, George Wright, had fought with the Second Maryland Infantry just as Charlie had. Although Charlie hadn't known Wright well, as he was with a different company and was several years Charlie's senior, they had fought alongside one another for most of the war.

It could have just as easily been Charlie killed at Petersburg. His hair had grown long enough to cover over the scar which the bullet had traced into his scalp. An inch to the right, and he would have been hit between the eyes, which was likely the intention of the Federal who pulled the trigger. But a slight movement, either of his own or of the man who wielded the gun, had robbed the bullet of its fatal purpose and it had instead only grazed him.

If he had died that day, Abigail would have never known how much he loved her, how much she had changed his life. Like Mariah, she would have had to learn of his death through the harsh and impersonal medium of the newspaper. The letters he had written and sent to Abigail and Jeremiah had been displaced in the chaos of the war's end and the disruption of the Confederate forces. Her last memory of him would have been that fateful December night when he had left in a rage without pausing to give her the time and explanation she deserved.

Thank you, God, for keeping me alive and for all the blessings you've brought into my life. I don't deserve even one of them, he silently prayed. Charlie wished he knew how to communicate these thoughts and feelings to Abigail, but he couldn't find the words. Instead he reached over and took her hand.

She startled at the touch, then laughed at herself. "Are you all right?" Charlie worried.

"I'm sorry, I was just lost in thought."

"So I see. I was just thinking about the Widow Wright, and how lucky I am to be alive and here with you today," Charlie told her.

Abigail gazed up at him and smiled. "I think I may have worn God's ears out praying for your safe return," she laughed.

375

"Now I thank Him every morning."

Charlie lifted her hand and pressed a kiss into it.

"We are blessed," she sighed. "Poor Mariah has been keeping her husband's farm going since he's been away, as well as caring for his mother and his younger sister. Now that he's gone, I don't know how she's going to manage."

"Doesn't she have anyone to help her? A property manager or an overseer?" Charlie wondered.

"I'm not privy to all the details. I only know that many of her former slaves have left, and the overseer as well. She doesn't have the financial means to hire anyone, and she's afraid that she may have to sell. I can't imagine trying to carry such a burden myself," Abigail shook her head sadly.

"How is it the property wasn't confiscated? I thought all property held by Rebels was being seized by the Federal government?"

"The house and properties were willed to George's mother when her father passed. Nothing was put in his name."

"Hmm. I suppose that was good thinking. I am sorry to hear of her predicament, however. I wonder if there isn't something we can do," Charlie wondered.

When they arrived, they were admitted into the house by a very young Negro girl and informed that Mrs. Wright would be sent for. Charlie was surprised that she was not there to welcome them, as their visit had been planned. But he thought he heard voices from the other side of the house, and assumed Mariah was preoccupied with her mother-in-law or George's sister.

After a moment, she appeared in the doorway of the parlor with a bright smile that did not match the sadness in her eyes.

Mariah Wright was younger than Charlie had expected, based on her husband's age. She was also surprisingly petite. Mariah was an attractive woman and wore the black of mourning well, her dark hair pulled back in a chignon and covered over with a snood.

Charlie stood when she entered the room and waited to be introduced while Mariah and Abigail exchanged greetings.

"And you must be Charlie Turner," Mariah turned to him, tilting her chin to look up at him. "I've heard a lot about you, and I'm very pleased to make your acquaintance. I understand that you served alongside my husband?"

"I did, ma'am," Charlie replied. "I'm afraid I did not know him well, but he was a brave soldier and a good man."

"Thank you," Mariah answered, her composure almost slipping at the kind words. She blinked away tears and rearranged her smile. "Please, will you come into the drawing room? The tea has been set up for us there."

Charlie and Abigail followed Mariah down the hallway, where she gestured for them to precede her. As he entered, Charlie had a strange feeling of history repeating itself. For sitting on the settee in the drawing room was none other than his brother, Jeremiah, with Clara beside him.

Chapter Thirty-Three

What is this?" Jeremiah demanded of Mariah, springing to his feet as Charlie entered the room.

Clara took hold of his arm. "It's my fault," she said, her voice surprisingly firm. "You need to reconcile with him, and you know it."

Anger blazed in Jeremiah's eyes as he glared down at her. Clara stared up at him, unflinching.

Jeremiah turned his fury on his brother. "I have no idea why my meddling wife should think I have any interest in hearing a word you have to say to me."

Charlie felt Abigail take his hand. He suspected that she and Clara had cooked this scheme up together. He only hoped it ended better than the first time.

"If it's any consolation, I didn't know you were going to be here either," he told Jeremiah, hoping to ease the feeling that he'd been ambushed.

Clara twisted her hands together at her waist, her yellow print dress swaying as she nervously shifted her feet. "I have another surprise for you, too," she admitted, giving Mariah a nod, who was paused on the threshold. Mrs. Wright gave someone in the hallway the signal to enter.

A white haired old man appeared at their hostess' side, standing almost level with her diminutive height.

"Davies!" Jeremiah exclaimed in shock. But then his bushy black eyebrows drew together as he declared, "You look even smaller in civilian clothing."

The old man ignored the jibe and strode up to Jeremiah, putting one arm around his chest in a fatherly hug as he patted Jeremiah's bearded cheek. "It's good to see you, Turner," he said affectionately.

Jeremiah grit his teeth. "I'd be pleased to see you under different circumstances, Chaplain."

Chaplain Davies then turned to Charlie and offered his hand. "You must be Charlie," he said cordially, seeming completely unaffected by the tension in the room. "Jeremiah's younger brother—the Rebel."

"I'm aware that my wife is to blame, Davies, but this really isn't any of your business," Jeremiah ground out. Charlie was surprised to see his brother behave so rudely to someone outside of the family.

"Well, I'm afraid I'd have to disagree," the little man answered with a half-smile. "I love you, son, and I'm not going to let you throw away something as precious as family without having at least made an effort to intervene."

"You cannot expect me—" Jeremiah exploded, but Chaplain Davies cut him off.

His entire demeanor shifted from friendly to commanding. He drew himself up to his full height of barely over five feet and ordered, *Everyone, sit down.* We're going to talk this out sensibly."

Immediately, the women and Charlie did as ordered. Jeremiah stood defiantly, his one good hand clenched into a fist by his side. The other hand, a rubber prosthesis, held its casual pose.

"I said *sit down!*" Davies insisted.

Charlie watched as his older brother obeyed, though Jeremiah's stony expression communicated his unrelenting attitude. He was only sitting out of respect for the chaplain, not out of any genuine desire to reconcile with his brother.

"Now then," the old man said, lowering himself into an armchair which faced the two sofas on either side of the low table laden with a porcelain tea set. Both their hostess and her servant had vanished, although no one was interested in refreshments after such a charged exchange.

"I understand that you have a legitimate grievance against your brother," the chaplain began, holding up his finger to silence Jeremiah as he prepared to respond. "I think it is safe to assume that we all know and sympathize with your position," he assured Jeremiah, whose lips were a thin white line between his mustache and beard. "But I've also been told that Charlie has offered his sincere apology and has a reasonable defense for his action."

"Reasonable?" Jeremiah's face mottled red as he exploded with rage. "There is no *reasonable* defense for shooting my hand off!"

"Tell me something," the chaplain replied serenely, as if they were having an ordinary conversation, "what happened after you were released from the hospital?"

Beneath his thick, black beard, Jeremiah's jaw worked back and forth before he finally ground out, "I was discharged and sent home."

"If I remember correctly, that was Charlie's intention," Davies' white eyebrows lifted in challenge.

"You were there, Davies. You know what it was like," Jeremiah nearly growled.

"I do." The chaplain turned his blue eyes on Charlie. "It was not your place to play God and decide who should be spared and how they should be saved. Would you agree that you overstepped your place when you made that decision?"

Charlie felt his throat tighten as he heard the condemnation in the chaplain's voice. He had just met the gentleman, but already his respect mattered greatly. Guilt and regret nearly strangled Charlie as he nodded, finally forcing the words past his lips, "I was wrong, and if I could go back and do it differently, I swear I would."

Davies nodded in acceptance of this admission. "It seems to me that you're not the only man I've met who's struggled with surrendering control to Providence. We like to believe that we have a firm grasp on our own life's outcome, or that we can somehow manipulate destiny.

"And while there are some things we *can* choose, there are many things in life which we either *cannot* or *should not* choose. And these must be left in the hands of God."

His voice softened as he continued, "I can't make your brother forgive you. I can only hope that he hears the love and regret in your voice, and that he can see past his own stupid pride to realize he isn't perfect either. He's needed forgiveness in the past. And as we forgive others, in the same way we shall be forgiven.

"Now that all of that has been said, I believe my job is done." Chaplain Davies leaned back in his chair and folded his hands in his lap. "What happens next is between you two."

Charlie took a deep breath. He felt the burden of

responsibility to make amends as he was the one who had committed the wrong. "Jeremiah," he said quietly, waiting until his brother's gaze had swung to meet his before continuing. "You have every reason to hate me. If our roles were reversed, I don't know if I could forgive you. Your friend here is right. It wasn't my choice to make, and I've regretted it from the second I squeezed the trigger."

He held out his left hand, wishing that somehow he could transfer it to his brother's wrist. "If I could remove my own hand and give it to you, I would! I can only appeal to you for forgiveness now because we are brothers, and because I love you," he finished, tears spilling from his eyes and trailing down his cheeks.

The coldness in Jeremiah's expression slowly melted away. He worked his jaw silently, struggling to maintain his aloof facade. But a raw cry escaped his lips as he sprang to his feet, moving toward his brother with outstretched arms.

Charlie met him halfway, encircling his brother in a bear-like grip, pounding him on the back and weeping. Held in an equally ferocious grip, Charlie could hardly breathe, and it took a moment for him to realize that the sound he heard was his brother's ragged sobbing.

When they had paused to take a step back and regard one another with new eyes, the chaplain stepped in between them. He took Jeremiah's cheeks in both hands, then stood on his tip-toes and planted a kiss on his forehead.

Jeremiah shook his head, an amused smile touching his lips.

Charlie cocked one eyebrow as he regarded the peculiar little man. "Is he…?"

"Crazy? Yes, I do believe he is," Jeremiah said, wrapping

his one good arm around Davie's shoulders. "But he's a good man, just the same. Even if he never minds his own business."

"I know I owe him a debt of gratitude," Charlie said, offering his hand to the chaplain. "Thank you for coming today. You've helped me to get my brother back," his throat constricted with emotion and he swallowed before continuing, "and a part of myself I couldn't do without."

"Come home. Father will be overjoyed to see you," Jeremiah said.

Charlie nodded. There was nothing he would like more.

As the carriage climbed the hill between the cornfields and the white house came into view, Charlie gripped Abigail's hand with tearful joy. "The last time I was here, I met Jeremiah in the barn. I felt like I was trespassing on my own family's property. When he told me to leave, I did. Now, I'm coming home as a son and a brother..." He could hardly believe the moment had actually arrived.

He lifted Abigail's hand to his lips and brushed a kiss across her knuckles. "Thank you again for orchestrating that meeting. On my own, I don't think I could have ever gotten through to him."

Although he had already thanked Abigail, Clara, and Chaplain Davies more than once, the gift of reconciliation with his brother was significant enough to warrant profuse gratitude.

"I'm just so glad that it worked!" she laughed.

As the carriage rolled to a stop, the front door of the house burst open and Francis Turner stepped out onto the brick walkway. He squinted at Charlie in disbelief, his shaggy white eyebrows narrowing into an unruly mass. He took a halting step forward, as if fearful that in his desire to see his son again, his eyes were deceiving him.

"*Charlie?*" His voice shook as he took another faltering step.

"Father, I'm home!" Charlie sprang from the carriage and ran to greet him. Francis was thinner than Charlie remembered, and he appeared to have aged considerably in the four years that he'd been away. But as Francis wrapped his thick arms around Charlie's neck in a bear hug, weeping into his shoulder, he felt as strong and solid as ever.

Jeremiah and Charlie had agreed that it would be easier for their father to be left in the dark regarding the conflict which had existed between the brothers, and its cause. All he needed to know was that both of his sons had made it safely home.

"Charlie!" his father cried, clinging to him so tightly that Charlie found it difficult to breathe. "You're alive! You're home!" he wept.

This time, Charlie's homecoming was everything he had hoped it would be. He was welcomed into the house and Francis called all the servants into the dining room to greet him. Old Joe and his wife, Mamie, Phoebe and her little boy, Joseph, along with young Silas, all gathered around him in jubilation. Hugs and handshakes and more tears followed, until Charlie felt the warmth of their love seeping into the cracks and crevices of his brokenness.

He was finally home.

"If I'd known you was comin', I would've made up your favorite supper!" Mamie lamented, wringing her plump hands together.

To his credit, Silas never gave away that Charlie had been there before.

"Don't worry, I'll give advance notice next time," Charlie promised the cook.

He explained to them all how he had been taken prisoner at Gettysburg and sent to Point Lookout Prison. After languishing there for nine months, he had managed to escape and made his way home to the Eastern Shore, only to be shot by members of the Home Guard. Charlie recounted how Abigail had found him, and how Mr. Sterret had hid him at Bloomingdale and nurtured him back to health.

It was difficult to explain why he had returned to Bloomingdale once he was paroled, instead of coming back to Laurel Hill. The simplest way was to say that he was unsure how he would be received since he had fought for the Confederacy.

"But as it turns out, Jeremiah and I were both invited to the home of a mutual friend today, and he assured me that all had been forgiven," Charlie nearly choked on the words, emotions flooding him as he spoke the partial truth.

"Of course all is forgiven!" Francis declared. "How could you ever doubt?"

"How did you escape Point Lookout?" Jeremiah wondered.

Charlie looked at Phoebe as he answered. "Men from the Third Maryland Colored Regiment were sent to guard us. Henry and Eli were with them. They pretended to be strangers, all the while planning my escape. I doubt I would have made it out alive if it hadn't been for their act of selfless courage."

Phoebe covered her mouth at this surprising news of her husband's involvement in Charlie's return. "I always knew that my Henry was a good man," she dabbed at her eyes, smiling proudly.

"Is he… safe? Have you heard from him?" Charlie worried.

"I gets letters from time to time," she assured him. "He gets white soldiers to write for him, and then Missus Clara reads 'em to me."

Charlie sagged with relief. "I owe those two men my life. I'll never forget that," he vowed solemnly.

Phoebe nodded in acknowledgment of the debt.

Despite her ebony skin, Charlie felt as though she was family, along with Old Joe and Mamie, and even young Silas and the baby. They were a part of Laurel Hill, and the best part of being home was being with his family again.

Chapter Thirty-Four

Jane and Judson's wedding was held at her parents' home on Chesterfield Avenue, in Centreville, not far from the wharf on the Corsica River. Vases of flowers filled the house, and the banister had been wound with a garland of orange blossoms. The June day was hot, but at least the sun was shining and the sky was powder blue, interspersed with tufts of cottony white clouds.

When they had chosen the date for their nuptials, Jane and Judson had presumed that the war would be over, and Abigail was glad that it had proven true. It was far easier to celebrate the coming together of the young couple knowing that the future held the hope of stability and peace.

When Jane had first become engaged to Louis Bland, who was killed at Antietam, she had intended for her wedding to be celebrated at the Methodist Protestant Church on Commerce Street, where her sister Clara's wedding had been held, and their parents' wedding before them. She had confessed to Abigail that she had lived that moment too many times in her dreams with Louis as the groom, and she needed her day with Judson to be different from what she had originally planned.

They had invited only family and close friends, but the house was nonetheless filled to capacity. The windows were opened to allow a breeze to move through, and the perfume of the many blooms both inside and out wafted on the air.

At the bottom of the stairs, Judson stood anxiously anticipating the moment when his bride would appear on the landing. A lock of blond hair had fallen over his forehead, and a nervous smile was fixed on his handsome face. The fingers of his left hand twitched in anticipation at his side, while his right arm was bent at the elbow with the prosthetic hand held against his waist.

The violin began to play and Clara, dressed in white as the matron of honor, slowly floated down the stairs. A little girl in white muslin with a pink sash followed her, sprinkling rose petals from a basket dangling on her elbow. Then at last, the bride made her grand entrance.

Jane's white satin dress and long lacy veil, attached to a wreath of orange blossoms, paled in comparison to the radiance of her expression. Her eyes were bright with anticipation, her cheeks rosy with excitement. Remembering the despondency of Jane's mourning, Abigail's eyes misted at the apparent joy on her friend's face as she descended the stairs to meet her groom.

Charlie stood beside Abigail in the main hall, dashing in a new linen suit bought for the occasion. As if feeling her eyes upon him, Charlie glanced down at Abigail and winked. Soon enough, they would be celebrating their own nuptials. Abigail blushed as a wide assortment of thoughts pertaining to that day ran through her mind. Charlie raised his eyebrows as if reading her thoughts, and her blush deepened.

His presence at the wedding with Abigail was something she did not take lightly. Not only was there a time when he was in hiding as a Rebel soldier, but now he and Jeremiah stood shoulder to shoulder as brothers and friends. There were many reasons to rejoice on this beautiful, summer day.

When the ceremony concluded, the newly married couple and the wedding party were moved into the parlor to pose for a photograph. The guests took this opportunity to slip outside for a breath of fresh air, strolling across the lawn or though the flower garden. Inside, the kitchen staff was busy setting up tables for refreshments.

Charlie steered Abigail to a secluded area behind a coppice of dogwood trees. This was the first time many of his former friends and colleagues had seen him since the war, and he was overwhelmed by the welcome he received.

There were a few who had either fought with the Union or lost sons in the Union Army, who glared at him as if he were personally responsible for the war and their loss. But the overwhelming reception had been positive.

Once concealed behind their leafy screen, Charlie's shoulders relaxed and he sighed audibly. "It's nice to have a moment alone. I was afraid I was going to suffocate in there, between the heat and the crush of people wanting to greet me. I swear, I feel as if I've returned from the dead!"

Abigail gazed up at him lovingly. "In a way, I suppose you have." The summer breeze danced around them and ruffled the tiered flounces of her pale blue dress.

He regarded her thoughtfully. "I suppose so. I'm blessed to be among the few who made it home, not only alive, but with all my limbs intact."

"Poor Mariah. I keep thinking about her trying to manage everything so bravely, all alone. I wish I knew of a way to help her," Abigail replied.

"Actually, I had an idea yesterday, when I paid Philip a visit at Mount Mill. My friend, Isaac Roberts, is still staying with the Allens, but he's on the hunt for a permanent situation. I know Mrs. Wright can't afford to hire anyone just now, but he might be willing to work for her in return for room and board. Roberts is an honest, hard-working man, and I'd vouch for him any day."

"That's an idea! I'll send word to ask Mariah if she would be interested," Abigail brightened.

"Now, give me a kiss before they call us back inside for the reception." Charlie leaned down to whisper in her ear, "I didn't steal you away just to talk." His lips trailed kisses along her jaw to her lips, and Abigail turned her face to accept his mouth eagerly. She wound her arms around his neck and clung to him, her dearest friend and the man whose name she would one day take.

Just then, the signal was given that the guests were invited to return to the house for refreshments. Charlie pressed a kiss to her forehead and offered his arm. "Shall we?"

As they strolled back across the lawn toward the Collins' house to continue the festivities, the sun warm against her skin and the breeze stirring her hair, Abigail considered how the hand of God was at work within the seasons to share a profound message of His presence.

In the winter, when the grass withered and the flowers lay brittle and brown, it appeared that nature had been abandoned to the cold. The months stretched out bleak and grim as nature slumbered, waiting for warmth of the spring sunshine to awaken it and the gentle rain to nurture it back to life. In the same way, there were seasons of grief and despair, when all hope appeared to be lost. But never was there a time when God was not at work to heal and restore.

Abigail remembered a day, which now seemed far away, when she and Charlie had sat by the creek near Mount Mill and watched the children splashing in the water. Sophie had caught a rabbit, and Charlie hadn't understood Abigail's concern for the creature.

"It's just a rabbit," he'd declared, predicting its end in the stewpot. When she had countered with a reminder that to the Yankees, he'd meant no more than the animal did to him, Charlie had become angry with her.

She'd been so disappointed in him. Shouldn't he, of all people, know that life was a gift to be protected?

Abigail had taken a deep breath, searching for the words which would help him to understand. "*'Are not two sparrows sold for a cent? And yet not one of them falls to the ground apart from your Father. But the very hairs of your head are all numbered. So do not fear; you are more valuable than sparrows.'*"

As much as God loved the world He had created and all of the creatures in it, He valued mankind above them all. If Providence nurtured the grass, trees, and flowers back to life every spring with all the loving care of a dedicated gardener, and if He saw the humble sparrow when it fell from its nest, how much more were the lives of men and women worth to Him? Although mankind might devalue the lives of their fellow man for varied reasons, such as differences of beliefs or skin color, they were all made equally in the image of God.

Now, at long last, the killing had ceased. The war had cast a gloomy pall over the nation for four long years, but finally the clouds were lifting. There would be no more widows weeping over the newspapers, no more mothers wondering if her son lay beneath the ground with nothing more than a wooden cross to mark his grave. Fathers were returning to their children, husbands to their wives, and even traitors to their country.

Abigail breathed in the fragrant summer air, grateful that once again they could look to the future with hope.

~

Charlie endured the cramped quarters and breathed the stuffy air within the house for as long as he could tolerate it. Once he had shared a light meal and a glass of punch with Abigail, and received more hugs, handshakes, and slaps on the back than he could count, he slipped out through the back door.

Standing on the patio, he blinked against the bright sunshine, relishing the open sky above him and the fresh air in his lungs. For a moment, he'd felt just as claustrophobic in the Collins' parlor as he had in the cellar at Bloomingdale.

He turned at the sound of the door clicking behind him, relieved to find that it was only Jeremiah who had followed him.

His brother tugged at the collar of his shirt, sweat beading his temples. "It's hot as blazes out here. Formal wear is miserable enough in cool weather."

Charlie grinned. "I couldn't agree more."

"It's good to have you back," Jeremiah told him yet again. "Since he saw you last week, I swear Father's had a new spring to his step and he's standing taller. It's as if a heavy burden has rolled right off his shoulders."

"I'm sorry for what I've put everyone through," Charlie apologized, not for the first time. "I guess sometimes you just don't realize how much you have until it's taken from you. Being home on the Eastern Shore, with my family and friends, it truly feels like I've come back from the dead."

"I can understand that," Jeremiah replied, leaning against the patio railing. "I can't imagine how you endured so many years of fighting. My one and only taste of it was at Gettysburg, and it will haunt me all of my life. When I came back to Laurel

Hill, it felt like a miracle. I realize now that I have you to thank for that. You spared me all of the battles that were yet to wage. And even if I don't necessarily appreciate your chosen method, I do value the love that was behind it."

He gripped Charlie's shoulder, his brown eyes glistening with emotion. "I'm sorry I was so slow to forgive. I guess I couldn't see past my loss." He glanced down at his prosthesis. "But losing you was even worse than losing a hand. I can live without it; I can't live without you."

Moved, and more than a little surprised, by his brother's heartfelt words, Charlie swallowed down the lump in his throat. "It's good to hear you say so. Your chaplain was right, I did overstep my place. But I thank God that He protected you and brought you home—and gave you a daughter. Henrietta is a darling!"

A proud grin split Jeremiah's bearded face. "She's growing into a little person more every day, learning to express her wants and emotions. It's such a curious progression to watch. One day she can't do more than eat and sleep, the next she's walking around and shouting, 'Dada! Come!' as if I'm the dog." He paused, thoughtfully. "I don't know that I'd have her without you."

"God is in control of life and death, but I like to give a helping hand when I can," Charlie teased. It felt good to be at ease and able to banter with his brother again.

Jeremiah tugged at his collar again, far more comfortable in a chambray shirt and felt hat, working in the fields. The sounds of laughter and merriment came to them through the open windows, and Charlie turned to his brother.

"I know Father said the farm is managing fine, but how are you really coping without me, Henry, and Eli?" Charlie wondered.

"The truth is we're very glad you've found a place of your own. You have a great opportunity at Bloomingdale, and it looks to me like you have a certain future there—of one kind or another," he grinned, referring to Charlie's interest in Abigail. "As for Laurel Hill, we *are* managing. Since the slaves have been freed, there are men looking for work during planting and harvest seasons, so we can always hire extra hands then. The rest of the time, we've learned how to get by."

"I'm glad to hear it." Charlie ran a hand through his sandy hair, remembering the way life had been at Laurel Hill before he'd enlisted in the Confederate Army. "It's ironic to think that I owe my life to the men who once lived at our home as slaves," he commented quietly. "I was the master's son, and it never occurred to me that the world could turn upside down and I could be under the authority of a black man. There were more than a few men at Point Lookout whose former slaves were sent there to guard them, and they saw it as an opportunity to take revenge. 'The bottom rung's on top now,' the Negroes said, and they took every advantage of their newfound power to drive that lesson in."

Jeremiah nodded, as if he could easily imagine the temptation of the former slaves who were placed as guards over their old masters. "Our father treated everyone with respect, whether it was an equal or a subordinate. That was your saving grace. They had no resentment, no reason to punish you. And they are good men, in their own right. Since gaining their freedom, many Negroes have wanted to adapt surnames. Old Joe and his clan have taken the last name Turner. Which is as it should be. Our families are inseparably connected."

The balmy breeze rustled the leaves of the dogwoods and maples in the yard, then stirred the roses and gardenias blooming in the garden before it blew like a puff of hot breath over the men standing on the patio. Charlie loosened the cravat at his throat, his mind still searching to find meaning in the havoc and horror of the last four years. While there was brokenness which could never be made whole again, there were also gifts which had been gained from the tragedy of the war.

The era of Reconstruction had begun, an attempt to forge a path through the chaos and lead the country back into unity and strength. There was a hard row to hoe ahead for them, but if Jeremiah could find it in his heart to forgive Charlie, then there was hope for the nation.

Through the open window, Charlie caught a glimpse of Abigail in her taffeta gown of cornflower blue, her dark hair curling damply on the back of her neck beneath her chignon. As she lowered herself into a chair to catch a breath of fresh air, her eye caught his. A smile curved her lips, and in her face, Charlie saw his future.

This was a new beginning for them all.

It was a unique time, when former enemies must learn to be friends; and former friends who had become enemies must make peace and begin afresh. They were all in it together now: North and South, Unionist and Rebel, white and black. There was but one country, the United States, and they must work together to build her into a strong, proud nation once again.

My Brother's Flag

On Maryland's Eastern Shore, the division of the Civil War is an inescapable reality for many households. For the Turner brothers, it means choosing politics over blood.

Although his younger brother goes south to join the Rebels, Jeremiah feels honor-bound to defend the Stars and Stripes even at the risk of meeting Charlie on the battlefield and facing a deeper conflict of loyalties.

His wife, Clara, is left behind at Laurel Hill to manage the farm with her father-in-law and his slaves. As the country is torn apart by opposing forces from within, Clara must find the strength to live in a world of uncertainty and change.

At the outbreak of the war, Charlie enlisted in the Confederate Army to defend States Rights while his older brother, Jeremiah, chose to fight for the Union.

Three years later, an emaciated prisoner of war, Charlie is determined to escape Point Lookout Prison and make his way home to face the conflict awaiting him there.

When Abigail Sterret discovers a wounded man near her home, she is moved by compassion at the sight of the gaunt Rebel soldier. Risking the consequences of aiding the enemy, Abigail shelters Charlie at Bloomingdale and nurtures him back to health. As his wounds heal, she discovers that Charlie carries more secrets than she supposed, and Abigail is more involved than she presumed.

And though war may end with the sweep of a pen, peace comes far less easily.

Watch For

From Fields of Promise

Belonging neither to the South where its sympathies lay, nor to the North which held it captive, Maryland's Eastern Shore must forge a new path through the havoc left by the Civil War.

Mariah Wright, a Confederate widow, has to find a way to keep her husband's farm from falling into poverty and ruin. Most of the slaves have headed north to freedom and there aren't enough hands to work the fields. Left with the care of her aging mother-in-law and young sister-in-law, Mariah strives to carry the burdens the war has left her.

Isaac Roberts, a veteran of the Confederate Army, returned from Appomattox to discover that the life he left behind has moved on without him. Disillusioned from the loss of a cause to which he has given everything and damaged from the savage realities of war, Isaac fears he has nothing left to live for.

With nowhere else to turn, Isaac accepts the challenge of helping a fallen comrade's widow save all she has left of her husband's legacy. As the fractured nation struggles to come together after four bitter years of fighting, Mariah and Isaac must find their place in a world which has changed forever.

Rebekah Colburn is the author of the Historical Fiction Series, *"Of Wind and Sky."*

Her desire is to bring history to life with rich stories, compelling characters and inspirational themes which will inspire and encourage her readers.

In 2001 she obtained a B.A. in Biblical Studies from Washington Bible College. Rebekah loves being outdoors and enjoys mountain biking, cycling, and cruising the local waterways with her husband.

She lives on the Eastern Shore of Maryland with her husband, teen-aged daughter, four spoiled cats, one rambunctious dog, and a whole lot of chaos.

You can contact Rebekah Colburn via:

Email: rebekahlynncolburn@gmail.com
Website: http://rebekahcolburn.weebly.com/
Facebook: https://www.facebook.com/ColburnRebekah
Twitter: https://twitter.com/RebekahColburn

Made in the USA
Middletown, DE
04 April 2016